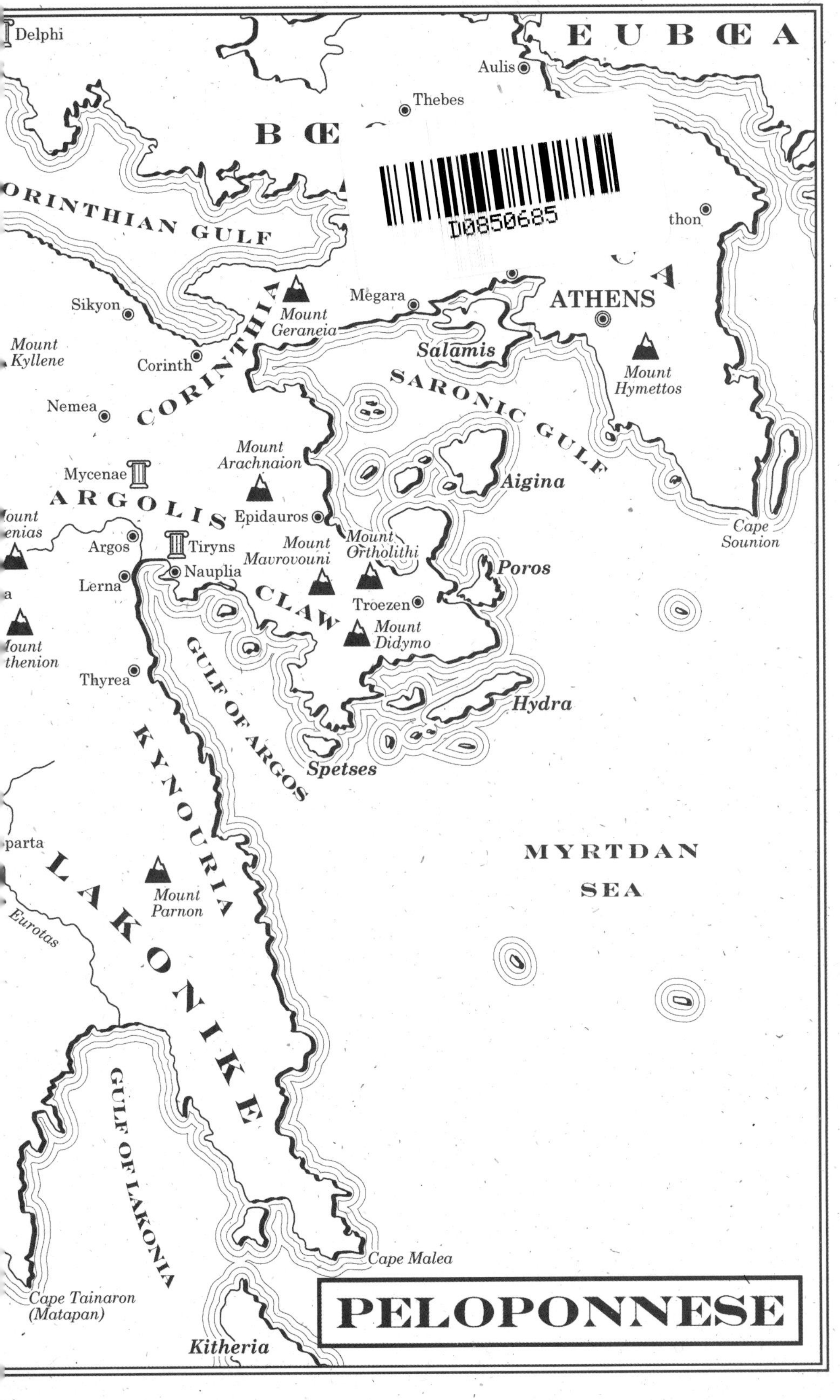
Delphi
EUBŒA
Aulis
Thebes
CORINTHIAN GULF
Sikyon
Mount Kyllene
Corinth
CORINTHIA
Mount Geraneia
Megara
ATHENS
Salamis
Mount Hymettos
SARONIC GULF
Nemea
Mycenae
Mount Arachnaion
Aigina
ARGOLIS
Epidauros
Argos
Tiryns
Nauplia
Mount Mavrovouni
Mount Ortholithi
Poros
Cape Sounion
Lerna
CLAW
Troezen
Mount Didymo
Thyrea
GULF OF ARGOS
Hydra
Spetses
KYNOURIA
LAKONIKE
Mount Parnon
Eurotas
MYRTDAN SEA
GULF OF LAKONIA
Cape Malea
Cape Tainaron (Matapan)
Kitheria
PELOPONNESE

ARCADIAN NIGHTS

JOHN SPURLING is the author of the novels The Ten Thousand Things (winner of the 2015 Walter Scott prize for Historical Fiction), The Ragged End, After Zenda and A Book of Liszts. He is a prolific playwright, whose plays have been performed on television, radio and stage, including at the National Theatre. Spurling is also the author of two critical books on Graham Greene's novels and Samuel Beckett's plays (with John Fletcher), has been a frequent reviewer for newspapers, magazines and BBC Radio, and was for twelve years the art critic of The New Statesman. He lives in London and Arcadia, Greece, and is married to the biographer Hilary Spurling.

ARCADIAN NIGHTS

THE GREEK MYTHS REIMAGINED

JOHN SPURLING

OVERLOOK DUCKWORTH
New York • London

First published in hardcover in the United States and the United Kingdom in 2016 by
Overlook Duckworth, Peter Mayer Publishers, Inc.

NEW YORK
141 Wooster Street
New York, NY 10012
www.overlookpress.com
For bulk and special sales please contact sales@overlookny.com,
or to write us at the above address.

LONDON
30 Calvin Street, London E1 6NW
T: 020 7490 7300
E: info@duckworth-publishers.co.uk
www.ducknet.co.uk
For bulk and special sales please contact sales@duckworth-publishers.co.uk,
or write to us at the above address.

Cataloging-in-Publication Data is available from the Library of Congress

A catalogue record for this book is available from the British Library

ISBN: 978-1-4683-1179-2 (US)
ISBN: 978-0-7156-5047-9 (UK)

In memory of my grandfather, J.C. Stobart,
who died before I was born,
and my grandmother, Molly Stobart,
who taught me to admire him and share his love of Greece.

I believe that our art and literature has by this time absorbed and assimilated what Greece had to teach, and that our roots are so entwined with the soil of Greek culture that we can never lose the taste of it as long as books are read and pictures painted.

from the introduction to J.C. Stobart's
The Glory That Was Greece (1911)

NOTES

1. The Greek language has no letter 'c' or diphthong 'ae', which come from Latin. Greek uses 'k' and 'ai'. For familiar names, such as Arcadia, Clytemnestra, Mycenae, I have used the Latin spelling, but for less familiar ones, the Greek. 'Herakles' is the main exception, since the Roman 'Hercules' is a composite figure, partly derived from the Greek hero, partly based on an old Italian deity.

The word 'Greek' itself is, of course, a Latin usage, probably derived from the tribe of the Graeci who inhabited the north-western coast of Greece and were the first 'Greeks' encountered by the Romans. The ancient Greeks called themselves 'Hellenes' and their country 'Hellas', while modern Greeks, dropping the aspirate, call themselves 'Éllenes' (three syllables with the accent on the first and a long 'e' in the second) and their country 'Elláda'.

The long 'e' at the end of Greek names such as Athene, Antiope, Hippolyte, should always be sounded.

2. 'Human kind,' said T.S. Eliot, 'cannot bear very much reality,' and their myths cannot bear very much real time. For example: Pelops and his bride Hippodameia seem to be contemporary with Perseus, the great-grandfather of Herakles; Herakles is contemporary with Theseus; Theseus marries the *daughter* of King Minos; yet Pelops' son Atreus, who should be at least two generations senior to Theseus, marries Minos' *granddaughter*.

CONTENTS

Contents

INTRODUCTION

'*Ti na kánoume;* – pause for no answer – *Den peirázei.*' ('What are we to do? – It doesn't matter.') Our neighbour in Arcadia rounds off her conversations over the fence with these useful phrases. They might come straight out of a Greek tragedy by Aeschylus or Sophocles, the hand-wringing words of a Chorus of old men or women contemplating the catastrophic downfall of Agamemnon or Oedipus, and they apply equally well to the long, rocky history of Greece. From ancient times it has been a story of foreign invasions, wars between city-states, venal demagoguery playing on popular gullibility, military dictatorships, civil war. Romans, Slavs, Venetians, Franks, Byzantines, Turks, Germans and Italians have come and gone. Just over a century ago my grandfather, J.C. Stobart, published his history of Greek culture, *The Glory That Was Greece*, and remarked in his introduction:

> The traveller is struck with the small scale of Greek geography. ... From your hotel window in Athens you can see hill-tops in the heart of the Peloponnese. ... In that radiant sea-air the Greeks of old learnt to see things clearly. They could live, as Greeks still live, a simple, temperate life ... the modern Greek still reminds us of his predecessors as we know them in ancient literature. He is still restless, talkative, subtle and inquisitive, eager for liberty without the sense of discipline which liberty requires, contemptuous of strangers and jealous of his neighbour.

Now, as I write, the cosy embrace of the European common currency has turned into a strangling squeeze of impossible debt, austerity and looming economic collapse unless the Greeks can meet the terms and make the sacrifices demanded by the Eurocrats and in particular the Germans (the Greeks' most recent invaders).

But whatever the hardships in the cities, where a large proportion of the population works for the government, the village people here in the Peloponnese go on much as they have for millennia. Their life was always hard and still is – based on their olive trees, a few goats, a donkey, chickens, and home-grown fruit and vegetables. True, they now have electricity, to which the government adds tax – probably the only way it can be easily collected from people who view the state chiefly as a source of unwelcome interference with their family-centred life – and piped water, though some, including our neighbour, have gone back recently to using the well behind our house. They still bake their bread in outside bread-ovens, wash their clothes and cook their meals over open fires in the courtyards and warm themselves in winter at the fireplaces built into the back of the houses, their fuel being the branches they prune from their olive trees after gathering the olives in January. But these days, of course, since most of the villagers are old – their children having migrated in better times to easier lives in the cities – they have pensions, so long as the government can contrive to pay them.

My wife Hilary and I came to visit this hill-side village, staying in an Athenian friend's holiday house, in 2006 and, seduced by the beauty of the sea below and the mountains behind, as well as the friendliness of the people, bought a house for ourselves. There were several for sale, in various stages of decay, as there had been since the 1970s, when a few German visitors acquired the more inaccessible houses and restored them. By the time we bought ours the village population of about three hundred was roughly sixty per cent Greek and forty per cent foreign, mostly Germans, who had somehow by their good manners and contribution to the prosperity of the village redeemed their nation's reputation and earned the goodwill of people their fathers had crushed and persecuted.

Our house – a traditional rectangular box with stone walls a metre thick – and its courtyard below and terraces above were completely redesigned and rebuilt by a young architect, son of a Greek father and German mother. He employed and worked with local artisans – builder, plumber, electrician, carpenter, blacksmith, plasterers and decorators – and Albanian labourers to do the heavy work, and, contrary to all the bad stories about foreigners' houses never being finished and costing twice the original budget, finished the job in a year at the agreed price. When it was nearly ready – sufficiently for us to move in – we held a ceremony on one of the newly built stone terraces above the house. I made a brief speech and poured a libation of Greek wine 'to the gods of this place' on the earth round a newly planted lemon tree.

The Greeks present at the ceremony looked surprised. They had, after all, been Orthodox Christians for about fifteen hundred years. But for me Greece was still the land of its ancient gods and their myths. I studied Greek, Latin and ancient history at school, visited Greece for the first time as a student in 1959 and, driving these days along the new roads from Athens to Arcadia, passing signs to Eleusis, Thebes, Corinth, Nemea, Mycenae, and through the narrow streets of Argos, still feel as much part of a world of myth and ancient history as of modern reality. I was against buying the house at first on perfectly rational grounds – I dislike travelling and we didn't have enough money – but on a sudden instinct changed my mind overnight.

When we got home to London and I unearthed the diary I kept on my first visit to Greece in 1959, I found an entry I had entirely forgotten: over a drink at a café, my friends and I speculated about where we would be living when we were old, and I said I would be living in Greece. At that time I was under the spell of Lawrence Durrell's four-volume novel, *The Alexandria Quartet*, and his travel books, and when I visited Greece again three years later, newly married to Hilary, we still had Durrell's *Reflections on a Marine Venus* in our rucksack. But we did not go there again until 44 years later and, whatever her motives for buying the house, my own must have included an element of home-coming, of partly belonging to a place which I had spent my teens studying and where so much of our Western civilisation began. The Ancient Greeks, after all, laid the foundations of our logic, philosophy, physics, chemistry, biology, medicine, astronomy, history, art, architecture, literature, drama, politics, and even religion, since the New Testament was written in Greek and much of its story and teaching is Greek-inspired.

Mine was probably the last generation to be educated in the Classics as standard and the last, therefore, to be on easy terms with the innumerable references to and recycling of the Greek myths in Western art, literature, drama, music and opera. Many people have retold them with many variations, and they remain, because of the way they were honed and refined by the great originators of Western literature – Homer, Hesiod, Herodotus, Pindar, Aeschylus, Sophocles and Euripides – the most profound, sophisticated and humane myths produced by any culture anywhere. And the point about myths of this quality is that they become ageless and universal. Their interpretation of human behaviour and motivation becomes exemplary, in the true sense 'classical', even when the characters involved, whether gods or mortals, are recognised to be fictional and possessed of powers which later ages understand to be impossible in reality. Stories have their own rules and the best stories, like these, create a world the reader can live in as long as the story lasts. The Greek gods, for all their superhuman powers, are swayed by human emotions, which makes them peculiarly fascinating to us ordinary mortals. We study animals and birds to see how less powerful creatures than ourselves manage their lives, but how would we do if we were also more powerful than humans and lived for ever? The Greek myths provide a sometimes charming, sometimes alarming study of the question. As for the heroes and heroines, playthings of destiny and the gods, they are larger than life, men and women we might like to be – bold, brave, clever, handsome, humorous, temperamental, vengeful, chivalrous, austere, cool – but equally powerless against death. Achilles, Odysseus, Orpheus, Herakles, Theseus, Perseus, Jason, Orestes, Medea, Elektra, Antigone, Helen, Penelope are the original patterns for most fictional and many real heroes and heroines, and we still call masterful women Amazons. The very words 'hero' and 'heroine' come from ancient Greek.

The cities associated with the heroes and heroines are specific, as are most of the places where their heroic deeds were done, and even the gods' principal locations are defined. Zeus was born and brought up in Crete, Apollo and his twin-sister Artemis were born on the island of Delos, Hermes in a cave on Mount Kyllene in Arcadia,

Aphrodite the goddess of love from the sea foam off the island of Kythera (Cythera), the sea-god Poseidon's palace was deep under the Corinthian gulf off the north coast of the Peloponnese, and they all live on Mount Olympos. Many of the gods and heroes are specially associated with the Peloponnese, no doubt because the myths date back to a time long before the Classical period dominated by the city-state of Athens in the sixth and fifth centuries BC, to that at least of Mycenaean (Peloponnesian) dominance in the late Bronze Age, nearly a thousand years earlier. And since it is in the Peloponnese that I have landed so unexpectedly in my old age, I have concentrated on the stories of the Peloponnesian heroes, Agamemnon and his ill-fated family, Herakles (more often known by his Latin name Hercules), Perseus and Theseus, only alluding in passing to such other classic stories as the voyage of the Argonauts, the Trojan War and the adventures of Odysseus. I have also included some stories about Apollo, since although he was not a specifically Peloponnesian god, he had a shrine on the hill behind our village and the local football team is named after him.

Why tell these well-known stories again? Because I've found that they are no longer so well-known – or only in the barest outline. And I've enjoyed making my own interpretation of them, adding details and dialogue, clarifying obscurities. For instance, Herakles is always depicted naked, except for his lion-skin, but surely when he was staying in a city or passing through one he must have worn something round his genitals so as to avoid shocking the fully-dressed citizens? I have provided a suitably mythical loincloth. I have also added a new twist to Theseus' triumphant defeat of the Minotaur in the Cretan labyrinth and cleared up the vexed question of why he abandoned his loving collaborator Ariadne on the island of Naxos. Those who know the stories well can perhaps enjoy spotting my variations and those who don't can be assured that the main thrust of the stories – the tune, as it were – is authentic. Apart from the original sources – Homer, Hesiod, Herodotus, Pindar and the Greek dramatists – my three main secondary sources were *The New Larousse Encyclopaedia of Mythology*, Sir William Smith's *A Smaller Classical Dictionary* and Robert Graves' *The Greek Myths*. This last incorporates so many ancient variations chased up by his assiduous assistants, Janet Seymour-Smith and Kenneth Gay, and circling dizzily like a swarm of bees from myth to myth, that the brain reels and the reader longs to be back in the straightforward child's version provided by Charles Kingsley's *The Heroes*. My version is for readers of all ages and for entertainment not reference.

Greece for many people is simply one of the Mediterranean holiday resorts, with sea, sun, beaches, mountains carpeted with flowers in spring, good food and drink, friendly and hospitable natives, and a lot of famous ruins. For me it is all that, plus an intense, intangible atmosphere of magical narrative into which the real landscape dissolves and re-emerges as something strange and wonderful and perhaps unique in the world, a place that is at once both fiction and reality. Yes, I can even claim that in Arcadia with a little imagination and some help from these stories, one can still ascribe the thunderbolt to Zeus, the earthquake to Poseidon, the rainbow to Iris, the course of the sun to Apollo, the olive trees to Athene, a sudden love affair to Aphrodite and perhaps an economic disaster to Hades, god of the underworld and keeper of the earth's riches. But none of these gods could look kindly on those who offend the quintessentially Greek maxim, inscribed on Apollo's temple at Delphi, ignored at their peril by mythical heroes and heroines, vote-hungry politicians, greedy bankers and the over-optimistic creators of the Eurozone: '*Meden agan*', literally 'Nothing in excess', or 'Don't overdo it!'

London, August 2015

AGAMEMNON

1. THE MURDER

Sitting on our terrace in Arcadia overlooking the Gulf of Argos, I thought that if we'd been there earlier – three millennia and a century or two earlier – we would have seen Agamemnon's fleet passing on its way to Troy. According to Homer, who was born some three centuries later, there were 100 ships with 15,000 Argive soldiers on board and 60 ships with 9,000 Arcadians. Arcadia at that time was landlocked and its modern mountainous coastline, a district called Kynouria, was part of Argolis. But the Arcadians had a reputation as fierce warriors, so Agamemnon gladly lent them ships to take them to Troy.

When they came back, ten years afterwards, there were fewer ships. Thousands of men perished of wounds or disease on the shelterless plain of Troy. Many ships rotted on the beach and their timbers were burned to keep the men warm and cook their meals or to make funeral pyres for the dead. Many others were wrecked on the voyage home.

So when the remnant docked in Nauplia at the head of the Gulf and the Arcadians made their own way home past the Lernaian Marsh, it was a pitifully small army that marched up the road behind Agamemnon's chariot to his palace at Mycenae. And this perhaps explains why the *coup d'état* which immediately followed his arrival met with no resistance and why the most powerful king in all Greece, who had come home victorious with a cargo of rich spoils, could be murdered without anyone lifting a hand to save or avenge him.

Still, however few soldiers remained, they were hardened fighters. Surely they were a match for any force the conspirators could muster? No doubt. But the conspirators had the advantage of surprise and good warning of the army's return. Even before he left Greece Agamemnon organised a chain of beacon-fires to announce victory.

Each had its watchmen, charged with renewing the faggots and brushwood if necessary year by year and watching for its predecessor in the chain night and day. They could hardly have imagined that the job would last a decade and they must often have thought they would die of boredom, if not old age, at their posts, but none of them failed when the time came. As soon as Troy fell, Agamemnon's messenger ran to the top of Mount Ida, overlooking the Trojan plain, and the first beacon was set alight just as the flames shot up from burning Troy. The second was on the island of Lemnos, the third on Mount Athos, and so on southwards, via the island of Euboia, Mounts Kithairon and Aigiplanktos, across the Saronic Gulf to the final beacon on the Peloponnese, visible from the palace tower of Mycenae.

We too, from our terrace in Arcadia, looking north-eastwards, might have seen that last beacon high on Mount Arachnaion, behind the lower range where there is now a stately line of wind-turbines.

So the conspirators had plenty of time to make their final arrangements. The fleet would take many days, even if the wind and weather were favourable – and as it turned out, they were not – to make that crossing of the Aegean which had been leapt so easily by the message of fire. Nor could the victorious general and his troops have guessed that their triumphant beacons would help to betray them or that they would be received with anything but joy and celebration. And consider the topography of Mycenae.

The play by Aeschylus, written six to seven centuries after the event, when Mycenae was a forgotten ruin and the whole Mycenaean civilisation had been erased by successive invasions of Greek-speaking northerners, is set in the city of Argos. Agamemnon was indeed King of Argos, but that (or sometimes 'Argolis') was the name of the whole kingdom as well as its principal city, and although he had a palace there and another just outside Nauplia in the fortress of Tiryns, the heart of his extensive domains was Mycenae.

Mycenae is a natural acropolis, a conical hill set in the south-western flank of a range of higher hills, approached from the Argive plain by a steadily rising and winding road which ends at the famous Lion Gate. From there, within the massive walls of the fortress, a steep, narrow, twisting street between the buildings accommodating stores, shops, slaves, servants, administrators, guards and courtiers led up to the royal palace on the summit where, under the colonnaded porch of the palace, Agamemnon's wife Clytemnestra awaited him. Her lover Aigisthos, who was Agamemnon's first cousin, was out of sight inside the entrance-hall with some thirty well-armed men, none of them Argives, but mercenaries, malcontents and outlaws from other states whose only allegiance was to Aigisthos personally. In the open space in front of the palace was a small crowd of white-haired Argives, noblemen, merchants, municipal officials, well-to-do farmers who had been too old, even ten years earlier, to take part in the expedition to Troy.

Agamemnon's chariot, followed by the chariot carrying his principal prize from the war, a daughter of King Priam of Troy, the princess Cassandra, followed by the wagons carrying the lion's share of looted Trojan gold and silver, votive statues, precious cups and bowls, armour and weapons, fine robes, carpets and hangings, climbed the steep street with difficulty. The horses were tired after the twelve-mile journey from the ships. So were the soldiers marching behind the wagons. By the time Agamemnon's and Cassandra's chariots reached the plateau at the top, his soldiers were only halfway up the narrow street, cut off from their general and his Trojan mistress by the labouring wagons of treasure.

Now, as if Agamemnon had not already sufficiently offended the gods by violating a princess who was also a virgin priestess dedicated to the service of the god Apollo, Clytemnestra had prepared another offence for him to commit. This was before she'd seen and understood the offence to both the gods and herself represented by the woman in the second chariot. Clytemnestra ordered her slaves to unroll a crimson carpet, a huge length of blood-red silk stretching from the chariot up over the shallow steps of the portico, and invited Agamemnon to walk along it into his palace. He refused, saying it was wrong to tread on such costly stuff, wrong for a mortal to behave as if he were a god. She insisted. He refused again and again. Their increasingly vehement argument in front of the goggling audience of old men threatened to continue until his soldiers reached the top of the hill. Inside the entrance-hall Aigisthos began to lose his nerve.

'Gods above, woman,' he muttered in the hearing of his mercenaries, 'pull him out of the bloody chariot if he won't get down by himself!'

Finally Clytemnestra found the clinching argument:

'You are the mighty conqueror of Troy,' she said, 'the champion of Greece, the winner of battles and treasure beyond anything achieved by your ancestors. Allow me, a poor weak woman, to win this trivial argument!'

Fifty years ago in the huge stone theatre at Epidauros I first saw the red carpet rolled out and Agamemnon persuaded against his better judgment to walk it. Considering what it led to, you'd think people would have avoided walking on red carpets ever since, but no, you often see them, innocently laid out for visits by heads of state or when film-stars are drifting in for first-nights and prize-givings.

By the time his treasure and his exhausted soldiers reached the top of the hill, Agamemnon had disappeared into the inner rooms of the palace, been conducted to a ritual bath and, stepping out of the bath, been swathed in a thick towel by his wife. Then, as she held his arms to his sides in a tight embrace, his cousin Aigisthos came forward with a long knife – the kind used for sacrificing bulls or goats – and stabbed him to death. But fallen there, half-in and half-out of the bath, he was still breathing, still seeing with dimming sight, his blood streaming over the polished marble floor, when Clytemnestra stood over him with a double-headed axe – she had laid it ready out of sight behind the door.

'*My* sacrifice now,' she said, 'my sacrifice for yours, yours for mine!'

And she cut off his head.

This part we didn't see in the theatre at Epidauros – Greek drama, unlike Roman or British, keeps actual brutality off-stage – but we saw Clytemnestra reappear brandishing the bloodstained axe and we saw the corpses of Agamemnon and Cassandra brought out, for she too, after predicting Agamemnon's and her own fate to the shocked but disbelieving crowd of old men outside, had been taken inside the palace and slaughtered.

None of this happened, of course, quite the way it does in Aeschylus' play. Plays, especially Greek tragedies, condense and elide. Agamemnon's soldiers, when they finally reached the palace, were welcomed by Aigisthos and invited, with the assembled Argive elders, to a victory feast. Slaves brought out tables, sacrifices and libations were made to the gods, sheep and oxen slaughtered and roasted, brimming bowls of wine passed round, arms and armour laid aside. A few of them wondered what was keeping Agamemnon, why he wasn't presiding over the feast, but others guessed that he was making up for lost time with his wife, or with his Trojan mistress, or both, and soon enough they were all far too full of meat and wine, too relaxed to care. By the time they came to their senses next day their arms and armour, together with the Trojan treasure, had been locked away in the palace storehouses and with small gifts of gold and wine they were discharged and told they could now return to their towns or villages, greet their families and resume their normal life. As for their king and commander-in-chief, no, he was not available. If any of them wanted to know more, they were told he was indisposed.

One group, however, was not satisfied with this answer and demanded to see their general. Another group, looking for their armour and weapons, became angry when told they had been taken into safe-keeping and would be restored to them in a week or two. Both groups became more and more suspicious and others, overhearing their protests, joined them when they knocked aside the guards in the portico and crowded into the entrance hall. There they were met by Aigisthos and his mercenaries. Thoroughly frightened now, Aigisthos told his men to use their shields and push the soldiers out. That was ineffective, there were too few against too many, and suddenly two or three of the mercenaries began to use their swords. Soldiers fell bleeding and in a moment the hall became a savage slaughterhouse where Agamemnon's veterans fought with knives and bare hands against armoured men with swords. So it was that scores of the soldiers who had sacked Troy and butchered its inhabitants were themselves butchered in their own king's palace.

Rumours multiplied as the weeks passed and there was still no sign of Agamemnon or any definite news of him. Those of his soldiers who had not entered the palace got safely home to their families, but they dared not reveal to other families who were not so lucky that men they had last seen feasting beside them in Mycenae had since disappeared. They took refuge in vague commiseration: many comrades had died in the war, they said, and many more on the way home.

Clytemnestra and Aigisthos had been running the kingdom for the past ten years in Agamemnon's absence, so there was no immediate change to people's lives, only a groundswell of uneasiness as the assumption grew that a king who was never seen and for whom no public funeral was held, while his wife and her lover continued to exercise power, must have been murdered. But few within the borders of Argos would say so openly, and the other Greek leaders who had fought at Troy with Agamemnon had their own problems and were in no position to intervene. Some, like his brother Menelaos, king of Sparta, and Odysseus, king of Ithaka, were still trying to reach home, others, like Ajax, son of Oileus, had been drowned without ever reaching home. The second and more famous Ajax, the mighty warrior from Salamis, had gone mad and killed himself. Nestor had returned safely to his small kingdom of Pylos, but that was on the other side of the Peloponnese and he was very old. Achilles had died in battle, Diomedes had been wrecked on the coast of Lycia and captured by its king, a former ally of Troy, who was proposing to sacrifice him to Ares, the god of war. The gods were divided over the Trojan War, which was no doubt why it lasted so long. Ares, together with Aphrodite and Apollo, had supported the Trojans.

As for Agamemnon's three surviving children, one son and two daughters, they were still young. The daughters, Elektra and Chrysothemis, were in their teens, the son, Orestes, was only a child. During the planning stage of their *coup*, Aigisthos wanted to eliminate Orestes, since as soon as he was old enough he would be bound by customary law to take revenge for his father. The girls were not such a threat. Clytemnestra, however, would not agree in advance to kill her only son and since Aigisthos always gave way to her, the final decision was left till later. After the murder of Agamemnon and Cassandra and the slaughter of Agamemnon's soldiers, Clytemnestra reluctantly admitted that the boy would have to be destroyed, but she asked Aigisthos to do it without ever telling her how or when or where.

Her daughters, of course, could not help guessing that their father had been murdered and suspecting what would happen to their little brother. The younger daughter, Chrysothemis, was a sleepy, passive girl, always submissive to her domineering mother, but Elektra was more like her mother, with a powerful will and an independent mind, and she told their elderly nurse, who adored both her and Orestes, what she feared. One day when Clytemnestra and Aigisthos were attending a religious ceremony in Argos, Elektra and the nurse took Orestes out of the palace to visit one of the royal farms, worked by the nurse's son. Elektra returned to Mycenae, but the nurse and the boy, on donkeys provided by the farmer, crossed the border into Corinthia and later, afraid that the Corinthians might be intimidated by the superior power of Argos into handing them back, went on to Phokis on the far side of the Gulf of Corinth. Strophios, the king of Phokis, had married Orestes' aunt Anaxibia, Agamemnon's sister. Their son Pylades soon became his cousin's greatest friend and Orestes grew up in happiness and safety. But he had an unenviable task ahead of him.

2. THE CURSE

Even before the gruesome murder of Agamemnon, this family, the House of Atreus, had a curse on it – in fact, two curses. The first was acquired by Agamemnon's grandfather, Pelops, who gave his name to the whole peninsula, Peloponnesos, the island of Pelops. Pelops was the son of Tantalos, said to be a child of Father Zeus and a favourite of the gods; such a favourite that they even invited him to their divine banquets of ambrosia and nectar and when he invited them back, accepted. This was altogether too much for his sanity. He was beside himself with self-importance, promising his human friends that next time he was invited to Mount Olympos he would put aside a little of the gods' food and drink and bring it back for them to taste, and asking them meanwhile to find him the choicest foods and wines in Greece to set before the gods. He knew, of course, that the gods never touch human food or wine. They like us to offer them a prime ram or bull and to pour on the ground a libation of the costliest wine, but not for them to consume, only to demonstrate our love and esteem, our sense of gratitude for what earth gives us, our willingness to sacrifice the best things we have in their honour.

So when the twelve Olympian gods came to dinner at Tantalos' place in Arcadia – that made thirteen at the table, including the host – Tantalos did not expect them to eat any of the twenty or thirty courses he provided, nor to drink any of the choice wines from Thasos and Chios, Rhodes and Cos, and nearby Nemea. What he did expect them to do, as each delectable dish was brought in and placed on the table with its aroma wafting around the hall, as each superlative wine was opened and poured into the mixing-bowl and then both dishes and wine removed untouched, was to appreciate his very special, very expensive sacrifice. And they did. They smiled and laughed and sniffed the wonderful scents of the wines and the powerful aromas drifting round the hall from every sort of meat and game and fish and vegetable and herb. But Tantalos' disastrous mistake was the *pièce de résistance*. It was a huge casserole and Tantalos in his blind pride dared to set the gods a test. Could any of them, he asked, lifting the lid himself with a flourish so that the savour rose up in a rush with the steam, tell him what was in the casserole? A dreadful silence followed, but Tantalos thought it was only because they were flummoxed. He took a juicy piece of meat out of the pot and held it up for them to see. He even bit into it and chewed it with relish.

'Delicious!' he said, smiling slyly, 'But what can it be? It doesn't taste quite like anything else the good earth provides.'

Of course all the gods knew exactly what it was, but it was Demeter who spoke. She, the goddess of crops and fruits and the earth's plenty, had never smiled or laughed throughout the banquet, but sat there glum and silent. Her thoughts were on her daughter, Persephone, who had been kidnapped and then married by Hades, the god of the underworld, and had to spend half the year in that miserable place among the shades of the dead. Now suddenly Tantalos' boastfulness and self-satisfaction irritated her beyond bearing.

'You stupid, insufferable creature!' she said. 'Did you really imagine that we would want a sacrifice of that sort? Have we entertained you on Olympos and favoured you beyond all other men only for you to misunderstand completely what sort of gods we are? It's your son, little Pelops.'

Tantalos tried to explain that he had not meant to offend them, but on the contrary to show them that nothing he possessed, not even his son, was too precious to sacrifice to the masters of the universe, but his guests had already risen from their seats and vanished, leaving Tantalos in tears of shame and despair beside his casseroled son. Outside in the courtyard the rest of his magnificent dinner was eaten and drunk or carried away by the servants and the friends and neighbours who had gathered round his house. None of them, not even the servants who brought in the food and drink, had been able to see the gods, though they felt the earth shake and a great gust of wind go by as they left.

But how could little cooked and partly-eaten Pelops have become anybody's ancestor? Father Zeus took pity on him and Hermes, the god who escorts the souls of the dead to the underworld, boiled the gobbets in a cauldron with magic herbs and restored the boy to life just as he had been, except for the shoulder Tantalos had chewed. That was replaced with a piece of ivory, perfectly carved and fitted by the artificer-god Hephaistos.

As for Tantalos, he was taken down to Tartaros, the lowest level of the underworld reserved for the gods' worst enemies. There he stood in water up to his chest with a tree bearing every kind of ripe fruit – figs, apples, pears, grapes, apricots, peaches – hanging down over his head. But every time he tried to drink, the water receded and every time he reached for the fruit, a breeze blew the tree's branches aside. His was a life-sentence, and since no one in Tartaros ever dies that meant till the end of time – a fate worth remembering if you're ever tempted to serve up your son to the gods for dinner.

To return to little Pelops and the first curse on the House of Atreus: his restoration by Hermes had made him not just as he had been, but almost god-like in appearance, the most beautiful boy anyone had ever seen, his living skin as ivory-white as his artificial shoulder, his black eyes and black hair shining with the reflected light of heaven, his body and limbs strong and supple, his manner graceful and amiable. His first lover was Poseidon, brother of Zeus and god of the sea, a temperamental and vindictive god if you crossed him, but Pelops, being less vain and more intelligent than his father, never did. He only once, when he had grown up and fallen in love with a princess, invoked Poseidon's intervention in his favour.

Pelops had come to Elis, a kingdom on the western shore of the Peloponnese (then known as Apia), whose king had a beautiful daughter called Hippodameia. Many other likely youths besides Pelops wanted to marry this girl, partly because she was so beautiful and partly because she was her father's only heir to the kingdom. The problem was that her father, King Oinomaos, was himself in love with her and hated the idea of her marrying anybody, and, since he was a fanatical horse-breeder and chariot-racer, had devised a way of getting rid of the most pressing suitors and discouraging others. Whoever offered to marry Hippodameia had to take part in a chariot-race against her father. The course was a long one, about thirty miles, all the way from Elis to the temple of Zeus at Olympia.

The suitor, with Hippodameia beside him, was given a good start, while Oinomaos sacrificed to the gods. Then he set out in pursuit and, since he had the swiftest horses and a charioteer of genius (a man called Myrtilos), always caught up with the chariot carrying his daughter. As soon as he was in close range he took the spear from its sheath at the side of his chariot and threw it at the suitor's back. He was an expert spear-thrower and never missed, and Hippodameia was equally expert at seizing the reins from her dying companion and bringing her chariot to a gentle stop. Father and daughter then returned to Elis, unloaded and burnt the corpse, put the ashes in an urn, and added it to the growing row of identical urns outside the small temple where the race always started.

Pelops went to Elis simply to have a look at Hippodameia, as many others did because of her beauty and her reputation as a woman it was unwise to fall in love with her. There was always a large crowd, mostly of foreigners, waiting to get a glimpse of her whenever she left her father's palace, usually on horseback or in her chariot for an excursion in the country, sometimes on foot in a procession to the temple for some religious ceremony. She was always well guarded, but she seemed to enjoy being admired, as she did not hold her head high and stare into the distance as so many aristocrats do in public, but looked around the faces in the crowd as if seeking somebody she knew. However, the friend with whom Pelops was staying in Elis warned him not to catch her eye.

'You might as well look at Medusa,' he said, 'the Gorgon who turns people to stone when they look at her. Hippodameia, of course, is the exact opposite, not ugly and terrifying, but irresistibly seductive. People who catch her eye either try to marry her and end up in one of the urns outside the temple, or, not being well-born, rich or rash enough to present themselves as suitors, are overwhelmed with longing and frustration, dragged down by such melancholy that they often die of it, most frequently by hanging themselves.'

It wasn't that Hippodameia wanted to cause people's death or even that she didn't care, but that she was quite desperate to escape from her father and was always hoping to catch sight of the man who would be handsome and audacious enough to make an offer for her hand, as well as strong and skilful enough to win the chariot-race. So when Pelops joined the crowd round the temple and saw her enter, he did catch her eye and knew immediately that he must compete for her. While she was inside he inspected the dozen or so urns, each neatly inscribed with the name of a loser, and decided he would rather die with her father's spear in his back than by hanging himself later. At least in the first case, he thought, he would spend some time close to Hippodameia in the chariot and he hoped he might prove the urn-victor – each urn specified how far the ashes inside had driven the chariot before being overtaken by Oinomaos. But when she came out of the temple and this time looked at nobody but Pelops and looked at him with such an expression of encouragement and hope, and even turned her head so as to keep looking at him as the procession went up the road to the palace, then Pelops knew that this was his enticing fate and that he must somehow try to avoid even thinking about ending up in the row of urns.

He thought instead of Poseidon, who had several times during Pelops' boyhood appeared to him in the form of a young man, walked with him, slept with him and caressed him. Knowing what had happened to his father and knowing how careful one had to be with gods, leaving the initiative in any relationship always with them, never asking directly for any particular favour, Pelops went down to the shore and walked along the beach. He was entirely alone there, except that his mind kept picturing Hippodameia's face and the way she walked, so lightly and lithely, like an athlete before a race. The wind had been strong the day before, though it had dropped now, but the sea was still choppy and opaque, with small waves breaking on the sand. As he walked and pictured Hippodameia, Pelops began to shout over the noise of the surf:

'Hippodameia, Hippodameia, I want you, I want you, I want you!'

After a while he stopped and listened. He thought he heard a voice. He looked all around. There was nobody, he was still alone. He walked on, shouting over the surf as before.

'Hippodameia, I want you!'

Again he seemed to hear a voice and this time he pinned it down to the sea, the surf. And what the surf seemed to be saying was:

'Silly sop, silly Pelops, she's yours, yours, yours. Race, by all means, race, race, race! Myrtilos is what matters, Myrtilos is essential, Myrtilos saves you. Fix Myrtilos first!'

Now, as it happened, Hippodameia had fallen in love with Pelops at first sight just as irrevocably as he with her. After all, there could hardly have been two more beautiful people in the whole of Greece, though it may have been that Poseidon, to reward his former catamite, had already intervened in his behalf and asked Aphrodite, goddess of love, to spike her heart. Hippodameia realised at once, of course, that if this was the man she had hoped for so long, she could not rely on his also being a first-rate charioteer. She was almost that herself, but still not a match for Myrtilos. So she had also immediately decided that the only sure answer was to fix Myrtilos, and this was not so difficult in her case, because Myrtilos, like every other man in Elis, was in love with her. She therefore simply asked him, in the privacy of the stables, that if Pelops should become a suitor, he, Myrtilos, would somehow contrive not to catch up with them. Myrtilos replied that this would be difficult, since her father would as always be in the chariot with him, but he would do or not do what he could. She gave him her hand to kiss.

Meanwhile Pelops had gone to the palace, proved his credentials as a man of impeccable birth, breeding and wealth – his father had left him all his estates in Arcadia – and asked to marry the princess Hippodameia. King Oinomaos looked at him almost sadly, admiring his good looks and quite certain that they would soon be reduced to ashes, and had him sign the usual contract for the race and its sticky conditions. Pelops asked if he might view the chariots and the horses first and Oinomaos replied:

'Of course you can, dear boy. No trickery there. It's sheer speed and skill that will win you my darling daughter and nobody could be more delighted than me if you did.'

He was not being wholly hypocritical. He liked Pelops, as people always did, and thought that if he had to marry his daughter to anyone, Pelops would be a good choice. Also, he believed that his chariot-race offered a perfectly fair chance to the suitor, a better than fair chance, for that matter, since he always gave himself the handicap of sacrificing to the gods before he started. He was not at all the sort of person who would have barbarously nailed the losers' heads to his palace wall and thrown their corpses on a rubbish-heap, as some accounts have it. He thought of himself as a sporting man, a man who could be respected by everyone as a perennial winner, a champion chariot-racer and javelin-thrower, not as a father in love with his daughter who was prepared to murder any potential rival.

Pelops went to the stables, cursorily examined the chariots and horses and sought out Myrtilos, his real purpose.

'What are my chances?' he asked.

'Nil,' said Myrtilos, a small man in his thirties with a saurian skin and a face already much lined around the eyes and mouth from his constant speed-driving into wind and sun.

'Do you think the princess is worth taking such a chance for?'

'Absolutely.'

He spoke with so much conviction that Pelops immediately understood that Myrtilos too was in love with Hippodameia.

'Would you take such a chance yourself, then?'

'Yes, if I were not a mere charioteer.'

'But in your case, if you drove Hippodameia's chariot instead of her father's, you'd have a good chance of winning.'

'I think so. For that reason, quite apart from my humble status – though I may say that my ancestry is as good as anyone's – the king would never accept me as a suitor.'

There was a note of bitterness here, which Pelops observed. This man was not wholly devoted to his master. He probed a little more.

'Suppose that you were ill on the day of the race and couldn't drive the king's chariot?'

'The race would be postponed. But it's never happened.'

'Has none of the suitors ever tried to bribe you?'

'Of course. But I can tell you straightaway that I don't take bribes. There's nothing I want. Except ...' His voice trailed away and he laughed, a noise not unlike a horse snorting.

'Except the prize itself?' said Pelops. 'A bribe of the bride?'

Myrtilos laughed, snorted again. Pelops turned away, patted the neck of the nearest horse and said very quietly, almost as if he wasn't saying it at all or just murmuring to the horse:

'And if I were to offer you that?'

'You're joking.'

'Not really.'

'Why should you take such a risk with your life just for me to win the prize?'

'Doesn't the kingdom go with the bride – once the father dies?'

'So I believe.'

'Halves, then, on that.'

'Not bad, but not enough in itself.'

'No? But we can hardly halve the bride, can we? What about the first night?'

'The first night?'

They were almost whispering now, and Myrtilos was staring at Pelops as if he was not sure he was flesh-and-blood, which of course, considering his ivory shoulder, he wasn't entirely.

'The wedding-night,' said Pelops. 'After that she would be mine.'

Myrtilos said nothing. He was remembering that Hippodameia herself had already asked him to fix the race in Pelops' favour and beginning to think that it could be done.

'And half the kingdom,' said Pelops. 'Think about it! I shall take the chance in any case and if, with your help, I win – well, then you know what you can expect.'

And smiling politely he returned to the palace, complimented the king on his horses and chariots, thanked him for his kindness in permitting him to enter such a thrilling and imaginative competition, more than worthy of the legendary games which once long ago, he was told, used to be held at Olympia, and returned to his friend's house in a mood of euphoria.

The next day he made a costly sacrifice to Poseidon, whose temple he now realised was the very one from which the race started. Poseidon, of course, was the god of horses as well as of the sea. Coming out of the temple he stopped to contemplate the row of bronze urns and even patted one or two of them, but he was careful, unlike his father, not to presume.

'We shall see,' he said to the urns. 'Wish me luck!'

The race took place a week later, bringing huge crowds to the city and, since the news of it had quickly spread, all along the route. The two chariots were drawn up in front of the palace, grooms holding the horses' heads, Myrtilos already mounted in the king's. It was still dark, but warm and windless, the cloudless sky beginning to lighten, when Pelops arrived and was instructed to mount the empty chariot. Soldiers held back the crowd, leaving a broad avenue down to the temple.

Suddenly the sun came up and just as suddenly King Oinomaos and his daughter came running out of the palace and without a pause, sprang into the chariots, Oinomaos beside Myrtilos, Hippodameia beside Pelops. What a moment for him, what a moment for her! Their arms were touching, their faces only inches apart, their eyes searching each other's. But only for a moment. Myrtilos was already driving the king's chariot down the avenue of onlookers.

'You must catch up,' said Hippodameia, 'and draw level. That's how he likes it. What he calls a friendly trot down to the start.'

So, to cheers for their king and some bitter witticisms at Pelops' expense – 'Short but sweet!' 'Enjoy your ride, it's the only one you'll get!' 'Don't bother to make a will, you won't have any children!' – the two chariots proceeded side by side at a gentle trot, while the king waved his hand to his subjects and from time to time smiled genially at his daughter and her suitor. When they reached the temple, Myrtilos stopped his chariot and Pelops drew up beside it.

Oinomaos jumped down beside the urns and, looking at Pelops with a smile which seemed now more gloating than genial, said:

'Go on, boy! Don't hang around for me! The finishing post is the temple of Zeus. My daughter will show you when you get to Olympia.'

And he added over his shoulder as he went inside Poseidon's temple:

'If you do.'

Pelops flicked the horses with the loose reins and they were off, to shouts, this time mostly of encouragement, from the crowd, some of whom still persisted, against all reason, in laying bets on the suitor at risible odds. By the time they had crossed the river and were out on the flat, fertile land that lay between the sea and the low hills with their orchards and olive trees, the horses were at full gallop.

'Don't tire them too soon!' said Hippodameia, laying her lovely hand on Pelops' arm, 'they'll hardly make the distance as it is.'

'Does that matter?' asked Pelops. 'Have they ever gone the full distance?'

'I'm hoping they will today,' she said.

'I'm hoping not.'

'What do you mean? Do you want to die? Don't you want to marry me?'

'No and yes,' said Pelops. 'But I wouldn't care to live without you, and besides I have hopes that circumstances will arise ...'

'They always hope for that, my poor suitors, that one of Father's wheels will come off, that his horses will go lame or that a monster will come out of the sea and terrify them ...'

Pelops reflected that he might have asked his lover Poseidon for that. Well, I leave it to him, he thought, it's best not to second-guess the gods and I hope I understood his advice correctly.

'... but it never happens,' said Hippodameia, 'and up to now I haven't really been sorry – sorry at the time for the waste of a person's life, of course, but not in the longer term sorry on my own account.'

'But today ...?'

'You are different. You seem to me to be a favourite of the gods. I hope I'm right.'

Neither of them liked to mention having approached Myrtilos, but both were relying on it.

After about ten miles, with as yet no sign of pursuit, the road entered a village and turned abruptly inland, winding a bit now, along the bank of the mighty Alpheios, the river who was once in love with the Nereid Arethousa and whose brown current pursued her across the sea to Sicily, where she turned into a fountain. Pelops remarked on how well-dressed the peasants were, as they lined the road and shouted greetings.

'They are not in their working clothes,' said Hippodameia, 'they always wear their festival best for these events and treat it as a holiday, with feasting and dancing in the evening.'

'Macabre,' said Pelops.

'Not really. They don't get many days off and they always enjoy a good funeral.'

The sky was still cloudless and the sun very hot now. The horses were tiring and lathered with sweat, and so were Pelops and Hippodameia. They were glad of the occasional patch of shade from the plane trees, poplars and evergreen oaks growing beside the river.

'Did none of my predecessors try to avoid your father's spear?' asked Pelops, looking back and still seeing no other chariot. 'Did none of them duck or step aside?'

'Not much room to step aside, is there? One of them tried to, but he was a fat man and the spear pierced his belly. That was unpleasant.

He took longer to die than usual. This, by the way, is the furthest I've ever come.'

'Don't speak too soon!' said Pelops, ever fearful after his father's experience of provoking the gods and glancing back nervously.

Sure enough, as they turned a corner at the end of a straight stretch of the road, he thought he had seen a small cloud of dust in the distance.

'How far to go?'

'Not very far, I think. But as I said I've never been this far before.'

'Your father told me that you'd show me the temple of Zeus.'

'He always makes the same joke.'

The next time Pelops looked back, the cloud of dust was closer. His own horses were evidently exhausted and as they descended a slope towards a blind corner, they slowed and faltered. Taking the corner they slowed again to a trot, and they had not travelled far when, rounding the corner still at the gallop, came the chariot driven by Myrtilos, with the king beside him, his face a grinning mask of sweat and dust, his right hand already reaching for his spear. Pelops clutched Hippodameia's hand.

'I'm sorry,' he said. 'I'm afraid it was not to be.'

But at that moment the pursuing chariot swayed and wobbled. Oinomaos nearly lost his footing and was clinging to the side with one hand, still grasping his spear in the other. The wobbling chariot now began to swerve, and they saw Myrtilos suddenly jump clear and land in the undergrowth at the side of the road. As he did so, a wheel flew off the chariot towards the river, the chariot lurched and turned over, while the horses, still trying to gallop, dragged it on for two or three hundred yards before stopping.

Pelops and Hippodameia looked at each other with dazed expressions as Pelops brought his own chariot to a halt.

'What now?' he said. 'Will he still come after me on foot? Should we press on?'

'I don't know,' she said. 'I'm afraid he will be hurt.'

Pelops looked as if he thought this would be the least they could hope.

'He is my father, you know,' she said, 'and I love him, though I can well understand that you don't.'

But when they reached the overturned chariot they found Oinomaos dead, pierced by his own spear. Myrtilos, limping, joined them.

'What happened?' asked Pelops.

'What do you think?'

'It was deliberate?'

'What do you think?'

He would say no more in front of Hippodameia, who was weeping over her father's body, but he told Pelops aside that he had removed the axle pins and substituted wax. It had taken longer to melt than he expected and he was afraid it wasn't going to melt at all before they caught up with Pelops and Hippodameia. That was why he'd taken the last dangerous corner at such reckless speed. And he looked meaningfully at Pelops, as if to say, 'I've kept my side of the bargain, now you do the same for yours.'

It was only fitting, when Pelops had married Hippodameia and become king of Elis, that he restored the partly ruined temple of Zeus at Olympia, as well as the stadium, and re-started the Games. After his death, his grateful people – the Games brought them wealth as well as kudos – buried him near the temple and built a sanctuary, the Pelopion, over his bones. Perhaps a millennium later, his famous chariot race was commemorated on the eastern pediment of a huge new temple of Zeus. Twenty-one figures, sculpted in Parian marble by an unknown fifth-century master, are lined up ready for the contest, with Zeus at the centre, King Oenomaos, Myrtilos and their horses on one side and Pelops, Hippodameia and their horses on the other. Reclining in the corners of the triangular space are the river gods Alpheios and Kladeos. The battered remains of this masterpiece, magnificently displayed, can still be seen today in the new Archaeological Museum at Olympia.

Across the Gulf of Argos from our village in modern Arcadia we can see the low-lying island of Spetses. Beyond that to the south and beneath the sheer cliffs on our side, the Gulf opens out into the Myrtoan Sea, a subdivision of the Aegean, as the Aegean is of the

Mediterranean. The Myrtoan Sea, the books tell us, is named after Myrtilos. But how was it, after their successful chariot-race, that the happy bride and groom from Elis on the far side of the Peloponnese, came to be travelling on this side of it, in a chariot driven by Myrtilos? The explanation given by some storytellers is not very credible. Before the race, they say, Poseidon gave Pelops a golden chariot with wings and a pair of flying horses and with this equipment Pelops and Hippodameia were easily able to outdistance her father and Myrtilos, especially since the course was impossibly long for ordinary horses. It went from Olympia to the Isthmus of Corinth over mountainous terrain. Nevertheless, to make doubly sure, Myrtilos was still required to insert wax axle-pins and the king's chariot duly crashed just before it reached the Isthmus. After that, all three survivors took off for the island of Euboia and then down the east side of the Peloponnese in the flying chariot. The main objections to this explanation are obvious: first, there was no need for Pelops, once he had Poseidon's winged chariot, to make a bargain with Myrtilos; secondly, the king's earth-bound chariot, with or without wax axle pins, would never have made it as far as the Isthmus.

What happened was this: in the immediate aftermath of the chariot race there could be no wedding until a funeral had been held for the dead king and the period of mourning prescribed by the Council of Elders had been observed. Hippodameia was now ruler of Elis and until Pelops married her he had no kingdom to share with Myrtilos. His bargain, especially the second part of it, naturally preyed on his mind, since Hippodameia herself knew nothing about it. Myrtilos, however, since he was only a charioteer and there had been no witnesses to the bargain, was not in a strong position. Pelops, therefore, made him a new promise. He would marry Hippodameia, but he would not consummate the marriage until Myrtilos had received his reward, both of the bride and half the kingdom. Myrtilos had little choice but to agree.

As soon as they were married, Pelops carried his bride away for a honeymoon, a trip to see other parts of the peninsula, with Myrtilos driving their chariot. They stayed the night mostly with other kings and were royally received. But Myrtilos, accommodated with the servants and having no means of knowing whether Pelops was keeping his promise or not, became increasingly suspicious and sulky. One day, when the going over the bare Arcadian mountains had been particularly hard, they stopped to let the tired horses rest – it was midsummer and very hot. They found a patch of shade under a rock, but Hippodameia was thirsty and they had drunk all the water in their sheepskin flask. Pelops went in search of a spring, which he eventually found some way off. As he was filling his helmet, he heard Hippodameia shouting for help. Hurrying back he met her running towards him.

'Myrtilos!' she said. 'Myrtilos tried to rape me.'

Indeed Myrtilos, still pursuing her, was not far behind. Pelops ran straight at him and knocked him down with a single blow to the face.

'Is this how you keep your promise?' said Myrtilos, through broken teeth, squirming with pain on the rocky ground and trying to shield his face with his hands as Pelops leant over him and seemed about to hit him again.

'There was no promise of rape,' said Pelops, 'and you've certainly made it impossible now for me to keep my promise.'

'And my half of your kingdom? Is that another promise impossible to keep?'

'We'll talk about that another time.'

Hippodameia was all for leaving Myrtilos in the mountains as a prey for the lions, but Pelops argued that one could not count on lions – they had seen none so far – and told her he would find some surer way to lose him. So they rode on, and one can imagine the explosive feelings of hatred, guilt, fear and indignation that filled those three tight-lipped persons packed into one small chariot.

As the sun began to sink behind them they came in sight of the sea and were soon following a narrow track on the edge of the cliffs, looking for a way down to one of the fishing villages far below in small bays along the shore. The exhausted horses began to stumble and the dispirited Myrtilos, nursing his painful mouth, was hardly able to control the chariot, which swayed alarmingly towards the precipitous edge of the track.

'Watch out there!' cried Hippodameia.

'Wake up, you lousy lecher!' said Pelops.

Myrtilos' suppressed fury and sense of grievance welled up and he burst out:

'You are a pair! Didn't you both ask me to rig the race ? Didn't you, Pelops, make promises which you had no intention of keeping? Didn't I kill the king for your convenience? I wish I'd let him kill you. You are a pair of cheats and liars.'

That was all Pelops needed. He tore the reins from the charioteer's hands and threw them to Hippodameia, seized Myrtilos round the waist, lifted him bodily and tossed him over the side of the chariot and the cliff. They heard him scream, as he hurtled down towards the sea:

'My curse on you, Pelops. My curse on your seed!'

Not everyone's curses are effective, of course. But Myrtilos was the child of Hermes, the god of shepherds and travellers, who promised, as he escorted his dead son's soul to the underworld, to see the curse fulfilled. Pelops himself, ever the favourite of the gods, seems to have got away with no more than a ritual cleansing from the crime of murder, and the Peloponnese was named after him because by the end of his life he ruled most of it.

Part of the purpose of his honeymoon trip with Hippodameia was no doubt to put off his reckoning with Myrtilos – he surely never intended to kill him from the outset, or he would have done so sooner. His main purpose was to see the peninsula for himself, not quite as a simple tourist, rather as a king who meant to enlarge his dominions. He did not call on his fellow kings out of mere convenience or courtesy, but to observe their characters and even more their resources, both in specie and manpower. And since most of the Peloponnesian kings in those days were hardly more than the chief men and principal landowners in territories containing a market town and a few dozen scattered villages, he was encouraged by what he saw. So, having recruited and trained an army from Hippodameia's people, augmented by special forces (rough tough shepherds and hunters from his own domains in Arcadia), he set about acquiring the rest of the peninsula by a combination of political manoeuvre (allying himself with one king, against whom he later allied himself with another), friendly or unfriendly persuasion, and as the last resort, armed force. He didn't have to fight many battles. The kings he overthrew were most of them weak and lazy and their people fared much better under Pelops' unified rule than before. When at last he died of old age he was widely mourned and the Peloponnese reverted to a patchwork of small kingdoms.

3. THE BROTHERS

The curse fell on his seed. Argos, the largest and richest kingdom of the Peloponnese, was disputed between two of his many sons, Atreus and Thyestes, who agreed to put themselves up for election by the Argives. Since they were both notable astronomers and the Argives were passionate star-gazers, their election turned on which of them could make the most impressive contribution to their science – perhaps the first and last time in history or even myth that the choice of a ruler depended on such a test. Thyestes, the younger brother, observed that the sun rose in different parts of the sky according to the time of year, but Atreus said that it was not the sun that rose and set, but the earth, travelling in the opposite direction from the sun; and for good measure he made mathematical calculations to predict an eclipse of the sun.

Atreus was understandably elected king, took up residence at Mycenae and married a granddaughter of Minos, the late great king of Crete. It was surely this woman, Queen Aerope, who brought the sophisticated arts and fashions of her grandfather's highly civilised court at Knossos to Mycenae, so that when Knossos was destroyed by an earthquake, Mycenae succeeded it as the centre of Greek civilisation. She also brought to Mycenae the symbol of Cretan sovereignty, the sacred and sacrificial double-headed axe, with which her elder son Agamemnon was in due course beheaded by his wife Clytemnestra. Was it Aerope too who installed Cretan sanitation and a bathroom at Mycenae? And was it mere coincidence or the repetitive pattern of heredity that caused her son Agamemnon to die in that bath, or just out of it? Aerope's grandfather King Minos had also died in a bath, when boiling water was poured down on him from a pipe in the ceiling – the first recorded shower – constructed by his ingenious engineer, Daidalos, creator of the famous labyrinth at Knossos.

Unfortunately the innovating and civilising Aerope was seduced by King Atreus' envious brother Thyestes. Perhaps this was Thyestes' revenge for his failure to win the throne or perhaps it was simply that Aerope, like her grandfather, found monogamy boring and did not imagine the frightful consequences. Either way, it hardly mattered. The essential element in this appalling story was that the brothers Atreus and Thyestes detested one another. Myrtilos' curse had settled on them.

Concealing his black fury over Aerope's adultery, Atreus sent a message to his brother proposing to divide the kingdom with him and inviting him to dinner. The messenger was evidently a persuasive, ingratiating person and Thyestes came. Atreus welcomed him in person and led him into the great hall, where only two places were laid and no one else was present except guards and servants.

'No need for ceremony between brothers,' said Atreus pleasantly, 'and besides we have a matter to discuss which concerns us two alone.'

However, as they settled on their couches and the first courses were brought in, they did not discuss the kingdom but the stars.

'There is a constellation I have decided to name "The Charioteer",' said Atreus, 'after that poor fellow Myrtilos who fell over a cliff when he was driving Mother and Father on their honeymoon. What do you think?'

'Does he deserve such an honour?' said Thyestes. 'Didn't he try to rape Mother?'

'But he didn't succeed,' said Atreus, 'and certainly paid for his insolence.'

'And put a curse on our family,' said Thyestes.

'Do you think we should take that seriously?'

'We have had our differences,' said Thyestes, with a smile, 'but no more perhaps than most families.'

'Just so. But it's worrying to have a curse hanging over us and this might be a way of neutralising it. After dinner we'll go outside and I'll show you the constellation I mean.'

The main course was a casserole. But this time, unlike their grandfather Tantalos' casserole, it was not meant to please the guest and the host didn't touch it. It contained the juiciest parts of Thyestes' sons, including the latest, the child of his liaison with Queen Aerope, and while Thyestes was eating it, Atreus' suppressed rage suddenly got the better of him and he stood up:

'You have an appetite, don't you, Thyestes? Yes, you are a greedy man. You want to swallow half my kingdom and you've already helped yourself to my wife. And now you're eating up Aglaos, Callileon, Orchomenos and little Pleisthenes, my wife's bastard.'

At that, the servants brought in on silver platters the heads and hands and feet of the slaughtered children. Vomiting on the floor of the great hall, blinded by tears, lunging at his cruelly laughing brother, whose guards seized him and dragged him out into the night where his chariot waited for him under the starry sky, Thyestes shouted back at the ill-omened palace as he was carried away down the steep street:

'My curse on you, Atreus! My curse on all your House!'

After this Atreus' anger was still not satiated and he took his wife to Nauplia.

'On a bad day for me,' said Atreus as they stood on the jetty, 'you came over the sea from Crete and landed here at Nauplia, and now on a bad day for you, you can go back where you came from.'

Then he had his men carry her into the sea and hold her under until she drowned.

Thyestes, meanwhile, left his brother's kingdom and went to Delphi to ask Apollo's oracle what he should do to cure the horror of eating his own children and to punish his brother. Apparently the oracle replied that he must get a child with his daughter Pelopeia and this child would avenge him. This was indeed the truth, but can we believe that the god's oracle unambiguously encouraged incest? More likely, in view of what happened, Thyestes himself gave this twist to an oracle which merely told him that another son would, as sons were bound to by customary law, do the deed for him.

Leaving Delphi and crossing the Corinthian Gulf, Thyestes came to the city of Sikyon, where his daughter Pelopeia was a priestess in the temple. He arrived by night and found the city enjoying a festival. Inside a large tent erected in the public gardens he could hear laughter, music and dancing. In his desperate state of vengeful misery, hating the very thought of people enjoying themselves, he was about to turn away, when he saw a woman leave the tent and make for a nearby fish pond. He followed her stealthily. Reaching the pond, she removed her tunic and began washing out a red stain. Thyestes glimpsed her exposed breasts and saw that she was young and perhaps even a virgin. His misery turned to lust. Pulling his cap over the upper part of his face so as not to be known, he rushed forward, seized hold of her and clapping his hand over her mouth to prevent her from screaming, hurried her into a grove of trees. There he forced her to the ground and raped her. She was indeed a virgin. As soon as he had enjoyed her, Thyestes withdrew and hurried away into the darkness, forgetting that he had laid his sword aside during the rape. When he discovered its absence he was afraid to go back for it in case the girl's friends or relations would be looking for him. In fact, *he* was her nearest relation, for though he didn't recognise her in the dark, nor she him, she was his daughter Pelopeia. During one of the sacred dances performed by the priestesses, she had slipped in the blood of the sacrificial victim and stained her tunic. Now her skirt was also stained, with her own blood.

Thyestes left Sikyon that same night and fled eastwards past Corinth until he came to a small seaport. From there he travelled from island to island across the Aegean, until he reached Lydia on the coast of Asia Minor, where he had cousins and could hope to find a wife to bear him the son who would avenge him. But that son was already in the making. His daughter, though she didn't know it, was pregnant. She had found her attacker's sword and hidden it in the temple, but she couldn't, now that she was no longer a virgin, remain a priestess. However, her high birth gave her access to the queen of Sikyon, to whom she explained what had been done to her. The queen spoke to her husband, King Thesprotos, and this kindly couple took Pelopeia into the palace and treated her as their own daughter, little knowing that they were helping to fulfil the curse, the two curses now on the House of Atreus.

Atreus himself, whose kingdom was suffering from drought and a bad harvest, had qualms about what he had done to his brother and he too made a trip to Delphi to ask the oracle for advice. He was told to bring Thyestes back from Sikyon, so, like his brother shortly before him, he crossed the Corinthian Gulf, but this time arriving in daylight and going straight to the king's palace, where, as a more powerful ruler than Thesprotos, he was received with great respect. Thesprotos knew nothing of Thyestes' brief visit, of course, and, since the brothers' mutual hatred was common knowledge, suspected that Atreus only wanted to find his brother in order to kill him. He was therefore careful not to mention that the girl he was treating as his own daughter was actually Thyestes'. But Atreus caught sight of Pelopeia as she was going to draw water at the well, immediately took a fancy to her and asked King Thesprotos who she was.

'My daughter,' said Thesprotos, thinking to protect her with this insignificant lie.

'A lovely young woman,' said Atreus, 'excellent carriage, good colour in her cheeks, proud and spirited, I should say, by the way she holds her head up and looks around her. She does credit to her pedigree.'

'Thank you,' said Thesprotos and allowed himself a little private joke, 'Pedigree wins out.'

'I daresay you've heard that I recently lost my dear wife Aerope. I would like your daughter to take her place.'

Thesprotos was trapped. He could only reply that he was deeply honoured but would need to consult his wife and daughter. Both agreed that it was better not to tell Atreus the truth and that in the long run, if he ever discovered that Pelopeia was really his niece, that might even help to reconcile the brothers. They also agreed that, since her name implied her real pedigree and that Atreus might remember that his brother had a daughter called Pelopeia, she should change her name to Asteria. She herself was delighted at the prospect of becoming queen of such a prestigious kingdom as Argos and holding court in the great palace of Mycenae. She had no idea – how could she imagine such a thing? – of what her uncle/bridegroom had done to her brothers and her father in that very place.

They were married within days and Atreus returned in an optimistic mood to Mycenae with his new queen. He felt that in sending him to Sikyon to look for his brother, the oracle had really meant him to find Asteria (Pelopeia) and that this happy outcome amounted to absolution for his murder of Thyestes' sons. He was even happier when he learnt that his new wife was pregnant and made much of their new son, born a few weeks earlier than might have been expected. This son was named Aigisthos and was brought up in the palace at Mycenae with his older half-siblings, Agamemnon, Menelaos and Anaxibia. Pelopeia herself, of course, suspected that Aigisthos was really the child of the unknown rapist, but saw no reason to say anything about that to a husband who was prone to rages and fits of melancholia, but whom she could manage as long as she never directly opposed his wishes or inquired into his past.

So the two curses – Myrtilos' and Thyestes' – slumbered for many years, while the next generation of the House of Atreus grew up. Atreus and Thyestes were already growing old when Pelopeia, paying a visit to her supposed parents in Sikyon, was asked if she knew anything about the mysterious sword which had been discovered in the temple, hidden under the statue of Athene. Yes, she said, it belonged to the man who raped her all those years ago.

'It's no ordinary piece of bronze,' said Thesprotos, 'but of very fine workmanship. I hardly like to tell you this: it's engraved with the trident symbol of the House of Pelops. Its owner, your attacker, must have been some distant relative of yours, unless of course he was a thief and had stolen it.'

Pelopeia was not too dismayed. The attack had happened long before, she was the much respected queen of Argos and already married, after all, to a relative, her uncle, though he didn't know it. She took the sword back to Mycenae and gave it to her son, Aigisthos, now a boy of twelve. He was a physically weak child, but imaginative and addicted to the stories of heroes, and possessing the sword made him feel that he himself would grow up to be a hero. He kept it always beside his bed at night and strutted about wearing it by day. His elder half-brothers Agamemnon and Menelaos smiled at his pretensions and were sometimes irritated enough to mock him, but never in front of their formidable father or the boy's doting mother, their very young stepmother, scarcely older than themselves.

But through all these years Argos, usually one of the most fertile areas in Greece, had suffered from a lack of rain. As the drought worsened and the crops failed and famine threatened, the Argives began to blame their ruler. Unpleasant rumours spread about the disappearance of his brother and his previous wife. Atreus recalled that the Delphic oracle had told him to bring his brother back to Argos and that instead of doing so he had brought back a new wife, who had only borne him one son. Clearly the gods were seriously displeased with him. He knew that his brother had taken refuge in Lydia and sent a messenger begging him to return to Argos, swearing solemnly that no harm would be done to him and that he would have the palace at Tiryns to live in and all the eastern part of the kingdom to govern.

Thyestes came, not innocently and trustingly this time, but still looking for revenge, well aware that the Argives were blaming Atreus for their troubles and might even be stirred to open rebellion in Thyestes' favour. When he reached Mycenae he would not enter the palace, but stayed with one of the elders who had originally supported his claim to the kingdom and demanded that Atreus meet him in the open, without guards, in the presence of enough citizens to ensure his safety. Atreus, anxious to mollify both the gods and his people and if possible end the famine, readily agreed. So, in the open space in front of the palace portico, from where the chariot had carried Thyestes cursing down the street on that dreadful night when he ate his own children, the brothers met again.

The crowd of witnesses fell silent as Thyestes walked up from the street and Atreus came out of the palace. The brothers stopped some distance apart and stared at each other. Atreus moved first, stepping close to his brother and speaking in a voice too low for the crowd to hear.

'Well, Thyestes, your beard and hair are white.'

'As yours are, Atreus.'

'Just so. And in other ways too we are quits, aren't we?

'Are we? You have two sons and a daughter – three sons now, I hear – while I have only a daughter, a priestess vowed to celibacy when I last heard of her, though I have long since lost touch with her.'

'You took my wife, I took your sons.'

'A very unequal exchange. And you have a kingdom, I have none.'

'I will share it with you if you can agree that we are quits.'

'Then say it so that everyone can hear!'

Atreus did so.

'And one more thing,' said Thyestes. 'I require a pledge for your sincerity, a hostage. I will take your youngest son to live with me – he is after all my nephew and I shall treat him lovingly and gently and not at all as you treated your nephews, my sons. I will send him back to you as soon as I feel that I'm securely installed in the palace at Tiryns and truly sharing the kingdom with you.'

Atreus agreed. He no longer had much affection for Aigisthos, who was always afraid of him and clung to his mother.

There in front of the citizens the brothers drank together from the same cup, then each returned the way he had come. But when Atreus told Pelopeia that Aigisthos was to go to Thyestes, she was devastated and said she must go with him. This Atreus could not permit, afraid that Thyestes might seduce this wife as he had Aerope. It would do the boy good, he said, to be separated for a while from his mother. His own servants at Tiryns, which was less than ten miles away, would bring them regular news of Aigisthos and he did not think he would be absent for more than a few months. The child made even more fuss than his mother when told that he was to live with his uncle, but he had no choice. He was sent to Tiryns, where his uncle was now installed, and his precious sword went with him.

Thyestes was already taking advantage of his new powers as governor of eastern Argolis to weaken his brother's hold over the whole kingdom. He had little difficulty in finding men who had been pushed aside or passed over by Atreus and would be glad to see him overthrown, but he had to be careful that his conversations with them were not overheard by the servants at Tiryns, whom he intended gradually to replace but who for the moment had to be considered as spies for Atreus. He made frequent journeys through the territory he governed and held secret meetings along his route.

When Aigisthos arrived at Tiryns, Thyestes was just returning from one of his subversive trips and not in a good mood. His conversations with several local chieftains had been inconclusive and he thought one of them was not to be trusted, might even have been deliberately leading him on before reporting back to Atreus. As his chariot passed through the gate and drove up the steep ramp between the mighty stone walls built by a former king of the Perseid dynasty, it overtook the wagon carrying Aigisthos and his escort. Thyestes jumped down in the courtyard at the top of the ramp, ordered his servants to fetch the women from the palace and himself helped Aigisthos out of the wagon.

'Welcome to Tiryns, dear boy!' he said, 'But what's this? You're a bit young to carry such a big sword. I hope you don't mean to murder your uncle.'

'My mother gave it to me,' said Aigisthos, nervous and tearful, 'and it's a very special sword. I always keep it with me. Do you want to see it?'

And taking it out of his belt, he held it up so that Thyestes could see its fine workmanship and the Pelopian trident engraved on the blade. His uncle humoured him by looking at it with pretended attention. But what he saw jolted him into real attention.

'Your mother gave it to you? Where did she get it?'

'I don't know exactly. I think it came from my grandparents in Sikyon.'

'Very likely. I haven't met your mother. What's her name?'

'What's her name? My mother is the queen – Queen Asteria.'

'Yes, of course. My mind was wandering.'

Far from wandering, Thyestes' mind was working so fast he felt giddy. How could his own sword have come into the hands of Atreus' wife? Did she know that it belonged to him, and that it was he who had raped the woman at Sikyon? Why had she given it to her son? Would this mean that all his hopes of revenge were for nothing, that he must go on the run again? Somehow he must meet and speak to the queen privately and get answers to these questions, but what chance was there of that, given Atreus' jealousy?

In the meantime he devoted himself to making a friend of the boy, treating him as his own son (as he really was, though neither of them yet knew it), playing draughts and backgammon with him, seating him at his own table and beside him in the throne room on official occasions, demanding from all his servants the deference to Aigisthos which he had never had at Mycenae. Aigisthos' own tutor had come with him from Mycenae, but Thyestes often looked in on their lessons and himself taught him the rudiments of astronomy and mathematics.

All this was reported back to Atreus and passed on by him to Pelopeia. Her son was evidently happy and flourishing, but the more she was assured of this the more she missed him and wanted to see him again. Her health began to deteriorate; she was eating little and taking no interest in anything but news of Aigisthos. Atreus felt obliged at last to allow her to visit him, but she must stay only for the day and return to Mycenae by nightfall.

So when she arrived at Tiryns, Thyestes discovered that he was not welcoming an unknown woman called Asteria, but his own daughter Pelopeia. And when they had embraced and gone inside and were alone together, she told him how she had been raped on the night of the festival in Sikyon and adopted by King Thesprotos as his daughter and as such married to Atreus, who was still ignorant of her real identity. But what of Aigisthos, Thyestes wanted to know, was he Atreus' son or the child of her attacker? She could not say for sure, but she feared he was the latter.

Thyestes did not tell Pelopeia that he was the rapist, that the sword was his sword, and Aigisthos his own incestuous son. He sent her back that evening to Mycenae with instructions not to disturb Atreus, not to tell him anything except that she had found her son well and happy and that Thyestes now felt perfectly secure and would soon send his hostage back to Mycenae. His own course was clear. He had already gained Aigisthos' confidence, he must now gradually detach him from any lingering loyalty to Atreus and turn him into the perfect instrument of revenge. And remembering now what the oracle had told him all those years ago, he felt that the gods were with him and that he could hardly fail.

By the time Aigisthos returned to Mycenae he was fully prepared for his task. He believed that he was Thyestes' son and that Pelopeia/Asteria was not his mother but his sister; that his uncle Atreus was a monster who had stolen the throne and murdered all his elder brothers; that his precious sword was indeed his father's, who had given it to his sister, his supposed mother, to pass on to him, so that when the time came he could use it to avenge his father and his brothers. Aigisthos' weak character and strong imagination had been forged into a fierce desire to right his family's wrongs and prove himself a true heir to his legendary grandfather Pelops.

One night, as Atreus, tired and sleepy after a heavy meal, was about to retire to bed, he met Aigisthos in the corridor. The boy was trailing his precious sword as usual.

'Where are you off to, boy?' said Atreus. 'It's late and you should be in bed.'

Aigisthos said nothing but stood staring at him with what seemed to Atreus a look of insolence.

'You're getting rather too old to be always carrying that ridiculous toy around with you. In fact, it's not a toy but a dangerous weapon. I can't imagine why your mother gave it to you. I think you'd better give it to me before you harm yourself or someone else with it.'

Aigisthos still said nothing and went on staring at him.

'Come on, boy!' said Atreus, beginning to be angry, 'Give it to me and go off to bed!'

Aigisthos seemed about to do so, but instead grasped the hilt with both hands and, as he had been carefully taught by his father, plunged the blade under Atreus' rib-cage and upwards to his heart. With a great cry of pain and fury, Atreus fell dead at his feet. Guards and servants came running from all directions and surrounded the dead king and his boy murderer. He was still holding the bloody sword and looking about with an air of confidence and triumph, as if expecting to be congratulated. No one dared come too near him until Pelopeia appeared with some of her women attendants.

'What have you done, Aigisthos?' she said.

'I have killed my brothers' killer,' he said.

'What do you mean? You have killed your father and your brothers are both alive.'

Indeed Agamemnon and Menelaos were just pushing their way to the front of the crowd of servants.

'They are not my brothers and this is not my father. Thyestes is my father and this is his sword.'

'What nonsense! Who told you that?'

'*He* told me. My father Thyestes told me.'

'*His* sword?'

'Yes. And you are not my mother, but my sister Pelopeia.'

Then Pelopeia knew who had raped her in Sikyon.

'You gave me the sword,' said Aigisthos, 'so that one day I could avenge you and your dead brothers. And now I've done it.'

'Give me back the sword!' said Pelopeia. 'You have done a terrible thing, but so have we all. And now everything must come into the light. Your uncle murdered your brothers and mine, but you are my son as well as my brother, and your father was my father. I don't wonder that the rivers have dried up and the crops failed in Argos. Our family is its curse and we are all cursed.'

She took the sword from Aigisthos, turned the blade towards her own breast and pressed it home.

As soon as the news reached Thyestes, he and his supporters took possession of Mycenae and seized control of the kingdom. Atreus and Pelopeia were quietly buried in the royal cemetery just inside the Lion Gate. Aigisthos, who had been locked in a dungeon at Mycenae, was released and sent to the small neighbouring kingdom of Troezen to be ritually cleansed of murdering his uncle. But Atreus' three children, Agamemnon, Menelaos and Anaxibia, knowing only too well what fate awaited them at their uncle's hands, had already fled into the mountains of Arcadia and made their way from there to Sparta, where they were given asylum by its king, Tyndareus.

Thyestes ruled Argos for several years with increasing severity, since however much the Argives pitied him for the horrible murder of his sons, they could not forgive him for his own and his son Aigisthos' acts of rape and murder, and to judge by the continuing lack of rain and poor harvests, the gods were still displeased. When Agamemnon returned at the head of an army from Sparta there was little opposition. Hoping to end the curse, Agamemnon spared his uncle's life on the condition that he left the kingdom and swore never to return. Aigisthos, now fully grown, fled back to Troezen, but he did not seem a threat to Agamemnon, who had always despised him and considered that the murder of Atreus had really been committed not by the foolish, impressionable boy, but by his instigator, Thyestes.

While they were living in Sparta, Agamemnon and Menelaos married King Tyndareus' daughters, Clytemnestra and Helen. They hardly looked like sisters, though they were both certainly the daughters of Tyndareus' wife, the lovely Leda. Clytemnestra resembled her tall, sharp-faced father, but in those days, when the gods still frequently intervened in human affairs, many believed that Zeus himself had seduced Leda and was the father of the dazzling Helen. Her god-like beauty was often compared to Aphrodite's, and perhaps it was from anger at such a comparison that the goddess of love picked Helen to be the first cause of so much death and destruction to both Greeks and Trojans. People were really thinking of Aphrodite's statues, of course, since few had ever set eyes on the goddess of love herself. After King Tyndareus abdicated his throne, Menelaos and Helen became king and queen of Sparta and the surrounding territory of Lakonike; while Agamemnon and Clytemnestra, whose imposing figure and relentless will reminded people of the statues and stories of the goddess Hera, jealous consort of the multiprogenitive Zeus, became king and queen of Argos.

4. THE SACRIFICE

Sitting on our terrace in Arcadia overlooking the Gulf of Argos, I had thought of seeing Agamemnon's great fleet leaving for Troy and returning much depleted ten years later. But what about all the other fleets I might have seen? Seven hundred years after the War of Troy, in the Peloponnesian War between Sparta and Athens, when Sparta was strongest by land, but Athens by sea, Athenian triremes must have sailed past us to nearby Thyrea (now called Astros). Thyrea belonged to Athens' ally Argos, but had been seized and fortified by the Spartans. And I might have seen the Athenian ships returning victorious with a cargo of prisoners, including the Spartan governor, Tantalos, whose namesake was still doing time in Tartaros.

Then, after the Roman conquest of Greece in 27 BC, I would have seen Roman navies and traders coming and going from Nauplia, and later still the Byzantines, who still called themselves Romans. In the sixth century AD came Slavs and Avars from the north, in the ninth and tenth centuries Arab pirates from the south, and after the Fourth Crusade in 1204 Frankish knights from Burgundy and Flanders, Champagne Charlies who built castles all over the Peloponnese and turned it into the feudal Principality of Achaea. Geoffrey de Villehardouin captured Nauplia in 1210, but in 1388 the latest heir to the Franks, Marie d'Enghien, sold it to the Venetians, who lost it to the Turks in 1540, recovered it in 1686 and lost it again in 1715. In 1770 a Russian fleet sailed up the Gulf to Nauplia but didn't stay to occupy it.

In 1822 the Greeks at last recovered Nauplia from the Turks, but its two mighty fortresses were occupied by rival warlords conducting their own civil war, until sailing past me to the rescue of the benighted inhabitants came a British fleet, under Admiral Sir Edward Codrington, commander of the combined British, French and Russian fleets that had recently destroyed the Ottoman fleet at Navarino (now Pylos) on the far side of the Peloponnese. Six years later, after the assassination in Nauplia of Capodistrias, the first regent of newly independent Greece, the Greeks elected their first modern king, the young prince Otho, son of King Ludwig I of Bavaria. He too sailed past to claim his throne in Nauplia and returned a year later when his capital was transferred to Athens.

Then, on the night of 26 April 1941, I might have seen the disastrous evacuation of some seven thousand British troops in the face of the German invasion: huge explosions of light and sound as Stukas dive-bombed the British transport ships and destroyers, sinking several with the loss of many lives. Finally, in October 1944, after the German withdrawal, I would have seen a British fleet return to Nauplia to organise the surrender of the Germans' Greek collaborators, the Security Battalions, and their removal to the island of Spetses, just over there from where I'm sitting, on the other side of the Gulf, where it opens into the Myrtoan Sea.

After Agamemnon's 160 ships on their way to Troy had rounded Spetses, then called Pityoussa, or 'pine tree island', they turned north to rendezvous with all the other Greek fleets at Aulis on the coast of Boeotia. Sheltered from the north-east wind by the long island of Euboia, this was a good place for so many ships to meet and wait, but impossible to leave if the north-easterly persisted. As it did on this occasion, and day by day the troops became more and more restless. Agamemnon consulted the priest he had brought from Argos, a man called Calchas, whose father Thestor had been a notable prophet and taught his son to be an even better one. Calchas made sacrifices, consulted the omens, spoke to the gods in his dreams, and finally informed Agamemnon that Artemis, the goddess of hunting and wild creatures, was angry with him.

'What have I done?' asked Agamemnon. 'Is this still the curse on my family?'

'It's possible,' said Calchas, 'but I can't tell you exactly. Gods have long memories for injuries. Long ago, when you were passing through Arcadia on your way to Sparta, did you shoot any deer?'

'Of course I did,' said Agamemnon. 'We had to eat.'

'Arcadia is her own hunting ground,' said Calchas, 'and perhaps you were so unfortunate as to bring down one of her favourite animals.'

'How was I to know?'

'You weren't. It's all too easy to offend a god without being aware of it, but that is no excuse in the god's eyes. You might, on top of that, have been particularly proud of the accuracy of your aim and remarked to your companions – or even muttered to yourself under your breath – something like "Bravo, Agamemnon, what a shot! Artemis couldn't have done it better." That would have been ultra-offensive.'

'Well, I got some good shots, certainly. I've always been a first-rate archer –'

'Careful, sir, careful!'

'– but I don't recall comparing myself to Artemis. Even at that young age, when most people are boasters and show-offs, I knew that could only lead to trouble. Anyway, assuming you're right and that I have somehow offended her, what can I do now to appease her? This expedition against Troy is finished, everybody is going to go home unless the wind changes.'

'You will not like the remedy. I am even reluctant to say what it is.'

'Say it!'

'Remember I am only the messenger! Please don't shoot the messenger!'

'Say it!'

'You have three daughters. You must sacrifice the most beautiful to Artemis.'

'Iphigeneia! No! No! Nobody makes human sacrifices. You must have got your message wrong.'

'I'm afraid not. It's true that most of the gods dislike human sacrifices, but Artemis does sometimes demand them. She is a goddess, you see, who regards all creatures on earth as essentially wild, as either hunters or their game, and she has as little compunction in taking humans or even human young, if that suits her, as we have in taking a deer or a fawn or a lion-cub.'

Agamemnon called all the Greek leaders to his tent and told them what Calchas had told him.

'I cannot do it,' he said. 'Even if I could, my wife Clytemnestra would never allow it. We must all disperse and go home.'

The other Greek leaders sympathised with him, but refused to accept that there would be no war with Troy. Menelaos, in particular, though he was Agamemnon's brother, was adamant.

'The effect of your refusing to sacrifice your beautiful daughter Iphigeneia,' he said, 'is that I must sacrifice my still more beautiful wife Helen to her Trojan abductor. What does this tell the world about Greeks? That we sit down meekly under any insult and injury barbarians care to offer us?'

Odysseus, king of the little island of Ithaka, was cleverer.

'Send for Iphigeneia!' he said. 'There's no need to tell your wife why. In any case, I'm sure that your willingness to sacrifice your daughter will be quite enough to appease the goddess and she'll relent when she sees all the preparations made, especially if you promise to give Iphigeneia to her service as a priestess.'

'Perhaps you're right,' said Agamemnon, 'but my wife will not send Iphigeneia without some good reason.'

Odysseus thought for a moment, looked round the assembled leaders and said:

'Tell her that you want to marry her to the prince Achilles!'

'Achilles is not here. He's promised to sail directly from Thessaly to Troy.'

'Precisely,' said Odysseus.

So on this pretext, Agamemnon sent a message to Clytemnestra, who was only too delighted to send her daughter to Aulis for what she thought would be the most prestigious marriage any girl could make. But what Agamemnon – clever with his bow and spear, but not with his head – had not foreseen was that Clytemnestra herself would accompany her daughter. When they arrived, the wind was still blowing from the north-east and the pyre on which Iphigeneia was to be burnt after having her throat cut was already being heaped up. What could Agamemnon say to his wife now? He helped her and their daughter disembark, sent them to his quarters to settle in, and summoned crafty Odysseus.

'You've landed me in no end of trouble,' said Agamemnon.

'Women always outwit us,' said Odysseus, 'even the cleverest of us.'

'Well, what am I to do?'

'Your wife has the reputation of being the most formidable woman in Greece. She is, of course, the niece of my wife Penelope, Tyndareus' sister, who is the next most formidable.'

'And so?'

'And so, to judge by my own experience, any further attempt to deceive her will be useless. You must tell her the truth.'

'Tell her that I'm proposing to sacrifice our daughter!'

'Tell her that if Troy is to be punished for abducting her sister Helen, Greece must make this terrible sacrifice! If not, we end our expedition here and all disperse. That is the truth and you must show her our mighty armada and legions of soldiers and appeal to her sense of honour. This sacrifice is not yours or hers, it is demanded by a goddess, it is for the sake of all Greece. And aren't we all, kings and princes and soldiers alike, the pick of our people, ready to sacrifice our lives on the plain of Troy for the same cause, for the injury done to her own sister?'

In those words or as many of them as he could remember, clumsily, without Odysseus' fluent flow of rhetoric, Agamemnon told Clytemnestra the truth. The outcome was exactly what he expected. His wife's rage could be heard all over the camp. The lie about a marriage with Achilles infuriated her even more than the idea of her daughter being sacrificed. She wanted the priest Calchas to be put to death for his unholy and unsubstantiated prophecy and she swore that if Iphigeneia *were* to be sacrificed, she would never forgive any member of the expedition, least of all its commander-in-chief Agamemnon.

But Iphigeneia herself had heard the quarrel between her parents, the stumbling apologies and halting arguments of her father and the bitter recriminations of her mother. When at last they fell silent, staring at one another with smouldering hatred, this beautiful girl who had come expecting to be married to Achilles astonished them both by taking her father's side.

'No one's life is secure,' she said, 'and all of us have to die one day, perhaps even today or tomorrow. Every man here, as Father said, is ready to die for the honour of Greece and many of them surely will. Why should I, just because I am a woman, be more afraid to die than they are? Why shouldn't I show them the way to go into the underworld with courage? I thought I was coming here to marry Achilles. What a match, what an honour for me! But would he have considered it an honour? Let me show him that it would have been! My little brother Orestes is still a baby, but if he were my age he would be going to fight at Troy with all the other young princes, Achilles, Diomedes, Ajax. Do you think that King Agamemnon's eldest daughter is not as brave as if she were his son, as brave as any prince? If I am to be the first to sacrifice my life, I shall be the one that everyone will remember. Even my aunt Helen and the Trojans will hear of it and understand what it means to stir up Greeks. How could I return to Argos knowing that because I was afraid to die Troy was not punished? Besides, if the goddess Artemis demands my life, how can I refuse? Gods must be obeyed.'

Never was any sacrifice performed with such solemnity and emotion as Iphigeneia's at Aulis. Tens of thousands of men in full armour, their spears reversed to point at the ground, their heads bowed in sorrow and admiration, their eyes running tears, stood in complete silence as the girl, dressed all in white and garlanded with flowers, walked out alone to the altar where Calchas awaited her with the sacrificial knife. Ten years later, after the sack of Troy, when Odysseus demanded the sacrifice of King Priam's daughter Polyxena as an offering to the shade of the dead Achilles, there can be little doubt that this atrocity was meant to mirror at the end of the war the atrocity committed at its outset, to inflict on the Trojans what the Greeks had inflicted on themselves. And when Polyxena took the sacrifice to herself, insisted on going willingly to her death and slitting her own throat, she was surely imitating Iphigeneia's self-sacrifice and demonstrating that a princess of Troy could match the courage of a princess of Argos. But because one sacrifice marked the beginning of violence and slaughter and the other the end, there was a significant difference: Iphigeneia offered herself to her own people in a spirit of hope for their future, while Polyxena, in front of her burning city, with her people dead or enslaved, surrounded by the implacable ranks of her enemies, can only have felt despair.

One story has it that Iphigeneia did not die at Aulis, that at the last moment Artemis substituted a deer for the human victim and secretly carried Iphigeneia away to become her priestess at Tauris in a savage northern land (now the Crimea) beyond the Pontos Euxeinos (now the Black Sea). It might be comforting to believe that – except that as a priestess in Tauris she would have been offering human sacrifices – and perhaps many of the horrified witnesses of the sacrifice at Aulis afterwards preferred to believe it, but it must have been done with such secrecy, such divine subterfuge that none of those present knew it. Otherwise Clytemnestra would not have returned to Mycenae with such an incandescent rage for revenge that it had still not cooled ten and more years later when the burning beacon on Mount Arachnaion would have been not only the signal of her husband's triumphant return, but in her eyes the re-ignition of that monstrous bonfire at Aulis which consumed her daughter and for which Agamemnon would now at last pay with his head. Whichever is true, that Artemis accepted the sacrifice of Iphigeneia or that she only pretended to, the immediate result was the same. The wind changed and blew the Greek fleet to Troy.

5. THE MATRICIDE

So now the curses of Myrtilos and Thyestes passed to the third generation of Pelops' seed. Elektra had long since grown up and been married to that same farmer who had lent her the donkeys. This was her punishment for smuggling her little brother out of Argos. But she did not have to suffer the extra humiliation of bearing the children of a peasant, since her now elderly husband would not sleep with her and did not even expect her to perform the usual household duties of a wife. Elektra, however, in gratitude for his kindness and respect, preferred to cook and clean, draw water and help him with the animals and crops. She even felt satisfaction when she received a visit from her pliant sister Chrysothemis, still living in the palace with her mother and Aigisthos, and compared her white skin, soft hands and fine leather sandals with her own sunburnt complexion, calloused hands and bare, hardened, discoloured feet. She was sure that somewhere far away Orestes was growing into a man and that when he did it would be her mother's and Aigisthos' turn to suffer.

Meanwhile, from time to time she went secretly, dressed as the peasant she now was, with the flap of her cloak pulled over her face, and laid a few wild flowers behind her father's grave in the cemetery just inside Mycenae's Lion Gate. These precautions were necessary since to pay any respect to the former king was forbidden under penalty of death. She spoke to him in a whisper, but as if he could still hear her, reminding him of his days of glory in the war with Troy and promising that he would not go unavenged for ever. It's not likely that he heard her, since the shades in Hades' kingdom of the dead no longer have any knowledge of our world, unless a living visitor brings it to them, and there have been few of those. But Elektra was really speaking to herself, for, kind as her husband was, there was little she could talk about to him or the other peasant wives. She went about her work mostly in silence. She was like a once brightly-coloured song-bird that was fed and watered but, hanging in a dusty cage under the eaves of a low, dark house, had lost its bright plumage and ceased to sing. When she did speak to her father's shade, it was in bitter anger. Her mother's rage for revenge had ended with the murder of Agamemnon, but now, like an infection, it had passed into the daughter, who wanted nothing more than her mother's death.

Orestes, when he was old enough, was sent by his aunt Anaxibia, Agamemnon's sister, to consult Apollo's oracle at Delphi. He didn't have far to go, since Delphi was in his uncle's kingdom of Phokis. He went there to ask if he really must avenge his father's murder by killing his mother and her lover, his cousin Aigisthos. The god's reply was unequivocal: yes, he must. But wouldn't he be liable to be pursued by the three fearful Erinyes or Avengers – ancient goddesses of the earth and underworld, older even than the Olympian gods, who enforced curses and punished crimes against mothers in particular? Apollo's oracle assured him that, if necessary, the god himself would protect him from the Erinyes.

Orestes was a gentle young man, always in delicate health, subject to asthma and fainting fits, who had been happy living in obscurity at his uncle's court in Phokis, where he studied mathematics and astronomy, philosophy and music with passion and skill. The oracle's reply, though he had expected it, horrified him, and he did not entirely believe the god's promise of protection. Fortunately, his cousin and close friend Pylades, son of King Strophios and Queen Anaxibia, who had accompanied him to Delphi, was a more robust person. Pylades said he would go with Orestes wherever he went and help him do whatever he had to do. And he waved away his anxieties.

'What more do you want, Orestes? Apollo has given you his word.'

'The priestess at Delphi has given me Apollo's word, or what she says is his word. It's not quite the same thing.'

'You want to hear from the god's own mouth? I don't think that's likely, and if you did, it would probably drive you mad. People who see or hear the gods directly seldom come out of it well. Think of our ancestor Tantalos!'

'The oracle at Delphi is famous for giving advice which appears to be clear, but afterwards turns out to be ambiguous or even the opposite of what was thought by the recipient.'

'True, but that's because the recipient doesn't understand it properly or twists it to agree with what he wanted to hear. The oracle you've been given is perfectly clear and comprehensible and furthermore it's not at all what you wanted to hear.'

'The last part is what I wanted to hear, that the god would protect me from the Erinyes.'

'Yes, but it's absolutely straightforward. There it is, written down. Apollo *will* protect you. What other meaning can that have?'

'Words, words!'

'Your alternative is to do nothing, to disobey the oracle, to disbelieve the god's words. Is that sensible?'

'No. I have to do it. What was I born for except to be the carrier of the double curse on the House of Atreus?'

In this gloomy and reluctant frame of mind Orestes crossed the Corinthian Gulf and walked over the mountains to Argos. Pylades, of course, went with him, and tried to take his mind off his destination with observations of the stars by night and the places they passed through by day. But Orestes obstinately refused to be diverted.

'There it is!' he would say, as they lay in their cloaks under the night sky. 'The constellation named "The Charioteer" by my unlucky grandfather Atreus. The miserable Myrtilos himself, winking at us with his everlasting malice.'

'That man would sell his own grandmother,' said Pylades of a village shoemaker who had driven a hard bargain for a fresh pair of sandals.

'But I doubt if he'd murder his mother,' said Orestes.

'Somewhere about here must have been where Herakles killed the Nemean Lion,' said Pylades as they crossed the mountains to the west of Argos and descended into a deep valley.

'I wish he hadn't,' said Orestes. 'I'd like to meet that lion – any lion, for that matter, which would do me the favour of biting my head off.'

They stopped in Argos long enough to learn that Clytemnestra and Aigisthos were at Mycenae, then walked there through a long hot afternoon, arriving in time to find the Lion Gate still open. Pylades told the gatekeeper that he was the son of one of Agamemnon's soldiers at Troy and that he and his friend would like to visit the king's grave. The gatekeeper warned them that they were not permitted to show it any respect and must be careful not to leave any sort of offering to show they had been there, but, secretly disapproving of what had been done, as so many Argives still did, pointed to the cemetery just inside the gate. There they soon found the stone with its plain inscription: 'Agamemnon, son of Atreus'.

'Nothing more?' said Orestes bitterly. 'For the great king and commander-in-chief who led the Greeks to the conquest of Troy?'

'What more could they put?' said Pylades. '"Cut down by his wife and her lover in the hour of his triumph"?'

'I don't even know what he looked like,' said Orestes, 'I was a baby when he left for Troy and they didn't give me time to see him when he returned.'

'Bear that in mind!' said Pylades, anxious to stoke up Orestes' anger so that he would think less of the horror of killing his mother and more of the need to avenge his father.

'Shall I even recognise my mother?' said Orestes.

'I don't think that will be a problem. By all accounts she's a woman that stands out. She would have to be, wouldn't she, to have done what she did?'

'Will she recognise me?'

'It will give you an initial advantage if she doesn't.'

Behind the stone they found a few withered flowers.

'Someone has dared to disobey the edict and honour him,' said Orestes. 'I should like to do the same.'

'There are no flowers growing here,' said Pylades. 'Nothing but bare earth. I daresay your mother has it kept like that deliberately.'

'Cut off a lock of my hair!' said Orestes. 'I shall leave it in front of the stone. If anyone sees it there and reports to my mother, so much the better. It will frighten her perhaps.'

Pylades was unsure about this. They did not want to put Clytemnestra on her guard. On the other hand, he wanted to encourage Orestes' new mood of anger and determination, so he cut the lock of hair and Orestes, with a prayer to Apollo for success and a promise to his father's shade to build him a much greater memorial, laid it in front of the stone. Then, not wanting to draw any attention to themselves inside Mycenae, they went out of the gate again, just as the sun was setting, and walked down the road. There, in the low ridge overlooking the road, they found a shallow cave and slept the night in it.

Early next morning, Elektra paid one of her clandestine visits to her father's grave and was astonished to see the lock of black hair lying immediately in front of the stone. 'This is some brave person,' she thought, 'but who would put a lock of hair here except some close relative? And who could that be except my brother? Certainly the colour matches mine. Can I really believe that he's come at last? He's old enough now, and it seems he's bold enough. Then I will be bold too.' And she laid her small bunch of wild flowers beside the lock of hair, then quickly left the cemetery and lingered near its containing wall, mingling with the passers-by going up or coming down the street to avoid suspicion.

After an hour or so she was about to give up and go home when she saw two young men in travel-stained clothes enter the cemetery and make straight for the grave. She didn't recognise either of them – how could she when she'd last seen Orestes as a little boy and never set eyes on Pylades? – but her pulse raced as she watched one of them stoop down, pick up her flowers and put them to his lips before dropping them on the grave again. When he looked around to see if he was being observed she turned away and began to walk up the street behind a group of peasant women. But when she returned she saw the two men leave the cemetery and pass out of the Lion Gate, and she followed them as far as a grove of trees, where they stopped and sat down in the shade, deep in conversation. After a while, when they stood up and were about to go away down the road, she decided she must speak to them.

'Are you looking for somewhere to stay?' she asked, keeping her face partly covered with the flap of her cloak.

'Indeed we are,' said Pylades.

'I have a room to let,' said Elektra.

'Inside the walls?'

'No, but not far off, just down the hill on that farm. You can see the roof.'

'Show us the room!'

'Come with me!'

They walked on down the hill.

'Where are you from?' asked Elektra.

'From Athens,' said Pylades quickly before the less wary Orestes could say 'Phokis'.

'Strangers or Argives coming home?'

'A little of each,' said Pylades.

But Orestes had had enough of this circuitous caution.

'Excuse me,' he said, 'but you look like a villager and speak like someone from a noble family. What is your name?'

'My name is Elektra.'

'And your father's name?'

'Why should I hide it? My father lies in that grave you visited. His name is carved on the stone. Agamemnon, son of Atreus.'

'It was you who left the flowers?'

'Who else would dare to, but his own daughter?'

'Didn't he also have a son?'

'He had a son.'

'Who else would dare to honour his grave, but his own son?'

Elektra threw back her cloak and scanned his face.

'What is your name?'

'I am Orestes,' he said and moved forward to embrace her.

But she stepped back, still doubtful.

'How am I to know that?' she said.

'This is my friend and our cousin Pylades, prince of Phokis. He will confirm that I am Orestes.'

'How am I to know that he's Pylades?'

'Such suspicion! Is this the atmosphere breathed by the people of Argos?'

'Are you surprised? When their king has been murdered and his murderers rule the kingdom? You might have been sent by my mother and her lover to gain my confidence and find a way to destroy my brother Orestes. How they long to do that!'

Orestes pushed the hair back from his temple and showed her an old scar.

'Perhaps you remember that, Elektra? When I was running with one of the deer-hounds and tripped and fell and cut my head on a rock. You picked me up covered in blood and took me to our nurse to clean and bandage the wound.'

'Yes, I do remember.'

'And this,' Orestes reached inside his tunic and drew out an ivory ring on the end of a leather string. 'This ring was my father's and I believe he had it from his father Atreus. You gave it to my nurse when you sent us away from Mycenae and she kept it carefully and gave it to me when she was dying. She told me it was made from my great-grandfather Pelops' ivory shoulder, but I never quite believed that. All the same, it's carved with the trident of the House of Pelops, though my father's device was the lion. Look!'

Then at last Elektra was sure that he was her brother. There on that dusty road, their eyes full of tears, they took each other in their arms. Pylades' eyes too were wet, but he brushed the tears away as he kept looking up and down the road in case they were being watched.

They slept the night at the farm worked by Elektra's husband, who, when he came back from the fields, shared his wife's joy at the return of her brother and brought out his best wine to celebrate. Then they finalised their plan with the farmer's help.

'Queen Clytemnestra takes few precautions,' he said. 'She doesn't seem to know the meaning of fear, except in others. Most people do fear her and that makes her feel invulnerable. But Aigisthos is different. He's always afraid. He goes everywhere with four or five armed men around him.'

'Even inside the palace?' asked Pylades.

'I never go into the palace,' said the farmer, 'so I couldn't be sure of that.'

'What is he so afraid of?' asked Orestes.

'You, mainly,' said Elektra, 'but also the Argives in general. They hate and despise him. They have some sympathy for our mother, for what made her kill Agamemnon, if not for her adultery, but none at all for the adulterer who crept into her bed when her husband was at war and stabbed him while his wife embraced him.'

'All the horrible details are known, are they?'

'When did Greeks ever stay ignorant for long of the details of any family's troubles?'

The farmer asked what he could do to help. He was old, he said, and not afraid of death, and would like to see justice done before he died.

'Nothing that might shorten your life,' said Pylades. 'But if you can lay your hands on a bronze funeral urn and lend it to me, that would be a great help. You will get it back.'

'A new one, empty? Or one that already has ashes in it.'

'One with ashes might be better. But it should be a well-made urn, a handsome urn, nothing that looks too cheap. And wherever you get it, the loan must be secret.'

'I have a friend,' said the farmer, 'who keeps the urn meant for his own ashes in his house. Not something I would care to do myself. I'm sure he'll lend it and say nothing about it. And if you want it to contain ashes, that's easily done.' He pointed to the pile of ashes in the courtyard where Elektra cooked and heated water.

Since the farm supplied the palace with its produce, Elektra's husband knew most of the servants there and made careful inquiries about the movements and habits of Clytemnestra and Aigisthos. There were certainly guards at all the doors into the palace, he reported, but Aigisthos' bodyguard went off duty once he was safely inside. The exception was when the queen and her lover sat on their thrones in the great hall and heard petitions or issued decrees. Then Aigisthos' bodyguard stood close to him.

'The thought of him sitting on Agamemnon's throne makes me sick,' said Orestes.

'I imagine *she* sits on the king's throne,' said Pylades, 'and her paramour on hers.'

On a day when they knew that Clytemnestra and Aigisthos were both inside the palace and had no public business to transact, Orestes and Pylades, both armed and wearing their travellers' cloaks, entered the Lion Gate, walked up the narrow winding street and reached the portico.

'Tell Queen Clytemnestra that we have come from Phokis,' said Orestes to the guards. 'We have news for her, which she will prefer to hear in private. She will judge for herself whether the news is good or bad.'

The guard summoned his officer, to whom Orestes repeated his request. The officer went inside and returned some minutes later to admit them to the entrance hall. There they waited longer, sweating inside their cloaks with the heat and their own apprehension, until a guard at last admitted them to the throne-room. Entering from a door at the back, Clytemnestra came forward to meet them. Aigisthos entered behind her and the pair stopped in the middle of the hall.

'From Phokis?' said the queen.

'From Phokis, yes,' said Orestes, in a low voice, looking down at his feet.

'And your news?'

'It concerns your son Orestes.'

'What of him?'

'I regret to say it is not good news.'

'What is it? Speak up!'

'Your son is dead.'

'Is that certain? How did he die?'

'He was never very strong. He caught a chill after exercising too vigorously and his breathing, you know, was difficult at the best of times. He quickly got worse and the doctors could not save him.'

'So my son is dead.'

'Forgive me for being the one that brings you this sad news!'

'Do you have any proof ?'

'Only this,' said Pylades, stepping forward and holding out the borrowed bronze urn which he had kept concealed under his cloak. 'This contains his ashes, since it was too far at this time of year to bring the body for cremation here.'

Clytemnestra took the urn and looked at Aigisthos. If she had shown any sign of sorrow then, Orestes would perhaps have been unable to do what he had come for. But he saw the smile that passed between his mother and her lover, saw the bowed shoulders of Aigisthos straighten, saw his mother pass the urn to him with her whole face lightening, with a look almost of joy, saw Aigisthos jauntily set it down on the floor and even push it aside with his foot. Truly, he saw that he had brought them the best news they could hear.

'Well, then, he is dead,' said Clytemnestra. 'We thank you for bringing us the news and the poor boy's ashes. You will be entertained.'

Only then did Orestes raise his head and look his mother in the eye. For a moment her eyes were troubled, as if she thought she had seen the face before but couldn't remember who it belonged to, then she turned to leave. Pylades instantly drew his sword and intercepted her, while Orestes also drew his and went for Aigisthos. Aigisthos' cry of alarm as he tried to escape and stumbled over the bronze urn on the floor brought guards running into the room, but they stopped when they saw Orestes thrust his sword with savage fury through Aigisthos' body and, withdrawing it without a pause as his victim collapsed with a yell of pain, turn to threaten the queen. Pylades, meanwhile, went and stood over the dying Aigisthos writhing in blood on the floor and told the guards not to throw away their own lives for the sake of two criminals who richly deserved to die.

'Don't you know your own son?' said Orestes to his mother, and raising his voice so that the guards could hear him: 'Yes, I am Orestes, son of Agamemnon, sent here by command of the god Apollo to punish my father's murderers.'

'You have killed Aigisthos,' said Clytemnestra, 'and perhaps for that you have right on your side. But surely you would not kill your mother?'

Orestes, with his blade pointed at her, hesitated.

'Look!' she said and bared her breasts. 'These nourished you. You came out of my belly and sucked from these. You would not kill your mother.'

'Must I do it?' Orestes asked Pylades, his eyes still on his mother, his sword wavering.

'It's what you came for,' said Pylades. 'It's what the god told you to do.'

'And gods must be obeyed,' said Orestes, repeating without knowing it the very phrase with which his sister Iphigeneia justified her own sacrifice.

'What god can tell you to kill your own mother?' said Clytemnestra, kneeling in front of him with her breasts held in her hands.

'Apollo himself, the god of light and the sun. The same light, the same sun that shone on that day when my father returned from Troy and his own wife cut off his head,' said Orestes, and with sudden resolution, pierced his mother's throat with his sword. But as she fell forward choking with blood, he flung the sword away, knelt beside her and held her in his arms as she died.

The account that has Orestes swing his sword and sweep his mother's head from her shoulders with a single blow cannot be true, since the bronze swords of that time before the use of iron had no cutting edge. She herself had used an axe to behead Agamemnon. But all accounts agree that from that moment or soon afterwards Orestes went mad. He was in no state to occupy the vacant throne of Argos. Some say that a son of Aigisthos took it, but that is unlikely. Did he have any children at all and would the Council of Elders have elected a son of the murderer of their great king Agamemnon? All the accounts, of course, date from long afterwards and perhaps the whole story was invented. Yet the Trojan War was not invented, nor the destruction of Troy, nor Mycenae and its period of wealth and power. Agamemnon and his unlucky family were surely not altogether mythical people.

Elektra was the person to hold the kingdom together when Orestes went mad, and with her kindly old husband's heartfelt consent she divorced him and married Pylades. But first Pylades had to get Orestes, pursued by the Erinyes, back to Delphi to claim Apollo's promised protection. That was not straightforward. Apollo had promised more than even he, the god of light and order, could easily perform. Although the new gods of Olympos had crushed the old gods of the earth – those that had sprung up during the chaos of its creation – or at least pushed them down out of sight into caves and crannies or even, in the case of the defeated Titans, to the depths of Tartaros, they could not be altogether eliminated. They were no threat to the immortal Olympians themselves, but could be deadly to humans, whether as the heaving, spewing volcanic mountains under which the Titans lay pinned, as poisonous or ravening monsters such as the Lernaian Hydra or the Nemean Lion, or as inward disorders, mental or physical, causing madness and death.

Orestes, therefore, could find sanctuary and temporary sanity inside the temple of Apollo at Delphi, but the Erinyes sat outside, waiting to seize him and drive him to beat his own head in on the rocky ground or pitch himself off the precipice below. Only the ever-faithful and practical Pylades, taking possession of his sword inside the palace, then accompanying him, bound on the back of a horse, to Delphi, had so far prevented his suicide. But he could hardly stay in the temple for the rest of his life. Apollo and his priestess had to find some way to release him from his torment, from the Erinyes he could hear howling for his blood beyond the walls and whom, whenever his eyes and ears closed in exhaustion, he could not prevent entering his dreams to deprive him of sleep.

6. THE TRIAL

It grew dark as I sat on our terrace recalling the story of the House of Atreus and the curses of Myrtilos and Thyestes. Just as the sun was setting, a cruise liner with tiers of lighted cabins, a floating apartment block, had passed on its way from Nauplia to the Myrtoan Sea and from there perhaps southwards to Crete and Knossos or northwards to Athens, Aulis and Troy. Now the street lamps came on in our village and the small seaside town below, and lights were blinking along the shore on the far side of the Gulf. Suddenly I noticed an owl perched on the electricity pole to my right, grooming itself before flying over me towards the hills behind in search of its dinner. The owl, I remembered, was the bird of Athene, the armed goddess of strategy, wisdom and culture, and is depicted on the Greek one euro coin, as it was on the coins of ancient Athens, whose temple on the Acropolis was dedicated to her and once contained her colossal statue, made of wood, ivory and gold by the great fifth-century sculptor Pheidias.

Six or seven centuries before the Parthenon was built, it was to Athens that Apollo's priestess at Delphi finally sent Orestes. The old gods and the new had come to an agreement. Orestes was to be tried for the crime of matricide by a jury of twelve Athenian citizens and the trial would be presided over by Athene herself. The Erinyes were to plead for his punishment and Apollo for his acquittal. Athene declared at the outset that if the votes were equal, she would decide for acquittal. The dice, you might say, were loaded against the Erinyes, except that the jury was equally scared of both sets of gods, and in the play by Aeschylus both openly offer bribes as well as threats. The arguments for and against Orestes' guilt count much less than this divine pressure.

Apollo admits that he ordered Orestes to kill his mother, as punishment for her murder of his father. The Erinyes reply that it is their ancient right, established long before the coming of the Olympian gods, to punish matricide. Apollo's dubious response is that mothers are only receptacles for the father's seed and that therefore the father is really the mother. The Erinyes reiterate their ancient right, indeed it is more or less their sole argument, warning that they will unleash every kind of pestilence on Athens if they are baulked. Finally the nervous jurors vote by placing a black or white stone in an urn and the result is a tie. Athene accordingly pronounces that Orestes is acquitted and the Erinyes explode with predictable fury – the Romans called them the Furies. They are mollified eventually, bought off with Athene's promise of a permanent site in central Athens, a cave on the Areopagos – the hill where the trial took place, next to the Acropolis – and special worship, respect and regular sacrifices from the Athenians, who will in future call them not the Avengers but *Semnai theai*, venerable goddesses of the earth and underworld. Aeschylus' play – the third in his trilogy, the *Oresteia* – was called after their other soothing name, *Eumenides* or 'Kind gods'.

So Orestes went free. But whether the Erinyes were not as easily mollified as Aeschylus suggests or whether Orestes' mind had been permanently unbalanced, he still suffered from periods of madness. He ruled over Argos and married his first cousin Hermione, the daughter of Menelaos and Helen, and after Menelaos' death became king of Sparta as well as Argos. But travelling one day through Arcadia on his way from one kingdom to the other he was bitten by a snake

– it was perhaps in springtime when the snakes in Arcadia are most active – and died. His successor, his son Tisamenos, was slain in battle by the Herakleidai, descendants of Herakles. They were reclaiming the kingdom which had belonged many generations earlier to the House of Perseus, from whom Herakles was descended, and their return may have coincided with the Dorian invasion of the Peloponnese and the end of the Mycenaean civilisation.

At any rate, this was the end of the House of Atreus and its curses. As I left the dark terrace and the sky now sparkling with constellations (Auriga or 'The Charioteer' among them) and went inside our house, I heard Athene's owl hooting in the distance and our neighbour's savage dog, Artemis, howling maniacally further along the street.

APOLLO

I. THE RESCUE

Two hours' walk from our house, on the highest point of the ridge overlooking the Myrtoan Sea, is the sanctuary of Apollo the Shepherd. Nothing is left of its buildings except an outline of stone in the open ground behind the chapel of the Prophet Elijah, which occupies the centre of this more or less circular space, walled, and surrounded with mountain oaks. But along the north and south sides of the chapel, large blocks of marble, which were no doubt once part of Apollo's temple, provide seating for weary pilgrims. The walk is mostly uphill, with dips down to two dried-up riverbeds, by way of ancient donkey tracks made of green and black boulders, and a modern dirt road which twists round the hill past olive groves, a vineyard, a communications' mast with a throbbing engine and, nearer the top, oak trees. Apollo's special trees are the laurel, the poplar and the palm, but as the son, vice regent and appointed prophet of Zeus, conveying his father's commands and warnings to mortals through the oracles of Delphi and Delos, his presence here evidently rates a halo of the oaks usually associated with Zeus.

Some English guests who walked to the sanctuary with me were amused by the presumption of the Christians in replacing the Greek prophet with the Jewish one. Apollo and Elijah share another aspect too, their connection with the sun. Elijah, whose name in Greek is Elias, was carried up to Heaven in a fiery chariot. The ancient Greek for sun is Helios, Elios in modern Greek. The ancient Greeks imagined it as a chariot racing across the sky, and Apollo, among his many other functions, is the god of the sun. So is Apollo's counterpart among the ancient Persians, Mithras, many of whose aspects were adopted centuries later for Christ. Mithras was the mediator between mankind and the Supreme Being, called the Eternal; Sunday or Sun-day, the seventh and last day of the week (seven being his sacred number) was known as 'the Lord's day'; his birthday was celebrated on 25 December and his rebirth at Easter; the secret rituals of his cult included baptism and a sacred meal; he would preside over the Last Judgment and welcome his faithful followers into Heaven as a father to his children. What magpies those Christians were! Or is it just that new religions are like company takeovers and promote the same goods or gods under new names?

Apollo himself was not born in a stable, but, together with his twin sister Artemis, even more humbly, in the open, sheltered only by a palm tree. Their mother Leto, a Titan's daughter pregnant by Zeus and pursued all over Greece by the jealous anger of Zeus' wife Hera, finally found refuge on the small uninhabited island of Delos. Perhaps the similarity of Hera's name to Herod's gave the Christian storytellers the idea, after the birth of Christ, of sending their holy family on the same sort of flight from persecution. But even when Leto's flight ended and her birth pangs began, when the Olympian gods, like Christ's herald angels, had flown in to welcome the new immortals, Hera deliberately delayed the arrival of the birth goddess Eileithyia and kept Leto in agony for nine days and nights. However, when the twins finally emerged, the whole island became a carpet of flowers, just as the hillsides all around our house do every spring.

Greek gods grow up as rapidly as spring flowers. Within a few days of his birth, Apollo went to Mount Parnassos, the lair of the monstrous serpent Python – Hera's accomplice in the pursuit of Leto – and wounded him with an arrow. Python crept into the sanctuary of Gaia (Mother Earth) at Delphi, but Apollo followed him in and finished him off. So, from the very beginning Apollo had a record of conflict with the older gods. The original shepherd god of Arcadia was the disreputable, lecherous Pan, but Apollo usurped most of his functions, including his habit of pouncing on pretty nymphs. One might imagine that the youthful, athletic, clean-shaven, radiantly handsome Apollo would have been more appealing to the nymphs than the old, ugly, goat-legged, horned and hairy Pan, but women's tastes are often surprising – at least to men – and there are several instances of nymphs running away from Apollo, notably Daphne. As he closed with her, she was turned by Gaia, still at odds with Apollo, into a laurel, which became Apollo's favourite tree.

Still, there were a great many nymphs as well as mortal women who did not run away from Apollo, or not fast enough, and he had many children, some by members of his particular group of followers, the nine Muses. For Apollo was not only the god of the sun and of shepherds, but also of music and the other arts, as well as of disease and healing, which he delegated to his son Asclepios. Asclepios' own sanctuary-cum-hospital has been excavated at Epidauros, now most famous for its theatre, and he was such a successful healer that Zeus was afraid humans would cease to die. He loosed a thunderbolt at his medical grandson and struck him dead. But this made Apollo so angry that, not being able to punish his father, he killed instead the one-eyed giants, the Cyclops, who had manufactured Zeus' thunderbolts. And this in turn made Zeus so angry that he punished Apollo by giving him a year's hard labour as shepherd and general dogsbody to a Thessalian king called Admetos.

Fortunately Apollo liked his master, well-known as a generous and hospitable person, who gave liberal dinner-parties to his guests and laid on festivals and public entertainments for his subjects. In any case, Admetos must have been careful not to offend his divine servant by asking too much of him in the way of hands-on tasks such as lambing, shearing or removing parasites. But at the end of the year Admetos, who was barely middle-aged, was suddenly struck down with a fatal disease and there was now, of course, no Asclepios to cure him, nor it seems could Apollo himself save a man whose death had already been scheduled by fate. The best he could do was to have a word with Death, who relented only so far as to demand a substitute. If Admetos could find anyone willing to die instead of him, he could at least live until he was a bit older. Admetos, lying on his sickbed, called in his friends and subjects, but there were no takers.

'You're a good man, Admetos, a kind host and a popular monarch and we shall all miss you dreadfully, but really it's too much to ask. I have my own life to live – only the one, after all, and I can't just throw it up, not even for you.'

That was the general response in the kingdom of Pherai. Finally Admetos turned to his parents, the former king Pheres and his queen. Tired of ruling, they had retired to their pleasant house by the sea and passed the throne to their son. Surely one or other of them would be only too happy to lay down the burden of old age, the painful joints and muscles, the rotting teeth, the grumbling insides, dimming sight and fading memories, and allow their son his proper time in the sun? But no, they were not at all happy to do so, they wouldn't hear of it – or actually, it seemed, couldn't hear it.

'What's that you say? Your voice is very faint now, poor dear Admetos, and our hearing is not what it was. Death, you say, will take someone else? Of course he will. He will take us all in time. Yes, as you say, our time is pitifully short now, but don't worry about us, we will make the best of what we have left. No, we are not unhappy, except to lose you. But what can we do? It seems quite unfair that Death has come for you before he comes for us, but don't be too sad for us, losing our dear son, we shall survive for a while, we shall try to be happy for as long as death spares us, we shall sit in the sun and think of you ...'

'Among the gibbering shades! You refuse to take my place, then?'

'We gave you our place, didn't we, our place on the throne? No, we can't take it back. But your son will soon be old enough and your wife is a fine woman who will hold things together in the meanwhile.'

'But you could die instead of me. Apollo himself has arranged that.'

'Yes, we know how friendly you are with Apollo and it's rather surprising he can't arrange for you not to die. Gods are so powerful and he's more powerful than most.'

No, the old sods were going to cling on to their miserable existence, sitting in the sun, eating and drinking, mumbling to each other about their various symptoms, sleeping most of the day and all night, served hand-and-foot and carried to and fro by their slaves, to the bitter end. But when Admetos told his pretty young wife Alcestis about the negative response of all his friends and subjects and above all the meanness and selfishness of his parents, she replied immediately:

'There's one person you haven't asked. I'll do it. I'll die instead of you.'

'You? No, no, I couldn't have that, I couldn't bear that.'

But in the end he could and did. Apollo informed Death and Death agreed to take Alcestis instead of Admetos. Admetos began to recover and Alcestis to sicken. He got out of his bed and she got into hers. And now Admetos began to realise what he'd done. He'd escaped death only to ruin the life he'd recovered. How could he go on living without the one person who loved him so much that she was ready to die for him? How could he hold up his head in public when everyone knew that he'd taken his wife's life in exchange for his own? What could he say to his children when they asked him why their mother had had to die so young?

'It was her or me, you see, and we chose her.'

Such are the gifts of the gods. Miracles, interferences with the laws of nature, are never free lunches. The gods, of course, are well aware of this, so they seldom perform miracles for short-sighted mortals, and even when they merely offer advice in the form of prophecies they know that misunderstandings and probably wrong actions will follow. Unlike the older gods, who care nothing for humans except to punish them for their crimes, the Olympians often feel pity for them, especially for the shortness and misplaced ambitions of their lives. But what can they do when these inadequate creatures have false ideas, barely controlled emotions, bad heredity, aggressive instincts, short lives and to some degree free will? It takes a hero of the calibre and strength of Herakles, another son of Zeus, but by a mortal woman, to force events to a more satisfactory conclusion.

Herakles happened to be passing through Pherai, on his way north to steal some man-eating mares which belonged to a barbarous king in Thrace, on the very day Alcestis was expected to die. Herakles feared neither god nor man nor monster. He'd already had a fight with Apollo, when, after a bout of the madness which sometimes seized him, Herakles had visited Delphi to get advice and the priestess refused to answer his questions. He'd tipped her off the sacred tripod and was dragging it out of the temple and about to throw it over the cliff when Apollo stopped him and the two came to blows. The fight was broken up by their mutual father, Zeus, who threw a flash of lightning between them. But on this occasion, Apollo, having settled the substitution of Alcestis for Admetos, had already left Pherai when Herakles arrived. The Olympians, whether out of tact or disgust, prefer not to witness the decay and death of mortals, though they don't flinch from seeing or even causing sudden death. There were gods helping the principal warriors on both sides in the Trojan War and even sometimes taking part in the battle themselves, though usually wearing the appearance of one of the mortal warriors.

Herakles was welcomed by the distraught Admetos and given rooms in a distant part of the palace, well away from the dying Alcestis. Admetos, hospitable as ever in spite of his misery, knew that if he told Herakles about Alcestis, his distinguished guest would insist on staying the night somewhere else. Nevertheless, sitting at his wife's bedside, taking leave of her forever, Admetos could not entertain Herakles properly and personally and, having told the servants to provide him with food and drink, forgot all about him. Herakles, considering his rudely neglectful host to be a man of false pretences whose hospitality had been ludicrously overpraised, drank himself into a destructive rage, singing lewd songs, smashing the furniture, throwing the food and the cups and dishes at the ceiling or through the window, pissing against the walls, terrifying the servants, and finally to their great relief passing out in a huge heap of mighty limbs and bulging muscles on the floor.

Alcestis died early in the morning and Admetos gave orders for her body to be carried to the family tomb – a large domed chamber in the side of a hill beyond the city-walls – and for the funeral to be held the next day. Then he retired to his private room to grieve alone and no one dared disturb him with news of his guest's behaviour the night before. Herakles himself came to his senses towards evening and seeing what he had done was deeply ashamed. He went into the courtyard, fetched water up from the well and drenched himself, while the servants observed him covertly from various windows and doorways without daring to go near him. Wondering where everybody was, he sat down on the wall round the well and began to pick a thorn out of the sole of one of his feet. And now three or four serving-women who had escorted the body of Alcestis to the tomb and only just returned from sitting there all day in sad attendance, entered the courtyard on their way back into the palace. They stopped in amazement at the sight of this huge naked man sitting on the side of the well.

'You there!' said Herakles. 'Where is everybody? What's going on? Is there some festival in the town to which I haven't been invited?'

'No festival, sir,' said the one of the women, still goggling at the man's enormous dimensions, 'but a funeral, alas!'

'Whose funeral?'

'The queen's, of course. She died in the night.'

'The queen's? I don't understand. You can't mean the queen of this city, Admetos' wife Alcestis?'

And so it all came out and Herakles learnt the truth about Apollo's deal with Death, Admetos' escape and Alcestis' self-sacrifice. Now Herakles could perfectly understand why he had not been properly entertained and was even more ashamed of his own behaviour. He discovered from the women where the tomb was, went back into his wrecked room and knotted his green and purple snakeskin round his loins. His parents had preserved the colourful skins of the two snakes strangled by their infant in his cradle, and when he grew to manhood his mother had lovingly sewn them into a loincloth, which he wore only for public appearances and is never depicted in his statues or the pictures of his exploits, since he preferred to be naked when in action. Then he threw his outsize lion skin (taken from the Nemean Lion) over his head and, with his massive club balanced on one shoulder, strode down through the city to its outer gate. He paid no attention at all to the crowds of people who came out of their houses to watch this great celebrity pass and who assumed, having already heard from the palace servants about his disgraceful drunken fury in a house of mourning, that the king must have expelled him from the city.

It was now nearly twilight and the gatekeeper warned Herakles that the gate would not be opened again until dawn. Herakles glanced at the gate and remarked that the keeper was not to worry.

'You won't be returning, then?'

'Very likely. But if I need to come in, I can open it myself.'

'I doubt it, sir. Not from outside. Look at the timber it's made of! Look at the bronze bolts!'

'Yes, I just have. No problem.'

Admetos, meanwhile, had remembered his guest and decided that he would have to tell him of Alcestis' death and apologise for his failure to look after him in due form. But when he heard that Herakles had left the city just as night was coming on, he was appalled and immediately ordered a groom to ride after him and bring him back. The groom returned an hour or two later to say that he had ridden far along the road but seen no sign of Herakles. He reported that the gatekeeper had seen him go out of the city and that he had said he might return, threatening to break down the gate if it was closed. The gatekeeper, he said, was worried sick about what damage might be done to his gate and would keep watch all night. If Herakles did return, the gate would be opened to him.

'What can he be doing?' asked Admetos. 'Can he have turned off the road and be sleeping somewhere in the open rather than spend another night in my unlucky palace?'

The poor king spent another sleepless night, pacing up and down his private room, blaming himself alternately for the death of his wife and the injury to his guest. But just before dawn, when he was seated in his chair, his head dropping on to his chest and his eyes closing at last, he heard what sounded like a roll of thunder and woke up thinking wretchedly that now his ill-treated guest would be soaked in the storm. Then there was an urgent rapping on his door and a servant opened it.

'What is it?' asked Admetos, weary and confused. 'Was that thunder I heard?'

'No, sir, it was Herakles at the outer door of the palace.'

'Well, let him in, let him in at once!'

'I did, sir. He's here now.'

He stood aside and Herakles entered the room carrying Alcestis in her winding sheet.

'Why, why, what?' cried Admetos. 'Oh, my poor dead wife!'

'She's not dead,' said Herakles, drawing back the sheet from her face. 'See, there's even a little colour in her cheeks! She must be put to bed immediately and given a little warm milk and honey and a finger of wine. Fetch her women!' he said to the servant. 'And cancel the funeral!' he said to Admetos.

But when the women had taken Alcestis from him, he sank down on a stool.

'It took all I had,' he said, 'all that even I, Herakles, had. That time I wrestled the Nemean Lion to the ground and strangled him, that other time I cut off the myriad heads of the Hydra, they were nothing to this.'

'But how can she be alive?' asked the bewildered Admetos. 'Death had already claimed her.'

'Claimed but not collected,' said Herakles. 'When I reached the tomb and made your guard admit me, he was already there and just about to take her.'

'Who, what?'

'He looked easy game – thin, smoky white, something the wind could blow away, but when I hit him with my club he just drifted aside. I had to drop the club and take him in my arms. Gods above, what cold! And how he fought to escape! All night I wrestled him and every so often I had to let him go, my hands were frozen, my arms, my whole body lumps of ice. But every time he tried to take Alcestis I went for him again and at last I got my hands round his throat – something between bone and a nasty soft ooze – and my knee into his pelvis and he began to rattle and wheeze and I thought to myself, "What will happen if Death dies? Shall we all live for ever? What will become of the world then? There'll soon be too many of us. And too many evil monsters, if I can't kill any of them any more." So I let him go and he was off in an instant. There I was alone in the tomb with your wife and it was growing lighter and she was definitely breathing, so I picked her up and brought her to you. Send somebody to fetch my club, would you? I left it in the tomb. Yes, I think I gave Death a real fright.'

He tumbled off the stool and immediately fell asleep on the floor. For a moment Admetos feared that he was dead, but then the dust he'd disturbed as he hit the floor got into his nose and made him sneeze. Admetos pulled his lion skin over him to keep him warm and hurried away to see Alcestis and sit beside her.

2. THE DUEL

Apollo has the strange habit of going north every winter, just when all the birds are flying south. The Argonauts on their journey to fetch the Golden Fleece from Colchis (now Georgia), once caught sight of Apollo on his way north. They had landed on the small island of Thynias in the Black Sea and suddenly saw the beautiful god taking off into the air, his golden hair blown across his cheeks, a silver bow in his left hand and a quiver of arrows on his back. Nothing is said of his clothes, so presumably, like his statues, he wore none. The whole island quaked as his feet leapt off it, and a tidal wave rushed high up the beach. None of the heroes dared look him in the face or meet his eyes, but they all bowed their heads as he passed over them and headed away across the sea.

Mortals rarely see gods except in the outward appearance of men or women, and when they do are astonished by their giant size, something like the great statues of Zeus or Athene which once occupied their temples at Olympia or Athens. When Demeter, disguised as an old woman, entered the palace of the king of Eleusis and threw off her disguise, she touched the palace ceiling. On another occasion, according to a man who had been cutting down sacred trees and incurred her anger, 'her footsteps touched the ground, but her head touched Mount Olympos'. When Ares, the god of war, was helping the Trojans on the plain of Troy, he attacked Athene, who was helping the Greeks, with his spear. She hurled a stone at him and knocked him down, and his prone body, according to Homer, covered sixteen acres.

Apollo spends the winter with the Hyperboreans, people 'beyond the influence of the north wind'. Where do they live? In Britain, according to one source, but we are not so lucky. The land of the Hyperboreans is a place of perpetual sunshine, producing plentiful fruits, and its people are vegetarians who enjoy long lives in peace, knowing nothing of violence or war. They neither work nor suffer from anxiety or disease, but dance and sing and worship Apollo. Perhaps he flies over the Arctic Circle and down the other side of the globe to a secret island in the South Pacific, but it's difficult these days to imagine where exactly he would find the Hyperboreans.

It was Arcadia that became Western literature's idea of a classical Eden, but that was mainly due to the Roman poet Virgil in the first century BC. The ancient Greeks saw Arcadia as the back of beyond, a wilderness given over to wild animals, sheep, goats and savage yokels. Long before Elijah took over from Apollo on our hilltop, Apollo the Shepherd and god of music must have taken over from Hermes the Shepherd, inventor of the lyre, who had taken over from Pan, inventor of the pipes named after him, the goat-god of the original inhabitants, known as Pelasgians. Later generations rearranged this succession in the opposite order: Hermes, they said, was the younger brother of Apollo and Pan was Hermes' son. But the people of our village, who now worship Christ and his prophet Elijah, still speak a dialect called Tsakonika and this dialect is probably that of the Pan-worshipping Pelasgians, since its structure predates the Dorian dialect of the last wave of Greek speakers to invade the Peloponnese. Dorian Greek was the language spoken by the Spartans of classical Greece. The previous waves of invaders, Achaeans or Ionians, perhaps brought the worship of Hermes with them and the Dorians the worship of Apollo.

Apollo, the golden-haired god of order, light and the arts of music and poetry, whose famous inscriptions at Delphi are 'Nothing in excess' and 'Know yourself', who protected Orestes from the Erinyes, who lived on earth for a year as Admetos' servant and saved his master from death, also has a less attractive side. His encounter with Marsyas, the subject of a gruesome late painting by Titian, is a lesson in the basic relationship between mortals and immortals. What they dislike above all are pushy people, those so pleased with their own accomplishments that they presume to compare themselves to the gods. Not that the Olympians demand the same abject humility in their worshippers as the Middle Eastern monotheistic religions. The Olympians respect human pride and do not require the kneeling and self-abasement that Christians and Muslims go in for. Ancient Greeks worshipped their gods standing up, with their arms raised to heaven. But if ancient Greek mortals are not expected, like Christians, to feel permanently guilty, to be constantly acknowledging their sins and failings, they must always be aware of their limitations.

Marsyas, depicted by Titian as a satyr, half-human, half-goat – but usually by ancient artists as a silenos, with the tail, ears and hooves of a horse – was a talented player of the flute. This was not the transverse flute we are used to, but the ancient aulos, a pair of long pipes joined at the mouthpiece. He was so pleased with his music that he boasted it was more beautiful than anyone else's and far surpassed any music that could be played on that new-fangled stringed instrument, the lyre. Foolish creature! Gods hear such boasts and don't take them lightly. Marsyas was invited by Apollo, master of the lyre, to prove his claim. The judges of the competition were a Phrygian king called Midas and the nine Muses, who, as Apollo's followers, might be considered to be biased, but Marsyas, convinced of the superiority of his instrument and his playing of it, does not seem to have objected. Nor did he object to the terms of the competition, which was really more like a duel. There was no prize for the winner, but for the loser a penalty to be imposed by the winner.

Marsyas played first. It was a lovely, lively, liquid sound like a stream rushing down a rocky bed, and the Muses could hardly keep from dancing to it. They even joined hands and swayed to and fro, but Apollo's stern eye on them prevented them moving their feet. Then Apollo played. His music was gentler, more mysterious, its rhythms more complicated, suggesting poplars rustling in a breeze with bars of sunlight breaking through and sprinkling the ground with the darting shadows of their foliage. The Muses, no longer trying to dance, stood entranced. Apollo stopped playing and demanded sternly:

'Name the winner!'

Midas voted for Marsyas, but the Muses said they needed to hear more before deciding. Marsyas played a slower, sadder tune, a kind of lament, mostly in the deeper notes of his instrument, and the Muses again wanted to dance, but more torpidly, as a wide river flows between high banks. Marsyas smiled as he took his instrument from his horsey lips and thought about what penalty he would impose on Apollo. But Apollo also smiled as he re-tuned his lyre. He began with a simple skipping beat, then started to sing to his own accompaniment; a song of joy at nature's fertility, a song of lovers walking through fields of flowers as they looked lustfully into each other's eyes, at last lying down together surrounded by autumnal asphodels and the wild irises of springtime, seasons and sexual opposites merging in this magical meadow. Now the Muses couldn't help dancing, holding hands and moving sideways in a sinuous line, first one way, then the other, as Greek dancers still do. And as they moved, new flowers sprang up under their feet, the trees grew new leaves, birds perched silently on their branches, deer and foxes, mice and moles, lizards and snakes came out of their hiding places in bushes and under rocks to listen. Even the cicadas went quiet and the butterflies settled on the ground with their many-coloured wings spread in the sun.

Apollo stopped singing and laid his instrument aside. The audience of animals, birds, reptiles and insects looked at each other with astonishment and quickly ran, flew, scuttled, slid out of each other's way, but Marsyas could not run anywhere and knew he'd had it. Midas voted for him again – he was certainly biased, perhaps because the aulos came originally from his own country, Phrygia. Are the judges for modern musical, literary or artistic prizes any less swayed by their own prejudices and loyalties? The Muses, of course, voted for Apollo, who pronounced the penalty. Midas was to grow ass's ears and Marsyas was to be skinned alive, or to use the technical term, 'flayed'. As Titian depicts it, he was tied upside-down to a tree and servants performed the excruciating operation on his hairy pelt.

'You play the flute very well,' said Apollo graciously as they made the first cut, 'however, next time you boast about its beautiful sound remember that you can't play it and sing at the same time.'

But poor foolish Marsyas was never going to boast again, or play the flute.

King Midas perhaps deserved his new ears. This was his second unfortunate encounter with a god and a silenos. His first was with Apollo's artistic counterpart Dionysos, the god of wine and stimulants, of deafening music with cymbals and drums, of sexual orgies and drunken disorder. One of Dionysos' followers, an old, fat, Falstaffian silenos who had been the god's guru, had somehow got into Midas' palace garden and been found there totally drunk, thrashing about among the rose bushes. He was trussed up with garden twine by Midas' gardeners and brought before the king for punishment. But Midas treated him well, had him de-thorned, bandaged and put to bed until he sobered up, then wined and dined him. Dionysos, coming to collect his old teacher and pleased with Midas' kindness, told him to ask any favour he wanted. The king, who was a big spender and whose finances were in Dionysian disorder, asked that everything he touched should turn to gold. The god, if he had been more compassionate – but gods are seldom compassionate – might have cautioned him. No doubt he was slyly amused by the man's stupidity. Midas couldn't take a bath or pick a fruit from his orchard or go to bed with his wife or mistress or try to eat a piece of bread and cheese without the inevitable consequence. Finally, rich but starving, he appealed to the god to release him and was told to wash in the source of the river Paktolos. The treatment was successful and the river ran with gold for a long time.

After his second mishap Midas went back to his kingdom across the Aegean and concealed his huge pointed ears under his Phrygian cap, swearing the man who cut his hair to keep the secret on pain of instant execution. Hairdressers, however, are professional gossips and in those days the equivalent of journalists today. Even in recent times Greek village hairdressers would cut men's hair in the cafe and the news they passed on would be an important part of the cafe's attractions. Midas' barber was so tormented by this succulent item of news he dared not reveal that he went out to a lonely spot in the country, dug a deep hole, whispered the secret into it and filled up the hole. That seems to have relieved him of his anxiety, but one might ask how the secret nevertheless got out. Perhaps it was not until after Midas' death, when his body was being prepared for cremation or burial, or perhaps it was because, as the story says, a clump of reeds grew out of the hole made by the barber and, rustling in the slightest breeze, whispered Midas' embarrassing secret to all who passed by.

3. THE RAPE

Apollo's twenty or so known children, by nymphs, muses or mortals, were all male. There were presumably some girls too, whose names are not recorded because they didn't become the founding fathers of dynasties or cities. Our own reigning monarch's pedigree in my old copy (1953) of Burke's *Peerage* begins with the Norse god Woden, ancestor of the Anglo-Saxon kings, and includes for good measure Noah and Adam. Indeed, any of the several hundred thousand people alive today who are descended from King Edward III can claim the same pedigree, and if there's any truth in the widespread stories of creation and the flood, we must all be descended from Noah and his wife or, in the Greek version, from Prometheus' son Deukalion and his wife Pyrrha.

The Greek stories never suggest that the Olympian gods created the human race; rather, according to Pindar, 'men and gods are of the same family; we owe the breath of life to the same mother'. According to Hesiod, until Zeus ousted his father Cronos 'meals were taken in common; men and the immortal gods sat down together'. Zeus, however, having castrated his father, taken his place as ruler of heaven and earth and put him into retirement somewhere beyond the earth, was afraid of sharing Cronos' fate and ran a strict regime of absolute power over both gods and men. When several of the senior gods, including his wife Hera, his brother Poseidon and his son Apollo, rebelled and tried to tie him up he summoned a giant with a hundred arms and fifty heads to his aid and swiftly quelled the revolt. Poseidon and Apollo were punished with a year's hard labour for the king of Troy. But Zeus was more severe with mortal dissidents and when the Titan Prometheus stole fire and gave it to mortals, he unleashed a nine-day flood in order to eliminate the human race altogether. Prometheus, however – his name means 'one who foresees' – warned his son Deukalion, who built an ark, survived the flood with his wife, and disembarking on top of Mount Parnassos as the flood receded, offered a sacrifice to Zeus. Zeus was mollified and responded by promising to grant Deukalion his first wish. Deukalion asked for the renewal of the human race.

The Greek gods may not have had the same internal organs as humans – a fluid called ichor served them for blood and they consumed only ambrosia and nectar – but they certainly had seed and frequently increased the human population on an ad hoc basis. Not that they did this as a favour to us. They were attracted to beautiful mortals, mostly women, occasionally men. The goddesses Hera, Athene, Artemis and Demeter are not reported to have had sexual relations with mortals, but Aphrodite, the goddess of love, herself fell in love with Anchises and bore him the Trojan hero Aeneas. Her other notorious mortal love affair was with Adonis, a keen hunter who was gored by a wild boar and became the vivid blood red anemone which flowers in early spring in the sheltered parts of the hills round our house. The male gods too sometimes fancied men. Zeus loved Ganymedes, a prince of Troy, and brought him to Olympos as his cupbearer, Poseidon loved Pelops, and Apollo loved Cyparissos and Hyacinthos.

Cyparissos was a grandson of Herakles and another passionate hunter, but became such a miserable companion after killing his favourite stag by mistake that Apollo gave up on him and turned him into a cypress tree. His memorials are everywhere along our coast, but especially round cemeteries. Apollo's love for the beautiful and athletic Hyacinthos, a prince of Sparta, ended more abruptly. The lovers were throwing the discus together when the wind caught the discus – no plastic frisbee, but made of stone – and blew it against the boy's head, cracking his skull and killing him. One version has it that Boreas, the north wind, and Zephyr, the west wind, were also in love with Hyacinthos and killed him out of jealousy. But if they were both blowing their kisses towards him at the same time it was probably misadventure, not murder. Apollo turned Hyacinthos into the flower named after him.

But on the whole Apollo preferred women. In his play *Ion*, Euripides tells the story of a girl called Creousa, the unmarried daughter of an early king of Athens, who was picking wild flowers on the lower slopes of the Acropolis when she was spotted by Apollo, dragged into a nearby cave and raped. Their child, Ion, whom Creousa bore in secret and left in the same cave to die, became eventually the ancestor of the Ionians, most of whom lived in classical times along the coast of Asia Minor, now the western coast of Turkey. Their distant descendants are back in Greece now after the forcible ethnic exchange that took place in 1923, when the 800,000 Turks living in Greece were swapped for the 1.5 million Greeks living in Turkey, a Stalinist solution carried out under the auspices of the League of Nations. The dire consequences for people uprooted and resettled among resentful and unfriendly compatriots in a small, already over-populated country with meagre resources were still evident after the Second World War.

When Creousa visited the cave surreptitiously a few days later she found no corpse. All traces of her baby, including its basket and wrappings and an ancestral necklace of entwined serpents which she had clasped round its neck, had vanished. She assumed, what she had hoped all along, that some kindly peasant had found and adopted it. She went sadly home to her father's palace and in due course married a man called Xouthos, who after her father's death became king of Athens. Many years later she and her husband were still childless and went to Delphi to get advice from Apollo's oracle. It was Xouthos, in fact, who consulted the priestess, while Creousa, very nervous and unsettled by this visit to her long-ago secret rapist's headquarters, stayed in their hotel room – Delphi was always a tourist mecca, with souvenir stalls, eating places and all levels of accommodation. She gave her attendant women permission to tour the sights – temples, statues, monuments to victory in war or sport – before gathering outside the priestess's sanctuary to wait for Xouthos and hear what advice he had received.

He emerged exultant, smiling happily, swivelling his head from side to side, evidently looking for something. Just below him, sweeping the temple steps, was a boy in his teens. Xouthos no sooner caught sight of him than he ran down the steps and put his arms round the boy.

'My son, my son!' he said.

The boy tried to push him away.

'No, no!' he said, 'you're mistaken. I'm just an attendant here, just a servant working for the priestess.'

'The priestess herself told me that you were my son,' said Xouthos.

'How could she do that?' asked the boy. 'She doesn't know who my parents are. She found me as a baby, left by some unfortunate woman on these very steps, and she took me in and brought me up, and as soon as I was old enough gave me the job of keeping the place clean and stopping the birds from roosting on the pediment and shitting everywhere. Look, there's a couple of doves up there now! I must get my bow and arrows. Let me go, please!'

'All I can say,' said Xouthos, 'is that the priestess told me that the first male person I met when I came out of the temple would be my son. Why? I've no idea. What does it matter? I asked the advice of Apollo and this was his answer. Perhaps you don't know who I am?'

'No, I don't,' said the boy, 'and it strikes me that you might have met anyone when you came out of the temple. That old man there, for example,' pointing to a very bent old slave standing with the women at the foot of the steps.

'It was you I met first,' said Xouthos, 'and it certainly would have been unfortunate and not at all what the priestess meant if I'd met that fellow first, since he's been a slave in my wife's family for about fifty years and is far too old to be my son or the son of any living man. I must tell you, dear boy, that I am the King of Athens and it would surprise me a great deal if you aren't absolutely delighted to find yourself from this moment on not a sweeper or a bird-scarer, but a prince and the heir to a great kingdom.'

'I see, that's nice. But, you know, I'm very happy as I am. This is pleasant work in a beautiful place. And what more could anyone ask than to serve the great god Apollo?'

'Apollo evidently means you to serve him from now on in a higher station. Or do you suppose that the advice I received from his priestess was incorrect?'

'No, I couldn't suppose that. The priestess has been a mother to me and Apollo himself a father.'

'Then you *are* my son. You are my son and I want to celebrate this wonderful news with a great feast for all the people of Delphi. Put away your broom, dear boy, and come with me! We have arrangements to make – a marquee, food, drink, tables, servants – and since you've lived here all your life, you'll know all the best people to supply these things.'

'This is very sudden and confusing,' said the boy. 'Do you mean that Apollo wants you to adopt me or that he's saying I'm really your son?'

'Undoubtedly the latter. You really are my son.'

'Then who is my mother?'

'That I'm afraid I can't say.'

'Can't or won't?'

'It's a puzzle to me too, I must admit. But I did come to Delphi long ago, when I was very young, and took part in one of the Dionysian mysteries here.'

'You had sex with someone you didn't know?'

'Well, probably, yes. There were a lot of maenads – girls in a very excited state.'

'So you might have got one of them pregnant with me?'

'That's the only rational explanation I can offer. But I remember nothing about it – no details. I can only assume that Apollo is better informed than I am. Now, come with me! We have work to do, celebrations to look forward to. Do you have a name, by the way? I shall call you Ion, because you were the first to meet me.'

And putting his arm round the boy's shoulders, Xouthos led him away, still protesting that he really had no wish to be a prince. Princes, said Ion, led a very unenviable life; always in the public eye, always in danger of being assassinated, always anxious about their status and their wealth and their popularity. And he wouldn't even be a legitimate prince, but a foreigner with an unknown mother. People would no doubt be polite to his face, but behind his back they'd despise him. He really would prefer to go on being who he was, the person who kept Apollo's temple clean and had nothing else to worry about.

Most of this conversation had been overheard by Creousa's women and the old slave, so that when Creousa finally appeared to discover what advice her husband had received, they were able to tell her that he'd already found his son. This was not at all what she wanted to hear. Now he had a son and she didn't. Xouthos himself was a foreigner to Athens, only reigning as its king because he was married to her. Now the heir to the throne would be another foreigner, a boy whose unknown mother had conceived him during a drunken orgy. Creousa, egged on by her women and the old slave, became angrier and angrier the more she thought about the way her husband was treating her, bringing in some by-blow of his own to usurp the throne of her ancestors. As for her husband's public celebration, she would have nothing to do with it. She hoped this upstart sweeper would drink himself stupid and open her husband's eyes to his utter unsuitability. She wished she could poison the wretched creature.

'Why not?' asked the old slave. 'Give me the poison and I'll make sure it goes into his wine.'

Now, as it happened, Creousa did have some poison with her. It was given to her grandfather Erichthonios, the first king of Athens, by the city's patron goddess, Athene: two drops of the Gorgon's blood, one that killed and one that cured, contained in a double phial on a golden chain. The heirloom had passed to Creousa on her father's death and she wore it on her wrist. She gave it to the slave and he tottered away towards the open space where they were already erecting the marquee, a hundred foot square, and bringing out costly tapestries from the oracle's treasury to hang inside.

Ion was proving a first-rate organiser and, as Xouthos said, he knew everyone in Delphi. They all liked him and were only too pleased to celebrate his sudden good fortune. The circular tapestry on the ceiling showed the sun setting, the moon rising and night leading on the constellations. Along the walls were tapestries from the East: sea battles between Greeks and Persians, hunters pursuing deer or lions, monsters that were half-human, half-animal. And near the door was a gift from Tiryns, a tapestry showing Perseus cutting off the head of Medusa, the Gorgon.

When the tent was ready and the tables laid with food and wine bowls, a herald stood up on a rock in the town square and shouted a general invitation to the banquet. These invitations to festivities in the seaside town below our village are issued now by the municipal authority (the *demos*) over loudspeakers in the town and in our village square.

The old slave had already found Xouthos and been put in charge of mixing the wine with water (in those days the Greeks never drank it neat) and handing it round to the people of Delphi as they entered the tent. When they had all eaten and drunk and Xouthos was about to make a speech announcing that he had found the son he had come to Delphi for, the old slave sent all the attendants round to recharge the wine cups and himself selected and filled a large gold cup.

'Apollo will have to look for another sweeper for his temple,' he said, as he handed the cup to Ion, 'but it will be hard to find your equal. Gods are seldom so lucky as to have their temples swept by princes.'

Ion, who had little experience of human nature but had learnt the ways of gods since childhood, was horrified.

'I never heard such unlucky words,' he said. 'Do you mean to insult the gods or to injure me?' and he poured the contents of the cup on the ground.

As he did so, one of the doves which had been pecking at the fragments of food dropped on the floor of the tent, darted forward and sipped from the pool of wine. Moments later, shaking and choking, it fell over and lay on its back with its claws in the air, dead. The old slave was already trying to make his way unobtrusively out of the tent as Xouthos shouted, 'Seize that man and bring him to me! This was poison he meant for my son.'

Caught and tortured until, with broken limbs and blind in one eye, he was nearly as dead as the dove, the old slave confessed that he *had* put poison in the cup and that he'd been given the poison by his mistress, Creousa. The people of Delphi, transformed in an instant from party-goers to a howling lynch mob, rushed out of the tent to find Creousa. She, warned by one of her attendant women, who had followed the old slave to the tent and seen what happened, ran up the steps into the temple, took hold of the altar and claimed the god's protection, just as Orestes was to do one day when he was pursued by the Erinyes.

Xouthos, meanwhile, who, as a ruler himself, feared illegality and riotous behaviour, persuaded the Delphian magistrates to convene a special court and, citing the slave's confession, demanded the death sentence for his wife. The case was still being heard as Ion, at the head of the mob, burst into the temple and confronted Creousa.

'What right have you,' he shouted, 'to claim sanctuary from Apollo when you meant to murder Apollo's servant?'

'Everyone has the right to claim sanctuary,' she said.

'Only the innocent, not the guilty.'

'Guilt has to be proved.'

'It has been proved. Your slave has admitted that you gave him the poison and that it was meant for me.'

'What else could I do? My husband picks up some stray from the temple steps, claims it's his son – what son? a whore's mistake? – and means to bring him into my home, to set him on my throne – mine, inherited from my father, not his – he is a foreigner, king only by his marriage to me. So a foreigner's bastard is to usurp the kingdom of my ancestors? No, let me die by all means sooner than that!'

'Then come away from the altar and die! I've no wish to take your precious throne. It wasn't I who wanted to break into your home, even before I knew what kind of stepmother you'd be. Your quarrel is with your husband, not with me, yet it was me you tried to poison. Come on! You've no right to Apollo's protection. Leave the altar or I'll pull you off it myself!'

And, backed up by the crowd filling the temple, he might have done so if the priestess had not come out of her inner sanctum and stopped him.

'Have you learnt nothing in all your years here?' she said. 'Violence in a god's temple is violence against the god. Whatever this woman has done to you or tried to do is for Apollo to punish, not for you. You ceased to be a servant of the temple when Apollo named the King of Athens as your father, and even as a servant of the temple you have no business to attack someone who has claimed sanctuary here. Now, before you leave and take these people with you, I have something to give you. Wait here and stand well back from the altar!'

The priestess went out and returned with a baby's cradle.

'This was yours,' she said, putting it down in front of Ion. 'This was what you were lying in when I found you on the temple steps eighteen years ago.'

Everyone craned to see it, but Creousa could see it close to and, forgetting her fear, left the altar to touch it. Ion stepped forward to seize her, but the priestess intervened.

'No!' she said. 'No violence. If she goes with you willingly, so be it, but you must not touch her yet.'

'This is mine,' said Creousa. 'Was mine, long ago.'

And when she had identified the contents, the cloth woven by herself with a head of Medusa to represent Athene's aigis, the necklace of gold serpents worn by every royal Athenian child, the wreath of olive leaves from the tree planted by Athene on the Acropolis, the whole story came out. Creousa was Ion's mother and his father was Apollo.

But how had the cradle and the baby it contained travelled from a cave in Athens to the steps of the temple at Delphi? In Euripides' play the mystery is cleared up by the goddess Athene. She appears in person to confirm that Ion is indeed the child of Apollo and that, on his instructions, when Creousa abandoned her baby in the cave, Hermes had brought it to Delphi. Xouthos, who has meanwhile got a verdict from the Delphian magistrates that his wife is to be thrown from a crag to her death, is not best pleased to discover that the longed-for son is after all hers not his, but is mollified by promises that he and Creousa together will produce two more sons, Achaeos and Doros, who, together with Ion, will be the eponymous ancestors of all future Greeks: Ionians, Achaeans and Dorians.

Apollo emerges from all this with a mixture of credit and discredit. He saved the child and arranged for it to grow up in health and safety; on the other hand he conceived the child without the mother's consent and gave her no help or comfort in her secret pregnancy (except, says Athene, to make it an easy birth and easy to conceal from her parents) or in her distress at abandoning it, or in all the years since. He contrived to prevent the mother killing her son and the son killing the mother, but at the cost of much misery for both and the torture of the unfortunate old slave. He passed the business of saving the child to his brother Hermes and the business of final explanation to his half-sister Athene, who admits that Apollo sent her because he wished to avoid hearing any reproaches.

Euripides is often accused, and was accused in his lifetime, of bringing the gods into disrepute, of showing them in a bad light.

Isn't it rather that in re-interpreting the old stories he can't help highlighting the difficulty of the relationships between mortals and immortals, between powerless creatures with short lives and powerful forces that last for ever? Whether any gods exist is still a vexed question, but there can be no question that the only view we have of them is our own, coloured by our own superstitions, traditions, sacred texts and theological dogmas. The Greek gods may sometimes seem as morally uncertain as we are, but the prophet Elijah's Old Testament Jehovah certainly suffered from fierce jealousy of rival gods and he is just as vindictive towards mortals who offend him as the Olympians. The Christians' three-person god is a complex abstraction, a theological compound of a remarkable rural preacher/teacher in Roman Palestine with the Jewish Jehovah and traditions from all over the Eastern Mediterranean, including Greece and its great philosopher Plato. But for story-lines and the human touch, Christianity relies as much on its saints and martyrs as the Greeks did on their heroes or demigods. Saint Nicholas, for instance, patron of sailors as well as children, who has a chapel overlooking our favourite beach beside the Myrtoan Sea, seems to have inherited Poseidon's function as marine overseer, together with a storyline borrowed from the myth of Dionysos.

The attraction of Apollo, especially to writers, artists and musicians, is that he is a god of outstanding physical beauty and presence, responsible for harmony and order after the earth's early period of violent upheaval – look at him calming the chaotic wedding feast of Lapiths and Centaurs in the sculptures from the west pediment of Zeus' temple at Olympia. Dionysos may be needed, as Nietszche suggests, to break things up again, to get the juices flowing, to reintroduce the wild and barbaric and reinvigorate what has become sclerotic and academic, but after more than a century of that, the appeal of Apollo's watchwords, 'Know yourself' and 'Nothing in excess', is all the greater. Not that in his intimate human encounters he always seems quite master of his own emotions, whether of love or anger, but this too is part of his attraction, that he gets caught up in the knotty problems and contrivances which all human affairs inevitably entail, that he behaves sometimes more like a man than a god.

HERAKLES

1. THE MARES

Several new houses are being built and some old ones reconstructed on a site overlooking our village square. The big bags of concrete waiting to be mixed are labelled 'HERAKLES'. Son of Zeus and the mortal Alkmene, the Superman of ancient Greece, Herakles remains the most famous of all the Greek heroes and has the most stories attached to him. He was born in Thebes, but his family came from Argos and many of his celebrated Labours were performed in the Peloponnese. He should have been the king of Argos, except that from the very beginning he was up against the goddess Hera, Father Zeus' wife and sister, whose main role in Greek mythology seems to be to persecute her husband's mortal mistresses and their children. Hera made sure that Herakles' cousin Eurystheus, who was conceived after him, should be born before him and would therefore inherit the kingdom which Zeus had intended for his son Herakles.

Even this did not mollify the angry goddess. When Herakles was still in his cradle she sent a pair of snakes to finish him off. Alerted by the frightened screams of his mortal twin, Iphikles, their father and mother came running into the babies' room to find that Herakles was holding a lashing snake in each hand. He smiled sweetly at his horrified parents, squeezed both snakes to death and dropped them on the floor.

Little Iphikles' father, Amphitryon, was not, of course, little Herakles' real father. While Amphitryon was away exacting revenge for the murder of his wife's two brothers – this was Alkmene's bride-price – Zeus had taken his place in Alkmene's bed and, in order to ensure that she would bear a truly remarkable hero, stayed there for a night the length of three nights, ordering the sun to stand still – or rather, as Zeus would have known but most Greek storytellers did not, stopping the earth rolling on its axis. When Amphitryon returned to his wife's arms he found her exhausted and astonished that her husband still had the energy for another night of lovemaking. Nevertheless she did her best to satisfy him and the result was twins, one by Zeus and one by Amphitryon.

We last met Herakles on his way to Thrace, having wrested Admetos' wife Alcestis from the arms of Death. His task in Thrace, the eighth of his Twelve Labours, was to capture four man-eating mares belonging to the local king, Diomedes, and bring them to his cousin Eurystheus, whose palace was at Tiryns. These Twelve Labours were the consequence of another attempt by Hera to ruin Herakles' life. She sent him mad, and in his madness he mistook his wife Megara, daughter of King Creon of Thebes, and their six children for enemies and killed them. When he recovered his wits immediately after the slaughter and saw what he had done, he broke away from the soldiers sent to arrest him and went into the palace armoury intending to kill himself, bolting the door from inside so as not to be prevented. But the goddess Athene, who had instructions from Zeus to look after him as assiduously as Hera tried to destroy him, appeared to him while he was still hesitating over which of the innumerable weapons available he should take down from the wall and turn on himself. She told him that Zeus had not brought him into the world to leave it so soon and that his great strength and fierce spirit were intended to benefit mankind.

'Where was the benefit of killing my beloved wife and children?' he asked.

'That was not the will of Zeus,' said Athene.

'Then Zeus is not all-powerful?'

Gods never criticise each other in front of mortals, so Athene avoided mentioning Hera's jealousy.

'In the short term his will is sometimes frustrated,' she said, 'by the free will of others, whether mortals or immortals. But in the long term, often by winding, zig-zag paths, he reaches his goal and achieves his purpose.'

'And along those crooked paths, our sufferings, my great loss and sorrow and despair, are nothing to him?'

'Zeus did not create mortals, any more than men created animals.

He may sympathise with your losses and sorrows, he cannot by his nature share them. No more than you can share his knowledge of the future and of where the paths will eventually lead. You can only trust him and be sure that from a man such as you he expects more, even in such dreadful circumstances, than self-pity and self-harm.'

The Labours, to be imposed by the cousin he particularly despised, were his penalty and expiation, an ancient and more exacting version of our own Community Service Orders. Most of them entailed ridding the world of dangerous monsters, though one or two, such as fetching the golden apples of the Hesperides and stealing the girdle of the Queen of the Amazons, were merely frivolous. It may be that Eurystheus ran out of ideas for really useful tasks, or more likely that he didn't want any more live monsters brought back to Tiryns. The storytellers say that he asked for them to be brought back alive, but since he was so terrified by them that whenever Herakles reappeared with another over his shoulder Eurystheus took refuge in a large bronze urn, this was surely Herakles' own humorous wheeze, a way of getting back at his taskmaster and perhaps hinting that he'd do better to set tasks that didn't involve monsters.

Herakles had arranged for a few friends to meet him on the coast of Thrace, since he guessed that extracting the mares from King Diomedes' stables would provoke a battle with the king's equally savage warriors, the Bistones. It was easy enough to get at the mares, given that Diomedes' servants had orders to feed them with unaccredited strangers – those without visas, as it were. Accordingly, as soon as Herakles turned up at the palace entrance and begged for something to eat, the guards seized him and two of them marched him round to the stables. They were particularly contemptuous of such a huge man with such a powerful physique who submitted so meekly to having his hands tied behind his back. He had left his weapons – his club and his bow and arrows – as well as his lion skin, with his friends on the beach and was wearing only an old tattered cloak and a pair of patched leather trousers, so that they took him for a vagrant from some distant part of Asia.

The groom on duty at the stables was delighted to see him.

'Now what shall we do with you?' he said.

'A little something to eat!' whined Herakles, rolling his eyes.

'Oh, more than a little something,' said the groom, pulling back the tattered cloak and eyeing the mighty torso of the strongest man in the world. 'As we say here, I should think you could eat like a horse.'

He and the guards had a good laugh.

'In fact, in your case I'd say more like four horses,' and he pointed jovially to the four man-eating mares snorting and stamping in their stall and straining at the heavy iron collars and chains that prevented them from breaking out.

'They do look hungry,' said Herakles and, bursting the rope round his wrists, raised both arms and felled the guards on either side of him with simultaneous blows to the back of their necks. Then, as the groom turned to run, Herakles caught him by his lank Thracian-style hair and told him to unlock the mares' collars and hitch them to the king's four-horse chariot, which stood in a shed nearby. The groom, stuttering with terror, told him they must not be released before they'd eaten human flesh, but after that they became perfectly calm and amenable.

'That's fine,' said Herakles. 'Then give them their breakfast!'

And he made the groom drag the two guards into the stall, where the mares immediately started to devour them. While they were doing so Herakles and the groom brought out the chariot.

'What would you say now?' asked Herakles contemplating the mares with blood dripping from their jaws and the torn corpses at their feet, 'Have they had enough or will they need a second course before they'll pull the chariot?'

'They won't need any more,' said the groom.

'Just as well,' said Herakles, 'you're too puny to go far between four horses. Release them, then, and hitch them up!'

Half an hour later the two remaining guards at the palace entrance were appalled to see the four mares gallop past drawing the king's best chariot, whose only occupant was the recently arrested stranger in his tattered cloak and patched trousers.

It wasn't far to the beach, where Herakles gave the mares to his friend Abderos to look after while he and his other friends prepared to do battle with the Bistones who would surely be in hot pursuit as soon as King Diomedes heard of the theft. The friends had not been idle while Herakles was absent, but according to his instructions had dug a long trench in the level ground above the beach between the two swift rivers that entered the sea at that point. Herakles was still damming the rivers with rocks and debris when a cloud of dust on the road announced that the Bistones were coming, several score of them, all on foot except for King Diomedes in his second-best chariot drawn by two vegetarian stallions.

Even with Herakles at their head, the dozen or so friends did not feel hopeful about the outcome, but they did as they had been told and dug through the last barriers between the river and the trench, leaping away as the river poured into its new course. Herakles quickly filled the last gaps in his two dams, and as the Bistones broke into a charge they suddenly found themselves confronted with a double torrent and surrounded by a rapidly expanding lake. What could they do but turn and run back up the road? But the king's chariot in the lead took the full force of the two diverted rivers and overturned, spilling Diomedes and his charioteer into the water. Both jumped clear and the charioteer managed to flounder to safety, but the king was not so lucky. He probably never knew what hit him – it was Herakles' massive club and the blow on Diomedes' bronze helmet shattered his skull. Herakles pulled him out of the water and laid him on the beach, then, picking up his bow and arrows, went to help his friends finish off those Bistones who had escaped the water and still wanted a fight.

But when they returned triumphant to the beach they were met by a dreadful sight. Abderos had led the mares to a small grove of fir trees and tied them in pairs to two stout trunks, then sat down nearby on a rock to watch the battle with the Bistones. Two of the mares, however, had chewed through the ropes that held them and, hungry again, had caught Abderos from behind and were even now consuming his corpse. The other two mares were desperately straining at their ropes to join the feast and would no doubt soon be free. Herakles sent his friends to collect as many fallen Bistones as they could carry and himself fetched King Diomedes and threw him in front of the two tethered mares before driving the other two off the corpse of Abderos with his club. All four then set about tearing the flesh off their former owner. And strange to say, when Herakles' friends returned with assorted Bistones, the mares showed no interest in them and indeed never afterwards ate anything but grass and hay and the occasional apple. But before hitching them to Diomedes' best chariot and riding back to Tiryns, while his friends dispersed to their various cities and islands, Herakles buried the bones of Abderos and promised his spirit to return one day and found a city named after him.

2. THE COWSHEDS

Herakles had used his trick of diverting rivers once before, for his fifth Labour. This was a filthy job. In the north-western corner of the Peloponnese there was a king of the Epeans called Augeias, who owned a huge herd of pedigree cattle, 30,000 of them. But their sheds had not been cleaned for 30 years – in those days the Greeks did not value manure as a fertiliser – and there was so much dung in them that the cattle were having to be kept outside. Winter was approaching and King Augeias was wondering what to do about it, when his son Phyleus remarked jokingly that only a superman like Herakles could hope to shovel shit on that scale. Augeias immediately despatched a messenger to Tiryns and Eurystheus enthusiastically agreed to send Herakles, adding that the whole job was to be completed in a single day.

When Herakles arrived he inspected the cowsheds and walked about the neighbourhood, admiring the great herds of fine cattle in all the fields around.

'What do you think?' asked Augeias. 'Can you do anything about it?'

'Oh, yes, no problem,' said Herakles. ' My fee is 10 per cent.'

'Ten per cent of what?'

'Of your cattle.'

'Three thousand head of cattle!' said Augeias, who was evidently a mean man or he would have paid labourers to clean his cowsheds regularly. 'I thought you did these jobs for nothing.'

'This one is exceptionally unpleasant,' said Herakles, 'not really suitable for a son of Zeus, and I feel I'm entitled to some small reward. What do you think?' turning to Augeias' young son Phyleus who was standing beside them.

'It seems fair to me,' said Phyleus, a brave boy who was afraid of his father but had been taught by his mother always to tell the truth and was besides thrilled to be consulted by such a famous hero. 'I don't know who else would or could do it for twice that fee or even the whole herd.'

'All right, I agree,' said Augeias sulkily, with a furious glance at his son.

So the moment dawn broke next day, Herakles, completely naked, set to work knocking down one wall of the cowsheds and diverting the courses of the two nearby rivers, the Alpheos and the Peneos. Just before dusk he dug away the banks and the two rivers raced towards the sheds. There was a brief period of flooding as the water encountered the dung and Augeias' servants' quarters were inundated, but very slowly the massed cowpats began to slide and shift and suddenly with a mighty whoosh the two currents regained their power and scoured Augeias' cowsheds from end to end. Herakles threw down his last spade – he had bent or broken dozens – and smiled at the king.

'No problem,' he said. 'I'll be on my way with the three thousand cattle in the morning.'

'No, I don't think so,' said Augeias. 'It was the rivers that cleared the cowsheds, not you, and you've cost me every spade in my kingdom.'

'You made an agreement,' said Herakles.

'Did I?'

'There were no get-out clauses, no ifs or buts. Your son was a witness.'

'Was he?'

Both men turned to look at Phyleus, who blushed all over at the embarrassing choice he had to make between supporting his father or telling the truth.

'There were no ifs or buts,' he mumbled.

'This is your inheritance, son,' said Augeias.

'But you did agree and I thought that was fair.'

'Then you'll get no inheritance at all.'

'Better that than inheriting a broken promise.'

'You don't know what's good for you, son, and as far as I'm concerned you're no longer any son of mine. You can leave my kingdom and go on the roads as a beggar! As for you, Herakles, you've done what you were told to do and can go home to your master before I call out my fighting-men.'

Some say that Herakles did so and came back later to exact his revenge, but it's hard to imagine a man of his temper behaving so meekly under such provocation. No, Herakles picked up the king and dangled him upside down by one leg over the rushing waters of the Alpheos.

'Did you make an agreement or didn't you, king of shit?'

'All right, I did.'

'Nobody messes with Herakles. Remember that in future!'

'I will, I will.'

But the wretched man had no future. Whether on purpose or because his hands were greasy with sweat, Herakles dropped him and he was swept away through his own well-scoured cowsheds and out to the dung-dark sea. Then, resuming his lion skin, picking up his club and bow and arrows, shooting or clubbing a few of the foolish king's more foolhardy guards who tried to stop him, Herakles rounded up a good number of the cattle and, taking the young Phyleus with him, drove them home to Tiryns, where he gave them to a farmer to care for on his behalf.

He did not forget the courage and honesty shown by the boy Phyleus, but a few years later returned to Augeias' kingdom with a small force of friends, defeated and expelled Augeias' younger son, a surly and unpopular ruler like his father, and installed Phyleus as king. And while he was in that part of the Peloponnese, Herakles revived the Olympic Games, which had ceased to be held sometime after the death of Pelops. The marble metopes of the Temple of Zeus at Olympia, carved by an unknown master in the fifth century BC, depicted Herakles' Twelve Labours, and their fragments are among the treasures in the Archaeological Museum there. Why twelve rather than the ten Herakles had originally been assigned? Back at Tiryns, cousin Eurystheus declared that since Herakles had received a fee the cleansing of the cowsheds could not count as a Labour, so, with another that had already been ruled out, ten Labours became twelve.

3. THE HYDRA

Driving to our village from Argos one passes through a little town called Myli at the head of the Gulf. Is this the place that features in the first section of T.S. Eliot's *The Waste Land*?

> There I saw one I knew, and stopped him, crying: 'Stetson!
> You who were with me in the ships at Mylae ...'

superimposing, if so, the First World War and its American reinforcements (Stetson) on the War of Troy and invoking all such wars to date – the poem was published in 1922. But was Myli the port from which Agamemnon's argosy sailed to Troy? More likely it was Nauplia, since Myli in ancient times was a town called Lerna and most of the shore at the head of the Gulf was a marsh. The marsh has been eliminated now, but this is still a most unprepossessing place, a long curving road with a shallow sea and dreary-looking beach on one side and holiday homes on the other. Nearer to Nauplia there's a factory with tall chimneys emitting a great cloud of white smoke and a sulphurous smell, plus a series of grotesque nightclubs in various Hollywood/Mexican styles. Stetson, now a Greek cowboy home from finding his fortune in the USA, has put his mark on the dried-up marsh.

In Herakles' time it was a serious bog, inhabited by the Lernaian Hydra, and his second Labour was to kill this monster, which was said to have a body like a dog's and nine heads. The bog itself was dangerous enough – even some fifteen centuries later, in the reign of the Roman Emperor Nero, it was unfathomable and sometimes swallowed unwary travellers – but the Hydra was poisonous, breathing out lethal fumes from all its heads. Although the marsh was only a few miles from Tiryns, Herakles travelled there by chariot, driven by his young nephew Iolaos, son of his twin half-brother Iphikles. Herakles had probably been warned in advance by the goddess Athene that he might need his charioteer's assistance, as indeed proved to be the case. It was Athene too who showed him the monster's lair under a plane tree at the source of one of the rivers which fed the marsh and suggested that he light a bonfire and fetch it out with a shower of burning arrows. After that Athene withdrew and left him to it.

The creature, when it emerged from the ooze onto dry land and rushed angrily towards Herakles, had a body the size of a large pig, its skin was mottled and waxy like a toad's, and its nine snaky necks, writhing hideously from every part of its body, overtopped Herakles, though the heads, puffing poison, were relatively small. It was more like a giant octopus on legs than a dog. Herakles shot two arrows into it as it approached. These increased its fury but seemed to have no other effect. As the Hydra reached him, Herakles held his breath and swung his club horizontally across all the heads at once. The Hydra was momentarily dazed and sat back on its haunches, while its necks, which had become tangled, sorted themselves out. Herakles took the opportunity to pull out his arrows – he always disliked losing them – but was dismayed to see that two new necks and heads grew out of the wounds. With his head turned away, he drew a deep breath and, as the now eleven heads reached towards him again, swiped them again. This went on for some time until it became clear to Herakles that however hard and often he hit the heads, he was doing them no real damage. He and the Hydra could go on like this for ever, except that even Herakles could not continue swinging his club for more than a day or two, so the Hydra would eventually get the better of him. The next time the necks reared up again, he threw his club aside, drew his long knife and slashed off the nearest head. The neck started to gush green slime and then – horrible to see – grew two more heads. Herakles slashed again and cut off both heads. Slime poured out and four heads grew. Herakles cut off a different head, but again two heads grew in its place. This was a monster now with fifteen poisonous heads instead of the original nine. What to do? His nephew was watching from behind the chariot.

'Iolaos!' shouted Herakles, retrieving his club and retreating a few yards, 'bring brands from the fire!'

Then as the Hydra followed he stopped it with another side-swipe to its fifteen undulating necks and kept swiping until Iolaos joined him with a red-hot branch in either hand.

'Now when I take off a head,' said Herakles, 'you must cauterise the neck.'

It worked. Herakles cut, Iolaos applied his smouldering branch to the green slime, the neck shrank and shrivelled like the stalk of a dead flower, and no more heads grew. Soon they were down to the original nine, but now the Hydra gained an ally. An enormous crab, the size of a round shield, came out of the marsh and sank its pincers into Herakles' left foot. Herakles shouted with pain, stumbled and would have fallen and been easy prey for the Hydra's poisonous breath, but Iolaos caught his arm and kept him upright. With a mighty kick Herakles dislodged the crab, turning it upside down – its pincers waving uselessly in the air – and went on beheading the Hydra.

It was still not a won battle. Two or three times a puffing head came perilously close to Iolaos' face and he fell back without cauterising the neck that Herakles had just exposed, allowing more heads to grow. But by midday the monster was down to three heads and had had enough. It turned and began to run back to its lair. Herakles, seizing the burning branch from Iolaos, ran after it, sliced a head with one hand and cauterised it with the other. Now there were only two heads and the creature, despairing of reaching its lair, turned sideways into the marsh. Herakles followed, sliced, cauterised and now there was only one head left. The Hydra's body was already sinking into the mud and Herakles was up to his thighs in it. Iolaos began to be alarmed.

'Leave it, uncle, leave it! Don't go any further!' he shouted, but Herakles was determined to finish the job and with one more stroke of his knife severed the last head, cauterised the neck with the last few inches of his burning branch and plunged his knife downwards into the creature's body, now invisible beneath the surface of the marsh. The dead Hydra took the knife with it into the depths and neither was ever seen again. But Herakles himself, up to his middle in mud, was now in immediate danger of being sucked down. His struggles to escape only made him sink lower, his great strength was useless. It was lucky he had brought the chariot, not to speak of the charioteer, who immediately untied the two horses, still wearing their harness, from the tree round which they had been grazing, tossed the reins to Herakles, who had sunk now to his armpits, and urged the horses up the slope from the beach. Slowly the hero's mighty torso emerged, his belly and buttocks, his massive thighs, and suddenly he was free, dragged like a great marble statue coated in stinking sludge onto firm ground.

'Thanks,' he said. 'Time for lunch.'

But Iolaos pointed to the fire, which had begun to spread. Together they beat and stamped it out, leaving the hot centre still smouldering.

'We shall need that,' said Herakles and, taking his club to the crab, which was still lying on its back, feebly gesticulating with its claws, he beat it to death and threw it on the fire.

While it was cooking Herakles washed himself thoroughly in a clear spring near the Hydra's lair and picking up his two arrows from the ground where he had thrown them, returned them to his quiver. It didn't occur to him that these arrows were now steeped in the Hydra's deadly poison and he would only discover this later to his great sorrow. When the crab was nicely done they scooped out its flesh with Iolaos' knife, ate it with some bread and olives they had brought with them, and afterwards lay down for a siesta in the shade of the trees.

Although its intervention was a mere footnote to the story, this giant crab nevertheless rose in due course to the stars as the constellation Cancer, my own sign of the zodiac, and in memory of its loyalty to a fellow monster twinkles modestly beside the head of Hydra, largest of all the constellations.

Herakles and Iolaos returned to Tiryns in the evening and Herakles entertained Eurystheus and his courtiers over dinner with a full account of his battle with the Hydra, plonking his left leg on the table to show them the gashes left by the crab's pincers. Everyone was amazed and grateful, except Eurystheus.

'All very well,' he said, 'but I can't count it as one of your ten Labours. You had too much help from Iolaos. And besides, what proof is there that the Hydra is really dead? You say it sank into the marsh, but there are no independent witnesses, only your own nephew. However, the next one I've got for you should be a lot easier and I hope this time you'll stick to the rules.'

4. THE STAG

The Arcadian Stag was not a monster. On the contrary, it was a most beautiful dappled creature with golden antlers and brazen hooves. Some said it was a hind, but if so what was it doing with antlers, unless it was a reindeer? Perhaps the confusion arose because it had been roaming the Arcadian mountains with its four attendant hinds when the goddess Artemis, whose favourite hunting ground was in those mountains, spotted them. She captured the four hinds and used them to draw her chariot, but the stag escaped. It frequently came down into Argolis and ate the farmers' crops, but was too swift and cunning ever to be caught, and no one dared to shoot or harm it in any way for fear of angering Artemis. So Eurystheus told Herakles to catch it and bring it to Tiryns.

Herakles travelled in his chariot as far as the mountains, but then dismissed Iolaos and continued on foot. Otherwise, as he said:

'These Labours will keep sprouting like the Hydra's heads and I shall grow old in my cousin's service. Which is no doubt what he intends, since he must know that as soon as I'm through with them, my final Labour – a free bonus service to all his subjects – will be to turn that bronze urn of his upside down with him inside it.'

It was several days before the stag appeared, stepping delicately down from the upper slopes to feed on somebody's vineyard. Herakles, who had been hiding near this spot because it was relatively high up and isolated and he guessed might prove a temptation to his quarry, crept out and came within a few feet of it. But a dry stick cracked under his foot, the stag's head went up and in a second it was off up the hill. Herakles ran after it. He was a faster runner than any man in Greece, then or since, but still no match for the stag, which after an hour's pursuit vanished into a forest of chestnut trees. Herakles went back down to his hiding-place to collect his possessions – lion-skin, club, bow and arrows, a bag of provisions and a coil of rope for lassooing and trussing the stag – then climbed the hill again and spent the night under the chestnut trees.

In the morning he saw the stag – its golden antlers and polished bronze hooves glinting in the sun – silhouetted on the next hill, and carefully worked his way round the hill so as to approach it with the breeze blowing towards him. But again the animal heard him, again it galloped away, and again Herakles pursued it, this time for three hours, since the ground was more open and the running easier. He hoped to tire it out, but it was he who tired first and returned disconsolately to his possessions among the chestnut trees.

Thereafter he sighted and pursued the stag almost every day, always in vain. But it surprised him that although every day he had to return over the whole course they had run to fetch his possessions, the stag never seemed to spend the night far away, but appeared on some nearby eminence as soon as the sun rose. Once, exhausted, Herakles overslept and was awakened by a gentle snorting and a stamping of bronze hooves quite near his sleeping-place. He rose cautiously to his feet, but it was not until he began to move towards it that the creature turned gracefully on its slender legs like a dancer and made off into the distance. Herakles realised then that the stag was enjoying this daily chase, that it never mingled with the herds of ordinary deer on the mountains and must have been lonely and bored until he came on the scene. On the days when he did not see it at once, he discovered it later returning from another foray off the mountain into somebody's crops, but most days they ran their race up and down the high ground from Mounts Ktenias and Parthenion in the north to Parnon in the south.

But how was he ever to catch it? It would have to be by some trick. One morning he pretended to be asleep again and when the stag came closer and snorted and stamped as before, took no notice. The stag came closer still, lowered its head and with the tip of one brazen hoof flipped a small shower of leaves and dirt on to the sleeper's head.

When Herakles still took no notice, the stag snorted again and this time touched his foot, protruding from the lion skin. Herakles was up in a flash, but the animal leapt in the air, turning as it leapt and galloped away up the hill. Herakles shook his fist in the air and shouted:

'You are a joker, I see, and you are taking the piss out of Herakles. This cannot go on. Even if this were not one of my Labours, I would catch you for my own sake, if it takes the rest of my life.'

The seasons came and went and Herakles became a familiar sight to the shepherds and goatherds and their boys, who pastured their flocks on the mountains in the summer and led them down to the valleys in the winter. When the simple rations Herakles had brought with him were used up, he obtained more from these people or, if they had none to spare, went down into the villages. The stag seemed to shadow him, for it was never far away when he returned up the mountain. But on one occasion, rounding a crag, he came face to face with a lion. The lion glared at him for a moment or two, put its shaggy head on one side, opened its jaws and snarled.

'Are you looking for a fight?' said Herakles. 'Don't try it! See what I'm wearing!' and he pulled the head of the Nemean lion skin down over his eyes. 'That beast was twice as big as you. So move over, little Leo, before I clout you with my club!'

The lion snarled again, but with less conviction, then turned and slunk away into a cleft dense with undergowth.

On another occasion, higher up the mountain, on a narrow track almost overgrown with broom bushes, he was suddenly confronted with a two-legged creature such as he had never seen before. It had the hairy thighs, legs, cloven hooves and horns of a goat, but the head, body and arms of a man. Its eyes and beard were those of a man, but its flat nose and prehensile lips were goatish. Herakles was taken by surprise and stopped in his tracks, then relaxed and bowed his head.

'Great God Pan!' he said. 'You startled me.'

Pan smiled. It was what he liked doing to passers-by and he was no doubt particularly pleased to have been able to startle Herakles, even if he did not, like most of Pan's victims, take to his heels in panic.

'I wonder if you could help me?' asked Herakles. 'How can I catch the Arcadian stag without doing it any injury?'

'Have you got time?' said Pan.

'How much time?'

'A year?'

'That long?'

'Or longer?'

Everything Pan said ended with a question mark and a crooked smile.

'But how?' asked Herakles, 'that's the question.'

'You're asking me?'

'Your help would be invaluable.'

'Aren't you supposed to do these things without help?'

'True, but if you were to advise me ...?'

Pan only smiled and raised his bushy eyebrows.

'A net, do you think?' asked Herakles.

'Have you got one?'

'Or a hole in the ground?'

'Who would walk into a hole in the ground?'

'If it was disguised with sticks and leaves. No, I don't think the creature would fall for that. He'd see me making it.'

Pan was evidently losing interest. He scratched his oversized, goatish genitals.

'I'm sure that some sort of surprise is the answer,' said Herakles, 'the sort of thing you're so good at.'

Pan smiled a wide, happy smile and vanished.

Herakles had begun his pursuit of the stag in early spring. Now it was late autumn and the shepherds and goatherds were taking their flocks down to the valleys. Most of the wild animals in the mountains – the deer, the lions, the wild pig – were also making for their winter quarters lower down. Only Herakles and the stag still raced over the heights, though they too spent their nights lower down in more sheltered spots.

Their relationship had become extraordinarily close within its special limits. Herakles did not feel any longer that the animal was mocking him. It would wait for him when he stopped to get his breath or urinate and sometimes watch from a short distance when he was eating his austere meals, and he was sure that the look in its large golden-brown eyes was friendly and sympathetic. Why should it not be? He himself felt the same towards the stag, indeed he had begun to think of himself less as a hunter than a competitor and he longed to embrace the creature, not as a captured quarry but as a respected rival, an athlete with a body and a will even more perfect and concentrated than his own. He had abandoned any idea of trapping or tricking the stag as beneath the dignity of either of them. Either he must one day overtake it or it must come of its own free will to him. Until then they must race their race and relish one another's sole and exhilarating company in a landscape that grew emptier as it grew colder.

The last weeks of autumn and the first of winter were wet. This hardly mattered to the two heated runners, except that they had to slow down over slippery rocks. The stag tended to gain in these circumstances since four feet are better than two over treacherous surfaces, but it would soon pause briefly for Herakles to make up the distance. The gap between them was usually about half a kilometre, but once when Herakles did slip and fall and was lying there for a moment disconcerted, the stag came back towards him and did not turn and make off until it saw Herakles get to his feet, rub his bruised thigh and start running again.

But once the winter had set in, it became very cold. A sprinkling of snow fell on the tops of the mountains, then more, and the whole terrain over which they raced turned white. The snow was not thick enough at first to slow them down too much, but in the new year more fell. All tracks were invisible now and their own footprints were wiped out overnight. Herakles noticed that the stag had become thinner and a little slower and guessed that it was not finding enough to eat, whereas he himself, paying weekly visits to the nearest village, was carrying up heavier bags of food and felt even stronger and more energetic in the cold weather than he had during the heat of summer. His strategy now was to try to drive the stag down off the open mountain so as to corner it in a fold of the lower hills where it could not run so easily and its superior turn of speed would be neutralised. The animal understood, of course, what he was up to and would always break for higher ground. In this way they gradually moved northwards to the western slopes of Mount Kyllene, the second highest peak in the Peloponnese, where the borders of Arcadia, Achaia and Corinthia meet.

Here, as the snow began to melt and the first spring flowers appeared, the stag, desperately hungry now, at last turned downwards in search of fresh green leaves. Before long they were following the River Ladon, at this point, close to its source, a small brook. But the banks soon became higher and the stream, swollen by melted snow, broader and deeper. The stag was finding plenty to eat here during the nights when they rested, but it was evidently in territory it did not know and in leading the way showed signs of uncertainty. The ground on either side was growing steeper, and one morning Herakles saw that they were coming to a point at which the river narrowed and became deeper to pass through a rocky gorge. The bank they were on was barred by a sheer cliff. The stag, of course, had already seen what lay ahead, and it suddenly darted sideways towards the river.

'No, no!' shouted Herakles, forgetting that he was trying to catch the animal and thinking only of its safety. 'It's too deep and fast. You'll be carried away.'

Either the stag heard him and understood his alarm or it was simply daunted by its own view of the river. It stopped on the bank. But then as Herakles came nearer, it began to descend and entered the water, which rose round its body as it walked cautiously forward into the current. Herakles reached the bank and stood there for a moment above the stag, the closest he had ever been to it, except for that occasion when he was pretending to be asleep. How small it looked now, how vulnerable, as the water lapped round its sides and it stumbled on the boulders in the riverbed! Surely it couldn't make the crossing without being swept away? And now the water was up to its neck and it lost its footing altogether and was struggling to swim against the current. Herakles ran a few metres further along the bank, plunged into the river just below the stag and, setting his feet firmly on the riverbed with the water up to his waist, caught the animal in his arms as the current carried it down towards him. It struggled for a moment or two and then became quite still as Herakles waded to the bank muttering soft silly words as if to some beloved boy or girl who had finally submitted to him:

'Got you, sweetheart! That river nearly had you, didn't it? What a chase you've given me! What a joy to have you safe! No harm, no harm, I promise you. Herakles kills monsters, but he loves beautiful creatures and you are the most beautiful of all the creatures he ever saw. You'll come with me now to Tiryns, I'll carry you there myself.'

Whenever Herakles pursued the stag he wore his rope wound many times round his waist – it was all he did wear – but he had no need of the rope. As he hoisted the stag on to his shoulders it made no attempt to escape. It lay across the back of Herakles' neck with its head resting on his thick, bushy hair and its legs dangling either side of his chest, and Herakles held the pairs of slender legs in his huge hands without too much pressure, since the stag was entirely relaxed, and so, when Herakles had collected his lion skin and weapons, they set out for Tiryns.

Soon after they left the river and began to climb a narrow path, they met an old woman in black, her face barely visible inside the hood of her winter cloak. She didn't seem unduly surprised by the sight of this huge man, from the back of whose head apparently sprouted two sets of golden antlers.

'*Ya saas, kyría* (your health, lady)!' – or words to that effect in his more ancient Greek – said Herakles politely and waited for her to move aside.

'That stag is not yours,' said the woman, still barring his way.

'Excuse me!' said Herakles. 'I've been chasing this stag for nearly a year now and if it's not mine I'd like to know whose it is.'

'I'll tell you,' said the woman. 'It's mine.'

Herakles smiled indulgently. This person was evidently out of her mind and no doubt that was why she was wandering alone far from her village.

'By what right is it yours?' he said.

'By ancient right.'

'Ah, that's easy to say. But you'll have to prove it. I'm taking this stag – mine by right of possession – to King Eurystheus at Tiryns. If you want to make an issue of it, you'll have to come to Tiryns yourself and put your claim before the king. Now I'm already quite tired and I have a long way to go, so be so kind as to step aside or I may have to give you a nudge.'

'Herakles,' said the woman, 'you are a big fellow, but I warn you that if you give me a nudge you will regret it.'

'I always regret discourtesy,' said Herakles, 'especially to a woman, especially to an old woman, especially to one that knows my name, but I have a shortish temper and people that bar my way tend to inflame it.'

With that, he took a step forwards and was about to take another and brush the woman aside, when she put out one hand, placed it flat on his chest and with the gentle touch of a breeze but the force of a hurricane pushed him back.

'Herakles,' she said, 'I have four hinds with golden horns and bronze hooves. This is the stag that foolishly ran away when I captured them. My hinds are missing him and he is missing them. Since I wished to reunite them, I put it into Eurystheus' head to set you this task, and when you have shown him the stag you must bring it to my temple at Aulis.'

As she spoke she grew many times taller than Herakles, her black cloak and thin black dress dissolved to reveal feet in golden sandals beneath a dazzling white *peplos* and above it, the face of a young woman of unearthly beauty, with golden hair piled under a golden circlet. She held a bow in one hand, and a strap passing over her shoulder and between her breasts secured the quiver of arrows on her back.

Herakles bowed his head, recognising Artemis, avoiding meeting her eyes.

'I will do what you say, great goddess,' he said.

'You shall have light feet and a swift journey to Tiryns,' she said and suddenly the sun was shining in Herakles' eyes and the goddess was no longer there.

At Tiryns the stag was kept in the king's stable, where it was fed royally and admired by crowds of visitors. Herakles himself visited the stag every day. It would eat from his hand and he would rub its nose while he reminisced aloud about their year together and apart in the mountains. Then, when both were thoroughly rested and refreshed and Herakles had shaved the beard he had grown in the mountains, they left together, Herakles riding a horse, the stag trotting beside him, travelling northwards across the Isthmus of Corinth and past Athens to Aulis. Some storytellers say that Herakles was still pursuing the stag and that the chase took them all over Greece, but this was because they were often seen to be running, the stag in front and Herakles behind, just as they had over the Arcadian mountains, for the sheer pleasure of reliving the experience. On these occasions the horse, loaded with Herakles' lion skin and weapons, cantered along beside Herakles if the terrain allowed it, or, on narrower tracks, trotted steadily in the rear.

Why did the stag never attempt to escape in earnest? Animals, no less than men, are subject to the gods, and although the stag had once run away from Artemis, it had learnt from its loneliness in the mountains that that had been a mistake. Now it was submitting to the will of the goddess and it knew that as well as Herakles did, though not in so many words or with any knowledge of their destination. When they reached the temple, Herakles patted the stag and rubbed its nose.

'You're going to the ladies now,' he said, 'and I'm sure they'll appreciate you as you'll appreciate them, but don't forget your old friend and pursuer, Herakles! He won't forget you.'

Then he delivered the stag to the priestesses of the temple and returned to Tiryns to be given his next assignment.

5. THE BOAR

In the sculptures from the Parthenon and the Temple of Zeus at Olympia depicting the fight between Lapiths and Centaurs, the centaurs are horses with four legs and the full torsos and heads of men where the horses' necks and heads should be. That was how Pheidias and his contemporaries imagined them in the classical era. But in mythical times, in the days of Herakles, they were not such clumsy combinations – three-quarters horse and half-man, making more than one whole. They were half of each, men down to the waist with the hindlegs and tails of horses, and they walked, therefore, on two legs, not four. Is it likely that the Lapiths – a tribe of ordinary men – would have invited four-legged creatures to their king's wedding-feast? How would they have fitted round the table or reclined on the couches next to their hosts?

They were not, however, even on two legs, the best guests for a wedding. Huge, hairy and wild, followers of Dionysos, the god of wine and orgies, prone to lust and violence, they got blazing drunk whenever they could. King Peirithoös must have thought that it was better to invite them than not, given that they lived in the neighbourhood and might have burst in anyway without an invitation. But the drinking had hardly got going, the women were still at the table, when the centaur Eurytos seized the royal bride and made off with her towards the bushes, whereupon the rest of the centaurs followed suit with the rest of the women. The Lapiths and their other guests leapt off their couches, battled fiercely with the centaurs, who were much bigger and stronger but fortunately outnumbered, rescued the women and drove the abductors away. This happened in Thessaly and afterwards the centaurs were forced to leave the area altogether and take refuge far away to the south, in the mountains of Arcadia.

But just as some men are hooligans and some philosophers and some both at different times, so the centaurs were not all or always brutes. One of them, Chiron, was a famous teacher of hunting, medicine, music, gymnastics – not easy to teach if he had four legs – and the art of prophecy. He himself was taught these diverse skills by Apollo and Artemis and his own pupils included Jason, the leader of the Argonauts, Peleus, king of the Myrmidons, and his son Achilles.

Herakles, who was two-and-a-half metres tall and nearly as big as the centaurs, got on well with them, especially the two most civilised ones, Pholos and Chiron. He was not one of Chiron's pupils but had acquired his outstanding skill at archery from Eurytos, the instigator of the trouble at the Lapith wedding-feast. So when King Eurystheus gave him the task of capturing the Erymanthean Boar, Herakles decided to visit his old friend Pholos on the way. The boar had been ravaging crops and killing people in the area of Mount Erymanthos, the third highest peak in the Peloponnese, and the centaurs, after their flight from Thessaly and the angry Lapiths, had settled in some caves overlooking a deep ravine on the southern slopes of this mountain.

Pholos was delighted to see Herakles, sat him down on one of the handsome stone seats he had carved from boulders, roasted a goat for him – though he ate his own portion raw – and brought out from the back of his cave a barrel of wine, a gift to the centaurs from their patron Dionysos. It was, of course, a peculiarly fine wine, fit for gods let alone centaurs, its grapes grown and picked by satyrs, pressed by the delicate feet of nymphs and maenads, selected and blended by the god himself, aged in oak barrels, and it had been maturing in this particular barrel for some time, since Dionysos had specified that it was not to be opened until the centaurs were visited by Herakles. Did Dionysos know what the outcome would be? He must have done, since he shared the Delphic oracle with Apollo and could look into the future. Whether he deliberately *caused* that future with his gift of fine wine is a more difficult question, since the gods are not always masters of fate, even if they know what it will bring.

At any rate, as soon as Pholos opened the barrel and ladled the wine into a mixing bowl, it gave off a heavenly aroma, so powerful that all the centaurs in the nearby caves could smell it. They guessed immediately what it was and rushed furiously to Pholos' cave to remonstrate, arriving just as he and his guest were toasting each other in the rare vintage. Pholos tried to remind them that this was the very occasion for which they had been given the wine by Dionysos, but with centaurian hotheadedness they shouted him down, complaining that he was keeping to himself what belonged to them all, and set about pulling Herakles and Pholos off their seats with the intention of throwing them both down the cliff and drinking the wine themselves. Herakles and Pholos retired further into the cave, where the meat was roasting, and beat them back with flaming brands from the fire, but when Herakles saw his old archery master Eurytos, who had gone back to his own cave for his bow, setting an arrow to the string, he ducked just in time and picked up his own bow and arrows. His aim, as always, was true. He shot Eurytos in the groin, so as to bring him down without killing him, but recoiling with shock and pain Eurytos fell backwards over the cliff and was shattered on the rocks far below.

The scuffle now became a serious fight. The other centaurs fetched weapons and Herakles shot and killed or wounded several before a heavy shower of rain made the rocky apron in front of the cave so slippery that the remaining centaurs withdrew for fear of sliding into the ravine. Herakles and Pholos had a brief breathing space and took the opportunity to drink some more of the wine that had caused the fracas, but as soon as the shower passed their enemies were back and Herakles found that his bowstring had got wet and loosened, so that his shots fell short or missed their targets. He dropped the bow and used his club until at last those centaurs who were still on their feet seemed to have had enough and retreated. But just as he was restringing his bow, he saw a centaur coming cautiously on to the apron in front of the cave. Swiftly selecting an arrow from his quiver, he set it to the string and shot the intruder in the knee. Alas, it was his particular friend Chiron, who had come not to attack him but to try to make peace and tend the wounded. Now he himself lay there wounded, in terrible pain. Herakles and Pholos went to help him.

'What is it?' said Chiron. 'What sort of arrow is that? Something frightful! I never had such torture.'

Pholos pulled the arrow out of the wound and looked at the arrowhead.

'Nothing special that I can see,' he said, turning to look at Herakles.

But as he turned, the arrow slipped out of his fingers and the point nicked his foot.

'Careless!' he said, and the next moment his eyes widened, his mouth fell open and he collapsed where he stood, dead.

Now Herakles realised what had happened. This was one of the arrows he had retrieved from the Hydra. It was steeped in the Hydra's poisonous blood. He had killed his friend Pholos and as good as killed his friend Chiron. Unlike the other centaurs, Chiron was immortal. He could not die of his wound, nor could he ever get rid of the excruciating pain in his knee. Skilled as he was in medicine, he could find no antidote. So he lived on, crippled and perpetually tormented, until at last, the storytellers say, he persuaded Zeus to give his immortality to Prometheus and was able to die.

Distressed as Herakles was, blaming himself for what was not really his fault, he did not remember that his quiver contained one more of these poisoned arrows. His fate kept it for another day, far in the future, when it would kill another centaur and indirectly and ultimately himself. Meanwhile, he was only too glad to have to put his mind and strength to capturing the Erymanthian Boar. It didn't take him nearly as long as catching the Arcadian Stag. The boar was very big and made at least one attempt to charge Herakles and gore him to death with its huge tusks, as another boar had once served Aphrodite's beloved Adonis. But Herakles clouted the boar's snout with his club and vaulted over its back in the manner of a Minoan bull-jumper. After that the animal ran away whenever it saw him and the chase ended in the winter, when it blundered into a snowdrift and couldn't free itself. Herakles lassoed it with his rope, dragged it out of the snow, clubbed it senseless without killing it, tied its legs securely – he had no such relationship here as he'd had with the stag – and carried it over his shoulder to Tiryns.

On his way, passing through a forest, he met an extraordinarily handsome boy gathering firewood. The boy had heard of Herakles – who had not? – but had never seen him, and stared with astonishment and admiration at this famous hero carrying an enormous live boar on his shoulder. Herakles was equally astonished by the boy's beauty and stopped to speak to him, discovering that his name was Hylas and that his father was king of the Dryopes, a people driven out of their homeland and now dispersed all over Greece, living as best they could – foraging, hunting, labouring in the fields and vineyards – in small groups in out-of-the-way places.

'If you decide you want a better life,' said Herakles, 'come to Tiryns and ask for me. I can teach you a few more useful skills than picking up sticks.'

Hylas opened his mouth but could find nothing to say. Suddenly he took to his heels and disappeared among the trees. Herakles continued on his way, but soon heard running feet behind him. Turning his head, stepping to the side of the track and grasping his club more firmly in case it was a vengeful centaur or some other enemy, he saw Hylas.

'I asked my father,' he said. 'He told me that opportunities like this come only once in a lifetime and I should take it.'

'Well done!' said Herakles. 'You can start by carrying my club.'

Arriving at Tiryns, Herakles, with Hylas proudly carrying the club beside him, walked up the street to the palace, while the people, seeing the boar snorting and struggling on Herakles' shoulder, shrank into doorways and alleyways for fear it might escape. Inside the palace itself, Eurystheus viewed the animal from his bronze urn.

'Well,' he said, 'so that's the Erymanthean Boar! Did you have much trouble catching it?'

Herakles explained how it had fallen into a snowdrift.

'Oh, I see, you mean anyone could have scooped it up?'

Herakles laid it on the floor beside the urn so that its tusks were scraping the bronze.

'What do you want done with it now?' he asked, fiddling with the ropes round its legs.

'Are those ropes secure?' asked Eurystheus.

'Fairly secure,' said Herakles, 'but it's a big beast and you can never tell with ropes. Chains would be better.'

'Well, you can kill it now,' said Eurystheus, shrinking down inside his urn, 'and give it to my cooks.'

But Herakles saw no reason – it was not in his contract – to supply Eurystheus' kitchen, so he took it back down to the town to give to the townspeople. As he was doing so he met his nephew Iolaos, with the news that Jason and his Argonauts were gathering in Thessaly to sail to Colchis, in what is now Georgia, in order to win, as they put it, or steal, as the Colchians saw it, the Golden Fleece.

'I must join them,' said Herakles. 'Opportunities like this come only once in a lifetime.'

With that, he simply dumped the trussed boar in the market-place and set out on horseback, with Hylas on another horse beside him, to join the Argonauts.

What happened to the boar, who killed it, who ate it, is not recorded, but aeons later the travel writer Pausanias was told that its mighty tusks were still to be seen in Apollo's temple at Cumae in Italy. He thought this unlikely.

6. THE ARGONAUTS

Herakles' love for Hylas was unusual. He generally preferred women, in fact he fathered 66 children by 60 different women. True, 50 of those were the daughters of King Thespios, with whom Herakles was staying while he was hunting the lion of Kithairon, an earlier and more ordinary beast than the lion of Nemea. This was when Herakles was just eighteen years old, before he started his Labours. Thespios recognised a future hero when he saw one and, being fond of all his daughters equally as well as anxious for grandchildren with the best possible heredity, sent them in turn, night after night for 50 nights, to sleep with Herakles. Some say he had them all in one night, but that is clearly improbable, even for Herakles, who does not seem to have noticed that it was a different daughter each night. All 50 daughters conceived and bore sons, and the eldest bore twins.

The Argonauts, who included the singer Orpheus and many mortal sons of gods, were surprised and delighted by the arrival of Herakles. They had feared he would not be allowed to interrupt his Labours. Since they were rowing themselves whenever the wind was adverse, an oar wielded by Herakles was obviously going to give the ship jet power. But in the end he wasn't much use to them, and the cause was Hylas.

The Argonauts, rowing lustily to the rhythm of Orpheus' lyre, began by crossing the Aegean Sea, stopping first at Lemnos, where they found that the island was almost entirely populated by women. These women had neglected the worship of Aphrodite and been afflicted with an unpleasant smell. Their men responded by making regular visits to sweeter smelling women on the mainland, and their wives and daughters accordingly conspired one night to murder them all. Only Queen Hypsipyle had qualms at the last moment and hid her father. Whether Aphrodite had relieved them of the bad smell by the time the Argonauts put in to the harbour or whether it made no difference, her rites of love were rapidly and energetically observed by a shipload of salt-stained, sex-starved heroes coming ashore to an excited mob of exceptionally willing women.

Lemnos, as a result, was soon repopulated by a new generation of the sons and daughters of heroes, though none were the children of Herakles. Jason, as the leader of the expedition, lay with Queen Hypsipyle and gave her twin sons, and it may be that Herakles was too proud to sleep with any lesser woman. His relationship with Jason had been awkward from the beginning, for although Herakles made the ship go faster and was the strongest man and the best shot with a bow even in that distinguished company, he was not an easy person for the younger and less experienced man to give orders to. Or he may have been too besotted with Hylas to spare a thought for any woman.

The Argonauts' next port of call was the land of the Doliones, an island close to the mainland in the Sea of Marmara, where they were hospitably received by King Kyzikos and sent on their way with gifts and good wishes. Unfortunately, during the night the wind changed and blew them back on to its shores. The Argonauts did not realise it was the same island, the inhabitants took them for enemies, and there was a fierce fight in which the visitors slaughtered many of their hosts including King Kyzikos. When the sun came up and they saw their mistake, they were deeply upset, cut their hair in sorrow and apology and buried the king and the other dead with great ceremony.

Further along the coast towards the Bosporus, after an exhausting day of competitive rowing against the wind, which Herakles easily won, they landed on the mainland for rest and supplies. Herakles, who had broken his oar, pulled up a large fir tree and whittled himself a replacement, while Hylas went to fetch water. When, after an hour or two, he had not come back, Herakles set off to look for him, and when after several hours more Herakles had not come back either, the rest of the Argonauts debated what to do. Jason was not altogether sorry to lose him, but others declared that he was the mainstay of the expedition. At any rate, after searching and shouting for some time and after fierce disagreements which nearly came to blows, the Argonauts finally accepted Jason's argument that Hylas, Herakles and his brother-in-law, a Lapith called Polyphemos who was also missing, had found something better to do, and they sailed on without them.

Herakles, meanwhile, had not found Hylas, but had eventually met Polyphemos beside a small lake. Polyphemos told him that he heard Hylas cry out, ran towards the sound assuming that he was being attacked and, coming in sight of the lake, saw the boy being kissed and fondled by three water nymphs who, when they saw Polyphemos with his sword drawn, dived below the surface taking Hylas with them. Herakles immediately dived in himself, but the lake was deep and dark and he could find no trace of the boy or his abductors. He came out at last and lay on the bank beside Hylas' discarded water pot in utter misery. Polyphemos tried to comfort him:

'The boy was too beautiful,' he said. 'If he had not been taken by those nymphs, you can be sure one of the gods would have wanted him. Ganymedes was seized by an eagle sent by Zeus himself and surely Hylas was at least as beautiful as Ganymedes.'

'Losing a boy to Zeus is one thing,' said Herakles, 'but losing him to a bunch of bloody water-nymphs is quite another. You're sure that's what you saw? It wasn't just that he slipped in and drowned? Or could he, like Narcissus, have seen his own reflection and fallen in love with it?'

'He was pulled in by water nymphs, as I said,' said Polyphemos.

'Then he must have drowned anyway.'

'I'm afraid so. The nymphs can't have realised that he wouldn't survive under water.'

'Gods above! How stupid is that?'

'Women ...' said Polyphemos. 'I love them dearly, especially your sister, my dear wife Laonome. But their quick tempers and lack of patience sometimes get the better of their commonsense. They don't always consider consequences. And women are more collective creatures than we are, they seldom work things out freshly for themselves, but tend to pick up their ideas from each other. Think of those murderous women of Lemnos! Do you imagine men would ever have behaved like that, cutting off their noses to spite their faces? When we sack a city we don't kill the women, do we? And besides, these were water-women – probably nobody ever told them that humans are made differently and don't breathe like fish.'

‘I never loved any woman as I loved Hylas,’ said Herakles. ‘Men are made to get children and women to bear them, but love is not the same as that animal instinct. Love is aroused by pure beauty and a meeting of minds.’

‘Did Hylas have a mind?’ asked Polyphemos. ‘I never heard him put two words together.’

‘He did to me. He was quite innocent of the world and was always asking me questions.’

Polyphemos refrained from saying what he thought, that Herakles’ love for Hylas sprang as much from the boy‘’s massaging of his hero’s vanity as from the hero’s possession of the boy’s beautiful body.

‘It’s a dreadful loss,’ he said. ‘But somehow you must reconcile yourself to it. All life is gain and loss until at last we lose everything. But the memory of your deeds, Herakles, will never be lost and so in some sense you will gain what you lose. You will lose your life but gain immortality.’

‘My life is worth nothing to me now. Take your sword and put an end to it!’

But Polyphemos was wiser than to go down in history as the man who killed Herakles with only half his deeds done. Besides, he thought that Herakles’ passion for Hylas was out of character and would probably pass in a day or two.

‘Do it yourself!’ he said, ‘I’m going back to the ship. They’ll be tired of waiting for us.’

Indeed, when they returned to the shore to find that the Argonauts had abandoned them, Herakles’ fury almost drove the memory of Hylas out of his head. He wanted now to find a village or town, commandeer horses and gallop after the ship, not so as to take any further part in the expedition but to put an end to it by hammering the crew and breaking up the Argo. But the district was not at all populous and by the time they did find a village it was far too late to hope to catch up with the ship. In any case the village had no horses, only donkeys.

The name Polyphemos is better known as that of the one-eyed Cyclops blinded and outmanoeuvred by crafty Odysseus. But this human Polyphemos, Herakles’ brother-in-law, though his opinion of women is disputable and was probably mostly based on his wife’s character, who may well have shared her brother Herakles' 'quick temper and lack of patience', this Polyphemos too deserves to be remembered as the kind of sensible friend – like Orestes' cousin Pylades – that every hero needs.

7. THE BIRDS

Herakles returned to Tiryns and took up his Labours again. First, he was to dislodge a flock of large and dangerous birds which had gathered in the trees around Lake Stymphalos and were attacking the farmers' sheep and goats and sometimes their children. The lake was on the border between Arcadia and Corinthia, on the route he had taken when returning with the Erymanthian Boar. Passing sadly one evening through the forest where he had first met Hylas, it occurred to Herakles to seek out the boy's family. They might easily blame him for the boy's death and try to take revenge on the person who had indirectly brought it about, but Herakles could be kind-hearted as well as ruthless, and in any case he was still grieving and wanted to share his grief with the only other people in the world who would feel it as deeply as he did. The family's first reaction to the bad news he brought them was bitterness and anger, but as Herakles stood there in front of them, his weapons laid on the ground, his head bowed, his face wet with tears, their anger melted away. They spent the night drinking, mourning and praising Hylas' beauty and good nature.

'He will not be forgotten,' said Herakles.

'Not as long as his name is linked with yours,' said Hylas' father. 'In the short term it's a terrible misfortune for him, for you and for us, but in the long term such an opportunity comes to only a few.'

The next day Herakles pulled up a fir tree and shaped it into an oar to be set up as a memorial to Hylas' brief glory as one of the Argonauts. Then several of the Dryopes accompanied him to Lake Stymphalos, where with a fearful noise of shouting, beating bronze pots and pieces of wood, they drove the angry, shrieking birds into the air. They were indeed enormous, vultures surviving from the

Pleistocene era, with wing-spans of five metres. Herakles shot several down into the lake and one on to the shore before the rest dispersed, never to trouble that region again.

Taking kind and sad leave of the Dryopes, Herakles carried the dead vulture back to Tiryns and, without telling Eurystheus it was dead, draped it over the top of his bronze urn, while he demonstrated how the birds had been driven into the air by striking the side of the urn with his club. When the bird's stinking corpse had been removed by the king's guards, Eurystheus was helped, more dead than alive with terror, nausea and earache, out of his urn. Immediately he ordered Herakles to go to the island of Crete and capture a feral, fire-breathing bull. The storytellers say that he was to bring it back to Tiryns alive, but it's hard to imagine how a bull that breathed fire could be conveyed in a wooden ship, and besides, if Herakles really had succeeded in crossing the Myrtoan Sea from Crete with a bull that still breathed fire and presenting it to his cousin, Eurystheus would surely have been pot roasted.

8. THE AMAZONS

Herakles' visit to the Amazons was suggested by Eurystheus' daughter Admete. Someone had told her that Hippolyte, the queen of the Amazons, wore a girdle given to her by Ares, and Admete thought she would like to wear it herself. She was evidently not a very clever or imaginative girl, or she would have guessed that a girdle given by the god of war to the queen of a tribe of female warriors was unlikely to be the sort of pretty fashion-accessory worn by feather-brained domestic princesses like herself. However, since Herakles had now more or less cleared the Peloponnese of monsters, his range had to be extended and Eurystheus no doubt hoped, on every occasion when his cousin set off to perform another Labour, that this time he would be worsted and would not return. Admete's whim must have seemed to offer the best odds yet. Very well, so he had strangled the Nemean Lion, sliced up the Lernaian Hydra, caught the Arcadian Stag and the Erymanthean Boar, dispersed the Stymphalian Birds, killed the Cretan Bull, cleared the Augeian cowsheds, even brought back the man-eating mares of Diomedes. But how could he survive an encounter with a whole tribe of women who regularly defeated and slaughtered tribes of men in pitched battle and would be outraged by the mere appearance of a man inside their territory, let alone one who had come to rob their queen of her most famous possession?

The Amazons did, of course, sleep with men from time to time, in order to keep their population steady, but they did so on their own terms, taking the best specimens of captured warriors and killing them – as well as any male babies – once they had done their job of fertilising an Amazon. Many of them were beautiful women, but they were also skilled with bows and double-headed axes, and the men of the neighbouring tribes knew better than to tangle with them. Depending on whether they were left- or right-handed, they bound one of their breasts flat under their chitons and it was this custom which gave rise to the false rumour that they actually cut off one breast so as to be able to draw back their bowstrings or cast their javelins more easily. And the fact that they wore the other breast fetchingly exposed gave them an immediate advantage over male opponents, whose concentration on the business of defending themselves was often fatally diverted.

The Amazons lived beside the Black Sea, in the territory called Pontos on the northern coast of what is now Turkey, and their city, Themiskyra, was built beside the mouth of the river Thermodon. Herakles went there by sea. The Amazons allowed men in ships to dock and trade their goods within a strictly limited area of the harbour, and Herakles' strategy was not to conceal his identity, as he had with King Diomedes and the Bistones, but to show himself openly and, trading his fame for hers, as it were, ask for an interview with Queen Hippolyte. The news that this celebrated hero had landed in their harbour was swiftly carried to the palace and word came back that the queen would receive him, though he must be unaccompanied by any of his crew and must leave his weapons on the ship. It was only a short distance from the harbour to the palace and at least half the population of the city lined the street as Herakles, wearing his snakeskin loincloth and lion skin, strode up it, staring about him at these formidable women with as much curiosity and admiration as they showed in staring at him.

Queen Hippolyte, tall, young and golden-haired, received him in her great hall in the presence of her chief warriors. She reminded Herakles of his encounter with Artemis, except that the goddess was infinitely taller and had not displayed her right breast – Hippolyte was evidently left-handed. There were several minutes of complete silence while she and her visitor appraised each other. The queen spoke first:

'That was a very large lion,' she said. 'I've seen and killed lions myself, but never anything on that scale.'

'It *was* large,' said Herakles, 'but the problem was not so much its size as its invulnerability. Its skin could not be pierced by a spear or arrows. I had to wrestle with it and strangle it. Even when it was dead I had to skin it with its own claws.'

'And is it still the same now, still unpierceable?'

'Oh, yes.'

'So, in effect it's like wearing a suit of armour.'

'Just so.'

'An enemy would have to strangle you, then?'

Herakles laughed and patted his bare chest.

'I don't wear it belted up,' he said. 'But, tell me, is that the girdle that Ares gave you?'

'Not at all,' she said. 'This is a pretty thing I inherited from my mother, quite light and flexible. The gold ornaments come from Colchis, which, as you know, is famous for its gold and goldsmiths, not to speak of its Golden Fleece, which I hear has been stolen by your friends the Argonauts.'

'They *were* my friends,' said Herakles, 'but they have some explaining to do.'

'What is your mission here? I hope you've not been sent to steal anything from us.'

Herakles looked round at the assembled Amazons and concluded that his mission would be hopeless if he revealed it in public, so he asked if he could speak to the queen in private. Hippolyte looked him now in the eyes, very seriously.

'I mean you no harm,' he said.

'Come, then!' she said and, taking his hand, led him through the door at the back of the hall into her own private room, closing the door behind her.

'If your mission is not to kill or rape or kidnap me, as I first assumed,' she said, 'what can it be?'

Herakles pointed to the wall, on which were hanging Hippolyte's double-headed axe and her bow and quiver.

'You came to take my weapons?'

'No, but what is that hanging beside them?'

'That's the girdle you mentioned, the one given me by Ares. As you can see, it's a warrior's belt, heavy with bronze discs and the great bronze sword in its scabbard, fit for the god of war, but hardly for a woman. I never wear it, even in battle. I prefer to ride light and trust to my axe and arrows.'

'It's that I came for,' said Herakles. 'My foolish cousin's foolish daughter wanted it, but I think she would really prefer the one you are wearing.'

'That she can't have,' said Hippolyte, 'but the other, perhaps. What would you give for it? Your lion skin?'

'If you insist.'

Herakles took off the lion skin and held it out. But Hippolyte smiled.

'It would fit me no better than Ares' girdle,' she said. 'I thought myself tall until I confronted you.'

Herakles dropped the lion-skin on the floor and smiled in return, standing there naked except for his snakeskin loincloth.

'You made me leave my weapons in the ship,' he said. 'What else have I got to give you?'

Hippolyte, smiling still, eyed his loincloth.

'Take it!' he said. 'It was made from the snakes I strangled in my cradle. I value it greatly as a memento of childhood, but I would like to think of it hanging on your wall in place of the god's girdle.'

Hippolyte stepped forward, undid the knot on Herakles' hip and dropped the snakeskin on top of the lion skin.

'You shall have it back,' she said and, undoing her own girdle, slipping deftly out of her chiton, untying the pad that flattened her left breast, stood naked before him.

They stared at each other's bodies for some time in silence. The queen spoke first:

'That's a very large cock,' she said, 'Do you think it will fit?'

'It generally does,' he said. 'When the will is there.'

'The will is there, yes.'

'Then we can but try.'

Which they did, and soon enough it did fit, very pleasurably for both.

'My foolish cousin and his foolish daughter little imagined,' said Herakles, when they were lying sated side by side, 'that they were sending me on my best Labour yet.'

'I would make you king of the Amazons and save you any further labours except this one,' said Hippolyte, 'but I'm afraid that our laws allow no man to remain in our city after he has performed his only useful function.'

'You mean to kill me, do you?'

'No, I mean to keep our bargain. You have given me what you had to give, I shall give you the girdle of Ares.'

'I care less for that than I do for its owner. If I cannot stay with you here, will you come with me? I will make you queen of any city you care to name, in Greece or Asia.'

'Now you're boasting, Herakles. You're not king of any city, but merely the servant of the contemptible king of Tiryns.'

'Apollo served Admetos and both he and Poseidon served Laomedon, King of Troy. These were punishments decreed by Father Zeus, but they did not lose their power or status as gods once their service was completed.'

'Do you compare yourself to gods?'

'Far from it. I am as mortal as you. But you must have heard that what I undertake I do, and that what I undertake is more than any other man could even think of doing. When I want a city I shall have a city.'

'I'm already queen of a city and a people. Why should I want any other?'

'Because you would also be queen of Herakles and because we fit so well.'

'Yes, we do fit well.'

'Can you really pretend that this life of yours among women, murdering your casual lovers – terrified out of their manhood, no doubt, more often than not – bearing children to conquered slaves, destroying your sons like unwanted puppies, is the best you could have? Queen you may be, but queen of a misshapen state, queen of an anomaly, queen of women who make war before they can make love and whose daughters cannot escape the same unnatural fate.'

'You are holding up a mirror to the world in general, the world of men, in which most women are forced to live as child-bearing slaves, beaten and raped out of any residue of love, in which sons are valued, but not daughters. If our state is misshapen it is because it cannot be otherwise in this world misshapen by men. If we did not make war on men and exclude them, we would be their slaves like all the other women in the world. It's simple enough, isn't it, Herakles? You, who can do anything you undertake, might think of undertaking this: change your world of men so that women can be their equals and we Amazons will change our state so that men can be our equals.'

'I will found such a city and you shall be queen of it.'

'Found it first and then send for me!'

They laughed and made love again, then Hippolyte got up and washed and put on her clothes. Herakles also washed, tied on his snakeskin loincloth and, taking the girdle of Ares from the wall, fastened it round his waist. He retrieved his lion skin from the floor and hung it over his arm.

'You had better wear it,' said Hippolyte, 'and pull it round you to conceal the girdle. I would not give much for your chances if my people were to see you strutting away with your prize.'

'And what of your chances when they find out it's gone?'

'Leave me to manage my own people! But I will walk down to the harbour with you, so that when they find out they will know it was not stolen.'

'If you bear a child, the son of Herakles and Hippolyte, what will you do with him?'

'With *him*? You know what our laws require. With *her*, she will no doubt be strangling snakes in her cradle and grow up to be such a queen of the Amazons as will extend our power far beyond the borders of Pontos.'

'And this is what you bought with the girdle of Ares?'

'A good bargain, don't you think? And so I shall tell my people.'

'I must warn you that my children are most often sons.'

'But mine most often daughters.'

Unfortunately – or perhaps fortunately – there was to be no such child, male or female, from this legendary union. As Herakles and Hippolyte walked together from the palace to the harbour they were surrounded with the queen's chief warriors and followed by a great crowd of gaping Amazons, whispering among themselves, speculating about what this might mean, their queen showing such unprecedented favour to a man. Was he her prisoner or she his? Would she allow him to sail away alive? Or was she hostage to him and in danger of being abducted? And there were no doubt some women in the crowd, though they could not have admitted it to their friends, who, admiring the god-like couple, secretly wished that their laws were not so strict and that they too might walk and talk openly with a man.

When Herakles and Hippolyte reached the harbour enclave, they clasped hands and looked into each other's eyes for the last time. Then Herakles turned and went inside the barrier alone. But whether it was again the goddess Hera's continual malevolence towards Herakles, as some storytellers say, or whether it was Hippolyte's understandable pang at the thought of losing this man she couldn't help loving, something made the queen step forward after him beyond the barrier, calling out:

'Herakles! Don't forget to found that city!'

He turned with a delighted smile.

'No, and be sure I'll send for you, Hippolyte!'

But, as he turned, his lion skin swung open, revealing the belt of Ares round his waist. With a great cry of rage and horror, the queen's guard of warriors rushed forward brandishing their weapons. Herakles drew the bronze sword from the belt and laid about him. The men from his ship, whom he had warned to be armed and ready at all times in case he had to steal and run away with the girdle, came immediately to his assistance with bows and spears. The battle was fierce and brief. Leaving a swathe of dead and wounded Amazons and a few dead comrades of their own, Herakles and his crew regained the ship, cast off and rowed away. But lying among the dead by the harbour barrier was Hippolyte herself, caught unarmed in the middle of the furious melée and pierced through the throat by the bronze sword of Ares. Herakles only heard much later, after he had delivered the fatal girdle to Eurystheus' silly daughter, that he had unwittingly killed the lovely woman who gave it to him in exchange for a child she would now never bear.

9. THE APPLES

The accounts of Herakles' last few Labours have him roaming the Mediterranean world from Arabia, Egypt, Libya and Morocco to Spain, Portugal, France, Italy, the Balkans and the Black Sea; and even beyond the Pillars of Hercules, which he himself set up on either side of the Strait of Gibralter, to the fringes of the Atlantic Ocean. His complicated and sometimes contradictory adventures in the course of his missions to collect Hippolyte's girdle, the red cattle of the three-headed giant Geryon and the golden apples of the Hesperides included defeating predatory tribes, founding cities and fathering children, as well as destroying monsters, giants, bandits and evil rulers. Most of these subsidiary activities were presumably inserted by local storytellers so as to attach his prestigious name to a district, a city or a dynasty, much as we now put his name on a bag of concrete or boast that other assorted celebrities 'slept here'. I once came across two modest terrace-houses facing each other on a narrow street in Bonifacio, on the southern tip of Corsica, which cap most such boasts: one side claimed the Emperor Charles V, the other Napoleon Bonaparte, though not, of course, at the same time.

Shall I claim that Herakles, who spent so much time in Arcadia, visited our village and, in the ravine beside it, blocked the river with immense boulders? The storytellers say that he did that to the river

Strymon, on the border between Macedonia and Thrace, either so as make a bridge for Geryon's cattle as he drove them back to Tiryns or to punish the river god, who had aggravated him and whose stream had previously been navigable. The river god in our case has been more or less permanently disabled, since our local authority (the *demos*) pipes the water from higher up so that the bed is quite dry. Very occasionally the river god recovers his powers and unleashes a spate, which has been known to carry away unlucky donkeys tethered in its path or cars parked in the wrong place in the seaside town below. Contracts for Greek houses contain with good reason a clause forbidding building within so many metres of the course of a possible spate. Meanwhile the *demos*, with the help of funds from the EU, has transformed part of the ravine into a public square, with drinking fountains, a viewing platform and a terrace – a kind of mini-spa. Even if Herakles didn't personally place the boulders, he was surely here in spirit with his bags of concrete, and the *demos* might just as well put his name to this place as so many of their ancient predecessors did to theirs, all round the Mediterranean.

When Herakles set out on his eleventh and penultimate Labour, to fetch the golden apples of the Hesperides, he had no idea where to find them. Somebody, probably his guardian goddess Athene, told him that he should ask the sea god Nereus, son of Poseidon and Gaia, the earth goddess. Athene could have given him the information herself, of course, but the gods treat mortals much as sensible parents treat children, helping them only enough to help themselves. Nereus was not an easy person to get directions from, since he lived at the bottom of the sea, but by his wife Doris he had 50 sea nymph daughters called the Nereids whose favourite bathing place was the mouth of the River Po in northern Italy. Herakles therefore took a ship from Patras in the Peloponnese up the Adriatic Sea towards what is now Venice, as one can still do, and soon discovered the Nereids swimming and sunbathing and playing ball games on the beach. Their father, they said, frequently came up from the bottom of the sea to watch them – they were certainly a lovely sight, whether, as the earliest Greek vase painters and sculptors depicted them, they wore wet and clinging dresses or, as in later depictions, nothing at all. They advised Herakles to wait around until their father turned up and, although several days passed before he did, this must have been a very welcome break in very pleasant company for the indefatigable hero.

Nereus, when he did appear, walking ponderously out of the sea and up the beach, was not such a pretty sight as his daughters. Barnacles, mussels and other sea creatures clung to his body and limbs, his hair and beard were tangled with seaweed and he smelt violently of fish. The Nereids had warned Herakles that their father could be gruff and grumpy and that if he refused to answer questions the only solution was to wrestle with him.

'Wrestle with him?' said Herakles. 'Are you sure about that? If anybody asked me a question and got no answer and then immediately started to wrestle with me, I'd not only not answer his question, I'd wrap him round a tree.'

'Dad enjoys a good wrestle,' said one of the Nereids.

'It amuses him,' said another.

'The thing is,' said a third, 'that he keeps changing shape.'

'Just as you've got a grip on him,' said a fourth, 'he'll turn into a seal ...'

'Or an octopus ...' said a fifth.

'Or a shark ...' said a sixth.

'Or a lion ...' said a seventh.

'Or a buzzard ...' said an eighth.

'Or a toad ...' said a ninth.

'Or a worm ...' said a tenth.

And by the time all 50 Nereids had suggested some creature Nereus might turn into, Herakles had begun to understand the scope of their father's sense of humour.

'What you have to do,' said the first Nereid, 'is keep hold of him, whatever he turns into, and when he finally gets tired of the game and turns back into himself, you can ask your question and he'll probably answer it.'

'But suppose he doesn't, or doesn't know the answer?' said Herakles. 'Is it really worth all this hassle?'

'Oh, you needn't worry about that,' said the Nereid. 'Dad loves showing off his knowledge, once he's had his bout of wrestling, and he knows absolutely everything, past, present and future.'

So as soon as Herakles had asked politely where he could find the golden apples of the Hesperides and Nereus had looked at him contemptuously and belched his terrible fishy breath straight into his face, Herakles grabbed him round the waist and kicked his legs from under him. Only to find himself belly-to-belly with a stinging jellyfish, and, still grasping it in spite of the pain, being squeezed in his turn by a python. But he had no sooner got the python's neck between his hands than it became a vast basking shark with no neck at all and many times his own size. Still he held on and fell on top of the whale-like creature, when it shrank to a sea urchin and spiked him savagely in the chest before metamorphosing into a mullet and almost sliding out of his grasp into the sea before Herakles caught it by the tail, which turned into a butterfly. Herakles closed his great fists around the fluttering insect and said:

'Aren't you afraid I'll crush you to death, old man?'

But it was already an ant, crawling between his fingers and over the back of his hand, and as Herakles covered it with his other hand, the ant became a heron, then a bee, then a stork, then a rat, and still Herakles held on, as the rat became a fox and the fox a bear and the bear a porpoise ... and suddenly at last Nereus himself, the old man of the sea.

'You did well, young man,' he said. 'The butterfly usually has them, because they're afraid if they crush it they'll never get the answer, so they open up a bit and away I go.'

'But if you *were* crushed?' asked Herakles.

'Nothing to worry about. My reactions are quick and I'd turn into something else. Besides, I'm immortal. What is your question?'

Having enjoyed his peculiar form of exercise, Nereus became relaxed and friendly. He not only told Herakles that the Garden of the Hesperides was in the Atlas Mountains on the southern side of the Mediterranean, he gave him essential advice on what he had to do to get the golden apples. The tree which bore the apples, he said, was given by his mother Gaia to Hera as a wedding present when she married Zeus, and it was planted in the goddess's own walled garden, where it was guarded by a dragon. The giant Atlas had been Hera's gardener until he joined the other giants in attacking Mount Olympos and attempting to overthrow the Olympian gods. After their defeat, most of the giants, who were immortal and couldn't be got rid of altogether, were buried deep under various mountains. Atlas, however, was given the task of standing on top of the mountain range that bears his name and holding up the sky on his head, while his four daughters, the Hesperides, took on the job of looking after Hera's garden.

'So I have to avoid Atlas, charm his daughters and kill the dragon.' said Herakles. 'But if the tree belongs to Hera, my enemy ever since I was born, she is going to be less than amused.'

'For that reason I suggest that you don't kill the dragon or charm his daughters or avoid Atlas. On the contrary, go straight up to Atlas and ask him to fetch the apples.'

'Why should he do that?'

'Because you'll offer to hold up the sky while he's doing it – I'm sure you're capable of that – and he'll think that the golden apples you want are his golden chance to leave you holding the sky.'

'And he'll be right. How can I get him to take it back?'

'I leave that to you, dear boy. Atlas was never the smartest giant on the planet and I doubt if his brain has been quickened by the weight of the sky.'

'No. He must have a very sore head by now.'

'Bear that in mind!'

Herakles took friendly leave of Nereus and his 50 daughters and boarded a ship sailing to Libya, where he encountered another competitive wrestler. Like Nereus, Antaios was a son of Poseidon and Gaia, but whereas Nereus was immortal and lived in the sea, his father's element, Antaios was mortal and depended on his mother's element, the earth, for his extraordinary strength. He did not wrestle for amusement but in order to kill his opponents. He was building a temple to his father Poseidon and his favourite materials were the bones of the passing travellers he had beaten, especially their skulls, with which he was decorating the roof. The sailors on Herakles' ship had warned him about Antaios and had no intention of going anywhere near his part of Libya, but Herakles was intrigued and asked to be landed on a beach near the temple of skulls. The sailors who took him ashore in a small boat made Herakles wade the last several metres and swiftly rowed back to their ship.

Antaios came out from his workshop near the temple and welcomed Herakles enthusiastically, taking him on a tour of the racks where the skulls and other bones were drying and then to the temple itself, with its macabre roof, glistening white under the brilliant African sun.

'Impressive!' said Herakles.

'My life's work,' said Antaios.

'Still a few gaps,' said Herakles.

'It's slow work. People don't come by as often as they used to.'

'I daresay they would if the entrance fee wasn't so expensive.'

'I charge nothing,' said Antaios.

'Nothing but their lives. It's hard to go home and tell your neighbours what you've seen on your travels if you have to leave your skull behind.'

'Well, at least you've turned up to leave yours.'

'We'll see about that.'

Then they both stripped off and came to grips. Antaios was if anything taller and broader than Herakles, but they were almost equally matched in strength, and the struggle was intense. Herakles had landed in the early morning and by late afternoon he was beginning to tire. Every time he wrestled his opponent to the ground, Antaios came up with renewed vigour.

'This is the Hydra's heads all over again,' Herakles thought. 'The more I throw him, the stronger he gets. What does that tell me?'

It told him that Antaios, the son of Gaia, was being refreshed by contact with his mother earth and that if he, Herakles, continued this way he would soon be contributing his skull to Antaios' grisly roof. So exerting all his reserves of strength, Herakles lifted Antaios off the ground, held him there clasped in both his arms like a lover as Antaios struggled wildly to get his feet on the earth, and then, as he felt the man weaken, tightened his grip, squeezed harder and harder until at last Antaios' ribs cracked and gave way, the air was forced out of his lungs and with a fearful moan of despair he gave up his last breath. Herakles flung him down dead on the sandy soil and, almost exhausted to death himself, collapsed and lay beside the corpse.

When he recovered he dragged Antaios to the workshop where, near the drying racks, was a high platform on which fresh bodies were placed for the vultures to pick clean before the bones were transferred to the racks.

'I'd very much like to add you to your roof,' he told Antaios as he carried him up the steps and laid him on the platform, 'and I'll look in, if I can, on my way back with the golden apples in case the birds have finished with you. But I'm afraid the temple will never be completed now and your life's work will only be remembered because I aborted it.'

Then he picked up his lion skin, his weapons and the knapsack in which he kept his snakeskin loincloth for public appearances, together with a flask of water and some dried crusts of the kind Greek villagers still take with them into the mountains, and set off towards the setting sun. He thought he would prefer to sleep at some distance from Antaios and his tourist-trophies and he was too tired to shoot anything, let alone cook it, for his supper.

After many days he came in sight of the Atlas mountains and, nearing the summit, saw what at first looked like a great pillar reaching into the sky but gradually resolved into the figure of the giant. Herakles approached, laid down his weapons and his knapsack and sat on a rock to rest. When he had sat there in silence for some time, Atlas, who had glanced at him several times from the corners of his eyes, said:

'Who are you, little fellow?'

'I am Herakles, son of Zeus.'

'Never heard of you.'

'Most people have.'

'After my time. What do you want?'

'I've been sent to fetch some of the golden apples from Hera's garden.'

'Have you just? Then you might as well pick up your things and go home to wherever you came from, because those apples are private and very well guarded.'

'But you know where they are?'

'Of course I do. I planted the tree and I was the gardener until things went wrong.'

'What went wrong?'

Atlas gave a long, laboured account of the war of the giants with the Olympians, full of still smouldering resentment and self-justification, especially against Hera for not making any allowances for him personally, although he had served her faithfully as her gardener.

'But then you joined the Giants' Rebellion,' said Herakles. 'And surely this punishment is better than being buried *under* a mountain like the other giants? I may tell you that I am a victim of Hera's anger, too, not for anything I've done myself, but solely because Zeus fathered me on a mortal woman.'

'But at least you're free to get about,' said Atlas. 'You can't imagine the boredom of standing here forever, rooted to the spot with a permanently aching head.'

'You'd welcome a break?'

'Gods above, don't even make me think about it!'

'Well this is what I suggest: you fetch me some golden apples and I'll take your place in the meantime.'

'You'd do that?'

'I would. With pleasure.'

'But there's the dragon, curled round the tree, a dangerous fire-breathing creature. It wouldn't let me anywhere near the apples. Only my daughters, the Hesperides, can go past the dragon.'

'Then ask your daughters to fetch the apples!'

'They'd never do it. They once took some apples on their own account and were given a severe warning by Hera that if it happened again they'd be shut in a cave for the rest of time.'

'Nothing for it, then,' said Herakles. 'I'll have to kill the dragon and fetch the apples myself and you won't get your break. Which way do I go to find the garden?'

Atlas was silent. Giant tears rolled down his giant cheeks.

'Three points,' said Herakles. 'Hera can hardly blame your daughters for taking the apples, if they do so because their father tells them to. What would the world come to if daughters disobeyed their fathers? Secondly, you can take the blame on yourself, since what can Hera do worse to you than what you're already suffering and who would she get to take your place? Thirdly, the real blame lies with me and I swear by all the gods that I shall only borrow the apples. They will be returned to the garden as soon as I've shown them to my cousin Eurystheus.'

Atlas began to look more cheerful and asked for clarification. Herakles repeated what he had said several times, until the giant had fully understood all three points.

'I'll do it,' he said at last.

'Then give me the sky!' said Herakles, 'but first you must swear by the River Styx, whose oaths bind all immortals, even Father Zeus, that once you have brought me the apples you will take the sky back.'

Eager now to get rid of his burden as soon as possible, Atlas swore the oath. Herakles piled up a few rocks beside Atlas to make a cairn the size of a small mountain peak, and climbed on top of it so as to approximate to the giant's height, while Atlas, sliding carefully sideways, transferred the weight to Herakles' head. Then, rubbing his own head with both hands, flexing his shoulders, swinging his arms, Atlas skipped down the mountain, kicking loose rocks aside in his joy as if they were pebbles.

The sky was the strangest weight Herakles had ever borne. It had no substance or hardness or edge, but only pressure, and the pressure was at first almost intolerable, giving him a headache far beyond any hangover he had ever suffered, making his lungs feel as if they would burst and his heart beat as if he were running up hill, inviting his legs to buckle, hurting the soles of his feet as they gripped the pile of rocks. But gradually, as he resisted the desire to crumple and lie down, his body and head adapted to the pressure and he began to feel a strange normality, almost a comfort in being wedged between earth and sky. It was as if he were awake and asleep at the same time, except that he had no dreams.

'So this is what it's like to be the top of a mountain,' he thought. 'Everlasting endurance and sameness, without any sense of past or future, without memory or anxiety. In many ways it's harder to be a man than a rock.'

And when, after several hours, Atlas returned with three apples, Herakles felt an odd reluctance to hand back his burden and return to his old self. Atlas was equally reluctant to change places.

'I tell you what, little fellow,' he said, juggling the apples, which were made of solid gold, 'you're doing this job so well that I've had an idea. Why don't *I* take the apples and show them to your cousin, then I can make sure they come safely back here afterwards?'

'Yes, that's a very good idea,' said Herakles, and for a moment he almost meant it. But then he reflected that unlike Atlas he was mortal and would die of hunger and thirst long before the giant returned. 'But I must say that I've got a tremendously sore head. And what if winter sets in before you're back? I might perish of cold and the sky would fall. So before you go, would you mind just holding it a minute while I fetch my lion skin?'

'No sweat!' said Atlas.

He put down the apples and they swapped places.

'Thanks,' said Herakles, climbing down from the cairn, collecting his lion skin, weapons and knapsack. 'On second thoughts, though, I fancy I'd better do the job myself. My cousin's a stickler for the rules and he might discount this Labour altogether if he saw that you'd helped me.'

He picked up the apples and put them in his knapsack.

'See you!' he said with a friendly wave, but got no reply.

Atlas just stared at him with hopeless reproach. Nor did Herakles ever see him again. He returned to Tiryns by way of Libya and Egypt, calling at Antaios' place on the way so as to add his skull, by now picked clean, to the temple roof.

'And no one will ever know which was yours,' Herakles said to it. 'You look just like all your victims and you take up no more space, in spite of your arrogance and your boastful ugly architecture. Let this be a lesson to you! You had every advantage. Your father was the god of the sea and your mother the goddess of the earth and yet you completely wasted your life wasting other people's.'

After Eurystheus had been shown the golden apples, Athene delegated Iris, the gods' messenger, to return them to Hera's garden.

10. THE DOG

The twelfth and last Labour was the hardest. Eurystheus had determined not to have any more live monsters brought to Tiryns, but he was almost entirely certain that this Labour would not only defeat Herakles but be the death of him. He was to go down to the kingdom of Hades and bring back Cerberos, the three-headed dog which guarded its gate. He had to prepare himself by becoming an initiate of the Mysteries in Demeter's temple at Eleusis. When Demeter's beloved daughter Persephone was abducted by Hades, who ruled the underworld as his brother Zeus ruled the earth and sky, Demeter in her grief devastated the earth with rain and cold. The crops failed, the cattle died, famine and disease spread among men and the service of the gods was neglected. It was agreed then between Zeus and Hades that Persephone should spend the winter with Hades in the underworld and the rest of the year on earth with her mother. So the worship of Demeter, the goddess of harvest and plenty, became associated with her daughter Persephone's part-time job as queen of the underworld, and her worshippers could prepare themselves for their future as flittering shades and perhaps gain some advantage over non-initiates by going through a series of rituals at Eleusis. But since Eleusis was dominated by the nearby city of Athens, this opportunity was normally offered only to Athenian citizens and Herakles was no such thing.

It happened, however, that the current King of Athens, the hero Theseus, had preceded Herakles on a live expedition into the underworld and failed to return. The priests of Eleusis were ready to accept Herakles as an initiate on condition that he brought Theseus back, and evidently he would more easily accomplish that if he was also bringing back the fearsome dog that guarded the gate and prevented anyone leaving once they had entered the underworld.

There were various entrances to Hades' kingdom. The one chosen by Herakles on Athene's advice was Tainaron, better known now as Cape Matapan, where in more recent times, during the Second World War, the British defeated the Italians in a naval battle. This is the most southerly point of the Peloponnese, the tip of the mountainous Mani peninsula. Hermes, whose business it was to conduct dead souls to the underworld, accompanied Herakles to the cave mouth at this desolate spot and Athene was there too. They were both disguised as local villagers, but Herakles was not deceived and thanked them warmly before turning to go into the dark.

'Be careful how you behave, Herakles!' said Athene. 'Be stern with Charon, who will not want to ferry you across the River Styx, but don't lose your temper down there and be particularly polite to Persephone and Hades themselves. The reason they are keeping Theseus and his friend Peirithoös, king of the Lapiths, is that there was a stupid oath sworn between the two of them. Having both recently lost their wives, they thought they would like to marry daughters of Zeus, so Theseus was to abduct Helen of Sparta and Peirithoös Persephone. The oath required them to assist each other and since the first abduction succeeded, Theseus had to go to the underworld to help Peirithoös abduct Persephone. What childish bravado! My uncle Hades naturally took it as a serious insult to himself and his queen and has kept both of them prisoner for the last four of your years. You may be able to free Theseus, who was only an accomplice, but I don't think there's much chance for Peirithoös. Now is there anything you want to ask of me before you go?'

'I have my lion skin, my club and my bow. Those are all I ever need, except for patience, strength, courage and your advice and good wishes, great goddess.'

'Think more carefully!'

'A flaming torch, of course!' he said, contemplating the pitch-black passage he was to descend.

'It would hardly last you to the bank of the Styx, let alone beyond.'

'Well, I shall have to feel my way and perhaps my eyes will gradually become used to the darkness. They must have light of some sort down there, even if the sun never touches them.'

'I have never been there myself, but I don't think so. Deeper down, of course, is Pyriphlegethon, the river of fire, which divides black Erebos and the palace of Hades from Tartaros, where the Titans are imprisoned. There must be light enough there, but you will not be going as far as that.'

'How shall I manage, then?'

Herakles leant against the wall of the cave. All his usual confidence deserted him. He felt suddenly weak and disconsolate. His great shoulders drooped, his knees bent, tears welled in his eyes. Athene smiled, not with disdain for a hero faced with failure, but with the tenderness she always felt for a few particular men whose intelligence and determination fought constantly against their own mortal weaknesses as well as the hostility of one or other of her fellow immortals. She loved Herakles as later she loved Odysseus.

'I'm sure you will manage.'

'How can I rescue Theseus and overpower Cerberos if I can't see them?'

'Close your eyes, Herakles!'

He did so, releasing the tears, so that they ran down his cheeks. At the same time he felt a gentle puff of air on each of his eyelids.

'Open your eyes now and go down to Hades!' said Athene. 'I have given you what you need.'

But when he looked to thank her, he found he was alone, facing only the sea and the evening sky, the surf lapping on the rocks below him, a seagull crying. The two gods disguised as mountain villagers had disappeared. He wiped his cheeks with his hand, checked his weapons, shouldered his pack of provisions and turned again towards the dark passage. It no longer seemed so dark and as he descended he had no difficulty in seeing his way. Athene had given him night vision.

Arriving after many hours at the bank of the Styx, he found a jostling crowd of shadows, the recently dead, waiting to be ferried across by Charon, who was in no hurry to oblige them and was testing every coin presented to him for his fare between his mouldering teeth. Being newly dead in those days was a little like going through security in an airport today, except that these shadows did not form an orderly queue, had no bags to be searched, no jackets or belts or shoes to remove, nothing at all, in fact, except their miserable naked semblances and the coins their relatives had placed between their cold lips. And there was only ever one self-important official on duty who, if he rejected your coin or if you had none, barred your passage and left you to wander for ever on that bleak shore, a soul lost between life and death. Airport security would seem almost pleasant by comparison.

The crowd scattered as Herakles walked straight up to Charon.

'Wait your turn, scum!' said the boatman without looking up from the coin he was examining.

Herakles knocked the coin out of his hand. Charon fell back into his boat and, looking up at the aggressor on the bank with his lion skin and his club, instantly changed his expression from fury to fear.

'I need to cross,' said Herakles. 'If you don't mess with me, I'll not mess with you.'

He stepped into the boat and sat down, while Charon, his black teeth chattering behind his grimy white beard, pushed off and laboured to row them across, using his single long oar in the manner of a Venetian gondolier. He was not used to such a weight, or really any weight, in his ferry, and made a slow and clumsy job of it.

'I don't reckon with living customers,' he said, when Herakles advised him to try harder or he would take the oar himself and throw the oarsman into the river.

'You must have had a couple of them quite recently,' said Herakles.

'And that was right outside the regulations.'

'Well, you'd better prepare yourself. I shall be coming back with one or both of them and a dog.'

'A dog? What dog? There's only one dog in Hades that I know of and I wouldn't take that dog or any other dog in my boat for any money.'

'Don't worry! No money will be offered.'

'All the same, I won't have dogs in my boat. Filthy beasts! They leave piss and hairs wherever they go.'

'Your boat is already as filthy as you are and when I come back you'll take whatever I tell you to take, even if it's a dog with three heads and a snake for a tail.'

'Oh, if that's your game, no worry! Cerberos will have you by the balls before I ever see you again, bad luck to you!'

Cerberos, however, could not have been more ingratiating when Herakles arrived at the gate of Hades soon after disembarking from the boat. All three of his heads were dipping and dobbing, his tongues drooling, his six ears laid back, his six huge eyes fawning, his serpent tail flapping happily, as Herakles passed through the great marble archway, which was lit on either side by long flares of natural gas (Athene had been wrong in thinking there was no light at all in Hades) and over which was carved on the outside 'WELCOME TO THE KINGDOM OF HADES', but on the inside 'NO EXIT'.

Bat-like creatures were fluttering everywhere around him as he strode forward into the darkness beyond the gate, and there was a continuous whispering and squeaking, which he soon realised was nothing more than a recital of their own names – 'I was Menoetios,' 'I was Telamon,' 'I was Hippodameia', 'I was Phaedra', and so on. These were the most recent arrivals, still desperate to cling on to their individual identities. Herakles listened hard in case he might hear 'I was Hylas', but couldn't be sure that he did. Perhaps, after all, the boy had survived in the arms of the amorous water nymphs. One shadow seemed to say 'I was Antaios, son of Poseidon' and another, 'I was Hippolyte, Queen of the Amazons'. He had slain so many by mistake or on purpose and had lost so many others, friends, lovers, relatives and acquaintances, by disease or accident or old age, that any or all of these whisperers might once have been known to him.

'Shall I be like this,' he wondered, 'miserably insisting "I was Herakles" until oblivion sets in and it will no longer matter whether I was Herakles or some nameless slave?'

The thought at first depressed him, but then, as the whispering grew fainter and he understood that the silent shadows still fluttering round him were those of the longer dead, his spirits rose again.

' Of course I shall, but not yet. The more reason to do what I have to do, to finish the twelfth Labour, to be Herakles still and return to the bright world in triumph.'

He did not imagine that with other heroes, poets, philosophers, healers and rulers who had benefited mankind he might spend the afterlife in the flowery meadows and sunlit glades of the Blessed Isles or Elysium, somewhere in the west, on the borders of the Ocean that encircled the earth. That was an idea dreamed up by poets, who perhaps hoped to go there themselves, long after Herakles' time. In his time, whoever you were, whatever you had done, whether you were an Achilles or a Homer or an Agamemnon or a Plato, if you did not become an immortal or a constellation, you joined the shades in the underworld.

The night vision given him by Athene allowed him to see his way, but not to see very far. He seemed to be in a boundless space without walls or roof, though the smooth rock under his feet, the lack of any breeze and the cold, clammy atmosphere that he felt and smelt made him suspect that there was rock all around him. To test the acoustics and restore his courage, he shouted aloud:

'I am Herakles, son of Zeus, a living man in the kingdom of the dead.'

The sound echoed and re-echoed. Evidently he was in a vast cavern. The silent shadows surging round him disappeared at the sound of his voice, but they returned as the echoes died away. He had another thought: somewhere among the shadows must be his late wife Megara and their children, whom he had killed in his madness and who were indirectly responsible for his being here at all. He stopped walking and shouted again:

'Megara! Megara!'

And waiting where he was until the echoes faded and the shadows began to gather round him again, he held out his hand until he thought something lighter than a fly touched it.

'Forgive me, dearest wife!' he said, keeping his voice low. 'I didn't know what I was doing when I took away your life and theirs – our lovely children's. I was not myself, but the plaything of an angry goddess. The gods know how I grieved for you then and wanted to end my own life, and would have done if Athene had not prevented me. But now that I see with my own eyes what my madness made of you, when you might have enjoyed so many more years under the sun, I can almost wish, as the goddess Hera did, that I'd never been born to do you such harm.'

Tears filled his eyes and momentarily sharpened his vision, so that he seemed to catch a glimpse of his wife's sad face before the shadow in front of him drifted away among all the others.

Soon afterwards he came to another gateway, this time closed by a great door of adamant, a substance never found anywhere else, but often invoked on earth for its diamond-like hardness. And like a diamond, it was transparent. Through it Herakles could dimly see a courtyard set about with cypresses and beds of asphodel, and beyond that the steps and portico of Hades' palace. Remembering Athene's advice about behaving politely, he knocked on the door gently with his club and when there was no answer, knocked again harder and again harder still, until, exasperated, he put his shoulder to it, exerted his great strength and tried to force it open. His efforts were useless. This was a door that resisted even the mighty muscles of Herakles. Tired and frustrated, he leant against the door, when it suddenly slid silently sideways and he fell full-length across the threshold. Lying there bruised and disconcerted, he heard coarse laughter behind him and twisting his head round saw a huge figure all in black, its face hidden in a black beard and a black helmet, its pale eyes glistening as if with moonlight through the visor.

'The Lion recumbent!' said this figure, his sarcastic voice deeper and more reverberant than any Herakles had ever heard. 'Welcome to my kingdom! No, don't try to get up! I do not permit mortals to enter my palace and if you have a favour to ask me you can do so from where you are. It shows proper respect.'

'Great Hades, king of the underworld,' said Herakles. 'Since all we mortals are certain one day to be your subjects, we cannot but show you proper respect and I am honoured to lie at your feet.'

'So you should be,' said Hades. 'Mortals tend to forget, when they worship and make constant sacrifices to my brothers Zeus and Poseidon, that their days on earth or at sea are extremely few compared to the aeons they will spend in my kingdom.'

'Believe me,' said Herakles, 'it's not because they forget you, Great Hades, but rather because they have you constantly in mind and, since they are by birth and nature creatures of the sun and air and fear the dark, do everything they can to placate your brothers, so as to spin out those few days on earth as long as possible.'

'Is that so?'

'In fact I would go so far as to say that although Father Zeus rules earth and sky and Poseidon the sea, the ruling force for mortal men is inevitably you, sir. And consider the pyres we build for our greatest warriors when they die, and the domed tombs for our kings. Aren't these sacrifices and monuments to you? And since mortals are always fighting and regularly losing their kings, these sacrifices happen somewhere nearly every day and the monuments are nearly as frequent.'

Herakles was at first surprised to discover that such a powerful god could be so jealous of his brothers and so ignorant of the minds of men, but then he remembered that all his own troubles came from Hera's jealousy of his mother, and guessed that Hades had no experience of men's minds, which they had more or less lost by the time they reached his kingdom. But he felt that at least he was not annoying, was perhaps even pleasing this terrible god, and was ready to continue his ignominious flattery as long as it took to stimulate whatever generous instincts Hades might have.

Hades laughed again, the same harsh sound as before, something between the bark of a fox and the braying of a donkey. His whole kingdom seemed to crouch under it like a small animal mesmerised by a predator.

'I knew you had a reputation for brute force and some cunning. Your solution to the cleansing of Augeias' cowsheds amused me, your quick thinking when it came to the problem of the Hydra's heads was impressive and you did well to outwit that proud Amazon. Of course you were prompted by Athene, but still your responses were very creditable.'

'Thank you, sir. Such praise from you ...'

'What I didn't know was that you were capable of this unctuous sycophancy. Where did you learn to talk like a courtier? Surely you don't trouble to flatter your despicable cousin Eurystheus?'

He laughed again, and this time its caustic, malicious tone jangled Herakles' nerves to the point of making him almost lose his temper.

'Lying on the ground at someone's feet tends to encourage sycophancy,' he said, trying to keep his tone lighter than his words.

'Is that it? I thought you were accustomed to conversing with gods.'

'They generally disguise themselves to make it easier for me.'

'Ah, yes. Athene spoils her favourites and Artemis has been more than kind to you too. And you are used to lording it over your fellow mortals. But in my kingdom, in my presence, you are nothing. I hope you understand that. A mere hulk of mortal flesh in the borrowed skin of a dead lion.'

Herakles said nothing, for fear that whatever he said, humble or proud, would only exacerbate what now seemed to be the god's real dislike of him. And then, somewhere behind Hades, he heard a female voice:

'Don't be a bully!'

'It takes a bully to tame a bully,' said Hades. 'Mortals like him, given unnatural powers, unfairly favoured by certain gods, grow conceited and troublesome. You know how he treated my poor servant Death. Death does what he has to do, it is not in his contract to be physically assaulted, terrorised and prevented from bringing souls to my kingdom.'

'I'm sure he never meant to offend you, but only to do a favour to a friend. In any case, Death will be able to go back for Alcestis at a later date, and for her husband into the bargain. It was only a postponement. And you can't say he is short of work.'

'That's irrelevant. The point is that I do not tolerate threats to my staff.'

'And what about your relations? Have you no feelings for them?'

'My relations do not come into this.'

'No? Herakles is the son of your brother and my own cousin. I think you owe him more consideration than to make him lie at your feet and be lectured when he has had the courtesy to undertake such a difficult journey and call on us for the first time. Your brother might well take your treatment of his son as an insult to himself and I certainly find it most embarrassing. As for your staff, how sensitive are they to threats or beatings? Does Death have any feelings at all?'

'Get up, nephew!' said Hades. 'My wife always has the last word.'

Herakles got quickly to his feet and found himself still dwarfed by both Hades and Persephone, who, here in their own realm, did not trouble to reduce themselves to mortal dimensions. Persephone contrasted strikingly with the black form of her husband. She too was dressed in black, but like her mother Demeter and the other gods of the upper world she shone with her own light. Herakles bowed his head so as not to meet their eyes and thanked them both.

'Whatever my wife may say,' said Hades, 'I don't think you came here just to make a courtesy call on your relations. All the same, I suppose one must observe the conventions. We cannot invite you into our palace, but we can offer you refreshment. A beaker of pomegranate wine perhaps?'

Herakles shook his head and politely declined, though he was very thirsty. He knew from his initiation at Eleusis that even to taste anything in the underworld, as Persephone herself had after she was abducted, was to become part of it. This was why Persephone had to spend half the year as Hades' queen in spite of the grief and anger of her mother. The initiates at Eleusis drank pomegranate wine in memory of Persephone's mistake, but that was merely symbolic. Here in the kingdom of the dead it would be a fatal mistake.

'No?' said Hades. 'State your business, then! What is it you want?'

'I have two favours to ask,' said Herakles, 'and I hope you will not be offended. Neither is on my own behalf, but at the request of others.'

'I'm listening.'

'The first is that you will be so gracious as to release two living men who very foolishly came here on a mission that they should have known was not only impossible but insolent ...'

Hades laughed his terrible laugh and turned to his wife.

'What do you think, Persephone? Have they been punished enough?'

'I have nothing against Theseus,' she said. 'He came only to honour his oath and whether among gods or men, oaths must always be honoured, whatever the consequences. But Peirithoös can hardly be punished enough for thinking that I might be a suitable wife for him.'

'Well,' said Hades, 'you may take Theseus, but not the other.'

'Thank you, sir.'

'But only if you can free him!' Hades laughed again. 'You will need all your strength and Theseus will not enjoy the experience. Not at all!' He was bubbling with his malevolent laughter: 'Ha, ha, ha! And then, sore as he will be – ha, ha, ha! – you will have to get him past my little dog at the gate. And get yourself past too. Ha, ha, ha! Yes, quite a problem for you to solve there, nephew.'

'Since you mention the dog,' said Herakles, 'I should say that that is the second favour. I would like to take Cerberos with me, you see, though of course I shall bring him back.'

'You want to borrow Cerberos?'

'Exactly.'

'You want to take him home to your cousin?'

'Exactly.'

'You want him to sit by your cousin's door and keep out strangers?'

'Not exactly.'

'No, he wouldn't be much good at that. He's trained to keep people in, not out.'

'Quite.'

'You want him to sniff the fresh air and run about in the green fields after rabbits?'

'Not quite.'

'You'll keep him on a lead in case he scares the sheep? Not to speak of the shepherds.'

'I daresay he'll need more restraint than a lead.'

'I daresay he will.'

There was a brief silence and then the storm broke. It was Hades laughing again, but this time so loud and long that it was as if a volcano were erupting. The pillars of the gateway shook, the adamantine door rattled in its grooves, small pieces of rock fell around them, the cypresses and asphodels in the courtyard swayed as if in a wind, Herakles felt the ground under his feet heave. For the first time he understood something of the real power of the three greatest gods. It was not just that they ruled their kingdoms of earth, sky, sea and underworld; they *were* their kingdoms and their kingdoms were them. People often referred to the underworld just as Hades – and rightly so, he realised, for there was no essential difference between the place he was in and the black figure towering over him, whose laughter shook the whole of his kingdom and must have disturbed even the Titans in Tartaros.

At last the noise and physical repercussions stopped. There was another silence. Herakles did not care to break it. It seemed clear that he would fail in this last Labour and even if he succeeded in returning to the upper world would have lost his reputation, would be a mere husk of himself, the hero emptied and emasculated, Herakles humiliated.

'What do you think of that, Persephone?' said Hades. 'Did you ever hear such cheek? I must admit I'm beginning to appreciate this little bastard relation of ours – he makes me laugh. I haven't laughed so much for quite a while – not since we sat those two insolent fellows on their Chairs of Forgetfulness. What is it about living mortals? There's something in them which they seem to lose when they're dead.'

'You should spend more time in the upper world,' said Persephone, 'or invite more of the living ones to visit us here. As for Herakles' request, why shouldn't he borrow Cerberos?'

'Well, isn't that obvious? He's our watchdog, he prevents anyone leaving our kingdom.'

'Does he? It seems to me he's only there for show. How can anyone leave our kingdom when they're mere shadows of themselves without bodies? Even if Charon were willing to ferry them back across the Styx, they could only float about on the far shore or back where they came from, frightening the living. And we have so many and will get so many more, since they breed like fleas up there, that we'd hardly miss a few.'

'You're right as always, my dear.'

And with a nod of his head which rumbled thunderously around the caverns of the underworld, Hades signified that he had granted Herakles' request.

'Of course, you'll have to catch your little doggie before you can take him away with you,' he said to Herakles. 'And you're not to do him any harm with your weapons, you must use your bare hands. That should be amusing.'

But before tackling Cerberos, Herakles, directed by Persephone, went to find Theseus. He and Peirithoös were seated, not far from the palace gate, side by side and completely naked, on their Chairs of Forgetfulness, staring into the darkness, oblivious of why they were there or even who they were.

'Theseus!' said Herakles. 'I've come to release you and take you back to the upper world.'

Theseus stared at him blankly.

'Get up!' said Herakles sharply.

Theseus took no notice. Herakles slapped his face.

'Get up, I said.'

Theseus tried to rise but couldn't. He was stuck fast to the chair. Herakles took hold of his hands and pulled, but couldn't move him. He heard the laughter of Hades.

'You see the problem, nephew. Now solve it!'

Herakles grasped Theseus by his upper arms and pulled again. There was a tearing sound and Theseus cried out in pain, but he was still stuck to the chair. Herakles crouched down, passed his arms under Theseus' armpits and clasping his hands at the back, rose to his full height with all the force of his thigh muscles, at the same time exerting the full power of his mighty arms and chest. Screaming with pain, Theseus came free, leaving the skin and much of the flesh of his buttocks on the chair. Recovering his memory at the same moment, but immediately conscious only of his raw and bleeding bottom and that Herakles had caused it, he tried to wrestle with his rescuer until Herakles, holding him tightly, explained all the circumstances.

'You are free to return with me to the upper world,' he said. 'Hades and Persephone have generously remitted your punishment.'

'And my friend Peirithoös?'

'I'm afraid not. He must stay where he is. He seems quite content, however, as you were until I freed you.'

They both took leave of Peirithoös, who remained lost in forgetfulness and took no notice of their words or Theseus' warm embrace. Then Herakles took Theseus' arm and led him away. He could see nothing in the darkness and walked with difficulty owing to the excruciating pain in his backside and the years he had spent sitting down without using his legs. But Persephone met them and applied a herbal salve to his buttocks which instantly dried up the blood and soothed the pain. One storyteller suggests that as a result of this experience all Theseus' later descendants were born with unusually flat bottoms, but in the light of our modern knowledge of genetics, this seems unlikely.

By the time they reached the entrance to the underworld Theseus had recovered the strength in his legs and was ready to help Herakles subdue Cerberos, but Herakles could not accept the offer, for fear Eurystheus would discount the Labour. The moment he saw the pair of them approaching, Cerberos went into watchdog mode, barking furiously from all three of his slavering jaws, raising his serpent tail with its hissing head. The usual method recommended for evading Cerberos was to throw him three honey cakes laced with poppy seed and while he was devouring them and becoming temporarily drowsy, slip past. But on this occasion there was no question of slipping past.

Putting down his club, bow and knapsack, wrapping his lion skin round himself as protection against the dog's teeth, Herakles went straight into the attack. He flung his arms round all three necks and, just as he had done with Antaios, lifted the huge creature clear of the ground and squeezed. Snapping viciously but vainly at the lion skin, snarling and at last gagging as his three throats became more and more restricted, Cerberos aimed his serpent tail at Herakles' right leg, but Theseus, watching closely by the light of the gas flares beside the gate, was quick enough to seize the snake behind its head and prevent it striking. And with that, threatened with suffocation before and behind, Cerberos went limp.

'Good dog!' said Herakles and slowly relaxed his grip.

'Fair enough, nephew,' said the deep voice of Hades, echoing round his kingdom. 'I saw that you had a little help from your friend, but you need not mention that to your contemptible cousin. You are a credit to your father and your whole family. Take the dog now, but don't omit to bring him back or there will be trouble!'

'Thank you, sir,' said Herakles, 'I shall be back with Cerberos as soon as my cousin has released me from my Labours, and if he does not I shall be back anyway, and so will he, since I will have pulled him out of his urn and made dog food of him. And my thanks also to the great goddess your wife.'

'*Kaló taxídi* (safe journey)!' said the sweet voice of Persephone.

And so, with Cerberos quite relaxed in his arms and Theseus following with the club, bow and knapsack, Herakles passed through the gateway labelled NO EXIT. As they came to the bank of the

River Styx, Charon was just unloading a boat-full of shades, shouting abuse at them as they swarmed ashore. But when he saw Herakles and Theseus with Cerberos, he fell silent, staring with horror and disbelief and shaking all over with terror.

'No, no!' he said, as Herakles stepped into the boat. 'That dog ...'

'This dog will have you by the balls, Charon, unless you take us all three quicker than a kingfisher flies to the other side. Though I daresay you've never seen a kingfisher fly along this gruesome river of yours.'

And when, straining desperately at his oar, in constant fear of Cerberos, in constant danger of swamping the boat, so low it lay in the water, Charon had delivered them to the other bank and was gasping with exhaustion and relief, he could only roll his yellow eyes and grind his rotten teeth as Herakles waved goodbye and remarked:

'I shall be back with Cerberos one of these days or nights. Something for you to look forward to.'

They took a different passage out of the underworld from the one Herakles had entered by, emerging near Troezen, where Theseus was born. It was more convenient for Tiryns and besides Theseus had a good-sized house there, where he celebrated his release from Hades and entertained his rescuer. Cerberos, once he had surrendered to Herakles, accepted him happily as his new master and behaved towards him with almost excessive obedience and anxiety to please, so that, although just setting eyes on him terrified the people of Troezen and those on the road to Tiryns, he hardly needed the three great bronze collars and chains which Theseus' armourer made for him.

But when Herakles finally reached the palace at Tiryns and led Cerberos into the presence of Eurystheus, the dog began to growl savagely, lashing his serpent tail and straining at the chain, his six great eyes bulging and his red jaws foaming. Was it just the sight of Eurystheus' head poking pitifully out of his urn that provoked him? So it seemed, but the truth was that at Troezen Herakles had taken the trouble to borrow a large urn from Theseus, put a slave inside it, and encouraged Cerberos to behave in this way. He didn't want, after all the trouble he had been to, to fail to frighten his cousin nearly out of his wits. So when Cerberos leapt at the urn, Herakles pretended to be trying to haul him off, while actually gaving him enough chain to knock it over and, as Eurystheus shrank into the bottom of it like a snail into its shell, allowing Cerberos to get one of his heads into the opening and shower the king with stinking saliva.

The Labours were over, Herakles had completed his penance. He led Cerberos back to the underworld, paid his respects to Hades and Persephone, and took affectionate leave of the monstrous three-headed dog with the serpent tail who, after all, as Hades admitted, was more bark than bite, more spin than substance, given that his services as a sentry were almost entirely ceremonial. As for Eurystheus, he never did recover fully from his encounter with Cerberos. His hands shook, he had incessant tics in his neck and his left eye and, having dislocated his spine by curling up inside the urn, could only walk slowly and painfully on two sticks. He was, one might say, Cerberos' only known victim.

11. THE FORD

His Labours completed, the accounts of Herakles' subsequent adventures become repetitious and confused as everyone tries to get in on the hero's super-celebrity. To take only one example, he again kills an innocent victim – this time a young man instead of a wife – in a fit of madness. Again he is ordered by the oracle at Delphi to undergo a penance, this time as a slave for a year, or possibly three, to a Lydian queen called Omphale, whose kingdom he cheerfully clears of bandits, enemies and a huge serpent, in the meantime fathering children with both the queen and at least one of her maids. The main variation in this episode is that he and Omphale indulge in some cross-dressing and role-swapping, with Omphale wearing his lion skin and appropriating his club and bow, while Herakles, dolled up in women's clothes, bracelets and necklaces, sits among her maids teasing out wool and spinning thread, or being combed and manicured by them. Lydia being on the eastern side of the Aegean, in Asia, this looks like an early example of the West attributing perverse and effeminate practices to the East, what Edward Said, in his once fashionable late twentieth-century book *Orientalism*, characterised as 'a Western style for dominating, restructuring, and having authority over the Orient'. These days, of course, the East retaliates with Occidentalism, as Muslim mullahs preach the decadence and sexual licence of the West.

For the last episodes of Herakles' life we leave the wild mountains of Arcadia and cross the Corinthian Gulf to the Greek mainland, where Aitolia, an equally wild land of mountains, lakes and marshes, shares the south-western corner with Akarnania. This region is best known in modern times for the city of Mesologgion (Mesolongi), where Lord Byron died of fever in 1824 and the Greeks sustained a siege by the Turks which ended in 1826 with the last defenders blowing up themselves, their enemies and the city. Two years later, as Greek independence dawned, the Turks gave it up again without a struggle.

In Herakles' time there was an Aitolian king called Oeneus, who ruled the city of Kalydon and had a beautiful daughter called Deïaneira. She was an Amazonian girl, a skilled chariot driver, javelin thrower and archer. There is no record of her actually taking part in any battles, but she was fully prepared to. Herakles, relieved to have finished with Omphale and his experiments with transvestism, and thinking now of settling down to a quieter life, liked the sound of Deïaneira. He was still remembering with pleasure and regret how well he and Hippolyte, the queen of the Amazons, had fitted. And by marrying the king's daughter he would become the heir to Oeneus' kingdom.

He made his way to Kalydon, where he found that Deïaneira's hand was to be the prize for a knock-out competition, a series of wrestling matches between her numerous suitors. The arrival of Herakles, however, caused all the other suitors, except one, to withdraw immediately. His opponent in this premature final was an almost equally formidable person, the river-god Acheloös, the river itself being the largest in Greece, flowing from the mighty Pindos mountains into the Ionian Sea. The god sometimes appeared as a serpent, sometimes as a bull and sometimes as a man. Even when he took the form of a man streams of water constantly poured out of his unkempt hair and beard and small aquatic creatures – frogs, newts, water-snails – nestled in his ears and nose and whiskers. Deïaneira had no doubt which contestant she preferred, though her father, since his kingdom was bordered by the river and he needed the god's goodwill to avoid floods or drought, wanted Acheloös to win.

The match was held in the *plateia*, the town square, in front of a huge crowd of spectators, and before it began, the contestants were invited to state their qualifications as potential husbands.

'If I win the lady's hand,' said Herakles, 'she will have Zeus for a father-in-law and she will be the wife of the man who strangled the Nemean Lion, cut off the Hydra's heads, caught the Arcadian Stag and the Erymanthean Boar, drove away the Stymphalian Birds, killed the Cretan Bull, cleaned Augeias' cowsheds, captured the man-eating mares of Diomedes, carried off the girdle of the Queen of the Amazons and the cattle of Geryon, fetched the golden apples of the Hesperides and tamed the watchdog of Hades. I hardly need to mention, do I, all the other services I have performed all over the known world and even beyond it?'

'But perhaps you do need to mention,' said Acheloös, 'that you murdered your first wife and her children. You may claim that this was a one-off fit of madness, but it was evidently not, since more recently, raving again, you threw your young friend Iphitos off the tower of Tiryns. I wonder how King Oeneus and his lovely daughter Deïaneira view their prospects with such a son-in-law. You are besides a stranger to this region and a vagabond. You have never been able to settle anywhere, except when doing penance for one of your killings, whereas I am not only a local god, *the* local god, but the Father of all Greek rivers. As for your claim to be the son of Zeus, you are either no such thing or your mother committed adultery.'

'Enough of this!' said Herakles. 'I'm not here to listen to insults to my mother and I thank you, Acheloös, for making me so angry that I shall easily tear your head off.'

And without waiting for the match to be started officially, Herakles threw off his lion skin and grappled Acheloös, throwing him on his back. Acheloös turned immediately into an enormous spotted snake and swiftly wound himself round the hero's legs, whereupon Herakles gripped him behind the head.

'I strangled two snakes in my cradle,' he said, 'and I still wear their skins from time to time. Do you want to end up draped round my privates?'

Acheloös' reply was to turn himself into a bull and, rising between Herakles' legs, charge round the *plateia* with Herakles perched on his back. But for all his bucking and prancing and swerving, scattering spectators, narrowly missing trees and stone walls, he could not shake his opponent off. Herakles simply rode the bull, holding on to its horns, as if he had acquired an enormous motorbike long before any such machine was invented, laughing and shouting with delight.

'Keep it up, Acheloös, old cow! This is the best ride I ever had.'

At last, exhausted, Acheloös stopped dead, arched his back and dropped his head so as to toss his rider. Herakles, taken by surprise, shot forward, but the strength with which he gripped the horns was so great that one of them broke off and, somersaulting gracefully, he landed on his feet with the broken horn still in his right hand. He held it up as Acheloös prepared to charge at him.

'Do you want to give me the other one too?' he said. 'A pretty sort of bull you'll be with no horns. You look silly enough with one.'

That settled the contest. Acheloös turned himself into a man and slunk away back to his riverbed, holding his right hand to the side of his head as if to cover a painful and shameful injury.

Herakles and Deïaneira were married and lived happily together in Kalydon, where Herakles as usual cleared the neighbourhood of brigands, dragons and marauding tribes, but also turned farmer and enjoyed cultivating olives and vines and breeding cattle and sheep. Acheloös did not punish the kingdom with floods or drought, wishing everyone to forget his ignominious defeat with a broken horn. Besides, he was a mature and generous-minded river and accepted that he had lost in a fair contest. It seemed for some years as if Oeneus had gained an ideal son-in-law and as if Herakles had at last won through to a prosperous and well-deserved retirement. Alas, though, his superhuman strength was also his weakness.

He was banqueting one night in the palace with his father-in-law and several of the chief citizens of Kalydon. They were celebrating a plentiful harvest and the birth of another son to Herakles and Deïaneira, who already had a son and a daughter. The toasts went round again and again and everyone, especially Herakles, was very loud and flushed.

'Here's to you, Herakles!' shouted one of the citizens. 'You've brought us the luck of your ancestors, the fortunate gods.'

'I don't think they eat so well on Olympos,' said another, gnawing the last flesh off a bone and throwing the bone on the floor. 'All they get is the smoke from our sacrifices. We keep the best bits for ourselves.'

'And our Ganymedes is just as pretty as theirs,' said another, as a handsome fair-haired boy called Eunomos, a relation of the king's, went round pouring warm water over their greasy hands.

'To our Ganymedes!' said another and they all raised their goblets and drank.

But in pouring the water over Herakles' hands, Eunomos, made nervous by all this attention, missed his aim and splashed water over Herakles' legs.

'Less Ganymedes than a careless ape,' said Herakles angrily and cuffed the boy on the side of his head.

Eunomos fell to the floor, breaking his pitcher, spilling the rest of the water, and lay there in a puddle amongst the broken sherds without moving. Herakles, sorry to have reacted too violently, reached down to help him up, but the boy still didn't move. He was dead.

The merry banquet ended abruptly. All rose from their couches, those who had not said anything inauspicious blaming those who had for angering the gods and inviting retribution. But Herakles refused to blame anyone but himself.

'It was I who hit him,' said Herakles, 'I, who lost my temper and forgot my own strength. This poor boy to whom I did so much harm in return for so little will be for ever on my conscience. I sentence myself once again to exile and penance.'

King Oeneus and the others tried to change his mind, but Herakles was immovable and Deïaneira, who loved him passionately and feared that if he went away for years on further adventures she would surely lose him to other women, insisted on accompanying him into exile. Their two sons and their daughter Makaria – Herakles' only known daughter – remained behind in their grandfather's care.

In those times when you killed somebody, whether by mistake or on purpose, you went to some other city to be purified before making whatever amends to the family and society in general were imposed by Apollo's oracle at Delphi. Herakles had been through this process more often than most. On this occasion he decided to go to the city of Trachis in Boeotia where a relative of his stepfather Amphitryon was king. From Trachis, once he had been purified, he could double back to Delphi to hear what penance he should undergo.

Soon after leaving Kalydon he and Deïaneira, travelling on foot, came to the other great river, the Evenos, that formed the boundary of Aitolia to the east, as the Acheloös did to the west. It had been raining heavily during the two or three days since the death of Eunomos and the river was very full. Herakles, carrying their baggage, his usual backpack and weapons plus two or three extra bags containing his wife's clothes, jewellery and other belongings, forded the swollen river by himself, but since a centaur called Nessos was earning a meagre living by carrying travellers across, Herakles thought it only fair to hire Nessos to carry Deïaneira. Unfortunately Nessos was not one of the philosophical, professorial centaurs like Chiron or Herakles' old friend Pholos, but one of the greedy, lustful sort, and when he was halfway across the river and saw that Herakles had reached the other side, he suddenly turned round and carried Deïaneira back to the bank he had just left.

Deïaneira screamed as Nessos threw her down on the bank and brutally parted her legs with the intention of raping her. Herakles immediately took an arrow from his quiver, fitted it to his bow-string and with deadly aim shot the centaur, who was crouching with his backside towards Herakles, in his stallion testicles. With a terrible cry Nessos fell over his victim, blood from his wound and sperm from his jutting penis spilling on the ground and on Deïaneira's shift.

'Forgive me, lady!' he said, as he lay squirming in agony beside her, 'I owe you something. My blood and seed have magic power.

Keep your shift safe and secret, and if ever Herakles wants to betray you with another woman, make him wear it and he will love you more than ever.'

By the time Herakles had crossed the river again and reached his wife, she had taken off her shift, rolled it up and concealed it under her cloak. Herakles embraced her tenderly and then turned to finish off Nessos. But he was already dead, and Herakles, pulling the arrow out of his wound, guessed why. This was the second arrow he had once pulled out of the Hydra and, like the one he had shot into Chiron's knee and which had then pierced Pholos' foot, was still poisoned. He dug a grave for Nessos and buried the arrow with him so that it could do no further harm, but he didn't think to tell Deïaneira why the arrow had been so instantly deadly, nor did she tell him about the stain on her shift. When Herakles had carried her over the river and they had repossessed their baggage, she put on a clean shift and hid the soiled one at the bottom of her bag. So it was that by not confiding in each other they stored up future disaster for themselves.

Or so we would see it, as a human problem, a failure of communication, an unlucky chance. But was it chance or fate that caused this particular arrow to remain so long in Herakles' quiver amongst the others without ever being used? The gods who know almost everything, except what it is to be mortal, would not have understood the question. Chance plays no part in their immortal lives and time is as visible to them in both directions as space to us. They would have observed, from the moment Herakles retrieved those two arrows steeped in the poisonous blood of the Hydra, that the first was destined to wound Chiron and kill Pholos and the second to kill Nessos and in consequence both Herakles and his beloved wife. But the consequence was also a human problem, since it could not have happened if Deïaneira had not loved Herakles so much or if Herakles had not been attracted to another woman. The gods could see that that would be so and therefore already knew the end of this story and that there could not be a different ending. The oracle at Delphi had even told Herakles himself in its usual cryptic manner: 'No one alive may kill Herakles; his downfall shall be a dead enemy.'

But if Athene, for instance, had shared her knowledge with Herakles, if she had warned him at the time of his battle with the Hydra not to shoot the monster with his arrows or not to retrieve them if he did, then surely there might have been a different ending? Very likely, but for that very reason she could not share her knowledge with him. Tragedy – the stark ancient Greek version, not our modern loosening of the word to mean any sad event – consists in this relationship between immortals and mortals, which is also, of course, the relationship between the readers or hearers of a classic story and the characters inside the story.

12. THE SHIFT

Herakles and Deïaneira were hospitably received in Trachis by its king, Keyx, who willingly performed the purification ceremony required by Herakles' killing of the boy Eunomos. In fact it suited Keyx very well to have his powerful kinsman at his side. He was on bad terms with Eurytos, the king of the Thessalian city Oechalia. The two cities were some distance apart. Trachis was in the mountains to the west of the pass of Thermopylae, where long afterwards, in the fifth century BC, Leonidas' 300 Spartans held the vast army of the Persian king Xerxes at bay until a Greek traitor led the Persians over these same mountains to take the Spartans in the rear. Oechalia was in the hills above the Peneios river, sixty miles or so to the north as the crow flies. But both cities laid claim to a fertile stretch of grassland, perfect for breeding fine horses and cattle, which was roughly equidistant between them, and there were frequent clashes as each side tried to drive the other away, with the result that neither got any advantage from the disputed territory.

Herakles himself had an old score to settle with King Eurytos. Immediately after completing his Labours he had travelled to Oechalia to take part in a contest for the hand of the king's daughter, Iole, intending then as he did later with Deïaneira to embark on a more settled life. Eurytos and his four sons were all expert archers, the king even boasting that he had been taught by Apollo and outclassed his master, and Iole was to be given in marriage to the suitor who could shoot better than any of them. In practice, therefore, as far as Eurytos was concerned, believing himself to be the best archer in the world, that meant nobody. However, after a series of tests of marksmanship – at targets, birds, apples balanced on slaves' heads, through the shaft holes of twelve axe heads placed in a line – Herakles easily defeated the whole family. But when, having carefully repossessed his arrows (the poisoned one perhaps among them), he walked across the arena to possess his prize, the seductive princess Iole, her father stepped between them.

'No, you don't,' he said. 'You couldn't possibly compete or compare with me and my sons if you were not using magic arrows. You gave yourself away when you went to so much trouble to retrieve them. That of course is quite unfair, quite outside the rules and I therefore declare the contest void.'

'You're mistaken,' said Herakles, keeping his temper with difficulty. 'There's nothing magic about my arrows and you're welcome to try using them yourself, or else to let me use your arrows.'

'*You* are mistaken,' said Eurytos, 'if you imagine that however crafty you are with your bow and arrows, magic or not, that I'd entrust my beloved daughter to a cut-throat like you, murderer of your first wife and children and until now a slave to Eurystheus. Slaves don't marry princesses, slaves who get above themselves are beaten and driven out of my city.'

And with that he ordered his guards to expel Herakles, who, already very attracted to Iole and not wishing to kill or injure any of her near relations, simply knocked the guards aside and, still keeping his temper, walked with dignity out of the city. He told himself as he did so that he would be back before long with a sufficient force of armed men to make Eurytos honour his promise.

But at the same time as Herakles left the territory of Oechalia, a herd of prize cattle was stolen from the king's fields and Eurytos was convinced that Herakles must have taken them. Three of his sons agreed, but the youngest, Iphitos, who admired Herakles and disliked the way he had been treated, argued that he was not a thief and that it was a wife he wanted, not a herd of cattle.

'Why was he so quiet and easy, then, when we threw him out of the city?' said Didaion, the eldest brother. 'That wasn't like the Herakles we've heard about. No, he was already plotting to go away with our best cattle if he couldn't have our sister.'

The upshot was that Iphitos offered to go after Herakles and see if he was driving the missing cattle back to Tiryns. And, of course, since Herakles had not taken the cattle and was travelling at his usual rapid pace, Iphitos did not catch up with him until he reached Tiryns itself. Herakles was surprised to see him.

'What's this?' he said. 'Have you come to apologise for your father's disgraceful behaviour and tell me your sister is mine after all?'

'I'm afraid not,' said Iphitos, who was still very young and naive, 'we lost a herd of prize cattle just at the time you left Oechalia and my father and brothers thought you might have taken them.'

If only he had thought to mention that he had come because he disagreed with them, the outcome might have been different. But Herakles, though inside he was seething with fury at this boy's apparent insolence, remained outwardly as calm and reasonable as he had when leaving Oechalia.

'Oh, I see,' said Herakles, 'you'd like to check whether I've got them here at Tiryns.'

'Well, yes.'

'Well, yes! Let's both go up to the top of that tower, then, and you can look around. You'd recognise them, I suppose, if you saw them?'

'Oh, yes, no problem. They're very special cows and I know them all individually.'

So they climbed the tower and stood in the baking sun – it was midday and there was no shelter up there – looking over the battlements at the flat fields round Tiryns, where there were many cattle grazing or lying in what shade they could find.

'Do you see your very special cows?' asked Herakles.

'No,' said Iphitos, shading his eyes, 'I really don't. I'll go back and tell my father and brothers that they were wrong and you're quite in the clear.'

But now, out there in the full sun, where even the stone battlements were almost too hot to touch, Herakles' fragile hold on his temper gave way and anger enveloped him. His whole body shaking, his eyes wide and staring, his face suffused with blood, he grasped Iphitos by the shoulders and bellowed into his face:

'Yes, you tell them that! You tell them that they are wrong on every count, in every direction, in every part of their ugly hearts and miserable minds, and that if we are talking about thieves, it is your lousy, cheating family that deserves to be hung up with hooks on your city walls and dried in the sun for daylight robbery. And we'll send you back to tell them all that the shortest way.'

Then he picked up poor innocent Iphitos with one hand and whirled him over the battlements.

It was this crime for which he had had to do penance again by becoming the servant of Queen Omphale in Lydia, his wages being forfeit to Eurytos in recompense for the killing of his son. It's not hard to understand his enthusiasm when his cousin Keyx asked him if he'd help to settle the business of the disputed territory with Eurytos and the Oechalians.

'Most certainly,' said Herakles. 'And to make sure that it's properly settled, I suggest we don't stop at the disputed territory. I'll summon all the friends and forces I can and we'll finish with this shit Eurytos once and for all.'

Accordingly, having assembled an army of his friends and admirers, with contingents from Arcadia, Laconia, Boeotia, Aitolia, Elis and many other places where he had put cities and peoples in his debt by ridding them of monsters or brigands, Herakles joined forces with the warriors of Trachis and marched through the disputed territory and across the River Peneios. Eurytos and his three remaining sons led the Oechalians out of the city to do battle and were swiftly overwhelmed. Herakles himself had the satisfaction of shooting down the king and his eldest son and the other two were killed by his soldiers. With most of their young men slaughtered in the field, the elders of Oechalia gave up the city, which from that time became a part of Keyx's much extended kingdom. But Herakles, leaving Keyx to organise the occupation of the city, went straight to Eurytos' palace to look for Iole. She was still not married, since no other suitors had risked competing with her father and brothers, afraid that even if they had been good enough archers they would incur the anger of Herakles.

Iole was naturally in a state of utter despair at the loss of her family and her city and she fully expected that, when Herakles burst into the women's quarters, he would kill her too in revenge for her father's treachery. She kneeled in front of him and bravely told him that she knew she deserved to die and was ready to, but Herakles had no such thought and raised her up.

'You are my wife, Iole. I won your hand in a fair contest and now I'm here at last to claim you.'

'But you have a wife already. You married Deïaneira. Everyone knows that.'

'That's true. I won her in another contest, but I won you first.'

'Will you divorce her then?'

'No, I can't do that. That would not be honourable. Besides, I love her.'

'Then how can I be your wife?'

'I don't know. I love you too. Very much so, the more I look at you again. It's a problem and I'll have to think of some solution.'

His immediate solution was to take her back to Trachis and ask Deïaneira to look after her. Deïaneira was understandably taken aback.

'What?' she asked. 'Are you asking me to look after your new mistress?'

'She's not my mistress, she's my wife – or should be.'

'I thought I was your wife.'

'Of course you are, but so by rights is she. I won her in an archery contest and then I won you in a wrestling contest.'

'You can't have two wives. People don't. It seems to me that although you won her before you won me, you never actually married her, whereas you did actually marry me.'

'You're right, of course. But what am I to do? I owe her this marriage and she owes it to me. It was only her father's cheating that prevented it.'

'Why do you have to marry her? You can go to bed with her if you want to. I shan't object and she can't object – she's your captive.'

'That wouldn't be right. I won her as a proud princess, I can't now treat her as a slave.'

'Well, at present she's a very unhappy person, having lost everything, and I will look after her and try to comfort her. Perhaps you could marry her to someone else. Your step-brother Iphikles, for instance, or your nephew Iolaos.'

'I think they already have wives.'

And so they left the subject for the moment, while Herakles crossed over to the nearby island of Euboia to build an altar and make sacrifices as a thank-offering to his father Zeus for the capture of Oechalia. He hoped that perhaps Zeus might help him solve the problem of having, as he saw it, two wives, when custom only allowed him one. But Deïaneira, left behind with Iole in Trachis and noting that Iole was both younger and more beautiful than she was, convinced herself that what Herakles really wanted was to get rid of her and marry Iole. Deïaneira was not the sort of woman to take the easiest and most obvious course, by poisoning Iole's food or arranging a fatal accident for her, or even by poisoning Iole's mind against Herakles. On the contrary, she was very kind and gentle to Iole, who responded with love and gratitude. They soon became close friends and Iole often declared that she had no such claim on Herakles as he seemed to believe.

'I'm sure it's because my father behaved so badly to him and cheated him of his rightful expectations that he's determined not to do the same to me. But I don't see it that way. Much as I would like to be his wife, I'm not. You are.'

As far as she was concerned, that was the end of the matter. She loved Herakles – most women did – but she had missed the chance of marrying him and now it was too late. Deïaneira was the lucky winner of this contest.

Deïaneira, on the other hand, felt that the contest had only just begun. Not to have something you very much want may be painful, but to be plagued with anxiety about losing something you've already got and very much value is worse. She did not worry about Iole's feelings for Herakles – she was sure that her renunciation of him was sincere – but she did worry wretchedly about his for Iole and whenever she looked in her polished bronze mirror she saw that worry was wearing away her looks and making it even more likely that when Herakles returned he must prefer Iole's fresh complexion and sparkling black eyes.

If she had known the story of Herakles' Choice, which was only added to her husband's biography much later, in a lecture by the fifth-century sophist Prodikos, she might have been comforted. In that story the young Herakles goes out and sits down at a lonely crossroads in the mountains (much as the young Christ went out into the wilderness in the New Testament story and was offered three choices by Satan) to brood on what he should do with his life. After a while he is accosted by two tall women, one ravishingly beautiful, called Pleasure, and the other, rather plainer, called Virtue. Pleasure offers to lead him on an easy path down the mountain to a life of wine, women and song, while Virtue offers him a hard, relentless struggle to the top of the mountain where he will be crowned with glory. Somewhat reluctantly he chooses stern-faced Virtue's path, with a lingering backward glance at the beauty of gorgeous Pleasure.

Not knowing this story and only partly knowing her husband – she was aware of his innumerable liaisons with women, but not aware of how seriously he took marriage and how punctilious he was in honouring his commitments, whether to men or women – she remembered the dying words of Nessos. Her shift, stained with the centaur's blood and semen, still rolled up, was hidden at the bottom of her chest of clothes. She didn't entirely believe what the centaur had said about its effectiveness as a love potion, but it never occurred to her that it might have any other effect, and she felt that at least it could do no harm and might really turn Herakles' love back towards her and away from Iole.

But Nessos had said she must make Herakles wear the shift, and how was she to do that? It was not as if she was another Omphale and could persuade him to wear women's clothes again. In any case, the shift was far too small for him to wear. She knew, though, that he was superstitious, and when she received a message from Herakles, brought by a young follower of his called Lichas, that he needed a new white robe to wear while he made his sacrifice to Zeus, she saw her opportunity. She and her handmaidens made the robe and then she cut the shift down its length and sewed it sideways inside the robe, an inner layer reaching from the shoulders to the waist. She instructed Lichas to tell Herakles that this inner layer was from an old garment of her own and that the women of her native city had the custom of doing this, whenever their husbands wore a new robe for an important sacrifice. They believed, she said, that it increased their husbands' love for them, and although there might be nothing in the belief and she had no doubt that Herakles loved her, she was really following the custom just to show how much *she* loved him. Then she wrapped up the robe and gave it to Lichas to take to Herakles.

Herakles was amused by Lichas' careful rendering of Deïaneira's message.

'These women,' he said, 'full of absurd ideas which they addle each other's heads with and then try to addle our heads with.'

'Are you not going to wear it, then?' asked Lichas.

'Of course I shall wear it. How can one ever be sure what's false and what's true in these superstitions? It can't do any harm to adhere to them, but it might do harm not to. And if I didn't wear it, Deïaneira would take it that I didn't love her and didn't care about her love. That's how it is with women. They take everything personally – everything has an emotional meaning, everything is a test of how much you care about them. It's often tiring and even tiresome, but it gets a lot more tiring and tiresome if you ignore it.'

'Best not to have more than one woman at a time, then?'

'You're absolutely right, Lichas, and, do you know, I think you've given me the very answer I was looking for. My father Zeus must have put it into your head. Lovely as Iole is, engaged to marry her as I am, I cannot have two wives and I cannot desert Deïaneira. Therefore I must find another husband for Iole. My mind is quite clear now.'

With that, he put on the white robe, took the sacrificial knife in his hand and approached the altar he had built on a promontory overlooking the sea, while attendants brought forward the many fine bulls he was to sacrifice and lit the fire on the altar. But as he cut the first bull's throat and carved off the parts of its body to be thrown on the flames, the heat of his body activated the poisoned blood of Nessos still smeared on Deïaneira's shift, the inner layer of the robe, and he suddenly threw down his knife and began to dance with agony. Those around him thought at first that he had fallen into one of his fits of madness and began to scatter in all directions.

'Help me, help me, Lichas!' he cried. 'Get this robe off me!'

Lichas, terrified, did try to help him, but though between them they managed to tear off most of the robe itself, breaking the threads that held it to the inner layer, Deïaneira's shift itself stuck to his skin.

'What is this thing she sewed inside?' he shouted.

'It was something of hers, some kind of underclothing. You know more about women's underclothes than I do.'

But as Herakles tore pieces of it away, his skin came with it and the poison entered even more potently into his own bloodstream. Now he became truly mad with pain, and believing Lichas had conspired with Deïaneira to kill him, seized him by the ankles and threw him down the cliff on to the rocks below. Then he tore up pine trees and made a huge pile of timber and brushwood beside the altar, on to which he climbed, ordering his attendants to set light to it. But they were all keeping their distance and wouldn't come near him after what he had done to Lichas. Finally, as he screamed and threw himself about on top of his pyre, unable to die – partly from his own great strength, partly because the Hydra's poison had lost some of its strength after so long – a shepherd, who had come up the hill to see what the trouble was, went to the fire still burning on the altar, took a brand from it and lit Herakles' pyre.

As it flamed up and the smoke billowed round Herakles, concealing him from the watchers, he ceased to scream, whether because the poison had already killed him or because, as later stories claimed, he was taken up by his father Zeus in a cloud, with peals of thunder, and made an immortal on Olympos. There, according to these softer storytellers, he was reconciled to Hera, married her daughter Hebe and became the gods' gatekeeper. But Homer thought he died like any other mortal and makes Odysseus meet his shade in the underworld.

As for Deïaneira, when the news was brought to her and she realised how she had been tricked by Nessos, she hanged herself. Some said that Iole married Hyllos, the eldest son of Herakles and Deïaneira, but he cannot have been more than four or five years old at the time. It was Hyllos who later led the Herakleidai, the sons of Herakles, in their first invasion of the Peloponnese, and slew his father's former taskmaster, his usurping cousin King Eurystheus. But this invasion was ultimately unsuccessful, as was a second, in which Hyllos himself was slain. It was not until several generations later that the Herakleidai finally became masters of most of the Peloponnese, and historians suggest that this legend reflects the triumph of the Dorians over the Achaeans.

Many ancient Greeks worshipped Herakles, whose cult had originally been brought by the Phoenicians and was derived partly from their own god Melkart and partly from the Babylonian sun god Baal, the bane of the Israelites and rival of their god Jehovah (or Yahweh) in the Old Testament. The Roman conquerors of Greece and the whole Mediterranean world combined Herakles with an ancient Italian deity, named him Hercules and believed that he guarded the household as well as the state, gave victory and enforced good behaviour and the faithful keeping of oaths. In those days, before the arrival of Christianity, people did not swear on the Bible, but by Hercules.

Looking up at his constellation, between Ophiuchus the serpent and Draco the dragon, from our terrace in Arcadia, I wondered about the coincidence of the first part of his Greek name with the name of the goddess Hera, whose anger pursued him all his life without ever being more than a dangerous irritation and goad. Of course, that was the point. Without Hera's interference at his birth, Herakles would have been king of Tiryns and the territory of Argos. No doubt he would have conquered the rest of the Peloponnese, but he would not have performed the deeds which made him so famous. Fate required that Hera should goad him; fate required that he should overcome all the dangers she put in his way; fate required Eurystheus. Without Hera there could have been no Herakles as we know him, no story. Little wonder, then, that their names should be so similar or that if, after his cremation, he became an immortal himself, he should be reconciled with the necessarily jealous wife of his father Zeus.

PERSEUS

1. THE CHEST

Herakles was born into the Perseid dynasty. His Argive ancestor Perseus belonged to a generation whose chosen mortals were still in easy touch with the immortals, saw them more often, albeit disguised, and were even employed from time to time on the gods' business. Tantalos, the father of Pelops, was one of these until he transgressed by inviting the gods to dinner and serving up his son in a casserole. Semele was another. All the Olympian gods attended the wedding feast of her parents, Cadmus and Harmonia, who was herself the daughter of Ares the god of war and Aphrodite the goddess of love. Semele became the mistress of Zeus and bore him the god Dionysos, but, like Tantalos, her vanity, or at least misunderstanding of the relationship, was her destruction. Persuaded by Hera, Zeus' perennially offended wife, that if she was sleeping with a god she ought to have the satisfaction of seeing him in all his glory, Semele nagged at Zeus night after night to throw off his disguise and appear as he really was. Finally, exasperated and perhaps by now tired of her, he did and she was vaporised. It was no doubt their bad experiences with these two, Tantalos and Semele, that made the gods wary of getting too close to the mortals of later generations.

Perseus was another son of Zeus, conceived not by a three-night stand in the absence of the husband, like Herakles, but perhaps even more flamboyantly in an inaccessible dungeon. Zeus may have been a serial inseminator, but there was nothing repetitive about his methods. Some of the Greek stories, however, *are* repetitive, so I will quickly pass over Perseus' remoter ancestry: the twin brothers from Egypt, Aigyptos and Danaos, who had 50 sons and 50 daughters respectively and got on so badly with each other that Danaos fled to Argos with his daughters and was there elected king. When Aigyptos sent his 50 sons in a fifty-oar ship to marry their 50 cousins, Danaos seems to have suspected his brother of trying to seize his kingdom by remote control. At any rate he took drastic action, giving each of his daughters a knife with instructions to use it on their husbands on the wedding night – a story similar to that of the ladies of Lemnos who, having murdered their husbands, received the Argonauts with such enthusiasm. And just as in that story, one Danaïd daughter, Hypermnestra, disobeyed and spared her husband, Lynkeus.

Their son Abas succeeded to the throne of Argos, but all the other daughters ended up in the punishment section of the underworld, for ever pouring water into jars with holes in the bottom. Tantalos reaching for fruit and water that always eluded him, Sisyphos rolling his stone uphill only for it to roll down again, the Danaïds with their leaking jars: futile effort, rather than flames and devils with pitchforks, seems to have been the ancient Greek idea of hell.

Abas, the sole descendant of those 50 murderous marriages, had twin sons, Akrisios and Proetos, who like their twin great-grandparents as well as those later brothers of the Pelopid dynasty, Atreus and Thyestes, were always up against each another. Akrisios got the throne and Proetos fled to Lycia on the eastern coast of the Aegean, only to return with the help of Lycia's ruler and, like Thyestes, take control of Tiryns. Akrisios, meanwhile, had married Eurydice (not the same Eurydice as married Orpheus), who bore him a single and exceptionally beautiful daughter. They called her Danaë after her great-great-grandfather. But distressed at getting no other children, especially no sons, Akrisios consulted the oracle at Delphi and was told that although this was the only child he would have, he could rely on being succeeded by his daughter's son, who would also be the cause of his death.

This was not what anyone would want to hear about their grandson, so Akrisios took the only action he could think of to prevent his daughter having any child at all, short of killing her. He locked her in a windowless dungeon in the cellars of his palace. The only access was by a trapdoor which covered a grating in the ceiling, with a ladder leading down into the cell itself. Apart from the lack of daylight and freedom, her life was made as comfortable as possible. She had a bed and lamps, she could wash, she wore the fine clothes of a princess, she had a loom on which to weave pretty textiles – she enjoyed weaving – she was given good food from her father's table and was visited regularly by both her parents. But she was served and guarded exclusively by women. No man, apart from her father, was allowed anywhere near the dungeon and the women who guarded her were always in pairs – one old and one young – so that they could keep watch on each other and not be seduced into letting Danaë out of the cell or any man into it. The guards even had separate keys, one of which opened the trapdoor and the other the grating below it. These were all useless precautions, of course, since the unknown son-in-law – or son-out-of-law – whom Akrisios was trying to avoid was no man but a god, Zeus himself.

The guards gave Akrisios the first inkling of trouble one morning when he went to visit his daughter.

'A very strange thing, sir,' said the elder woman, 'when we were about to close up last night.'

'What sort of thing?' asked the king, immediately sniffing danger.

'We had closed and locked the grating – *she* did that ...' indicating the younger woman.

'Yes, yes?'

'But the trap was still open – I had the key for that ...'

'Yes, yes?'

'And suddenly ... it was like ...'

'Like gold,' said the younger woman.

'What was like gold?'

'It poured past us, through the grating ...'

'Coming from somewhere over our heads and going straight down ...'

'Through the grating, like rain ...'

'Like a cloud ...'

'Like a shower of rain.'

'Not exactly rain. It wasn't wet.'

'No, more like dust than rain, but gold.'

'Yes, it was gold dust. A cloud of gold.'

'I don't understand you at all,' said Akrisios. 'A cloud of gold dust? It's not possible. It must have been a sudden burst of sunlight.'

'No, sir, it was evening. The sun had already gone down.'

'A flash of lightning, then?'

'But there was no storm last night.'

'And it was definitely more of a cloud than a flash.'

'You were imagining things,' said Akrisios. 'Or dreaming. You must have been mistaken.'

'Not both of us. We both saw it, didn't we?'

After that, Akrisios came on several successive nights to see his daughter's cell closed up, in case the phenomenon should reappear, but of course it never did. Zeus had been and gone and the consequence was not manifest for some months.

In the erotic painting by Correggio in the Villa Borghese in Rome, a just pre-pubescent Eros (pronounced, unlike the statue in Piccadilly Circus, *rose* with a short 'e' in front of it, *erose*) is helping to uncover Danaë as she lies back on her well-bolstered bed spreading her legs for the descending golden cloud. Titian's painting in Naples (stolen by the fat Nazi Hermann Goering in the Second World War) depicts a more passive Danaë and a much younger Eros, while the descending cloud contains gold coins. But since her prison was by then sealed and there were no observers, it's more likely that the shower turned quickly into the form of a handsome young man and that Danaë enjoyed a wonderful night of passion with a very experienced lover. Did she ask his name? Surely she did, and surely he told her, since she had many ordeals still to go through and would need the courage of knowing that her lover was a god and that their child was destined to be a hero.

When it was clear that she was pregnant – though, as he many times exclaimed, 'God knows how!' – her father had to make another difficult decision. He was not a ruthless or wholly selfish man, but he really did not want to be killed by his grandson. Perhaps it would not be a boy but a girl. In that case he could rest easy. No doubt persuaded by his wife and his undoubted love for his daughter, he decided to take the risk. Although he could get no satisfactory explanation from Danaë, who resolutely denied that any man had been near her, he released her from the dungeon and allowed her back into the relative luxury of the women's quarters in the palace. But when she finally bore the child and it was a boy, Akrisios began to fear that the oracle could not be circumvented. Nevertheless, he still shrank from directly taking his daughter's and his grandson's lives to preserve his own, so he devised another scheme with an outside chance of preserving all three. He had his shipbuilders in Nauplia construct a small sea-going chest large enough to hold both mother and child, a kind of miniature ark. Much the same fate, millennia later, but in 'a rotten carcass of a butt' rather than a custom-made chest, awaited Prospero and his daughter Miranda in Shakespeare's *Tempest*.

If we had been on our terrace in Arcadia on that day long ago in the Bronze Age, we might have seen the ship carrying this chest sailing down the Gulf of Argos, but it would have passed out of our view into the Myrtoan Sea by the time the sailors lowered the chest into the water and watched it float away eastwards, before swinging their own vessel round to return to Nauplia. Akrisios had ordered that food and water for at least a week be placed in the chest, but in fact they were hardly needed. A brisk Zephyr from over our mountains blew the strange craft due east for only about a hundred kilometres before it reached a small island called Seriphos, in the Western Cyclades. There, washed to and fro in the white-crested waves breaking on the beach, it was spotted by a fisherman called Diktys, who caught it in his net and dragged it ashore. When he broke open the chest and discovered its contents, he realised immediately not only that this was no ordinary flotsam or jetsam but no ordinary single mother either. This woman had the soft skin and wore the clothes and jewels of a princess and was more beautiful than any he had ever seen. As for the baby, in spite of being tossed about for several days by the waves, he was as calm as if he had been lying in a padded cradle and, as Diktys told his friends in the village, 'he has a strange kind of glow about him, something not quite earthly'.

Diktys' brother Polydektes was the king of Seriphos – not a particularly grand position since the island even in modern times has less than two thousand inhabitants – and as soon as Danaë had recovered from her voyage, Diktys took her and baby Perseus on a mule to his brother's house on the far side of the island, no more than about five kilometres over a not very high mountain. Polydektes was as impressed as his brother with Danaë's beauty, and hoping to make her his wife immediately found room for her and the baby in his own house.

Years passed and Perseus grew into a young man, handsomer and stronger than any of the other youths on Seriphos. He didn't arouse their envy or hostility since he was a friendly, helpful and modest person, joining in all their activities, sharing their games and their skills at fishing, mending nets and boats, repairing roofs and building huts. His mother had a much harder time, for she was constantly fending off Polydektes and could not so easily make friends with the village women. She occupied herself, as she had in her father's dungeon, by weaving textiles. She was lonely and often sad, but the thought that she'd been singled out by Zeus and the sight of Perseus growing into his full strength and manhood kept her from despair.

Polydektes, however, was losing patience. Beautiful as Danaë still was, she was nearly middle-aged and if she went on rejecting him she would soon be too old to bear his children. He began to think of ways to get rid of Perseus, whose upbringing had been her excuse for not wishing to marry while he was still a boy and who now as a man protected her. He was also afraid that Perseus' popularity and superior gifts might eventually lead the people of Seriphos to prefer him as king. So when word came that the king of Elis on the far side of the Peloponnese was advertising for suitors for his daughter Hippodameia, Polydektes announced that he intended to be one of them. But, he said, he was too poor to compete with the rich suitors from larger and more fertile kingdoms, unless his more prosperous subjects could each contribute a horse or its equivalent in gold to his dowry. Several of them, primed by Polydektes in advance, promised to.

'What about you, Perseus?' said Polydektes. 'I have been a father to you. Can you help?'

'I have neither horse nor gold,' said Perseus, 'but if you are really going to marry Hippodameia and not my mother, I will go anywhere and do anything I can to help.'

This was exactly what Polydektes was hoping to hear. Now he could send Perseus off to the mainland or another island on some fool's errand and marry Danaë while he was away. Why was Perseus so easily deceived? The truth was that he was finding life on this tiny, isolated island increasingly restrictive and was more and more unsettled by the tales of heroes and monsters that were recited by the island's storyteller whenever Polydektes held a dinner for his friends. At one of these gatherings recently he had been particularly excited by a story about the Gorgons, three terrible creatures with wings, bronze claws and teeth like boars' tusks, with serpents instead of hair. Two of them, Stheno and Euryale, were sisters and immortal, but the third, Medusa, was mortal. She had originally been a virgin priestess of Athene, but had been seduced by the sea god Poseidon in Athene's temple and the insulted goddess had turned her into a Gorgon, so hideous that no one could look at her without being turned to stone.

With this story still echoing in his mind, Perseus, full of youthful enthusiasm at the thought of leaving the island and embarking on some adventure, added:

'I would even bring you Medusa's head if that was any use to you.'

'Now that would be still better than a horse,' said Polydektes. 'That would be sensational! If I took something like that to Elis, I don't see how either the king or his daughter could possibly prefer any other suitor. It would be the clincher.'

What he didn't know, of course, was that, whatever gifts they brought, Hippodameia's suitors were required to take part in a chariot race with her father which invariably, until the arrival of Pelops, ended in their defeat and death. But, then, Polydektes had no intention of becoming Hippodameia's suitor. It was Danaë he wanted and he was certain now of getting her because surely no one at all, let alone an inexperienced youth like Perseus, could even find Medusa, far less cut off her head, and the task would keep him away for years, if it didn't kill him.

Perseus' first move, after making this rash promise which had been so swiftly accepted, was to visit Polydektes' storyteller in the hope of obtaining more information about Medusa. Some hope! The storyteller was an old man with white hair and beard, yellow skin and shaking hands who lived in a ramshackle hut with his sharp-faced and sharp-voiced wife. He had always had poor health and, being unable to compete as a fisherman with his stronger contemporaries, had taken to telling the stories he had heard from his mother, with embellishments of his own, as a way of earning a little gold from Polydektes and the other better-off inhabitants of the island, and dining and wining well at their tables. His wife, who did not get the benefit of the free dinners, was always hungry and bad-tempered, so that although the storyteller seemed convivial and cheerful enough in public when he was practising his craft and away from his wife, he was the opposite at home.

Perseus found the storyteller sitting morosely in his courtyard contemplating their livestock, which consisted of four or five hens and a cock. They couldn't even afford a goat or a donkey. In order to ply his trade and eat his dinners in other parts of the island, the storyteller had to walk and he would soon be too old for that. Storytellers' circumstances have not much changed down the ages. Perseus sat down beside him on a step and came straight to the point:

'Where can I find the Gorgon Medusa?'

The storyteller nearly choked with ribald laughter and the cock crowed in sympathy.

'Over the moon, I should imagine,' he said when he had finished convulsing.

'Cock-a-doodle-doo!' crowed the cock.

'What do you mean? She doesn't exist?'

'I didn't say that. What exists or doesn't exist is not my business. As far as I'm concerned, if they make a story they exist and if they don't, they don't.'

'No. I see,' said Perseus doubtfully.

'If I have them in my head, they exist. If I don't, they may exist, but not for me.'

'Cock-a-doodle-doo!'

'So are you saying the Medusa *does* exist? I need to know where.'

'In my head, stupid boy. That's all I can tell you. North or south, east or west, she may exist – in Libya or Ethiopia, in Persia or among the Hyperboreans, on the borders of Ocean or on the other side of the moon, who knows? Maybe she's living in a secret cave on this very island of Seriphos, I might find that in my head along with all the other rubbish that's stored there, but if I told you that for certain you couldn't be certain in your head that my head wasn't making it up as it went along. I couldn't even be certain myself.'

'Cock-a-doodle-doo!'

Perseus shook his head as if he had got a wasp in his ear, but thanked the old man politely and went home to tell his mother of his promise to Polydektes and to ask her if she had ever heard where the Gorgons lived. No, she hadn't, and she was extremely disturbed by this development, guessing at once that the whole thing was simply Polydektes' subterfuge for getting rid of her son and closing in on her. But she was unable to persuade Perseus to abandon this impossible adventure and in great distress she crossed the island to a small temple of Athene that stood on the cliff above Diktys' village. She wanted to ask Athene to intercede with Zeus – Perseus' father, after all, as well as Athene's – not to deflect her fate, whatever that might be, but to give her some guidance. Should she perhaps marry Polydektes, however much she disliked the idea, so that Perseus would not need to go through with his perilous mission?

Perseus accompanied her, sacrificed a goat on the altar, and then, begging her to ask the goddess where he could find the Gorgons, left her to pray alone while he went outside to look at the stretch of sea that had brought them here in their chest when he was still a baby. He was determined, whatever happened, to cross it again, but was trying to think what he could do to protect his mother while he was away. As he walked up and down with his eyes on the sea he became aware that he was being watched. There was a village woman in black standing under an olive tree just above the path where he was pacing. She beckoned to him and he went up to her and asked, a little abruptly because she was breaking into his uneasy thoughts:

'Yes, *kyría*, what is it?'

'Perseus!' she said.

He was not particularly surprised that she knew his name. On such a small island people knew who everyone was, though it was true he didn't recognise her. Most of her face was hidden by her black hood.

'Yes, I am Perseus.'

'You have a long way to go and Medusa is not easy to find. You must first find the Graiai and ask them.'

'The Graiai?'

'Three old women, sisters of the Gorgons, who live in the Atlas Mountains far to the south-west.'

'And they will tell me?'

'Not willingly. You will have to make them.'

'How can I do that?'

'They have only one eye and one tooth between the three of them and they are continually passing both to each other so as to see and eat.'

'What a frightful fate!'

'They are quite used to it. They were born old, but they are immortal and have been doing this for ever and will be doing it for ever, except for this one occasion when you visit them and interrupt them.'

'By asking about Medusa?'

'By putting your hand between them as they pass the eye and the tooth and capturing both.'

Perseus looked shocked.

'You will give them back. But only when they have told you how to find their sisters the Gorgons.'

Perseus smiled.

'Brilliant!'

The disguised goddess smiled too. He was a very handsome youth and his smile was particularly seductive. The Olympians, who are subject to sudden strong feelings such as lust, jealousy or anger, never themselves experience the slow ache of unhappiness which they so often observe in mortals. For that reason they never really appreciate their own everlasting happiness. So to see the happiness of mortals, however brief, even if it lasts only as long as a smile, always gives them pleasure, much as a cat's happiness when it purrs gives pleasure to us.

'But I must tell you,' said Athene, for it was she, who having left Danaë praying in her temple had come outside in person to answer her prayers, 'that this mission of yours is absolutely impossible ...'

Perseus' smile faded, but Athene still smiled since she had better news in reserve.

'Impossible for a mortal alone. But you will not be alone. I shall accompany you and so will my brother Hermes. You will seldom see us, but we shall never be far off.'

In fact it was Athene who had put the idea of decapitating Medusa into Perseus' head in the first place. Having punished Medusa by making her a Gorgon, Athene now wanted her devastatingly ugly head to wear on her cape (or *aigis*) when she went into battle. The job had to be done in this generation, since Medusa, being mortal, would not live beyond it and her unique head would simply rot down to a skull like any other when her spirit joined the shades in the underworld.

There is nothing so exhilarating for an ambitious person as to know that a god is on his side, and Perseus was duly filled with energy and self-confidence. But he was a sensitive and affectionate son and thought immediately of what this would mean for Danaë.

'But my mother,' he said. 'What's to become of her while I'm away? Must she marry Polydektes?'

'Certainly not,' said Athene. 'You will see that I've not forgotten your mother. Meanwhile, you must borrow a boat and row or sail across the sea to the Peloponnese. Then you must make your way over the Arcadian mountains to the waterfall below Mount Chelmos, where the River Styx disappears into the underworld.'

'Am I to enter the underworld?'

'By no means. Playing around the waterfall you will find the Stygian Nymphs. They will try to seduce you, but don't succumb! You must not lose your virginity to anyone until you have dealt with Medusa or you will certainly fail. Instead, use your charm and the nymphs' mutually competitive temptations to persuade them to give you three necessary things: an adamantine sickle, a satchel made of the pelts of giant bats and a dragon-skin helmet. All these objects belong to Hades and the nymphs are charged with looking after them. Hades himself seldom makes use of them and will not miss them for the time being. When the nymphs have given you those things, put on the helmet, which will make you invisible. Then you can easily escape their attentions.'

'That doesn't seem very fair on the nymphs.'

'Perseus, I am giving you instructions. Your part is only to understand, remember and obey them. There is no room for sentiment or discussion. Heroes singled out by gods cannot always have the compunction of ordinary men. You will need those three things and the nymphs do not need them. In any case they will get them back in due course.'

Perseus bowed his head, avoiding the goddess's fierce grey eyes, and was silent.

'Once you have escaped the nymphs, you will meet my brother Hermes and he will give you further instructions. Now repeat to me everything I've told you!'

Perseus did so, and as he finished, asked again:

'And my mother? You said you wouldn't forget her ...'

He got no reply. The figure of the woman in black seemed to grow into a great column of light and vanish, while a wind blew and the ground shook so much that Perseus could not keep his feet and fell flat on the path. He picked himself up, brushed the dust off his clothes and was about to re-enter the temple to find his mother, when he saw her coming out of it. At the same time he heard a voice behind him.

'Perseus!'

It was the fisherman, Diktys, who had rescued them from the sea. Both Diktys and Danaë had felt the ground heave and thought there had been a mild earthquake. But Perseus understood that their synchronised arrival was Athene's reply. Diktys, who was increasingly at odds with his brother Polydektes and did not fear him, offered to take Danaë into his house to be looked after by his wife while Perseus was away. He also lent Perseus a boat to take him to the mainland. When Perseus asked him how he knew that these were exactly the two things he needed at that moment, Diktys laughed:

'Perhaps I dreamed it,' he said, 'or saw it written all over your face, or perhaps, since everybody on the island knows what you've promised to bring to my brother and why he wants to get you out of the way, it was perfectly obvious.'

2. THE NYMPHS

After crossing the Myrtoan Sea and landing on the long curving beach directly below our village, Perseus left Diktys' boat in the care of a fisherman who knew Diktys and promised to look after it. Perseus then walked for many days over the mountains towards the north-west until, on the borders of Achaia, under Mount Chelmos, he came to a sinister ravine of rocks, worn and twisted into grotesque shapes, and above it the source of the River Styx. A long slender waterfall plunged down into a pool and a dark cavern, where the river was lost to sight as it flowed away into the underworld. Perseus climbed down the side of the ravine and stood on a rock facing the cavern, where the force of the waterfall drove a spear of silvery water deep into the black pool, sending up bubbles and a perpetual ring of waves over the surface. There was no sign of the Stygian Nymphs, so Perseus clambered down still further until he reached a little stony beach beside the pool. There, hot and sweaty from his journey, he laid down his small bundle of food and his cloak, with his belt and knife, and slipping out of his tunic dived into the pool. It was icy cold and he came out as soon as he had swum once round the pool, to find that his clothes, his satchel, his belt and his knife had all disappeared. He looked round, thinking that perhaps he had come out on a different beach, but saw at once that there was no other and at the same time heard laughter.

'Where are my things?' he said loudly and sternly.

'Come and get them!' said a female voice.

'Come and get them, come and get them!' said others.

Five naked nymphs, all very much alike, small and stocky, with black hair and dark skin, emerged from behind the rocks where they had been hiding. They were not all quite naked. One wore his tunic, another his belt strapped round between her plump breasts and her navel, a third had tied his lunch bag round her waist so that it dangled suggestively just under the thick dark hair of her pubis, a fourth had his cloak flung carelessly across her shoulders and only half concealing her breasts, and the fifth, entirely naked, was twirling his knife between her fingers. He made a dart for this last, who was nearest, but she easily evaded him and retreated to a rock, where she sat smiling and throwing his knife from hand to hand, so that he was afraid it would fall into the pool and be lost.

'What's your name?' she said.

'Perseus.'

'Should we know you?'

'I shouldn't think so.'

'Where do you come from?'

'Seriphos.'

'Where's that?'

'Over the sea. It's an island.'

'What are you doing here, Perseus?'

'Looking for the Stygian Nymphs.'

Laughter.

'What do you want with them?'

'Three favours.'

'Only three? There are five of us.'

'So I see. But are you the Stygian Nymphs?'

'What if we are?'

'Then I've come to the right place.'

'And supposing we're not?'

'I'd be very surprised if you were not, considering you look like nymphs or what I've always imagined nymphs look like, and that this is the River Styx.'

'Well, you're right, we are the Stygian Nymphs.'

There was a pause during which Perseus, standing there naked, was very conscious that five all but naked nymphs were staring intently at his body and especially at his penis, which, having shrunk from the coldness of the water, was now beginning to stir. His mind was very conscious of Athene's warning, but his penis had a mind of its own. He had never before seen women without clothes and he – it – liked what he saw. He went towards the nymph wearing his tunic and, as she retreated, sat down on a rock with his back to the nymphs so as to conceal his arousal.

'Can I have my things back?' he said.

'Come and get them, Perseus!'

They danced and ducked and jumped about displaying his things and their own charms, but he knew he would never catch them, so pretended to ignore them, and after a while the nymphs, like the shy wild creatures they partly were, came and sat on the little pebble beach around his rock.

'Are you a mortal or an immortal?' asked the nymph wearing his belt.

'A mortal,' said Perseus. 'And you, I suppose, are immortals?'

'Not entirely,' said the nymph with his cloak, 'but we live much longer than mortals and we don't grow old.'

'A nice life,' said Perseus, 'swimming and sitting in the sun all day.'

'We have to look out for satyrs and creatures like that. They always want to catch us and they have much bigger tools than you.'

'Much, much bigger and always at the ready,' said the nymph with the knife. 'When they turn up, we have to dive down quickly into the pool and go down the river into the darkness.'

'But if it was a god who wanted to catch us,' said the nymph with his lunch bag, 'we wouldn't run away. Gods are better looking than satyrs or centaurs and their children would be lovely. Are you sure you're not a god disguised as a mortal?'

'No, I'm not a god. But I believe I'm the child of one, Zeus himself.'

The nymphs were impressed.

'That's why you're so good-looking,' said the one in the tunic.

'Thank you,' said Perseus. 'Do gods come here often?'

'No, they seldom come here,' she said sadly. 'Just occasionally when they have to swear an unbreakable oath on the water of the River Styx, one of them flies in to collect a jar-full, but it's usually a goddess – Hebe or Iris – and she's always in a hurry and doesn't stay to talk.'

'What about mortals?'

'Not very often and when they do they're quite ugly and often old and have sheep or goats with them. We keep out of their way and they don't see us.'

Perseus and the nymphs stayed talking on the beach for the rest of the day. He was curious to know more about their life, which seemed to consist of very little beyond bathing and sunbathing and keeping watch for satyrs. But such a life evidently did not bore them or make them want something different. They were perfectly content. In that, they were more like animals than the humans they resembled, though they suffered from none of the physical disadvantages endemic to both animals and humans, were never hungry or sick, and did not grow old. When, after aeons rather than years, they died, they simply faded out of existence like clouds. They were astonished to hear about the life of humans, not really understanding that they had to work to live and that being mortal they were constantly faced with all the hazards of disease, accident, envy, quarrels, loss of their loved ones, famine, poverty, warfare and the miseries of old age and death, none of which had any meaning for nymphs.

As evening came on, Perseus began to feel cold and hungry – weaknesses quite alien to the nymphs, who were never cold or hot and could dive into the river to swallow fish or water plants whenever they wished. He showed them his gooseflesh and they looked at it and touched it with interest, while he explained that mortals could easily die if they were left naked without any covering or shelter or food after the sun went down. At that, they quickly returned all his things to him, caught him two or three fish, and watched fascinated as he rubbed sticks together to make a fire and cooked the fish. Then they sat in a circle round the fire and observed him eating, even trying some of the cooked flesh themselves, but not much liking it. And when he said that he was tired and must sleep now and wrapped his cloak around him and lay down, they all lay down around him with their arms and legs and heads touching him or resting on him, so that anyone looking down from above would have seen a strange sort of twelve-legged, twelve-armed, six-headed monster sprawled on the little beach beside the dying fire.

Perseus did not sleep well that night. The nymphs, who had no sense of time and little sense of night and day, were not used to regular sleep – they tended to snatch naps just as they snatched fish to eat, when they felt like it. They were continually shifting position as one got up for a while and another lay down for a while, and whenever they thought Perseus was fast asleep they would pull up the edges of his cloak to examine his chest or biceps or belly or buttocks or, when he was not protecting them with his thighs or by lying on his face, his genitals. His genitals enjoyed this, of course, and hoped for more, but Perseus forced himself to remain passive and, in spite of the constant coming and going all over his body of soft hands and fingers, thighs and breasts and bottoms, fought off his pressing desire. He told himself that when he had finished with the Gorgon, he would be returning here with the items he had come to borrow and would then be free of Athene's harsh restriction.

But as it grew light he decided that he could not go on resisting the nymphs' temptations indefinitely and must tell them what he had come for and be on his way. He would have liked to plunge into the pool to clear his head, but was afraid they would take his things again. Instead, when he had stood up and stretched and clasped his belt round his tunic, put his knife in the belt and his lunch bag over his shoulder, and was holding his cloak over one arm, he said quite straightforwardly:

'I was sent to you by the great goddess Athene. She said you could lend me three things that I need. I will return them to you, of course.'

'You'll come back, then?'

'Oh, yes, I'd be very sorry not to come back. The three things I need belong to the god Hades: an adamantine sickle, a bat-skin satchel and a dragon-skin helmet.'

He was expecting a blank refusal and that he would have to argue his case, but they made no difficulty at all. Two of them disappeared into the cavern and returned in a few minutes with the three items. All they were interested in was his promise to return.

'You are such a lovely boy,' said the one who had played with his knife, 'and you never even tried to rape any of us. That's so different from the satyrs. Perhaps when you come back you'll stay with us for ever.'

'Nothing I'd like better,' said Perseus, 'if the goddess and my fate will let me.'

Then he embraced all five nymphs several times and climbed out of the ravine, not even needing to put on the helmet to make himself invisible, but waving from time to time to the nymphs below until he reached the top of the cleft and lost sight of them.

'Phew!' he said aloud, as he peed into a bush, 'Those nymphs nearly finished me.'

'Bravo!' said a soft voice behind and he turned to see a person, dressed like a shepherd and wearing a broad-brimmed straw hat, smiling at him. 'Impressive self-control, Perseus! I could hardly have managed it myself. The Stygians are not the loveliest nymphs on earth – they live too much underground – but they are very inviting.'

'What am I to do now?' asked Perseus.

'You are to fly across the sea south-westwards, to the Atlas Mountains.'

'Fly? How do I do that?'

'With these sandals I've brought you. An old pair of my own, but still perfectly serviceable. In a cave on the slopes of those mountains you will find the Graiai and I think you already know how to make them tell you where to find the Gorgons.'

Perseus sat down and strapped on the sandals, then got to his feet and picked up his cloak and the helmet of Hades. The sickle was tucked into his belt, on the other side from his knife, the bat-skin satchel and his lunch-bag hung from their straps over his shoulders.

'Put on the helmet now!' said Hermes.

Perseus did so and was astonished to see that he could no longer see himself, though he could still see everything around him except Hermes, who had also disappeared. Then he felt the invisible god's hand grasp his own invisible hand.

'Come!' said Hermes, 'I will launch you on your way.'

They rose together into the air.

3. THE GRAIAI

Perseus found it a very strange and exhilarating experience to be flying over the mountains and valleys of the Peloponnese hand-in-hand with a god. He could feel his eyes streaming with tears in the wind of their flight and that the winged sandals on his feet were driving him forward, just as if he were swimming and had thrust them against a rock to give himself momentum, but he did not have to move his feet nor could he see them. They passed over the high peak of Mount Taÿgetos and were soon over the sea, turning westwards.

'I shall leave you now,' said Hermes. 'Keep the same course over the sea, with Zephyr always in your face, and when you come to land again keep on the same course until you reach the Atlas Mountains. Any questions?'

Perseus had any number of questions and began with the most urgent:

'How do I come down?'

'Just drop your legs and the sandals will let you fall. But if you find yourself falling too fast, just raise your legs again, then drop them again, and so on. All right?'

Hermes was impatient to be off. He had some souls to escort to the underworld before he could return to Olympos.

'And how do I get into the air again without you to help me?'

'Just jump and raise your legs as you do so! Like diving into water, but in the opposite direction. Quite simple, but may take a bit of practice if you haven't done it before.'

'No, I haven't.'

'Easiest off a cliff, if you can find a handy cliff.'

And with that, Perseus felt the god let go of his hand. Below him now was the open sea, empty except for the occasional tiny ship, and he suddenly found himself shaking with fear. What if one of his sandals fell off – or both? Wanting to check that the straps were still tight, he lowered his left leg so as to bring it near his hand and immediately began to plunge sideways. Terrified, he dropped his right leg, corrected his sideways movement, but was now falling like a stone towards the sea.

'Perseus!' he said to himself aloud, 'Are you destined to be a hero or a poor drowned corpse? Get a grip!'

Raising both legs, he flew upwards again and when he had fully recovered from his fright began to experiment with raising or lowering one leg, then the other, then both, until he felt as confident in this new element of air as if he were swimming in the sea.

The sun, which had been rising behind them over the Arcadian mountains when he and Hermes set out, had now overtaken him and seemed to be leading him to his destination as he came over land again. At last, with the sun still ahead of him, he sighted the Atlas Mountains and dropped down on the lower slopes to look for food and shelter. Forgetting, however, to remove his helmet, knocking and speaking and being quite invisible to the owner of the first hut he came to, he scared him so much that the man slammed and barred the door. After that, with the helmet in his hand, Perseus' youth and good looks and soft tone of voice soon found him a warm welcome in a farmer's house. Since he did not immediately remember to take off his winged sandals, they surely believed they were entertaining Hermes himself, and he could not lie down to sleep in the farmer's best bed until all the family's neighbouring relations had come round to have a look at him.

Next morning he set off up the mountain to look for the cave of the Graiai, which his hosts knew of but had never dared go near. Once he had waved goodbye and turned a corner of the path he put on his helmet and sandals and, after several false attempts, rose into the air, narrowly missing the top of a tree. Towards the top of the mountain, under a sheer rock face, he found a series of caves and dropping to the ground explored them carefully one by one, until at last he saw the Graiai, the three grey sisters, seated side by side on a stone bench in the shadows towards the back of one of them. Being quite blind, except for the one eye they were passing between them, their hearing was acute and they heard his footsteps immediately.

'Who's there?' said the sister in the middle and, grabbing the eye from her neighbour, pushed it into her socket and peered about, without, of course, being any the wiser, since he was still wearing the helmet of Hades.

The other sisters demanded the eye and it began to pass rapidly to and fro as the three of them became increasingly agitated. Perseus wondered how he was to enter the cave and get behind them without distressing them so much that they would be unwilling or unable to answer his question. He decided, as he had with the nymphs, on the direct approach.

'My name is Perseus,' he said, 'and I believe you can tell me where to find the Gorgons.'

'I can't see you,' said the old woman on the left, whose name was Pephredo, and who possessed the eye at that moment.

Perseus removed his helmet.

'You're very young,' she said disparagingly.

'Let me see!' said Enyo in the middle, snatching the eye and putting it into her empty socket. '*Very* young!' she said with equal disapproval.

'Too young!' said the sister on the right, Deino, having snatched the eye in her turn. 'Why should we tell you where our sisters live?'

But while Enyo in the middle was taking the eye again, Perseus clapped his helmet on and moved quickly round behind the sisters.

'Where are you now?' said Enyo.

'Let me see!' said Pephredo.

And as Enyo passed the eye to her, Perseus took it, flinching a little as he felt the jelly-like thing in his palm.

'Give it to me, Enyo, you selfish creature!' said Pephredo in a shrill, angry voice.

'I gave it to you, Pephredo.'

'No, you didn't.'

'You're lying. I felt you take it.'

'*You're* lying, Enyo. I never took it.'

'Then Deino must have it.'

'No, I haven't,' said Deino. 'I've got the tooth, but not the eye. Do you want the tooth?'

She held out the tooth and Perseus quickly took it.

'No, I want the eye, I don't want the tooth,' said Enyo.

'Well, why did you take the tooth if you didn't want it?' said Deino.

'I didn't take it.'

'Yes, you did.'

'Never mind the tooth!' said Pephredo. 'It's the eye I want. Where is the eye?'

'It's in my hand,' said Perseus, 'also your tooth. If you want them back you must tell me where the Gorgons live.'

'How dare you take what doesn't belong to you?' said Enyo.

'I'm sorry, ' said Perseus, 'but needs must. Please answer my question!'

'No, we won't,' said Pephredo. 'We are too old to be bothered with very young people and their stupid questions. We shall just sit here until you give us back what doesn't belong to you.'

'In that case,' said Perseus, 'you will never get them back. I shall throw them down the mountain and you will never see or bite anything ever again.' After a pause, he added 'Sorry!'

He was genuinely sorry. He had never treated anyone like this before, let alone three old women who might be his grandmothers or even great-grandmothers.

'Sorry!' said Enyo, 'He's sorry!'

'He says he's sorry!' said Deino.

'If he's so sorry, why doesn't he give us our eye and our tooth?' said Pephredo.

'Why don't you tell me where the Gorgons live?' said Perseus.

'Why do you want to know?'

'I want to visit them.'

'They don't like visitors,' said Deino.

'They'll turn you to stone,' said Enyo.

'That will teach him his manners,' said Pephredo.

'I am walking out of your cave now,' said Perseus, beginning to do so, 'and taking your eye and your tooth with me. For the last time, will you tell me where the Gorgons live or do I have to leave you blind and toothless?'

Which they finally did, and when Perseus had made each of them repeat the directions so as to discover any subterfuges or discrepancies in their accounts, he put the eye into Pephredo's hand and the tooth into Enyo's, politely apologised for disturbing them and took off gracefully into the air from the side of the mountain.

4. THE GORGONS

The Gorgons lived on a barren island of rock near the coast of Okeanos, the great band of water that in those days, say the storytellers, surrounded the flat disc of earth and into and out of which all rivers and seas flowed. If we now suspect this was the Atlantic Ocean and believe, most of us, that the earth is not flat but spherical, that makes no difference to the story.

As Perseus reached the rim of the earth, the sun was disappearing into Okeanos and the moon and night were taking his place in the sky. Perseus thought he should eat and rest before seeking out the Gorgons, so he dropped down on a flat expanse of land overlooking Okeanos. He was enjoying the supper of bread, cheese, wine and dates given him by his kind hosts of the previous night, but also worrying about a difficulty which had not previously occurred to him, when he heard a familiar voice.

'Perseus!'

He turned, but did not recognise the dark-skinned person in a white robe and hood who was standing over him. Only the voice told him that it must be Hermes. He stood up and bowed.'

'Here I am,' he said.

'Here you are. You have done well and come far and Athene is very pleased with you. But the hardest part is ahead.'

'I know, and I have been wondering how I can possibly cut off Medusa's head when I can't look at her for fear of being turned to stone. Or will the helmet of Hades by making me invisible also make me impervious to her terrible glance?'

'It will not. It is you looking at her that turns you to stone, not her looking at you. For that reason, even when she is dead, her face will have that effect on anyone seeing it.'

'Yes, I understand. But I have first to pick her out from her immortal sisters, whose heads cannot be cut off, and then make the fatal stroke to her neck with my sickle – all with my head turned aside or my eyes shut. I should have thought of this before. It's making me quite nervous about the outcome.'

Hermes laughed.

'Is there something I'm missing?' said Perseus. 'Some strategy that hasn't occurred to me? I'm sorry. You are a god and we mortals must seem very stupid, but I really am worried about what to do.'

'What you are missing, Perseus, is this.'

Hermes brought out from behind his back and held up, so that it reflected the last red rays of the sun in the west, a polished bronze shield. It was circular, just large enough to protect a man's head or chest.

'Do you see?'

'I see a beautiful shield, but if I protect my eyes with it, I shall still not be able to see to do what I have to do.'

'When you approach the Gorgons,' said Hermes, 'make sure that the sun is shining on their faces not on the shield! You must on no account, not for a moment, look at their faces, but, holding up this shield towards them, look only at their reflections in its polished surface. You will not be in any danger from their reflections, only from the direct sight of them.'

'Brilliant!' said Perseus, with his winning smile.

Hermes smiled back and gave him the shield.

'But how shall I know which of the three is Medusa?'

'The other two have grey complexions, Medusa's is much redder. And she generally sits in the middle.'

'Generally? What if ...?'

'As soon as her head is off, you must put it in that satchel and pull the neck of the satchel tight, then you must take to the air and I hope my sandals will be fast enough. The other two Gorgons will be after you and they have wings. You may need to dive and duck to evade them, but try to rise above them or, like falcons, they will stoop with a speed you cannot match and get their talons into you. And make sure when you've escaped them that you fly in the right direction or you will be lost over the endless unchanging expanse of Okeanos, where even gods might miss their way.'

'And then?'

But Hermes was no longer there. Perseus, still holding the polished shield, turned it to reflect the moon and stars and practised looking at the reflections but not at the sky. Then, tired, he laid it on the ground and, having carefully covered it with palm fronds, afraid that even in that deserted place somebody might see it shining with the moon's light and steal it, slept under his cloak.

He rose at dawn and, setting up targets of branches in the sandy soil, spent an hour or two rehearsing with the shield, the sickle, the helmet and the winged sandals, until he was confident that he had mastered all the skills he would need for his formidable task. The cutting power of the glittering glassy sickle particularly delighted him. It severed thick branches as if they were blades of grass. Not knowing that adamant could be found only in Hades' kingdom, he wondered why men were content with bronze when they could cut swathes through forests or enemy armies with axes or swords made of this magical mineral.

When he was ready he took to the air and flew along the coast looking for the Gorgons' island. The Graiai had told him that it was shaped like a tooth, but upside-down. Their sisters, they said, lived in the hollow between the protruding roots of the tooth-like rock, which was also gleaming white like a tooth. Perseus had some doubts about their simile, considering that since their lives were entirely focussed on their eye and their tooth they probably thought every island on earth was shaped like one or the other. Also, their own tooth was yellow, not white, though with only the one eye between them they had probably not seen their tooth since it was white many centuries ago. But after some time he spotted what from a distance did indeed resemble an upside-down tooth, gleaming white and set in a circle of foam. Before going any closer he practised his aeronautics, diving and soaring, turning at speed, sliding sideways, even looping the loop, so as to be prepared for his escape.

Finally, gyrating in smaller and smaller circles, he approached the island and saw that it was not made of white rock as appeared from a distance, but almost entirely covered with bird shit, the accumulated droppings of the innumerable sea birds that shared the island with the Gorgons. Only the cleft between the twin pinnacles was clear of guano, a patch of dark-grey rock littered with small bird-shaped rocks. As Perseus landed among them he realised with a shiver that these were once living birds which had looked at the Gorgons and been turned to stone. There were also occasional larger rocks, man-shaped – sailors no doubt who had come ashore here out of curiosity or after being wrecked. He was careful now, advancing softly and invisibly with the sun behind him, to look at nothing but the ground or the surface of his shield, which he turned this way and that to mirror whatever was in front of him. Anyone observing him would have seen only the weird phenomenon of a polished bronze disc moving slowly and jerkily a metre or two above the ground.

Suddenly the shield reflected what he had come for. Squatting on a broad terrace of rock, basking in the sunlight, were three monstrous creatures resembling huge birds with folded wings and legs and feathered bodies, but with arms and heads more like those of humans except for the bronze claws where their hands should be and the bronze tusks that stuck forward out of their mouths. Perseus stopped and waited, getting his breath, watching the reflections. The Gorgons seemed to be asleep, at any rate their eyes were closed, though their hair was moving as if ruffled by the sea breeze. No, Perseus saw in his shield as he went closer, it was not the breeze, it was the hair itself, scores of small serpents writhing and hissing on each of the three heads. They had seen this strange object approaching even if their owners had not.

Now he studied the three faces. The face to his left was certainly grey, but so was the one in the middle. It was the face to his right which was red. Could this be correct? Was Medusa not sitting in the middle, as Hermes had suggested, but on the right, or was the light playing tricks with him? He looked again and was sure. And now another doubt made him pause. Reflections in mirrors, surely, turned right to left and left to right? Was the Gorgon with the red complexion really sitting on the left? The more he thought about it, the more confused he became. He felt a terrible urge to look at the group directly in order to check. He fought it down and moved stealthily to his right, so as to mount the terrace from that side, the side where the reflection told him Medusa was seated, and as he came nearer and nearer he saw that the shield had not deceived him. This creature on the right of the group as he looked at it, but on the left from her own opposite point of view, and now from his own point of view as he stood beside her and slowly drew the adamantine sickle from his belt, was indeed the Gorgon with the red complexion.

The hissing serpents were now in a frenzy of alarm, but, anchored by their tails in her head, could not reach the intruder. Medusa shook her head as if her sleep was disturbed by their noise and movement and Perseus raised the sickle in his right hand, looking for the first time not at the reflection in the shield, but, since he was no longer in front of her but just behind her and could not see her face, at the neck itself. Then he struck. The adamantine blade, visible now that it had left his person and sparkling like an arc of solid light, cut through the bone and tendons of the neck as if they were rotten wood. Medusa uttered a single shriek as her head fell to the ground. Blood spouted from the severed neck as Perseus quickly replaced the sickle in his belt, laid the shield on the ground, slipped the bat skin satchel from his shoulder, opened it and stooped to seize the head by its snaky hair, relieved to find as he did so that the snakes themselves were as dead as their host and could no longer bite him. All this took no more than a few moments, but the other two Gorgons had been woken by their mortal sister's shriek. Perseus had just time to push the head into his satchel, draw the top of it tight, loop the strap over his shoulder, pick up the shield and jump off the terrace and into the air, before the two monsters, shrieking in their turn, were unfolding their wings and rising after him. They could not see him but they could see the shield and possibly also the satchel slung over his shoulder – Perseus wasn't sure if that was visible or not.

He soared upwards and they followed. He could hear the beating of their powerful wings, and it seemed to be getting closer. Now was the time for all the aerial dives and dodges he had practised, but the satchel over his shoulder was heavy – he had not allowed for that – and the Gorgons were as quick and agile as he was. He soon found that between the two of them, working from either side, he was being forced downwards. Nor did he dare look at them, except with the aid of the shield – another problem in this all-round space which he had not foreseen. He found it easier to keep his eyes closed and guess where they were by their wingbeats. His best hope, he realised, was to jettison the shield. Unlike the helmet, the satchel and the sickle, he had not been told to return it, and he hoped that Athene and Hermes would not be angry at its loss. As it fell, spinning and throwing back the sun's rays, the two Gorgons pursued it and Perseus surged upwards and away.

He was beginning to feel almost safe and to look about for the coastline when it suddenly occurred to him that the sun was not in his eyes but warming his heels. He was heading in the wrong direction, out across fathomless Okeanos instead of back towards the Atlas Mountains. He turned at once and, aiming north-eastwards, so as not to pass near the Gorgons' island, came at last to a coast he did not recognise. It looked bleak and inhospitable, but he was exhausted, so he landed as soon as he could, on top of a mountainous promontory. There he lay down in the shade of a rock, with the bat skin satchel and its deadly contents at his side, and was soon fast asleep.

5. THE PRINCESS

All the storytellers agree that after escaping the Gorgons, Perseus flew over Libya, which for the ancient Greeks meant the continent of Africa and in particular North Africa, the only part they knew of, and reached the coast of Ethiopia. But it seems unlikely that he drifted so far out of his way, considering that his main purpose now was to return to Seriphos, deliver Medusa's head to Polydektes and rescue his mother. What the storytellers were probably trying to do was reconcile Perseus' story with that of various even more ancient stories of Egyptian and Middle Eastern gods and heroes – a fruitful field for anthropology, but a blight on fiction, much as though one had to reconcile Perseus with James Bond. I prefer to take a leaf out of the English storyteller Thomas Malory's *Morte d'Arthur.* Whenever Malory wanted to insert material into his narrative which was not in his French sources he would remark slyly, 'as the French book saith'.

So, as the Greek book saith, Perseus woke up to find himself on the Rock of Gibralter, roughly where his descendant Herakles would later set up one of his Pillars to mark the western limit of the Mediterranean. He was able to drink from a spring but had nothing to eat except a few crusts left in his lunch-bag and was famished. Putting on the helmet of Hades and slinging the heavy bat skin satchel containing Medusa's head over his shoulder, he leapt from the cliff and, following the coast, began searching for a village or even a shepherd's hut where he might be hospitably received. Quite soon he heard a voice in his ear:

'Forget about breakfast, Perseus! There's no time to spare. Turn eastwards and cross the sea to Sicily. I will set you on your course.'

The god grasped his hand and they flew together over the sea at such a speed that it was as if they arrived almost as soon as they had started. In many ways our modern technology is still inferior to the powers of the Greek gods.

'What is it I'm to do now?' Perseus asked, but got no immediate reply, and as they approached a line of cliffs, Hermes withdrew his hand.

'Look about you and do what your heart tells you!' he said and was gone.

Perseus had not flown far before he saw something very strange on one of the rocky outcrops below. It appeared to be a naked person. Dropping lower he saw that it was a naked woman. Dropping lower still he saw that it was a young and lovely naked woman and that she was tied to the rock by a rope knotted into bronze rings. Then he noticed that there was a large crowd of people, clothed, on the cliffs overlooking the outcrop.

'This seems to be some kind of sacrifice,' he said to himself and, diving down to land on the cliff quite near the crowd, removed his helmet and approached.

'What's going on?' he asked an elderly man with a sad face who was standing slightly apart from the others.

'Altogether frightful!' said the man with relish. 'Andromeda is about to be devoured by a sea monster.'

'Who is Andromeda and what has she done?'

'She's done nothing at all. It was her mother, Queen Cassiopeia, who was vain enough to claim that she and her daughter were more beautiful than the Nereids. The Nereids complained to the sea god Poseidon and he sent a series of inundations which destroyed houses and crops and cattle and took many lives, together with a sea monster which has been regularly eating up the fishermen. King Cepheus consulted an oracle and this was what it recommended: their daughter Andromeda must be put out as a tasty tit-bit for the monster.'

'Why does she have to be naked?'

'Presumably the monster doesn't want the trouble of spitting out her clothes before biting into the tender flesh.'

Apart from the unpleasantness of the explanation, Perseus found the man's lip-smacking tone unsettling. In fact he was the local storyteller and was already beginning to assemble the titillating story he would relate to his audiences. Perseus edged his way through the crowd towards the king and queen standing at the front, near the edge of the cliff. As he did so, the whole crowd began to stir and shout and some of the women to shriek in terror.

'It's there! It's coming! Look! Look!'

Perseus looked with the rest at where people were pointing and saw, still some way out to sea, huge black coils breaking the surface of the sea, then a mighty tail thrashing spray from the waves, then the monster's scaly, dragon-like head, rising as it eyed its prey, sinking again as it thrust through the water towards her. Reaching the front of the crowd, Perseus could see Andromeda quite clearly. She was shivering either with fear or cold, or both together, but her face did not show fear. Rather, she seemed to have an expression of determined courage, her lips closed, her jaw set, her eyes open. Her only sign of nervousness was that with one roped hand she kept brushing away her streaming golden hair, blown by the wind across her face and body. Perseus had never seen the Nereids – they were visited many generations later by his descendant Herakles – but he was sure they could not be as beautiful as Andromeda, and he knew from his own experience that she was much more beautiful than the Stygian Nymphs. He was careful to keep the thought to himself. Even gods cannot read people's thoughts, unless they show them on their faces.

Now the monster was only a hundred and two metres away from its prey, and Perseus, in love with the girl at first sight and with no time to spare for preliminaries, went straight up to the king and queen.

'Will you give me the hand of your daughter?' he said.

They were appalled.

'What did you say?' asked Queen Cassiopeia.

'Is this some sort of joke?' said King Cepheus. 'Who are you and how dare you come here at this moment and make such a crude and cruel suggestion?'

'My name is Perseus, from the island of Seriphos in Greece. Yesterday I beheaded the Gorgon Medusa and today I will do the same for that monster if you will give me your daughter's hand in marriage.'

'You're mad!' said the king, his face turning red with fury. 'How could anyone kill Medusa? How could anyone kill that monster? He'd have to have wings. Someone get this lunatic out of my sight!'

'You have only moments to agree,' said Perseus, shaking off the hands that were beginning to grasp him and pointing at the monster, now within 50 metres of the rock. 'Give Andromeda to me or give her to the monster! Look at these, if you can't believe me!'

He showed the king his winged sandals, he drew the adamantine sickle and flourished it so that it sparkled like diamonds, then he put on the helmet and disappeared, only to remove it and reappear a moment later.

'In here,' he said patting the bat skin satchel, 'is Medusa's head, but if I showed you that you'd be turned to stone.'

'This is a god,' said the queen. 'Let him save her! Let him marry her!'

'Very well!' said the king. 'If you save her, you can have her!'

Perseus jumped straight off the cliff, putting on his helmet as he flew, so that the astounded spectators first saw a man transformed into a bird and then empty air, as if he had fallen to his death. Many were peering at the bottom of the cliff in search of his body, when somebody shrieked:

'Look!'

They saw the girl shrink back against the rock as the monster's huge head reared up towards her and, almost simultaneously, with a sudden flash of light from the adamantine sickle, they saw the monster's head fall away in a spray of blood, while its tail lashed the sea into a whirlpool of foam and its black coils sank slowly into the depths. Then they saw Perseus, his helmet in one hand, his sickle in the other, alight on the ledge beside the naked princess and speak to her for a moment before cutting the ropes that bound her to the rock.

Some storytellers have it that Perseus, after decapitating the monster, turned it to stone with the Gorgon's head. But how could that be when the monster no longer had eyes to see with, and where was the need? Perseus might, of course, have used the head rather than the sickle in the first place, but suppose the monster had had eyes only for the princess or the princess herself had also seen the face of Medusa? A stone princess would have been little better than a swallowed princess. No question, then, that the adamantine sickle was the weapon of choice and that the monster was not turned to stone but fed the fishes.

Perseus was by no means certain that his winged sandals would carry them both across the narrow gap between the outcrop and the cliff, especially since the cliff was much higher, but the way she looked at him with her green eyes and sweet smile, the mere thought of holding her naked body in his arms, made him determined to try. He had to put on his helmet again in order to have both arms free, so that all the crowd on the cliff saw was their naked princess rising through the air towards them, slowly but surely, her shapely bottom first, as the invisible Perseus, clasping her in a fireman's lift over one shoulder, willed his sandals not to fail him.

He got there, but made a poor landing, stumbling to his knees and almost dropping Andromeda. The queen's ladies-in-waiting hurried to take her from his arms and cover her with a cloak. Perseus removed his helmet and rose to his feet and as he did so the crowd drew back, muttering that this was indeed a god, most likely Hermes to judge by the winged sandals.

'Are you a god?' asked King Cepheus.

'No, I am not a god,' said Perseus, 'nor anything approaching one. But I give thanks to the immortals who lent me these sandals, this helmet, this sickle and this satchel, who directed me to this place and helped me do what I have done. They gave me no warning of your daughter's sacrifice, but since I arrived only just in time to save her, I don't think that can have been chance.'

'Well, whoever was my daughter's real saviour, you or the immortals,' said the king, 'we are grateful for what you have done. We will return now to our city and make sacrifices to the gods. And we invite you to join our celebrations.'

'I would not wish to claim your daughter's hand,' said Perseus, 'without asking her first. If she is unwilling, I will leave at once, but if she consents, then let us by all means celebrate our marriage as soon as possible.'

'You misunderstand me,' said the king. 'She will certainly be unwilling since she is already engaged to our neighbour, King Agenor.'

'You never mentioned that when I asked you for her hand in return for saving her,' said Perseus unhappily.

'Didn't I? It all happened so quickly. I was about to mention it when you leapt off the cliff. You left the words in my mouth.'

Perseus now understood what sort of man he was dealing with and began to be angry.

'I will remind you, sir, of exactly what you said: 'If you save her, you can have her'. Those words rang in my ears as I left the cliff, as I attacked the monster, as my blade cut through the monster's head and as I freed and lifted your daughter to safety. I find no room next to those words for further words taking back the promise you made.'

'I'm sorry,' said the king without any note of apology, 'but I'm afraid my obligation to King Agenor precedes any obligation I may have to you.'

'I think, on the contrary, that your words cancelled any previous obligation, but as I said before I will not marry your daughter without her consent. So let her choose between me and King Agenor.'

'She is in no state to make such a choice,' said the queen, 'and even if she were, I would have to forbid her to do so. She must marry King Agenor as arranged. We are obliged to you for your rescue and would like to show our gratitude by entertaining you in our palace, but let that be the end of the matter. You are a complete stranger to us and we cannot allow you on the strength of words uttered at a moment of extreme stress to claim a reward which is no longer ours to give.'

'Stranger I may be,' said Perseus, 'but I don't think any of your friends or relations were going to save your daughter from certain death. Your stress would have been a great deal more extreme if I had not arrived in the nick of time. She would not be marrying this King Agenor or anyone else. I think I have at least won the right to speak to the princess herself.'

At this point the crowd, which had been listening intently to the argument, began to join in. They were angry and ashamed at the double-dealing of their king and queen and impressed by Perseus' dignified restraint. Several shouted that the princess should be allowed to speak. Others remarked that it was entirely the queen's fault that many people had lost their lives or their livelihood and that her daughter had been exposed for the monster. As their mood grew uglier, the king said:

'We cannot resolve this matter here and now. Let us all return to the city! We will celebrate Andromeda's rescue and the stranger's courage in proper style and then, when she has rested and recovered from her ordeal, let the princess decide whom she wishes to marry.'

But as the crowd streamed away, carrying the princess and Perseus in triumph down to their nearby city, and as preparations were made for sacrifices to the gods and a public banquet in the *plateia*, the king sent a messenger to King Agenor telling him what had happened and advising him to come quickly and claim his bride.

Perseus too received a messenger as he sat among the people in the *plateia*, accepting their thanks and admiration and waiting for the celebrations to begin. One of the ladies-in-waiting who had been with the princess came and whispered to him that Andromeda had never consented to marry King Agenor. Her parents had constantly tried to persuade her, she said, and would probably in the end have compelled her, since they feared Agenor, who was a more powerful king and a fierce warrior. But Andromeda sent this message: if Perseus really loved her, nothing would make her happier than to be his wife, though she warned him that her parents and Agenor would do everything they could to prevent it and she did not want Perseus to risk his life for her a second time. Perseus told the woman to reply that he would prefer to lose his life than lose Andromeda.

The sacrifices had been completed, the meat was roasting, the wine was beginning to flow and all the citizens were toasting their princess and her saviour, seated with the king and queen at a special table in the centre of the *plateia*, when there was a sudden disturbance. The crowd scattered as a band of about fifty horsemen emerged from the main street and pulled up on one side of the *plateia*. Their leader, a heavily built middle-aged man with a thick black beard and a hawk's nose, jumped down from his horse and strode up to the table.

'Celebrations, are there?' he said. 'What is the occasion?'

Cepheus rose to greet him.

'Welcome, sir! You are just in time to join us. My daughter Andromeda was to be a sacrifice to the sea monster sent by Poseidon, but she was rescued by this young man at the very last moment.' Turning to Perseus, he said, 'This is King Agenor who, as I told you, is to marry our dear daughter.'

Perseus, unarmed except for his sickle and knife, looked at this large man in full armour and his retinue of armed warriors and knew that, whatever he said, Cepheus had so arranged it that Perseus must either fight or abandon his claim to marry Andromeda. He decided, therefore, that there was little point in trying to be polite or subtle with a person who looked and sounded and swaggered like a bully. The people would perhaps take his side but, nervously huddled at the edges of the *plateia,* they were unarmed and evidently already intimidated.

'You did tell me that,' said Perseus to Cepheus, 'but only after you had promised me that if I saved Andromeda's life you would give me her hand in marriage. That promise was made in the presence of many of your people and I regard it as binding.'

There was a subdued murmur of agreement from the crowd, but no one dared to stand out and be identified.

'Who is this whippersnapper?' said Agenor with a sarcastic smile.

'My name is Perseus.'

'And where did you spring from?'

'I was brought up on the island of Seriphos.'

'Never heard of it.'

'Probably not. But I was born in Argos, which I'm sure you *have* heard of, in the king my grandfather's palace.'

'And your father's name?'

'I believe it is Zeus.'

'You believe! Any puppy can believe that. It generally means that the mother was a whore.'

'Your offensive words,' said Perseus, 'and your brutish manners make it clear that you are no fit husband for the princess Andromeda. However, as far as I am concerned, in spite of her father's promise to me, the choice of husband must be hers.'

'Choice!' said Agenor. 'There is none. She is to marry me and I am here to take her.'

Perseus made no reply, but turned to look at Andromeda, still seated at the table. She looked at him for a moment, her green eyes shining, and smiled.

'I choose Perseus,' she said.

The people round the square drew in their breath. One or two clapped their hands in applause, but quickly stopped as they saw Agenor's hand go to his sword and his horsemen also touch their weapons. Many in the crowd began to slink away or prepare to do so. Cassiopeia whispered urgently to Andromeda. Cepheus said to Agenor:

'My daughter is naturally disturbed after her ordeal and grateful to the young man who saved her life. But you are right that she has no choice. She is to marry you.'

Perseus moved away from the table and stood face to face with Agenor. They were about the same height, but Perseus was half Agenor's width.

'What now, Agenor?' he said. 'Will you attempt to carry off the princess against her will and in spite of the promise made to me by her father? Or will you join our celebrations for Andromeda's escape from death and return to your own city in peace?'

'I will dispose of you, for a start, son of a whore,' said Agenor and drawing his sword from his belt thrust it at Perseus' midriff.

Perseus parried the stroke with the adamantine sickle. The sickle cut through Agenor's bronze blade and left him holding little more than the hilt. Astonished and dismayed, he flung the useless weapon down on the flagstones and retreated a few paces, as a muted cheer went up from the citizens.

'You take his side, do you, miserable people?' shouted Agenor. 'You will regret it when your homes are burnt and you are made slaves.'

He gestured to his warriors, who advanced further into the square, while one of them trotted forward and handed him another sword. Perseus, meanwhile, had stood his ground but made no attempt to attack his disarmed opponent, hoping that he might accept defeat without bloodshed. Seeing that he did not and that he was now again armed, Perseus ran at him and, dodging Agenor's sword, severed the hand that held it. Bellowing with pain and fury and with blood pouring from his wound, Agenor staggered backwards.

'Kill them! Kill them all!' he shouted to his warriors.

Most of the people began running away. The king and queen and their attendants, still seated at their table, rose and hurried towards the palace, but Andromeda would not go with them. She never took her eyes off Perseus and so was almost the only person, except for a few of the fugitives glancing in terror over their shoulders as they ran, who saw Perseus put on the helmet of Hades and vanish. Then, as the horsemen surged across the *plateia* and pulled up in confusion at Perseus' disappearance, she saw a fearful head with snaky hair rise suddenly into the air, its face, invisible to her, directed at the horsemen. And as they saw it, they froze, they and their horses, and turned to stone. To begin with, there were a few exceptions, horses which hadn't looked at the head and remained alive with stone riders on their backs, or living men whose legs were suddenly gripping stony flanks, but within a few minutes all were calcified.

Agenor himself, slumped against a monument at the centre of the *plateia*, trying to stanch his bleeding wrist, did not immediately look up; and so had time, as he raised his eyes in the sudden absence of hoofbeats, shouts and the snorting of horses, to see his stone warriors all around him, before he too, utterly bewildered, looking for Perseus, caught sight of Medusa's face hanging in the air and instantly became part of the monument he rested on.

Slowly in the silence the people filtered back, gazing with disbelief, shaking their heads, speaking in hushed voices, to see the fifty equestrian statues and the petrified but still life-like fallen king with the missing hand which their *plateia* had so suddenly acquired. Perseus, visible again without his helmet and having restored Medusa's head to his satchel, took Andromeda for the second time in his arms. Cepheus and Cassiopeia came out of their palace and, concealing their chagrin as best they could, ordered their herald to announce the wedding of their daughter to her saviour, who had also, single-handed, saved the city.

6. THE RETURN

As soon as the wedding had been celebrated, Perseus told his still shamefaced parents-in-law that he must return to his island and that Andromeda wished to go with him. There was no question of his winged sandals carrying them both over such a distance, so Cepheus provided his own stout sailing ship with 30 oarsmen to sail across the Ionian Sea and round the Peloponnese to Seriphos. He was glad enough to be rid of a son-in-law whose popularity far surpassed his own, even at the price of losing his daughter.

Before leaving, Perseus made sacrifices to Athene and Hermes, begging them to take his part with Poseidon, who might otherwise wish to revenge himself for the killing of his monster by rousing a storm and sinking their ship. He also made a sacrifice to Poseidon, pleading with him that it was not Andromeda but her mother who had insulted the Nereids. As their ship left harbour it was escorted for several miles by a school of dolphins, and Perseus took this to be Poseidon's sign of forgiveness. At any rate, the wind favoured them and their voyage was calm and swift.

The ship landed Perseus and Andromeda early in the morning on Diktys' side of the island, but the beach was deserted. Perseus led his bride immediately to Diktys' house and found it barricaded, with several villagers keeping watch outside. As soon as they saw Perseus, the door was unbolted and Diktys came out.

'My mother?' asked Perseus.

'Safe inside,' said Diktys, 'but not for long. My brother has announced that he will marry her, whether she agrees or not, and that he will come for her tomorrow. Tonight he is celebrating with his friends and we, as you see, are making what preparations we can to resist him. It's a miracle that you've arrived just in time to help us, but I'm afraid we are too few to hold out long against the numbers and weapons he can command.'

'Since I last saw you,' said Perseus, 'I have cut off Medusa's head, I have done the same to a sea monster that was sent to devour this princess, and I have defeated a force of 50 armed horsemen whose king wished to make her his wife against her will. I tell you this not to boast of my exploits but to show you that I will never let Polydektes have his way with my mother.'

After embracing Danaë, introducing her to Andromeda and thanking the sailors, who were sent home to Sicily with fresh provisions and polite greetings to Andromeda's parents, Perseus went up to the temple of Athene to make a sacrifice. He hoped that she or Hermes might appear to him again and give him instructions, but when they did not, told himself that gods do not intervene when they have no need to and that therefore he must act as he thought best and assume that they approved.

Taking leave of Andromeda, Danaë and Diktys, he set off alone over the hill to Polydektes' house, wearing the winged sandals and carrying the helmet of Hades and the satchel containing Medusa's head, with the adamantine sickle in his belt. He did not fly or wear the helmet because he considered that these magical things should be used only in emergencies and he had plenty of time to cross the island in the normal way. When he came in sight of the town he sat down for a while, waiting for the sun to set. He did not want anyone to recognise him before he entered Polydektes' hall.

As soon as it was dark he put on the helmet and entered the town. Already he could hear the noise and see the lights of Polydektes' celebration. The outer door of the house was open and the servants either side of it, sensing the presence of something solid, a displacement of air, but seeing nothing, looked at each other with startled faces as he passed between them. Perseus entered the hall, where Polydektes' friends and supporters, twenty or more of them, were reclining at the long table while servants brought them food and wine. Polydektes himself was at the far end, his face flushed, his voice loud and triumphant as he raised his cup of wine.

'To my lovely bride of tomorrow!' he shouted and all his guests raised their cups and repeated the toast.

Perseus, standing just inside the entrance, removed his helmet and waited. He waited some time, since they were all so intent on their food and drink and loud conversation that no one looked up or, if they did, assumed that this silent standing figure was a servant or the steward. At last, one of the servants, brushing past him with a dish of octopus, glanced at his face and immediately recognised him as the youth they had all long since given up for dead.

'Perseus!' he said, loud enough to be heard by the nearest diners.

And as they and then their neighbours glanced his way and fell silent, the conversation gradually died away all down the table.

'What is the matter?' shouted Polydektes from his place at the end, still oblivious of the intruder.

'Perseus is here,' said the man on his left.

'Perseus, Perseus!' repeated the guests.

Polydektes rose to his feet.

'Perseus!' he said. 'Welcome to our feast, dear boy! You crown our celebration. I shall marry your mother in the morning.'

'I don't think so,' said Perseus.

'What? Have you come home to tell me that you've failed in your task?'

'No, I've brought you what you asked for.'

'Have you indeed? A horse, is it? A little gold? I asked you for something a bit more special than that. Remember?'

'I remember very well. I have brought you the head of Medusa.'

Polydektes laughed and all his guests laughed with him. Perseus held up the bat-skin satchel.

'Here it is,' he said.

Polydektes laughed again.

'What a liar!' he said. 'Your trip abroad has not improved your character, Perseus. You used to be a truthful boy.'

'When I left Seriphos,' said Perseus, 'it was to fetch the head of Medusa so that you could take it to King Oinomaos of Elis and win the hand of his daughter Hippodameia. Now you say that you will marry my mother against her will. It seems that you are the liar.'

'No one calls me a liar,' said Polydektes, 'you had better withdraw that word or you'll regret it.'

'I will certainly withdraw it if you can say that you will not marry my mother.'

'Of course I shall marry her. Take this insolent boy out of my hall and give him a thrashing!'

Two servants moved uncertainly towards Perseus, but he pushed them aside.

'Must I show you what I've brought?'

'You're beginning to annoy me!' said Polydektes, picking up his knife. 'Liars should have their tongues cut out, and that's what I'm going to do to you.'

He left his place and moved up the table towards Perseus, while his guests gloatingly encouraged him.

'Do it, do it, Polydektes!'

'Get hold of the little bastard!' said Polydektes, brandishing his knife.

Many of the guests were now on their feet, but none quite dared to lay hands on Perseus. Even Polydektes stopped and stared as Perseus, holding his helmet under one arm, loosened the top of the satchel and put his hand inside.

'This is what I promised to bring you,' said Perseus. 'Do you really want to see it?'

'Yes, let's see it!' said Polydektes, 'Whatever you've faked up to look like the Gorgon's head. But don't think that's going to save your lying tongue or prevent me marrying your mother!'

Perseus pulled the head out of the satchel and held it up.

'This is the head of Medusa!'

They hardly had time to gasp before they were turned to stone, every person in the room, Polydektes, his guests and his servants, all except Perseus himself. Only the servants outside the room, those working in the kitchen or fetching more food and wine or guarding the doors, were spared, as Perseus put the head back in the satchel and left the house. What the servants saw when they did enter the silent room was soon spread round the town and all over the island, and eventually far beyond the island, so that long afterwards people came from all over Greece to gape at this interrupted feast, this silent assembly of guests with their mouths open in astonishment and terror, these wide-eyed servants bearing trays or wine jugs, and the angry, derisive host waving his knife, set for ever in stone.

7. THE GRANDFATHER

Perseus had no wish to stay any longer on the island. Most people were glad to be rid of Polydektes and elected his brother Diktys to be king in his place, but some who had lost relatives at the feast could not forgive Perseus. Every small community, of course, is full of private quarrels and resentments, but on an island as small as Seriphos they are harder to live with, and Perseus and his mother were still regarded as strangers. They decided to return to Argos so that Danaë could see her parents again and Perseus could introduce his lovely wife Andromeda to his grandfather and claim his place as heir to the kingdom. Akrisios had never told Danaë why he had set her adrift in the chest, and she believed it was because he was ashamed of a daughter who had borne an illegitimate child. She was sure that as soon as he met Perseus and Andromeda and heard the story of Perseus' heroic deeds, her father would easily forget the past and rejoice in the survival of his daughter and grandson.

Diktys provided a ship, which sailed up the Gulf and landed them at Nauplia, from where they immediately sent a messenger ahead to Argos to bring the good tidings to Akrisios. Poor king! Never did a messenger carrying what seemed the best of news meet with such a rebuff, such an expression of shock and dismay. By the time Danaë, Perseus and Andromeda arrived at Argos, not far behind the messenger, Akrisios was gone. He had remembered that Teutamidas, the new King of Larissa, far to the north in Thessaly, was holding funeral games in honour of his dead father, to which he had invited Akrisios among others. It was left to Queen Eurydice to explain to her daughter and grandson and her grandson's wife that her husband was urgently called away and much regretted not being able to receive them. She did not, however, explain the real reason for his absence – he had forbidden her to do that – with the result that Perseus decided that he too, as heir apparent to the kingdom of Argos, must follow his grandfather and also attend the games, so as to compete for prizes with all the other young princes of Greece. His grandmother failed to dissuade him, since she could give no good reason except that he must have had enough travelling already, and in any case felt that her husband's fate, after so many abortive attempts to evade it, was inexorable. Was he never to return to Argos as long as his grandson was there? Or would he try once again, deviously or directly, to get rid of Perseus? She hoped, of course, that the whole notion of him being killed by his grandson was false, that the oracle had been wrong or he had misunderstood it, and that if only the two could meet, all would be well and the dark cloud that had hung over their lives so long would be dispelled at last. She loved her husband, but she doted on Perseus from the moment she saw him, and was sure Akrisios would too.

Before leaving for Larissa, Perseus went up to a small, bare, conical hill, set among higher hills to the north-east of Argos. He had dreamed of it several nights running but never been there before. On top of the hill he made sacrifices to Athene and Hermes, asking them whether he should now return the adamantine sickle, the bat skin satchel and the dragon skin helmet to the Stygian Nymphs, and what he should do with the head of Medusa and the winged sandals. When he had made the sacrifices and sent his attendants back to Argos, he spent the night alone on the hill with the magical objects beside him and dreamt that he heard heavenly music. He woke to find that it was growing light and that the music continued. Hermes in his shepherd's hat and cloak was sitting near him, playing the lyre which he had himself invented by stringing lengths of sheep gut across the shell of a tortoise, over which he had stretched ox-hide. Perseus closed his eyes again and pretended still to be asleep, not wanting the music ever to stop, but Hermes laughed and slung the lyre over his back.

'It was meant to wake you up, not send you back to sleep,' he said.

'I wish you would play more,' said Perseus.

'Of course you do. It is not music you could ever hear enough of. The more I played, the more you would ask for more until you became so addicted to it that you'd be good for nothing else. Before you die I will play for you once again, but not today.'

'You've come to take back these borrowed things?'

'Yes, I will give Medusa's head to Athene to wear on her *aigis*, and return the sickle, the satchel and the helmet to the Stygian Nymphs.'

'I promised to return them myself.'

'I wouldn't advise it.'

'Shouldn't one keep promises?'

'In general, yes. But those nymphs would never let you go.'

'I'm sorry I lost the polished shield.'

'It served its purpose.'

'I still feel badly about those nymphs.'

'You have other purposes to serve. In the first place, your wife Andromeda and your descendants, one of whom will be an even greater hero than you. In the second place, when your grandfather dies, which will happen quite soon, you are to end the long quarrel between him and his brother Proetos by giving the kingdom of Argos to your cousin, Proetos' son, Megapenthes.'

'Am I to have no kingdom of my own to hand on to my descendants?'

'In return he will give you Tiryns, which he governs now, and you will build it into a great fortress. You will also ask him to give you this little hill and he will willingly do so.'

'I should think so. What use is this hill to anyone?'

'You will build another fortress here, commanding with Tiryns not only the plain of Argos, but the road between the Gulf of Argos to the south and the Gulf of Corinth to the north. This hill, called Mycenae, will make your descendants and successors, kings of the triple fortress cities of Argos, Tiryns and Mycenae, the richest and most powerful rulers in the whole of Greece.'

'Shall I see you again?'

'Perhaps.'

'And the great goddess Athene?'

'Perhaps.'

Hermes gathered up the precious objects, smiled and was gone. Perseus stood for a while on the hill looking sadly at the place where the god had sat and trying to hear the music again in his mind. Then he shook himself, went down the hill and walked across the plain to Argos.

When he reached Larissa he found that he was famous. His killing of Medusa and his rescue of Andromeda from the sea-monster had already begun to be told by storytellers with embellishments of their own. But try as he might, he couldn't meet his grandfather Akrisios, who had always just left the palace or was sleeping and couldn't be disturbed or was somewhere in the crowd watching one of the events at the funeral games. Perseus took part in several events – running, riding, boxing, wrestling, javelin throwing – without success. He had never been trained as an athlete and was up against the best performers in Greece. But he did better with the discus, although he had never thrown it before – perhaps his practice at aeronautics had given his body the necessary flexibility – and reached the final. Alas, trying too hard to put extra strength into his throw, he lost his balance and the heavy stone discus flew prematurely out of his hand and into the crowd of spectators, where it fatally injured an old man. Perseus, in great distress, ran to where the old man was lying on the grass and knelt beside him.

'Does anyone know who he is?' he asked the people around.

'Everyone knows him,' they said. 'He is a great king.'

'Then why is he here in the crowd and not in the royal enclosure with the King of Larissa?'

'He always seemed to be hiding,' they said.

'Why should he do that?'

'Nobody knows why.'

'What is his name?' asked Perseus.

'Akrisios, King of Argos,' they said.

'My grandfather!'

Perseus, in tears, bent down to kiss his grandfather's face, bloodied from the terrible wound in his head. As he did so, the old man opened his eyes and his lips moved.

'Perseus!' he seemed to say with his last breath.

Looking up from our Arcadian terrace in the autumn I can see the constellations of Perseus and Andromeda directly overhead, with Cassiopeia and Cepheus next to them. Why should Perseus' baleful parents-in-law have deserved this honour, when famous heroes like Jason and Theseus did not? However, it was not the gods or even such early astronomers as the unlucky brothers Atreus and Thyestes who named the classical constellations, but the much later astronomer, mathematician and geographer Claudius Ptolemaeus. Ptolemy, as he's generally known, lived in Alexandria in the middle of the second century AD and made a catalogue of more than a thousand stars. It must have been a wearisome business trying to fit those myriad pin-pricks of light into recognisable configurations, and perhaps when it came to the Perseus group he was at the end of a long night's star-gazing and glad to knock off four constellations at a blow regardless of merit.

THESEUS

1. THE STONE

Theseus does not rate a constellation, although, next to Herakles, he is the most famous hero of all. King of Athens, killer of the Minotaur, deserter of Ariadne, husband of Ariadne's sister Phaedra, abductor of the underage Helen, living visitor to Hades, lover of an Amazon queen and indirect murderer of their son Hippolytos, his record is perhaps too mixed, his heroic deeds too compounded with human error. Or it may have been simply that he came too late, long after Perseus, in the wake of Herakles, belonging to a generation which no longer had close contact with the gods. None of the generation immediately following his, the heroes of the Trojan War, became constellations, not even Achilles. Their world was already sliding from myth into history and we name only streets or squares, not stars, after historical heroes.

Theseus was born on the 'Claw', the easternmost of the four principal Peloponnesian peninsulas, in a city called Troezen, cut off from neighbouring Argolis by the mountains we see from our terrace on the other side of the Gulf of Argos – Mavrovouni, Ortholithi and Didymo. Even as late as 1959, when I first visited Greece, there was no motor-road connecting Troezen to Argos, as there was none connecting our village under the Parnon mountains to anywhere beyond Kynouria. Such places were accessible only by sea or donkey or on foot. Troezen always had less association with Argos than with Athens, just across the Saronic Gulf, and to this day its district is administered from the Athenian port of Peiraias. It was in Troezen that Aigisthos took refuge from his cousin Agamemnon, and it was here that Agamemnon's son Orestes came to be purified after killing his mother Clytemnestra and his cousin Aigisthos. Built on the lower slopes of a mountain, enclosed by mountains, Troezen overlooks a fertile plain and a large harbour sheltered by the island of Poros.

Theseus' grandfather, Pittheus, a son of Pelops, was King of Troezen and famous for his wisdom. His only daughter Aithra was engaged to be married to the Corinthian prince Bellerophon, who, riding the winged horse Pegasos, had killed the monstrous Chimaera (a fire-breathing goat with a lion's head and a serpent tail) and performed other heroic deeds. Unfortunately, whether out of curiosity or vainglory or both, he made Pegasos fly him up to the home of the gods on Mount Olympos. Zeus sent a gadfly to sting Pegasos under his tail, Pegasos bucked and rolled like an aircraft in a severe patch of turbulence and flung his rider back to earth. Pegasos flew on to Olympos, where Zeus employed him as a thunderbolt carrier, an early version of the mules which used to carry mountain artillery up to the north-west frontier of India and other remote parts of the British Empire. Bellerophon landed in a thorn bush and survived, but lost his memory and became a miserable vagabond, lame, blind and outcast.

When he failed to turn up to claim his bride, King Pittheus was caught in a dilemma. He did not know what had happened to Bellerophon and assumed that, like many heroes, he might be delayed indefinitely by difficult and dangerous adventures. But Pittheus wanted grandchildren, since he had no son, and his daughter might grow too old if she had to wait too long. His solution was irregular but effective. During a long visit to Troezen by his old friend Aegeus, temporarily exiled from Athens, Pittheus made him drunk and then helped him to bed in Aithra's room instead of his own. Theseus was the result, and Pittheus must have told his friend what he had done, since when Aegeus eventually returned to Athens, he gave instructions to Aithra that if the child was a boy and grew up to be sufficiently strong and intelligent, she was to send him to Athens to be heir to the kingdom of Athens as well as Troezen. How was she to know if he was sufficiently strong and intelligent? Aegeus said that he had concealed his own sword and sandals under a stone and if Theseus could recover them that would prove he was made of the right stuff.

The ancient city of Troezen stood a little to the north of the modern village of Trizina and there are still a few relics of it: one of the towers from the city wall, a temple to the Muses (where Pittheus reputedly taught the art of oratory), some sort of Asclepian complex – a clinic or a health and gymnastic centre – and the stone of Theseus. Except that it cannot be the stone, being far too insignificant and unremarkable and hardly capable of concealing a single sandal, let alone a sword. Some two feet high and four feet long, mainly rectangular, with a bite out of one side, it is more likely to have been a piece of the city wall, which to judge by the tower was made of the same hefty blocks as Tiryns.

Theseus grew up in awe of his cousin Herakles' exploits and by the age of sixteen was determined to rival them. He was not, of course, as strong as Herakles – nobody was – nor was he the son of Zeus, though the Troezenians later claimed that his real father was not Aegeus but Poseidon and contrived an elaborate story in which Poseidon slept with Aithra on the same night as the drunken Aegeus. Since this was not unlike the story of Zeus sleeping with Herakles' mother on the same night as her husband Amphitryon, Theseus himself may have been its original author. But what he lacked of Herakles' superhuman strength and divine assistance (but also divine obstruction from Hera), Theseus made up for with his sharp intelligence, persuasive charm and the gifts for organisation and public relations which he had perhaps inherited from his wise grandfather. Herakles was too much of a maverick ever to be a king, but Theseus was a born leader.

When his mother told him about the sword and sandals under the stone, Theseus immediately set about finding them. It took him the best part of six months, as anyone who has ever walked in the Greek mountains will readily understand. A sword under a stone in that part of the world is roughly equivalent to a needle in a haystack in more arable places. Theseus characteristically conducted his search in an orderly sequence. He began with the road his father Aegeus had followed down to the harbour from which he had sailed back to Athens. Theseus did not really expect to find anything there, considering how many people must have travelled back and forth along the road in the more than sixteen years since Aegeus' departure, but he needed to eliminate it before fanning out in an ever-widening circle round the city. His patience was inexhaustible. He perfectly understood that if his father's test was in the last resort that of the strength to move the stone – and he was quite certain that his own strength was at least equal to Aegeus' – its main purpose was to prove that he had the rarer qualities of determination, persistence, percipience and self-control.

Having examined and occasionally lifted or shifted every large stone on the lower slopes of the mountain within a radius of about a mile round Troezen, Theseus began to climb higher. He couldn't now follow a circular pattern, so he divided his search into vertical segments, probing the sides of each valley before following the stream that had created the valley up to its source near the top of the mountain. His mother and grandfather observed his efforts with admiration and pride.

'That boy will go far,' said Pittheus. 'Day after day, week after week, he comes back tired and empty-handed, but never shows the slightest disappointment or frustration.'

'I asked him about that,' said Aithra, 'how he could keep searching and never finding. He looked at me with surprise. 'But I do keep finding, mother,' he said. 'Every day I find another area where it isn't and can tick that off my list.''

'Remarkable!' said the wise and cultivated Pittheus. 'He already understands the value of the negative in the discovery of the positive, the contribution of the pause to the effectiveness of speech and of rests to the beauty of music.'

One day Theseus began exploring the valley immediately above Troezen, where an aqueduct brought water from the plentiful springs high above directly into the city. After eliminating the sides of the valley, he took the path that followed the aqueduct up to where it crossed the stream on a narrow, single-arched bridge, known now as the Devil's Bridge, though the ancient Greeks knew nothing of the Devil. Their world was full of malevolent monsters and bad people, some of whom Theseus was soon to meet, but they happily lacked the concept of any guiding evil spirit in the universe.

The stream far below the bridge was a tumble of boulders and Theseus had decided to climb right to the top of it and then descend boulder by boulder. He crossed the bridge and took the path that led upwards, still high above the stream-bed, among plane trees and oleanders. After a while the banks of the stream became less steep and the path closer to the water. Hot and thirsty, Theseus left the path and clambered down to a lovely place, shaded by the trees, where the stream briefly paused in its descent and formed a pool. Theseus drank from the water spouting down into the pool, then took off his tunic and bathed in the pool, afterwards choosing a huge boulder in the sun on which to sit and dry himself. As he slid off it, he felt it tilt a little and realised that in the pleasure of bathing and sunning himself he had not thought to check underneath it. When he did so, he saw that although the upper part where he had been sitting was almost spherical, the underneath was cleft like a giant's buttocks, with the two stone cheeks resting unevenly on the sloping rock below. Warily, in case this was the hiding place of some unpleasant creature, he put his hand into the dark cavity under the boulder and touched what might, he feared, be a snake. Nevertheless, he grasped it and pulled it into the light. He was holding the thong of a sandal. He pulled the whole sandal out and felt in the cavity again and brought out a second sandal. His heart beat fast with excitement. He stared at the two sandals for a long time in silence and joy. They were no ordinary sandals, but made of the finest leather, royal sandals, and they looked pristine. They had kept dry in their hiding-place above the water and the sun had never reached them to fade their ox-blood colour.

Theseus sat down on the pebbles bordering the pool and tied the sandals on to his feet. They fitted him perfectly. He stood up and walked to and fro over the pebbles. He was deliberately holding back, not immediately putting his hand into the cavity again, so as to prolong his enjoyment of the sandals and the promise they held that he would also find the sword. When he did finally reach into the cavity his hand felt the hilt he expected, but he couldn't draw it out. The blade was stuck fast under one cheek of the boulder's bottom. Perhaps his father had thrust it in deep on purpose, or the boulder had shifted over time, or he himself had pinned it there when he tilted the boulder in sliding off it. He put his shoulder to the stone and tilted it again, but the sword was still immoveable. His hero Herakles would simply have lifted the boulder and flung it aside, but Theseus lacked that level of strength. He made a few more attempts to shift it by brute force, then resorted to mechanics. Selecting a flattish stone he hammered it under the boulder with a rounded stone, then did the same with another and another. At last when he put his hand into the cleft and grasped the sword's hilt, it came free. With blood pouring from his hand where he had scraped it, he drew the sword out and saw that its ivory hilt was carved with the serpents of the House of Erechtheus, the royal line of Athens. Triumphant, he flourished the sword once in the air, thanked the gods, washed his bleeding hand in the pool, took off the sandals, put on his tunic, and carrying the sandals and the sword walked quietly and thoughtfully, without haste, down the path to Troezen.

He was already planning his next move, and when he had shown his finds to his mother and grandfather, he surprised them both. They had expected him to want to go straight to Athens to meet his father, and Pittheus said that he would send him in his own royal ship, so that he might be received on arrival at Peiraias with proper ceremony. But Theseus thanked his grandfather and said that he did not mean to leave at once, but to spend another year at least in training.

'Training for what, dear boy?'

'For the journey.'

'There's nothing to the journey. It's very short. My sailors are well accustomed to it and you will be required to do nothing but walk on to the ship and walk off it again the other end.'

'That's why I mean to go by land.'

'Go by land! That's crazy. It will take you weeks, if not months, to go round by land, and besides there are several notorious brigands along the route. You would need a very strong escort of soldiers to protect you and I don't see my way to providing them when you can so easily go by sea.'

'I don't want an escort, not even a single servant.'

'Then you will certainly be murdered.'

'That's why I need to train.'

'I really don't understand your reasoning.'

'It's simple. If I turn up in Athens in a royal ship, with a pair of my father's sandals and his sword, which I found under a stone with no great difficulty, what have I done? Who am I? Theseus, son of Aegeus, grandson of Pittheus. Good! I'm most fortunate and much honoured to have such a noble heredity. But none of this is mine, is it? Not the birth, not the ship, not the sandals, not the sword, not even the name Theseus. All borrowed, lent to me on account. I mean to pay part of the account on my journey to Athens, so that when I arrive people will not be saying, 'Theseus, who's he?' 'Oh, the son of Aegeus, the grandson of Pittheus, born with a silver spoon in his mouth, comes from Troezen, found his father's sandals and swords under a stone, and now he's heir to two kingdoms, lucky bastard!' No, when I arrive in Athens, let them just say, 'Theseus? He's the man that cleared the road of all those killers and by the way he's Herakles' cousin'.'

So for more than a year Theseus exercised his body with weight-lifting, running and jumping, and honed his skills at wrestling, archery and swordplay, learning from all the best athletes and warriors in Troezen, until he was confident that he had enhanced his natural abilities beyond all competition. Observing his reflection in a polished shield he saw with satisfaction that the slim youth who had failed to push aside the boulder now looked a little more like the image he retained from his childhood of his cousin Herakles, who had once visited Troezen. Finally, Theseus walked up the path beside the aqueduct, crossed the bridge and returned to the boulder. Then, after washing himself, glancing with approval at his muscular reflection in the pool, and praying to Poseidon, who had loved Pelops and who he had come to believe looked with favour on himself, Pelops' descendant, he went to the boulder, exerted all his strength and rolled it off its shelf of rock into the pool. He was ready now to make the journey to Athens.

2. THE JOURNEY

The first part of the journey, northwards between Mounts Ortholithi and Mavrovouni, was not especially difficult, but descending towards the sea at Epidauros Theseus encountered a huge hairy hunchback called Periphetes, who demanded a fee and brandished a formidable club bound round with hoops of bronze.

'How much?' asked Theseus.

'Your pack,' said Periphetes, circling round him greedily, 'and that nice-looking sword in your belt and those pretty red sandals hanging beside it and the belt itself. And, of course, your gold, which I can't see but which you've surely got hidden somewhere.'

'Will you leave me nothing?' said Theseus plaintively. 'I have a long journey ahead of me.'

'I'm sorry for you. You'll meet a lot of nasty people and if I don't take your things someone else will, so you might as well get rid of them now and avoid the trouble of carrying them. It's a favour I'm doing you.'

'You're too kind. But if I had a club like yours ...'

'Oh, indeed! This is a nice little club, well balanced, and does its business very sweetly. This club could take you out of trouble anywhere if you were strong enough to swing it.'

'So what price your club?'

'What price! This club will cost you your life, cheeky boy, if you make any more jokes of that sort.'

'Come on, then! Let's have it!'

Periphetes looked at him popeyed, not quite believing that this youth who had seemed so anxious to please was really asking to be pulped, then swung his club almost nonchalantly at Theseus' head. But Theseus was too quick for him. His head was no longer where it had been a second earlier, but butting hard into Periphetes' stomach, knocking him flat on the ground, while his club flew out of his hand. Theseus picked it up and, as Periphetes struggled to his feet, swung it.

'Cheap at the price of your life,' he said and struck him dead.

After that, with the club balanced on one shoulder just in the way Herakles carried his, Theseus continued his journey round the coast to Corinth. In the middle of the Isthmus, between the two seas, in a grove of pine trees, he met a robber called Sinis. Sinis was a tall and very strong man with a ready smile, who pretended to be a friend to travellers. When he saw one coming he would lasso the top of a pine tree and bend it down to the ground. Then he would say to the traveller:

'Welcome, my friend! You must be tired and hungry. Let me offer you something tasty! Just hold this while I get it for you! It's well secured, you see,' pointing to the rope wound round another tree-trunk.

But as soon as the traveller did as he said, Sinis released the rope. The pine sprang up, the traveller was catapulted into the air and fell down dead or stunned. However, if the traveller declined his offer, Sinis would knock him senseless, bend down a second tree close to the first and tie one of the traveller's arms to each tree. He would wait until the traveller recovered consciousness, remark smilingly, 'Feeling a bit better, son?' and release the trees, so that his victim was torn apart. Either way Sinis finished him off, if necessary, with his knife, robbed him of anything of value and threw his corpse into the sea.

Theseus pretended not to understand Sinis.

'You want me to hold this tree for you?'

'That's right. Just for a minute or two while I fetch you refreshment. Quite free. Nothing to pay. I love to send travellers merrily on their way.'

'Very kind of you. But what's your purpose with this tree?'

'To hold it down.'

'Why?'

Sinis looked at him suspiciously. This traveller, he thought, might have to be treated to Plan B, but he didn't like the look of his club.

'So that I can trim it,' he said.

'Oh, really? I didn't know pine trees needed trimming. But just show me what's the best way I can hold it for you,' said Theseus, edging round to get close to the rope wound round the other tree.

Sinis sat on the bent tree and smiled genially.

'Like this,' he said. 'Simple as simple.'

'People must be simple to be taken in by that,' said Theseus, releasing the rope. 'Or else they lose their wits at the thought of a free lunch.'

The pine sprang, Sinis flew through the air, hit another tree and lay spreadeagled in its branches. Theseus shinned up the tree to make sure he was dead and left him there.

'A free lunch for the crows,' he said, going towards Sinis' hut on the far side of the grove of trees to see if he really had anything to eat. But as he did so he saw somebody run out and disappear into a patch of undergrowth. Grasping his club he kept quite still, scanning the undergrowth until he saw one of the bushes move. Then he ran forward, pounced, and pulled out a young girl of about fifteen, trembling with terror, her dress ragged and dirty, her black hair tangled.

'Are you that man's slave?' he asked, pointing to the body in the tree.

She shook her head.

'What then? His wife?'

'He's my father.'

'Sorry about that, but I have to say that he's no loss to anybody but you. And he doesn't seem to have looked after you very well.'

'I hate him,' she said.

'Then you're well rid of him. Is there anything to eat in your hut?'

'Some bread. A few olives.'

'Nothing else?'

'We live mostly on whatever travellers have in their packs and the last few haven't had much.'

'Well, bring out what there is! All his talk of food has made me hungry.'

'I thought you would kill me.'

'I'm only interested in killing monsters.'

Sitting on the ground, they shared the food. The girl, who was called Perigune, had seen many travellers murdered by her father, but she had never seen one as handsome as Theseus with his long fair hair, blue eyes, long legs and perfectly tuned athlete's body. He was equally attracted to her, not because she was beautiful – she was thin and malnourished – but because up to now he had had nothing to do with women, apart from his mother, and was suddenly overcome with lust. He did not jump on her and rape her, however, but asked her what she would do now that her father was dead. She shrugged her shoulders, she had no idea, so Theseus invited her to go with him. Perigune smiled for the first time and showed Theseus where her father had hidden the coins and jewellery he had stolen from travellers. He told her to gather them up and bring them.

'They're not strictly yours,' he said, 'but their rightful owners have no need of them any more and they will help you get yourself a husband.'

'I don't want a husband,' said the girl.

'You won't survive without one,' said Theseus. 'This world, as far as I can judge, is made for men.'

They left the ill-omened hut and the body of its owner in the pine tree and walked on together across the Isthmus until they came to a pleasant place near the sea. There they bathed in a stream, looked longingly at each other's bodies and, inexperienced as they were, began to touch and caress each other, before lying down together and making love in the light of a full moon. It was a painful and difficult process for both of them, especially Perigune, but in the days ahead, as they went eastwards along the coast, stopping at villages to buy food but sleeping always in the open, they got better at their love-making and were soon stopping more and more often to attend to it.

'Now I have a husband,' said Perigune happily, 'and I shan't need all those valuables. Won't you take them?'

'Better you keep them,' said Theseus. 'It's a cruel world.'

One day they came to a village called Krommyon where all the people were indoors or in their courtyards and the fields were untended. They were being terrorised, it seemed, by a sow, which had killed several farmers when they were out working in their fields.

'A sow?' said Theseus. 'I've heard of a wild boar killing people – the Erymanthian Boar captured by Herakles – but does a sow even have tusks? How can it kill people?'

They told him that this was no ordinary sow, but a sister of the Erymanthian boar and child of the giant Typhon and the monster Echidna, mother of many other monsters, including Cerberos, the Lernaian Hydra and the Nemean Lion. This sow was as big and fierce as a wild bull. It would charge and knock a man down, then trample his face with its hooves and tear away the flesh with its teeth. Theseus did not quite believe them, but he promised to delay his journey for a week or two and rid them of the sow if he could meet it. He and Perigune, whom he introduced as his wife, were given the best room in one of the villagers' houses, while Theseus spent the days roaming the empty fields with his club and sword at the ready.

He had almost given up and was standing idly picking his teeth at the edge of a field, when just behind him he heard a crashing of bushes and was only just in time to fling himself sideways as the huge creature emerged and charged. It turned in a moment and would have been on top of him if Perigune, who had come out to call him in to supper, had not shouted in dismay and momentarily distracted its attention. Theseus leapt to his feet, stepped deftly sideways and brought his club down on the sow's snout. Roaring with pain and fury, a mass of livid flesh thinly covered with black bristles, with glaring red eyes and great teeth that looked more like those of a lion than a pig, it charged him again. Theseus stood his ground and at the last moment, grasping his club with both hands, brought it down with all his strength on the monster's skull. It stopped within an inch of him, shivered the length of its body and collapsed.

'Thank you, Periphetes,' he said to the club, which he had named after its previous owner, and kissed it. Then, drawing his sword, he thrust it through the sow's throat.

The villagers held a great celebration, including a monster pig roast. The flesh, however, was not very sweet – the sow, after all, had been mainly carnivorous and was almost as old as the hills, though it had only been preying on this village for the last two or three years – and several people fell ill the next day, including Perigune. Theseus was eager to continue his journey and asked if the village would take care of her until he could send for her, which, of course, they were most willing to do considering what he had done for them. Perigune was desperate not to be left behind, but she could hardly stand up and was clearly unfit to travel. Theseus refused to delay his departure, and although he never did send for her and probably never saw her again, he did make arrangements, as soon as he reached Athens, for her to marry one of the villagers. It was said that Theseus was the father of her first child.

Beyond Krommyon the mountain of Geraneia blocked the way to Athens and the rest of Greece. The road, such as it was, ascended steeply and became little more than a path on a ledge high above sheer cliffs. Here Theseus met, as he had been warned he would by the villagers of Krommyon, a brigand called Skiron, heavily bearded and heavily built, who did not even pass the time of day.

'Your money!' he said, 'And wash my feet!' And he flourished an axe and pointed to a large pot of water beside him.

Theseus stopped and looked at him and at the steep drop beneath them.

'If you're thinking of having a go with that little club of yours,' said Skiron, 'don't! You'll never know what hit you until you reach the sea and down there is a giant turtle which looks to me for its dinner.'

'I'm very short of money,' said Theseus, pretending to be frightened of him.

'Put all your things on the ground!' said Skiron. 'If you wash my feet to my satisfaction, I'll pay you for it.'

'Oh, thank you,' said Theseus, knowing from the villagers exactly what payment was intended. He put his club and all his other things on the path.

Skiron sat down against a rock and stretched his legs out.

'Now wash my feet!' he said.

Theseus picked up the pot of water and knelt down beside Skiron's feet at the very edge of the precipice. But as he saw Skiron raise his knees and draw back his feet so as to kick his victim off the cliff, Theseus seized him by the ankles and jerked him sideways, knocking the pot of water into the abyss as he did so.

'Sorry, Skiron,' he said, 'your water's taken a dive.'

Skiron, caught completely by surprise, struggled to free his legs and reached for his axe, but Theseus was too strong for him. Rising to his feet and stepping well back on to the path, he swung the writhing Skiron as if he was a club and flung him after his pot, saying, as he heard the man's long scream of despair, 'Wash your own feet when you get there, and feed the turtle!'

Robert Graves in *The Greek Myths*, first published in 1955, tells us that 'there is no record of an Attic turtle cult' and suggests that this episode is based on a series of icons illustrating the ceremony of killing a Sacred King, who was provided with a parasol to break his fall, and that the supposed turtle was the parasol 'floating on the waves'.

His earnest anthropological explanations often sound even more unlikely than the original story. These days, as the modern traveller speeds along the side of this mountain between Corinth and Athens, the motorway passes through a tunnel called 'Skiron'.

Theseus' next stop on his journey was the city of Eleusis, famous for its temple of Demeter and the Mysteries associated with her cult. The current king of the city was Kerkyon, a cruel and tyrannical ruler who had killed his own daughter in a fit of rage and was famous for his strength as a wrestler. Entering the city and going immediately to the well in the city square to draw himself a drink, Theseus met a tall, handsome woman who had just filled her pitcher and gave him water from it. Thanking her, he asked where he could find a room for the night.

'Don't stay the night,' she said, 'unless you're good at wrestling! Even if you are, I'd advise you to leave this unhappy city immediately. Its ruler, King Kerkyon, is a rough and ferocious man. He makes all visitors wrestle with him and they seldom live to tell the tale. You are young and I'm sure strong, but no one has matched him yet.'

'Thank you for warning me,' said Theseus, 'but I think I'll stay all the same. I learnt to wrestle in my home city of Troezen and would like to test my skill against such a dangerous opponent.'

The woman looked at him appraisingly and smiled.

'I will show you his house, then,' she said, balancing her pitcher on her shoulder and striding ahead.

But when she had pointed it out and Theseus turned to thank her, she had disappeared. He was baffled for a moment, since they were in an open street and there was nowhere she could have gone except into thin air. He wondered if she might be the goddess Demeter herself. If so, it was clear that she had no love for this man who ruled the city of her worshippers and would be glad to see him defeated. Theseus felt his confidence surge and boldly approached the king's house.

Kerkyon was delighted to see him. Travellers who knew his reputation generally avoided Eleusis, while those who did not were seldom worth fighting. If they refused he had them beaten to death by his guards, otherwise he soon broke their limbs or necks and sent them dead or dying out of the city. But this tall and handsome boy was clearly good for a round or two and Kerkyon sent his herald out to call an audience to the square. Meanwhile he offered Theseus a cup of wine, which he declined, drank one himself, and asked where his visitor came from and where he was going.

'From Troezen, on my way to Athens.'

'A long and dangerous journey. You must have had a few adventures on the way.'

'Several, yes.'

'How did you get past our friend Skiron on the mountain?'

'I tossed him out of the way.'

'That doesn't sound very likely. I'm afraid you're a boaster. Boasting won't help you here. Where did you get that sword and those fine sandals?'

'I found them under a stone.'

'Worse and worse. And that club with the bronze bands?'

'I took that from a cripple called Periphetes.'

'That sounds nearer the truth. Well, I'm glad to say that your career of casual theft, taking unfair advantage of the disabled, and boastful arrogance ends here.'

A crowd had assembled in the square, Kerkyon and Theseus stripped off and oiled themselves and the contest began. Kerkyon was no taller than Theseus, but much broader, with bulging muscles, and he immediately rushed at Theseus with all the confidence of a man who had never yet been defeated. Theseus began by dodging and retreating, watching his opponent carefully. He could see that Kerkyon relied entirely on his strength and had not learnt any of the skills which Theseus had acquired from his teachers in Troezen. The crowd was now growing derisive at the way Theseus continued to dance backwards and aside and evade Kerkyon, and the king himself was becoming angry. At last he closed in and flung his arms out in what should have been a crushing bear hug, only to find he was embracing air and that Theseus had stooped and grasped him by the legs. A great shout went up from the crowd as Theseus tipped Kerkyon over his shoulder and dropped him head-first on the paving-stones. Kerkyon staggered to his feet, blood pouring down his face, and charged at Theseus with his head down like a maddened bull. Theseus stepped deftly sideways, put out his foot and again sent Kerkyon crashing to the ground. Then, as the king struggled up for the second time, Theseus grasped him from behind, lifted him off his feet and threw him at the low wall round the well. Kerkyon lay there without moving, but lived long enough to hear the crowd's outburst of joy at the defeat of their hated ruler. They wanted to make Theseus king in his place, but he politely refused, saying that they did not want another wrestler as king, far less a foreigner, and after a thanksgiving sacrifice to Demeter and a general feast of celebration, he set off towards Athens the following day.

He was now in a fertile plain, with Mount Parnes to his left and the sea to his right, and soon crossed a series of streams which marked the boundary between Eleusis and Attica. At a place called Korydallos he came to an isolated house beside the road, where an old man sitting outside in the evening sunshine invited him to spend the night. Theseus accepted gladly and sat with the old man, admiring the view of the island of Salamis, while an old woman brought them wine and a frugal meal of soup, bread and olives.

'Have you come far?' asked the old man, whose name was Prokrustes.

'Only from Eleusis today,' said Theseus, 'but originally from Troezen.'

The old man was astonished.

'How did you cross the Isthmus?' he said.

'How does anyone cross it? I put one foot in front of another.'

'I mean, how did you get past that villain Sinis?'

'I had words with him.'

'Sinis is my son, you know. An evil man. People tell me he uses pine trees to catapult or tear apart every passer-by. I don't know how you escaped him.'

'So his daughter Perigune is your grandaughter?'

'Oh, yes. You met her then?'

'I met them both.'

'And Sinis let you pass unscathed?'

'He was scathed, but I wasn't.'

'Are you telling me ...?'

'Sinis took a ride on his own pine tree.'

The old man looked at him doubtfully, with his eyes screwed up and a deep frown on his heavily lined forehead.

'He's an evil man,' he repeated. 'My wife and I couldn't keep him here, he was always up to his tricks, annoying and frightening the travellers, and our aim is to make people happy and comfortable.'

'No pine trees here.'

'No. But in those days he was all talk. He didn't like having to wait on people. He wanted to get rich and have people wait on him. He wanted nothing to do with the hotel trade. So we told him to go and set up his own business somewhere else. He was making our guests feel uncomfortable.'

'Yes, he was evidently good at that.'

Theseus soon felt very sleepy. Prokrustes led him to a small dark room.

'You'll be comfortable here,' he said.

'The bed looks rather too short,' said Theseus, yawning. 'Haven't you got another room?'

'Only one,' said the old man, 'but I'm afraid that's already taken.'

'Well, this will have to do,' said Theseus and, hardly waiting for the old man to leave the room, removed his belt and tunic and dropped on to the bed. The lower part of his legs, almost up to the knees, hung over the end of what seemed to be a bed intended for a child, so he curled up in a foetal position and immediately fell asleep.

He woke up sometime later to find that he was lying on his back and that both his arms were strapped to the sides of the wooden bed. There was another strap across his chest. His head ached terribly and he still felt drowsy. He realised that the wine he drank at supper must have been drugged. His legs were dangling half over the end of the bed and in the dim light of a lamp in the far corner of the room he saw two shadowy figures.

'No, he really is too long, isn't he?' said Prokrustes' voice.

'You'll have to make him comfortable,' said the old woman's voice.

Theseus, in his woozy state, almost believed he was dreaming, but he suddenly felt himself grasped by the ankles and his legs stretched out.

'Yes, there's a lot to come off here,' said the old man. 'Hand me the saw!'

The light gleamed for a moment on a metal blade passing between the two figures and as it did so, Theseus pulled back his legs and kicked out with both feet. The old man fell back against the wall with a cry of angry surprise, the saw clattered on the floor, and the old woman stepped backwards obscuring the light. Now Theseus got his feet on the floor and, exerting all his strength, raised himself and the whole bed to which he was strapped and flung himself forward, pinning Prokrustes against the wall. Raising one knee he jabbed the old man in the crotch and as he fell down shouting with pain, stamped hard on his chest, breaking one of his ribs. Then Theseus turned towards the old woman, who dodged out of his way. Theseus put himself and the bed across the doorway.

'I am going to do the same to you,' he said, 'unless you untie these straps.'

But the old woman had picked up the saw and nervously threatened him with it. Theseus spun round and struck her with the edge of the bed. The old woman dropped the saw and, clutching her side, crouched near her groaning husband. Theseus moved slowly towards her.

'I will, I will,' she said in terror, 'but you must promise not to kill me.'

'I promise,' said Theseus.

'And my poor Prokrustes?'

'Your poor Prokrustes was about to saw off my legs,' said Theseus. 'I make no promises for him.'

When the old woman had released him from the bed, he resumed his tunic and belt and retrieved his club, sword, sandals and pack which the old couple had taken into their front room. Driving the pair of them in front of him – Prokrustes bent double with his hand on his injured chest, his wife supporting him and carrying the lamp – Theseus demanded to be shown the other room which the old man had told him was taken. He thought it likely that some other unlucky traveller might be there and liable to be treated to the same fate as he had just escaped.

The room was empty, but the bed, unlike his own, was an especially long one.

'What does this mean?' said Theseus angrily. 'You tell me this room is taken and you give me the one with the ridiculously short bed.'

The couple made no reply.

'Speak up!' said Theseus, threatening Prokrustes with his club.

'You were too tall for this bed,' mumbled Prokrustes and suddenly, with a long knife he had somehow acquired while they were in the front room, made a lunge at Theseus. Theseus batted the knife out of his hand with his club and knocked the old man backwards on to the bed.

'Now explain yourselves more clearly!' he said, seizing the old woman by one arm and forcing her to the floor beside the bed.

As he did so he saw in the light of the lamp which she still held that this bed, like the one he had slept in, was equipped with leather straps. Beginning to suspect the truth, he took the lamp from the woman and examined the rest of the room. Attached to the wall beyond the foot of the bed was a large drum from which dangled two ropes with looped ends.

'This bed is for people who are too short, I suppose?' he said.

'We try to make people more comfortable, you see,' said the old woman.

'Is that so? Then tie the straps on your husband's arms and chest and let me see how you make him more comfortable!'

Very reluctantly, in the face of threats from Prokrustes that he would kill her if she did so and more convincing ones from Theseus that he would cripple her if she didn't, the old woman tied the straps.

'Now these!' said Theseus, indicating the looped ropes dangling from the drum, and when she had put the loops round the old man's feet, 'Now turn that handle!'

She made a few turns until the ropes were taut and Prokrustes' legs stretched as far as they would go, he meanwhile alternately shouting curses at her and making desperate pleas for mercy to Theseus.

'You had no mercy on me or on other innocent travellers,' said Theseus. 'Am I to leave you here to drug their wine and make them "comfortable" according to your mad, perverted idea of hospitality. I have already cleared this road of your vile son Sinis and several other equally monstrous creatures, and now it's your turn.'

Brushing the old woman aside, he began to turn the handle himself, stretching Prokrustes' limbs and racking his body until he could bear the old man's screams of pain no longer, when he picked up his club and despatched him with a single blow to the head.

'You were this torturer's willing accomplice,' he said to the cringing old woman, 'but I promised to spare your life. I am going to Athens now, where my father is king, and if ever I hear that any traveller has been harmed or robbed by you, I shall punish you so severely that you will wish you were dead.'

Then he broke up the drum, took away the saw (which he later threw into the sea) and left the house as the red glow of dawn appeared over Mount Hymettos far in front of him.

3. THE TRIBUTE

When he reached Athens, Theseus was welcomed and made much of by his father Aegeus, but nearly murdered by his father's wife, Medea. She was a princess (and sorceress) from Colchis in what is now Georgia and had helped Jason and the Argonauts steal the Golden Fleece from her father, the King of Colchis. She sailed away with the Argonauts and when her angry father looked like overtaking them cut up her little brother, whom she had taken with her (perhaps for that very purpose) and dropped the pieces in the sea. Her distraught father, pausing to collect the floating fragments of his son for decent burial, was delayed long enough for the Argonauts to escape.

It should have been obvious to Jason that Medea was not a person to cross, but the silly hero, arriving finally after many adventures in Corinth and wishing to be its next king, discarded Medea in favour of the King of Corinth's daughter. Medea thereupon slaughtered her own and Jason's children and poisoned his new wife, escaping to

Athens where Aegeus, spellbound by her beauty and strong personality and pitying her terrible history, gave her asylum and married her. She naturally assumed that their son Medus would succeed Aegeus as king, so that the appearance of Theseus, this earlier and unknown son, possessing the sword and royal sandals left for him by his father to show that he was the true heir, was an unpleasant shock. She made an angry scene in private with her husband, who pointed out that he had saved her from the vengeance of the Corinthians but had made no promises about their son succeeding to his throne. She was in no way mollified, though she pretended to be, and at the banquet celebrating Theseus' arrival she put wolfsbane in his wine.

Theseus was saved by his father who, knowing his wife better by now and noticing the smile of vindictive satisfaction on her face as Theseus lifted the cup, knocked it to the floor. Again she escaped punishment, though Aegeus sent her and their son away to Asia and some say that she returned to Colchis and was reconciled to her father. The Georgians are charming and hospitable people, living in a beautiful land with a long history of civilisation, but what with Medea, Stalin and his sidekick Beria, their best-known contributions to the outside world have been peculiarly unwelcome.

Theseus, incidentally, is often listed as one of the Argonauts, but how is that possible if Medea was already married to his father and living in Athens when, as a youth still in his teens, Theseus first arrived there from Troezen?

Two years before his arrival, Athens had been attacked by Minos, King of Crete. One of Minos' sons, Androgeos, had visited Athens for the Panathenaic Games and defeated all comers at wrestling and throwing the discus and javelin. But as he was leaving Athens to visit the city of Thebes he was attacked and murdered, either by robbers or by his disappointed fellow sportsmen. No one was brought to justice and his bitterly grieving father blamed Aegeus and the Athenians. Cretan troops landed on the coast between Corinth and Athens and, capturing the small city of Megara as a base, devastated the countryside of Attica and drove the Athenians back inside their walls, where famine and disease soon forced them to sue for peace.

The price was a large annual payment, with an extra clause

intended to inflict the same pain (with interest) on Athenians as Minos had suffered by the death of his son. They had to send fourteen young people, seven boys and seven girls, to feed the Minotaur, a man with the head of a bull, who liked his meat fresh and was particularly partial to humans. His mother was Minos' wife Pasiphaë and his father was a bull – no ordinary bull but an especially beautiful one given to Minos by Poseidon to be sacrificed to him on the occasion of Minos' enthronement as King of Crete. Minos, however, liked the bull too much to sacrifice it and substituted another from his own herd. Poseidon was understandably annoyed and punished him by causing his wife to fall passionately in love with the bull. So after she had indulged in a few sessions of bestiality with it – the storytellers explain that she received its thrusts from inside the wooden replica of a cow – she duly gave birth to the Minotaur.

This man-eating monster, which his mother loved if nobody else did and would not allow to be killed, could obviously not be given free run of the palace at Knossos or its grounds. Minos therefore ordered his master craftsman Daidalos, who had made such a success of sculpting the wooden cow that the bull was repeatedly deceived into mounting it, to design a safe environment where the Minotaur would have room to run about without endangering the population of Knossos. Daidalos came up with the brilliant solution of a labyrinth, which the Minotaur could explore without ever quite getting the hang of it and into which his victims could be introduced so that he would have fun hunting them down through the innumerable winding passages.

Theseus had hardly settled into his new life as the heir apparent of Athens when the time came round for the third annual payment to Minos. Lots were to be drawn as usual and fourteen pairs of unhappy parents would learn that their sons or daughters were to be shipped to Crete to feed the Minotaur. As soon as he heard about this, Theseus went to his father and protested.

'This cannot go on,' he said. 'Send Minos the money if you must, but no more of our children!'

'If I don't,' said Aegeus, 'the Cretans will be back. I am trying to build up our military strength, but this is still a small city and it will be many years before we shall be strong enough to defy Minos. Meanwhile they will obliterate Athens and enslave us all. The loss of fourteen lives a year – painful as it may be – is surely the better option?'

'Then I will be one of the fourteen,' said Theseus.

'That I can't permit. Besides, it's a lottery.'

'Rig the lottery! No one's likely to object.'

'You're already past the age ...'

'Who's going to complain about that?'

'*I*'m complaining. I shall lose my son and heir. You might as well have drunk Medea's poison.'

'I don't intend to be eaten by the Minotaur, but to destroy it, as I destroyed all those monsters on the road from Troezen, and to return safely to Athens with my thirteen companions.'

'This is a far more dangerous and difficult undertaking. Even if you kill the Minotaur, how will you escape from Crete?'

'The ship returns to Athens, doesn't it? Let it wait in the harbour on some pretext – repairs, sickness among the sailors, whatever – and we will contrive to board it.'

'And Minos' ships will swiftly follow to wreak revenge on Athens.'

'The first thing is to kill the Minotaur. After that we'll see.'

Very reluctantly, but with a sense that this fearless and decisive son of his, conceived long ago on a drunken night in Troezen, already admired for his deeds on the road to Athens, was no ordinary man, but a true successor to his cousin Herakles, Aegeus gave way. Theseus was entered for the lottery, his name was drawn and he went aboard the ship with black sails that was to take him to Knossos with six other youths and seven girls. There were the usual mournful leave-takings on the quayside at Peiraias, where most of the population of Athens had assembled, but also an unusual lift of spirits as Theseus appeared and embraced his father.

'They are all counting on you,' said Aegeus. 'As I am. If you fail I shall have nothing to live for. But if you really succeed in killing the monster and returning, do me the favour of changing those black sails. I have had white ones stowed below decks and I shall have watchmen permanently scanning the sea for the ship's return. I shall know long before the ship reaches port what fate it brings me.'

'I am not afraid,' said Theseus, loud enough for those at the front of the crowd to hear, 'and you shouldn't be either. Look for the white sails!'

And as those who had heard what he said passed it on to those behind, his words were repeated again and again, so that all along the quayside 'look for the white sails' was echoed and re-echoed, while the ship with black sails slowly drew away and headed for the open sea and the island of Crete.

It should have reached Knossos in a few days, but was forced by a storm to take shelter in the harbour at Troezen. That at least was the excuse Theseus made to Minos a month later, when Minos was on the point of launching his navy to punish Athens for the ship's non-arrival. Theseus took pleasure, of course, in seeing his mother and grandfather again, and they were overjoyed to see him, but his real purpose in Troezen was to put his thirteen fellow hostages, the girls as well as the boys, into training with his own teachers. They had time only to learn the most basic routines of attack and defence, both unarmed and with weapons, but at least they were fitter and in better heart by the time the ship with black sails moored in the harbour of Amnisos, close to Knossos.

Theseus' six male companions were taken away to prison, but the seven girls were kept in the women's quarters of the palace. Minos, astonished that King Aegeus had sent his own son and heir as an offering to the Minotaur, ordered that Theseus be given a room in the palace and that he should be the last to enter the labyrinth.

'On the contrary,' said Theseus. 'I must be the first. Athenian princes do not lead from behind.'

'You seem to be a bold fellow,' said Minos, 'unless you're just a boaster, but let me warn you that no one comes out of that labyrinth alive. My stepson is a simple killer and I doubt whether even Herakles could match his strength. You may escape him for a while by hiding in the passages but you will be quite lost yourself in all the twists and turns and he will find you eventually.'

'I know the fate that awaits me,' said Theseus, 'and I would be ashamed to put it off for as long as your stepson takes to devour my thirteen companions. But I would be grateful if, before I enter the labyrinth, you would show me all the wonders of your palace and city. The whole world has heard of them but few have seen them.'

His aim was partly to flatter Minos and partly to give himself the time and local knowledge to plan a successful escape.

'That's easily arranged,' said Minos, 'since we have a day or two of celebration, with feasting, dancing and bull-jumping, before we introduce the first victim to the Minotaur.'

There are different versions of what happened next. The Athenian version in which Minos' daughter Ariadne helps Theseus is the best known, but the Cretan version denies the existence of the labyrinth and the Minotaur and substitutes a Cretan general called Tauros ('Bull') whom Theseus defeats at wrestling, after which Minos gives him the hand of Ariadne in marriage, remits all the penalties and is reconciled to Athens.

But this story would be nothing without the Minotaur and the labyrinth. Across the Gulf, as night falls on our terrace in Arcadia, I can see the flashing light that warns low-flying aircraft – or gods – of the row of wind turbines on the ridge in front of Mount Didymo, beyond which is Theseus' native Troezen. Pondering the conflicting versions of his most famous adventure, it comes to me in a flash that the key is Minos himself.

Minos was no mere Mugabe or Saddam with sadistic tastes and a terrorised population, but an outstanding ruler. He unified Crete, gave it laws, created such a formidable navy that it became the most powerful state in the Aegean, put down pirates, built magnificent palaces – whose excavated remains are still among the wonders of the world – commissioned painters and sculptors, ran an efficient bureaucracy, presided over a sophisticated and cultured court. History and archaeological evidence mingle with myth in our uncertain knowledge of that distant time in the Bronze Age before the rise of the Mycenaeans and the Trojan War. Minos' mother, the stories tell us, was the lovely and lively Phoenician princess called Europa – she gave her name to our continent – who playfully jumped on the back of a white bull and was carried off across the sea from Asia to Crete, where the bull turned out to be Zeus. Their child Minos belonged to that early generation of privileged mortals who still had close relations with the gods, since the gods were so often their parents. By the time Theseus met him, he must have been at least as old as Theseus' grandfather Pittheus, perhaps even a generation older still, and when he died he became immortal and was made one of the judges of the dead in Hades.

This was the man whom the young and self-confident Theseus came intending somehow to outwit and it hardly seems that ridding the road to Athens of a few not very bright brigands and monsters was anything like sufficient preparation. He soon began to realise this himself as he was conducted round the palace by its architect. Daidalos came originally from Athens and had fled to Crete after being condemned to death for the murder of his apprentice Talos. He admitted that he had killed Talos, who was also his nephew, but claimed that it was an accident. He had been angry with Talos for spoiling a fine piece of marble he was carving into a statue of Aphrodite, had clouted him a little too energetically and knocked him backwards against a small bronze figure of Poseidon. However, the evidence suggested that Daidalos had picked up the bronze figure and brained Talos with it, and his accusers said his motive was not a momentary fit of anger but professional envy. Talos, they said, was already a better craftsman than Daidalos and had not spoiled the piece of marble he was carving but on the contrary was making it smoother and more lifelike than Daidalos had been able to. Daidalos countered that it was his enemies who were guilty of professional envy and that they wished to destroy him because they could not compete with him. What with his short temper, his very high opinion of his own talents and his contempt for the intelligence of his accusers and judges, he did not make a good impression at his trial, though it is his view of himself as the most brilliant craftsman and inventor of that era which has prevailed, chiefly on account of the work he did for Minos. Yet just because he rated himself so highly and was always sensitive to slights and signs that he was not sufficiently appreciated, by the time he met Theseus he had become very critical of Minos, at least behind his back.

The palaces Theseus knew, his father's in Athens and his grandfather's in Troezen, were little more than large houses amongst other houses, all packed into a few streets within the defensive walls of the cities. Minos' palace was at least the size of a city in itself and several storeys high, with huge porticos, grand staircases and spacious courtyards, long corridors and pillared halls. It was all decorated in bright colours, with cheerful frescoes of court life, sports and religious rituals painted by Daidalos himself or his pupils, full of air and diffused sunshine from clever light-wells and windows that gave sudden views of the surrounding gardens and villas and the range of hills to the south; while the houses of Minos' courtiers and subjects spread out into the valley around without any constricting city wall. The sea and his navy were Minos' defence and the whole large island of Crete, with other sumptuous palaces in other parts of it, his sovereign territory. Theseus was dumbfounded and humbled. This was a level of civilisation he could not have imagined.

Daidalos was pleased with Theseus' reaction, but not inclined to give much credit to Minos.

'Luxury he understands,' he said, 'though he doesn't like the cost of it. Size and display he appreciates. But elegance, taste, no. Many's the time I've had to head off hideous vulgarities on the walls and fight for better proportions and more expensive materials for the rooms. And he didn't like the cost of the drains and waterpipes I insisted on, though he appreciates them now. There was a palace here before, of course, partly destroyed in an earthquake, which had been constructed piecemeal like a rabbit's warren with horrible poky rooms opening into each other. Some of that I've demolished or opened out, some of it remains. As a matter of fact, it was such a ludicrous muddle that it gave me the idea for the Minotaur's labyrinth.'

'Well, I have been thinking about that labyrinth,' said Theseus. 'Is there any easy way to get out of it? Supposing one were able to overcome the creature inside?'

Daidalos laughed.

'Are you asking me to betray the man I work for?'

'You don't sound as if you have much time for him. And, after all, you're an Athenian.'

'I have no love for Athens and, whatever I may think of Minos, I owe him my life and living. Am I to risk becoming an exile all over again by helping you, to whom I owe nothing?'

'Any city in the world would be proud to receive Daidalos and make use of his unique talents.'

'True.'

They walked on for a while in silence, then stopped for Theseus to admire a large reception room decorated with full-length, figure-of-eight shields.

'Good defence,' he said, 'but surely a bit clumsy in attack?'

'There is an easy way to get out, of course,' said Daidalos, with a sly smile.

'But you're not going to reveal it?'

'Use your head, boy!'

'You mean, remember every turn I take as I go in and reverse them coming out?'

'Even I wouldn't be capable of that.'

'Perhaps you have a plan of it which I could study in advance?'

'No, I made a rough sketch but added complexities as we built it.'

'So what use is my head?'

Daidalos gave him the same enigmatic smile, but said nothing more until they reached the great central courtyard.

'It's a handsome head,' he said, sitting down on a stone bench with his back to the courtyard's eastern wall. 'If you were going to be with us longer I'd even ask you to model for a fresco. Behind this wall, I should tell you, is a part of the palace I haven't been able to show you, a little labyrinth in itself. That's where our demented Queen Pasiphaë lives, with her ladies-in-waiting and her two unmarried daughters, Ariadne and Phaedra, who will soon go mad themselves if they are cooped up there much longer with a mother who cares nothing for them and dotes only on her bull-headed son.'

'But can she ever set eyes on him?'

'She spends half the day doing nothing else.'

'How can she do that?'

'Parts of the labyrinth are open to the sky. The Minotaur needs light and air like the rest of us. Pasiphaë sits on a terrace on the palace roof in the full sun – she claims to be the sun's daughter, you know. From there she gazes down at him, uttering shrill cries of pleasure and encouragement as he pursues and catches and tears up his victims. You may catch a glimpse of her and you'll surely hear her when you're in there yourself.'

'If parts are open, then it might be possible to climb out?'

'Do you imagine I didn't think of that? This is a man, though he has a bull's head, and he's taller than you. If you could climb out, so could he.'

Theseus sighed and looked glumly at the paved floor.

'You said there was an easy way to get out. But how could there be? A man with your brain will have thought of everything.'

Daidalos smiled again.

'Of course, but if you used the brain inside that handsome head you'd conclude that all you need to get out of the labyrinth is a simple ball of thread. Possibly two balls, in case the first runs out. Attach one end to the door as you go in and unwind it as you go ...'

'So simple!' said Theseus. 'What a mastermind you are, Daidalos!'

'But, of course, having found your way back along the thread, you will still need to get through the heavy bronze door, bolted on the outside. For that you will need help. Someone so keen for you to escape that he – or she – will risk the anger of Minos by pulling the bolts back.'

'And how shall I discover this person?'

'I leave that to you. But do you really think you can overcome the Minotaur? No one ever has, not even the strongest prisoners of war or hardened criminals.'

Minos held a banquet that evening for his principal courtiers, inviting Theseus to attend and seating him beside him. Theseus gave an enthusiastic account of his guided tour of the palace.

'You live like the gods,' he said, 'or at least as we imagine the gods live. People in Athens will not believe what I tell them.'

'Do you expect to be able to tell them?' asked Minos.

Theseus blushed.

'Your kindness and hospitality, the magnificence of your palace made me forget my predicament,' he said.

And to cover his embarrassment he went on to ask Minos question after question about his kingdom, how it was governed, how justice was dispensed, how the gods were worshipped and which gods in particular, how the ships were built and the sailors recruited and trained, how and with whom they traded, how the people were taxed and how above all the innumerable small enclaves cut off from each other by mountains, just as in his own country, had been united here into one great kingdom.

Minos answered all his questions in detail and at last, as the banquet was ending, said:

'What a shame that you will not be returning to Athens! You are evidently a serious young man and I'm sure you would have done much to turn that primitive city of yours into something with more of a future. You know, in other circumstances I would have considered you a suitable husband for one of my daughters.'

The guests were now to be entertained by acrobats, dancers and musicians, but first the court ladies, accompanied by servants carrying flaming torches, descended the staircase from an upper floor where they too had been dining. Before taking their seats at the side, the dark-haired women in their multi-coloured swirling skirts came one by one to pay their respects to the king. Theseus was again astounded. He had never seen women dressed and coiffed with such sophistication, he had never seen women who wore their breasts bare above their tight, wasp-waisted bodices. The women were led by Queen Pasiphaë and her two daughters and all stared as admiringly at this Athenian prince with his long, soft fair hair and blue eyes as he at them. As they turned to go to their own places, Pasiphaë, who never troubled to lower her voice for an aside, was heard to say to her daughters:

'He looks just like Apollo.'

The entertainments were as much more polished and skilful than anything Theseus had seen before as everything else in Minos' palace, but he was not so completely absorbed in them that he did not glance frequently towards the row of bare-breasted women at the side. And whenever he did glance that way he saw that the princess Ariadne was looking at him. So was her younger sister, Phaedra, but more shyly, looking away quickly if their eyes met, whereas Ariadne simply stared.

'My daughters find you fascinating,' said Minos.

'I am as strange to them, I suppose, as your kingdom is to me. It's like a dream. I could almost think that I'm already dead and have entered another world reserved for the favourites of the gods.'

'Yet it's a world that contains the Minotaur.'

'I have to remember that. A world, for me, as brief as a dream.'

4. THE BULL-JUMPERS

The next day was given over to public festivities in the great arena in front of the western facade of the palace. These festivities were held every year in honour of the three greatest gods, Zeus, Poseidon and Hades, who ruled the earth and sky, the sea, and the underworld respectively. Zeus was born on the island of Crete and had here fathered Minos on Europa; Poseidon's good will was essential to a state that depended on the sea for its trade and defence, and he had honoured Minos' enthronement with the white bull which later fathered the Minotaur; while Minos, after his death, was to become one of the judges in Hades' kingdom, though whether he already knew that in his lifetime is unclear. Perhaps it was *because* he honoured Hades equally with his brothers of the upper world that he obtained this privilege, though it's usually considered to have been in recognition of his own high reputation as a law-giver and just judge on earth.

Three altars on a raised platform dominated the arena, filled with a huge crowd of Minos' subjects, who had come from all over the island, and the celebrations began with the sacrifice to Zeus of a 100 goats. Zeus had been suckled on the milk of goats when he was newly born and hidden in a cave below Mount Ida so as to avoid being swallowed by his father Cronos, whom he grew up to castrate and dethrone.

The priests who were to conduct the sacrifice came out in procession from the palace, and were followed by Minos and his courtiers, with Pasiphaë and her daughters and ladies-in-waiting. Behind them came soldiers leading the fourteen Athenians, including Theseus, chained together by the wrists. Garlanded and dressed in black robes they were paraded as sacrificial victims, although they were not offerings to the gods, but destined to feed the Minotaur, one every other day, for the next month.

After the initial sacrifices and prayers, dances were performed by groups from the various districts of Crete, and then the roasted and dismembered goats, with wine and bread, were distributed to the crowd. The next part of the celebrations consisted of the Cretan sport of bull-jumping. During his tour of the palace with Daidalos, Theseus had seen a fresco depicting this event and asked Daidalos what it meant. Daidalos replied that he would soon see for himself.

The crowd fell silent as soldiers, carrying the tall figure-of-eight shields which Theseus had seen on a wall in the palace, formed a palisade in front of the crowd, while a group of young Cretans, both male and female, dressed in gaudy, skintight costumes, marched into the arena. Some carried spears and fanned out to stand at intervals in front of the soldiers guarding the crowd. The rest, unarmed, waited in a line facing the crowd until, driven along a corridor from the enclosure on the south side of the arena where it had been penned, a bull rushed into the arena and paused a moment as it realised that it was still not free but penned in by the crowd. And now the extraordinary spectacle began, as the young Cretans in their tight costumes ran forward to surround it. The bull lowered its head and charged at the nearest, who instead of running away grasped its horns, and, tossed upwards by the bull, somersaulted over its head, landed with his feet in the middle of its back, and somersaulted again over the tail, to be caught by a colleague behind the bull. And this happened again and again, for every time the bull charged, another acrobat performed the same feat, and if the bull thought to change the rules by turning away from them to charge the crowd, the spear-carriers quickly headed him back into the arena. When the bull grew tired and ceased to charge with the same momentum, he was driven out of the arena by the spear-carriers and another bull sent in. This happened two or three times, until the crowd began to be jaded, as people tend to be by seeing something, however skilful and seemingly impossible, repeated so often that it looks easy and ordinary. Now, after the last bull had been expelled from the arena, there was a brief pause. The acrobats again formed a line and the crowd, which knew what to expect, as the Athenian prisoners did not, waited in tense silence.

Suddenly three bulls, one after the other, thundered into the arena. The danger and difficulty for the bull-jumpers now became extreme as they had to concentrate, all of them at every moment, on avoiding the plunges not only of the bull they were leaping over, but of the two being leapt over by their comrades. The speed and intensity of the spectacle, as the three bulls criss-crossed the arena and the young men and women darted round and somersaulted over them, making an almost continuous pattern of bright streaks of colour across the white, brown and black masses of the charging animals, was like a display of lightning over and between mountains. And the thunder of this human and animal storm was supplied by the crowd clapping and shouting and beating their feet on the ground and the bulls bellowing in response. In the midst of the barely controlled mayhem several spear-carriers and two or three acrobats were injured, but swiftly removed from harm's way by the soldiers forming the second line of defence between the spear-carriers and the crowd. Then first one bull, then the second, then the third was driven up the steps towards the altars on the platform and as they ascended one by one they were met by an enormous man, almost a giant, who felled them in turn with a great double-headed axe, the special symbol, painted on many of the pillars in the palace, of Minos' kingdom. The young acrobats withdrew and Minos himself, ascending the platform with the priests, led the sacrifice of the three bulls, one on each altar, the brown bull to Zeus, the white bull to Poseidon and the black bull to Hades. After that more bulls were led out and sacrificed and the roasted flesh distributed to the crowd.

The last part of the celebrations was a wrestling match, in which the strongest men from all over the island competed for a crown of olive leaves. A herald called out the names of the contestants, with the village or town they came from, as each entered the series of knock-out heats. But the match was clearly a foregone conclusion, since one of the competitors was the giant who had felled the bulls, and every time he took part he threw his opponent with contemptuous ease. Theseus, watching him intently, asked the soldier nearest to him who this was and was told it was the king's chief general, known as Tauros, the very man who had led Minos' troops in their attack on Athens three years before.

'He looks as if he'd be capable of overpowering the Minotaur,' said Theseus.

'Very likely,' said the soldier, 'since Tauros wins this competition every year. No one can match his skill.'

Theseus did not consider from his own observation that there was much skill involved, only brute strength, and asked the soldier if he himself could try his skill against Tauros.

'You?' said the soldier. 'Tauros will break every bone in your body.'

'Nevertheless.'

'You'd have to ask the king.'

'Then ask him for me!'

Minos, from his seat among the nobles and ladies to one side of the platform, looked down dubiously at Theseus as the soldier passed on his request, shrugged his shoulders and nodded. The chain was removed from Theseus' wrist and the herald was called over to take instructions from Minos and to forewarn Tauros. So when Tauros had disposed of his last opponent and the crowd was beginning to applaud the winner without particular enthusiasm, since this outcome was as usual a foregone conclusion, Tauros himself shook his head and pointed with a sarcastic smile at the group of prisoners, while the herald announced:

'One final challenger for the crown. From the city of Athens, Theseus son of Aegeus.'

Some of the crowd applauded, others shouted derisively as Theseus threw off his black robe, anointed himself with the oil provided for the contestants and advanced to meet Tauros.

'I wouldn't have guessed that a man from Athens would have had the courage,' said Tauros. 'They shut themselves inside their walls sooner than meet me in battle.'

'I regret that I was not there at the time,' said Theseus, 'or I would have led them out and thrown you into the sea.'

'Well, I shall try not throw you down too hard,' said Tauros, 'since the Minotaur doesn't fancy dead meat, but I see that your courage is only insolence and I shall find it difficult to restrain myself.'

'I beg you not to hold back on my account. I would prefer to win against a man who was doing his best.'

They stood for a moment looking at each other, Theseus a mere sapling beside Tauros' mighty trunk, the latter smiling with derision and looking round at the crowd as if asking them to share it, the former with a stern face and eyes only for his opponent. Then Tauros strode forward intending to pick up Theseus in one movement and fling him to the side like a sheaf of corn. Theseus ducked and side-stepped, at the same time seizing Tauros' left arm and twisting it backwards. Tauros, carried forward by his own momentum and sideways by the pressure on his arm, stumbled and almost fell. Theseus kicked his right leg behind the knee and the giant crumpled on to his hands and knees. The crowd shouted with excitement at seeing the inveterate winner worsted, but then fell silent, unsure whose side they should be on.

Theseus stood back and waited for Tauros to get up, knowing that if he grappled with the man too soon he could not match his strength. Tauros, flustered and furious as much with himself as his opponent for having been humiliated, ran straight at him, but Theseus zigzagged backwards just out of his reach, so that Tauros looked more and more like his namesake, a charging bull, and the crowd, seeing him as it were led by the nose, began to laugh. Tauros, more flustered still, took his eye off Theseus for a moment to look angrily at the crowd, when Theseus darted behind him and, seizing one of his huge legs, brought him crashing to the ground. Again Theseus stood back to allow Tauros to get up, but as Tauros stood there dazed and shaken, blood dripping into his eyes from a graze on his forehead, Theseus launched himself head down at Tauros' stomach, at the same time seizing him round the chest and sliding him head down over his back. Winded by the blow to his stomach and stunned by the impact of the paving stones on his skull, Tauros lay prone. The crowd, shocked and amazed, was silent. Theseus waited, but when Tauros did not move he walked away, bowed to Minos and returned to his place with the Athenian prisoners.

Attendants came forward and carried Tauros away. The crowd began to shout, some that the Athenian had won the crown, others that his tactics had been cowardly and unfair and that, unlike Tauros, he had not had to come through the heats. Minos rose to his feet and the herald called for silence.

'We are not such a mean-minded people,' said Minos, 'that we cannot recognise courage and skill when we see it or give honour to a conquered city that sends us a victorious athlete. My own son Androgeos won the games in Athens and was treacherously murdered by envious Athenians, to their everlasting shame. We are nobler-spirited. The winner of the crown is Theseus son of Aegeus.' Beckoning Theseus to come on to the platform, he placed the wreath of olive leaves on his head and led the applause.

'Prettily done,' he said privately to Theseus. 'I can tell you that I'm not sorry to see Tauros humbled. Kings must always beware of over-mighty subjects.'

Then, taking Theseus' arm, he conducted him at the head of the procession of courtiers, ladies of court, priests and Athenian prisoners back into the palace.

5. THE MINOTAUR

Minos was surprised and delighted by Theseus' triumph and realised, as he lay in bed that night, that he had perhaps been given the means to rid himself of several long-standing problems. The worst was the Minotaur, whom he detested – as well he might – his wife's horrible progeny from a scandalous union which shamed them both in the eyes of the whole world. The most pressing was his elder daughter Ariadne, who should long since have been married but for whom he had so far found no suitable husband. Tauros was very keen to marry her, but Minos did not wish to give him any more power in the kingdom than he already had. Tauros was also a great partisan of the Minotaur, not because he liked him but because he liked his appetite for human victims, whether Cretan criminals or foreign prisoners of war or the miserable annual tally of young Athenians – those especially. It was Tauros who had imposed this penalty on Athens, though Minos, in his anger at the murder of Androgeos, had endorsed the idea. But in practice it sickened him and he would have stopped it after the first year if he had not been afraid that Tauros, who was held in awe if not much liked by his soldiers and the people in general, would have objected and used it as an excuse to seize power from a king going soft in his old age. As for the Minotaur, who though he had a bull's head was after all his stepson, he could not have him killed for fear of the anger of both Tauros and Pasiphaë.

But now fate had sent him this splendid youth Theseus, who seemed to be the answer to all these problems at once. He had already almost disposed of Tauros, for even if he recovered, his formidable reputation must be severely diminished. And if Theseus could so easily overcome Tauros, he might also overcome the Minotaur. Neither Pasiphaë nor Tauros could hold it against Minos if the Minotaur was killed by one of his victims. And could there be a better husband for Ariadne than Theseus? The marriage and the cancellation of the annual tribute would surely make Athens a friend of Crete instead of a resentful enemy, and when Theseus succeeded his father as king and transformed his city, as he surely would, into a much stronger force in the Greek world, Athens would become a useful ally and trading partner. Minos' son Deukalion was even now leading an expedition to found a colony in Italy and if the Cretans no longer had to worry about disaffection to the north, they could concentrate all the more intensely on opening up the west to their trade and influence.

Next morning Minos summoned Ariadne to his study and asked her what she thought of Theseus. She was not afraid to say – she trusted her father and she was a pragmatic, straightforward woman – that she found him attractive, both his looks and his courage.

'And what would you think of being married to him?'

'I would like nothing better. But how will he escape Minotauros?'

'You could help him.'

'How could I help him?'

'In several ways. Think about it!'

'And you would not prevent it?'

'By no means. But I would not wish your mother or anyone else to know that. Your help to him and my help to you, if you need it, must be absolutely secret.'

'And then? If Theseus does escape?'

'You must help him escape not just Minotauros but Crete too.'

'Then how can I be married to him?'

'You can go with him.'

'To Athens? Our enemy?'

'With this marriage, with the return of all our Athenian prisoners, Athens will cease to be our enemy.'

'So the prisoners must escape too?'

'Certainly. Do you think Theseus would be willing to go without them?'

'I would be sorry if he were.'

'Well, you must make careful plans with Theseus himself and then share them with me, so that I can discover any weak points.'

'How shall I be alone and secret with Theseus?'

'I shall summon him here now and leave you to receive him. You needn't tell him that I am your secret accessory. Of course, he is clever enough to guess that you couldn't do this on your own, but don't admit it – not at least until you are safely clear of Crete and any pursuit that I may have to order for appearance's sake.'

So Theseus went to Minos' study and, finding only Ariadne, almost believed that some god must be watching over him, since she was exactly the person – as Daidalos had hinted – whom he hoped to win over to help him. Not knowing that she was already primed to do so, he began by courting her and they were soon exchanging looks and words of love. In between these endearments, Theseus, afraid that her father might return at any moment, quickly told her how he planned to thread his way out of the labyrinth and what help he needed from her.

The next day was set for Theseus to be sent into the labyrinth as the Minotaur's first victim. Minos himself took almost fatherly leave of Theseus inside the palace, grasping him by both hands. He seemed as if he might even embrace him, but Theseus, very conscious that hanging from hooks sewn by Ariadne inside his loose black robe were two balls of thread and a golden hairpin, stepped quickly back.

'Are you fully equipped for your frightful ordeal?' asked Minos.

'I believe so.'

'We can postpone it for another day if you prefer.'

'I prefer to get it over with.'

'I wish you well and I'm sorry we shall not meet again.'

'Perhaps in the shades,' Theseus said with a smile.

'We must all meet there, but not to much purpose, except to flit and gibber.'

'At least I might flit past you and gibber my thanks.'

'Thanks for what?'

'For your generous treatment of me and the inspiring example of your well-regulated kingdom.'

'You are too kind. I am also sending you to the Minotaur.'

'But perhaps you would not be sorry if you were relieved of him?'

'What makes you think that?'

'In your place I would not keep such a monster even if he were my wife's child.'

'Can you read my mind?'

'Certainly not. But in some ways I feel that our minds are not dissimilar. That sounds arrogant. I mean that I would like to be like you.'

'Are you hoping to escape by flattery?'

'I am not so afraid of the Minotaur that I would say what was untrue.'

Minos looked at him steadily and nodded.

'How strange fate is! If your people had not murdered my son I might never have met a man I would so gladly make my son-in-law.'

'I will take the word for the deed.'

'In what way?'

'I will think of Ariadne as my reward if I overcome the Minotaur.'

'But even if you do, I cannot give her to you.'

'I understand that. Even great kings are not free to do exactly as they wish, but everyone may try, as in a labyrinth, to find some way out.'

Minos laughed and put his hand on Theseus' shoulder as he sent him out to the soldiers in the corridor who were to conduct him to the labyrinth.

'You deserve your reward.'

The labyrinth was on the opposite side of the palace from the arena where the festivities were held. The ground fell away steeply there towards the River Kairatos, allowing Daidalos to construct high walls without impeding any of the views from the palace. Unless one went up on to the palace roof, as Pasiphaë habitually did, one would scarcely be aware of the labyrinth's existence. She was there today, of course, eager to see her terrible son destroy the upstart prince from Athens whom she both fancied sexually and disapproved of as a too attractive and so far too successful enemy. She had been one of those watching the wrestling match who sided entirely with Tauros and resented his humiliating defeat. She insisted that both Ariadne and Phaedra should accompany her on to the roof, wanting them to see the cocky conqueror brought low. This was not at all where Ariadne had planned to be and she was forced to disobey her father's instructions by swearing her sister to secrecy and revealing that she meant to help Theseus escape. Phaedra promised to distract her mother while Ariadne went down to unbolt the door to the labyrinth, once Theseus, as she hoped against hope, had overpowered the monster.

The heavy bronze door was opened by the soldiers and Theseus walked through into a dark lateral corridor. He waited to hear that the bolts outside had been shot before removing his robe, sticking Ariadne's golden pin firmly into the ground and tying the loose end of one of his balls of thread to it. As he did so, a bull roared somewhere in the distance. Minotauros, as his relations called him, had heard the door bolted and was looking forward to his lunch. Unwinding the tethered ball of thread with one hand and holding the second ball in his armpit, Theseus set off down the corridor to his right, feeling his way along the wall with his free hand, making no sound with his bare feet. He did not want to be surprised by the creature in a dark, narrow corridor, where Minotauros would have the advantage of his strength and of being long accustomed to the layout as well as the lack of light, but to find his way to one of the larger, lighter spaces, preferably that in the middle, which Daidalos had told him was the largest and fully open to the sky. Theseus had got quite far into the labyrinth, turning left and right alternately, when he heard Minotauros roar again, this time from somewhere behind him. He had probably reached the door and been disappointed not to find his victim cowering there.

Some of the corridors Theseus turned into were blind alleys. On these occasions he rewound the thread as he retraced his steps, not wishing either to waste thread or to come that way again. His eyes were well accustomed to the darkness now, but the part of the labyrinth he had reached was often roofless, so that some light reached even the darker passages. He heard Minotauros roar again, louder and closer, and after some time, as he thought he must be nearing the centre of the labyrinth, a faint scuffling sound several passages away, as if the monster in his haste to find his victim was brushing against the walls. Theseus had several times recently come across bones discarded on the floor and soon the passages were littered with them. He must, he thought, be approaching the centre. The scuffling was now much closer, and as he returned from a blind alley into the passage he had just left, Theseus realised that Minotauros had turned into the same passage. Theseus quickly went back into the blind alley and pressed himself against the wall, breathing as quietly as he could and hoping that his pursuer didn't have a sharp sense of smell. Minotauros passed without noticing him and went on down the corridor. Theseus followed him, pursuer now rather than pursued, catching glimpses of his quarry from time to time in the places where it was lighter, but always staying well back.

Just as he was in sight of an open, rectangular space, Theseus' thread ran out. He quickly knotted its end to the loose end of the second ball and continued warily towards the open space. There was no sign of Minotauros and Theseus hung back in case his enemy was lying in wait in one of the three passages leading off the space. But then he heard him roaring some way ahead and the faint answering cries of a woman. He was probably complaining to his mother on the palace roof that he was hungry and the cow or goat or human sent in for him had not materialised. Theseus, paying out his thread, carefully stepping round the bones on the floor, turned and turned again – he had long since lost any sense of orientation – towards the sound.

Beginning to feel tired now from the constant tension of concentrating and a little unnerved by the evidence of all his predecessors' fate, he wished he had accepted Ariadne's offer of a weapon. She had wanted to give him a knife to tie to his upper arm where it would be concealed by the sleeve of the robe, but he had refused. Why? He had some scruple about an unfair fight, perhaps not wanting to assassinate Minos' stepson as his son Androgeos had been assassinated on the road out of Athens. This scruple now seemed ridiculous. What was fair about being introduced into this labyrinth to feed a ravenous monster, what was fair about fourteen young Athenians every year being submitted to the same horrible treatment? Minos' kingdom must be among the most advanced and civilised in the world, but this aspect of it was wholly primitive and if Minos himself, as he had hinted, did not approve of it, why didn't he stop it? He, Theseus, owed nothing in the way of fairness to any of these people, except Ariadne, and by not accepting the knife he had put her future in jeopardy as well as his own.

The bull's roaring had ceased and Theseus, not knowing now whether Minotauros was still in front of him or might not, following a different route, have got behind him again, proceeded with great caution, constantly glancing back and looking round every corner before he turned it. It was as well he did, since he suddenly saw, at the end of the passage he was about to enter, a huge shape blocking the daylight beyond. Minotauros, he realised, was almost as broad and high as the passage itself. No wonder he made a noise brushing the walls and disturbing the bones on the floor when he was in a hurry! Theseus drew his head back and retreated, looking for a side passage to hide in. Given the monster's size, it would be disastrous to meet him anywhere but in the open centre of the labyrinth. But there was no side passage and the scuffling and rattle of bones were growing louder. He was coming.

Theseus went quickly back to the corner and got down on the floor on his hands and knees across the passage in the darkest place. Now he could hear the bull's breath, a snorting and sniffing amplified by the enclosing walls. But as Minotauros turned the corner, peering no doubt down the length of the corridor and not at the ground, his shins met the kneeling Theseus and he fell headlong over him with a fearful roar of shock and anger. Theseus was up in a moment and running down the passage towards the daylight. As he emerged into a large, square, open space – surely the centre he had been looking for – with the sun overhead, Minotauros was already on his feet and racing after him. Theseus ran to the far corner of the square, hearing as he did so an excited cry from Pasiphaë on the palace roof far above:

'You've got him, my beauty!'

Minotauros, as he came out into the sunlight, turned his great white bull's head upwards and waved one of his human arms in acknowledgement, then, seeing Theseus, roared in triumph, put down his head and charged across the square, kicking aside the bones which were scattered all around. Up above, Pasiphaë accompanied his deep roaring with shrill screams of delight and encouragement. Theseus waited until the last moment and dived aside. Minotauros ran, horns first, into the wall and as he recoiled and shook his head, less with pain than surprise, Theseus struck the back of his head with a long leg bone he had found on the ground nearby. Again Minotauros shook his head, but more as if a fly had settled there than as if he had been dealt a blow which might have killed an ordinary man. Then, turning more swiftly than Theseus expected and lashing out with one arm, he knocked his adversary sideways and sent the bone flying out of his hands. Pasiphaë on the roof of the palace could be heard screaming with joy as Minotauros stood over Theseus and bent forward to thrust his horns into him. Theseus, unable to get to his feet in time, seized the monster's left ankle and tugged it towards him. Minotauros staggered but kept his balance and one of his horns gouged a long wound in Theseus' calf. Theseus, meanwhile, had regained his feet and, hardly yet noticing any pain in his leg, leapt on to Minotauros' back, crossing his legs round Minotauros' belly at the same time as getting his arms round his neck. Minotauros roared and tried to shake off his incubus, then backed towards the wall to scrape him off, but Theseus, squeezing the human diaphragm with his legs and the bull's throat with his arms, hung on and could hear Minotauros gagging.

Now, in a desperate effort to free himself, Minotauros ran into the nearest passage, where, unbalanced by the weight on his back and the terrible pressure on his throat and diaphragm, he stumbled over a human skull and fell forwards on to his knees. Theseus quickly unclasped his legs and, moving forward to sit astride the monster's shoulders, exerted all his remaining strength on the windpipe. Minotauros was already too weak to rise and at last his feeble struggles ceased and he collapsed and lay flat on the floor of the passage. But Theseus did not release his grip on the windpipe until he was sure no breath remained. Then at last he stood up, rolled the huge body over and made sure the heart had stopped beating. For a moment he thought of going out into the open square and raising his arms in triumph for the benefit of Pasiphaë, whose cries of malicious pleasure at what she believed would soon be Minotauros' victory had stopped when he entered the passage out of her sight. But no, he decided, it was better no one should know the outcome of the fight until he had time to reach the door of the labyrinth, which Ariadne had promised to unbolt as soon as she heard Theseus tap on it three times.

The only problem now was that he had dropped his ball of thread as he emerged from the passage on the far side of the square, and if he were not to show himself in the open he must follow the passage he was in and find his way back to the original passage, where he could pick up the ball and, winding it up as he went, retrace all the twists and turns he had taken through the labyrinth. He didn't think that would be too difficult.

But it was. The passage he was in turned away from the direction of the passage where his ball of thread lay and Theseus, taking further turns which he thought should lead him back, lost all sense of direction. He must, he thought, since he didn't pick up his thread in any of these passages, be in the eastern part of the labyrinth, on the far side of the central square from the way he had come in. He cursed Daidalos for the ingenuity of his design and himself for not using some of the discarded bones to mark the ends of passages he had already traversed. The absence of bones now suggested that he was far away from the centre where Minotauros had evidently spent most of his time. From time to time he passed through roofless corridors, but the walls were too high and the corridors too narrow for him to be able to see the sun, which must now be beyond its zenith, and reorientate himself. He did not despair, certain that at some point he must either come back to the centre or to a passage where he had passed with his thread, but he was deadly tired and his gashed calf throbbed with pain.

In the meantime Ariadne had slipped away from her mother and sister on the palace roof. They had seen Minotauros leave the central square and enter the passage with Theseus on his back and Pasiphaë at least seemed to assume that her son would soon drag his victim out into the open again and begin to devour him. Ariadne feared she might be right, but when neither of them emerged, she began to hope for a better outcome. Her hopes rose higher as time passed and there was no sound or sign of either Minotauros or Theseus. Phaedra took over the task of trying to calm the increasingly querulous Pasiphaë.

Ariadne went first to Minos' study to report what she had seen. Her father thought that since neither had emerged, Theseus was likely to have been the victor, though he conceded that both might be dead or even still struggling or pursuing one another through the labyrinth.

'And what if Theseus is dead?' she asked.

'Then all our plans are likewise dead,' said Minos. 'You will not go to Athens, having no husband to go with. The seven Athenian girls must remain in the palace and the six youths in prison. If Minotauros is also dead, perhaps they will escape death, but we will either sell them as slaves or keep them here in our own service. Meanwhile, you must be ready to open the door in case Theseus has indeed conquered, but if he has not come out by nightfall you had better return to me and I will cancel the secret arrangements I have made for releasing the prisoners and conveying them to the harbour.'

So Ariadne went to the door of the labyrinth and waited between hope and despair. If Theseus had won, why had his thread not brought him quickly back to the door? But if Theseus had lost, why was her mother on the palace roof constantly calling out for her son? They must, she decided, both be dead or fatally injured, and for her that was as bad an outcome as if Theseus had lost. Hours passed and the sun began to set. Ariadne prayed to Aphrodite, goddess of love, begging her to be kind to two lovers and promising to sacrifice to her as soon as their ship reached land. Aphrodite heard, no doubt, but knowing these lovers' future knew also that her kindness could only store up heartbreak for Ariadne.

Night came down and Ariadne, stiff and sorrowful, was about to leave her post and go to her father when she heard, very faintly, a tap on the door, then another, then a third. Joyfully, her blood racing, her eyes pouring tears, she drew back the bolts and pushed the heavy door open. There he was, Theseus! She took him in her arms, but they nearly fell together. He could scarcely stand. For the last many hours he had been limping on his inflamed leg, sometimes crawling, sometimes supporting himself on the walls, through Daidalos' fiendish invention, and by the time he at last found his thread he was almost too exhausted and feverish to go any further. Taking time only to support him to the top of the steps that led up from the labyrinth and help him to a dark angle of the palace building where no one could see him, Ariadne ran to her father, afraid that he might already have cancelled all the arrangements for their escape. She found him on the point of doing so, but hearing of Theseus' wound he told Ariadne to fetch medicines, salves and bandages before leading the Athenian girls out of the palace to the rendezvous near the prison. He himself would fetch Theseus.

Half sitting, half lying in his dark corner and seeing not Ariadne but a man standing over him, Theseus thought some soldier must have come to arrest him and struggled to his feet so as to fight him off. But the man, an old man, unarmed, retreated a few steps and said quietly:

'Not quite the shades yet, Theseus, though dark enough. I have come to help you. You've killed my ugly stepson, I suppose, and you shall have your reward, but you must be careful what you say afterwards. Put the blame on Ariadne, or give her the credit, but never let it be known that Minos had any hand in your escape!'

Theseus, limping painfully with his arm round the king's shoulders to a place where Ariadne was waiting with balm and dressings for his wound, beside two covered carts containing the seven girls and six youths from Athens, could hardly believe this was not a dream. Perhaps he had dreamed the labyrinth and the encounter with the Minotaur, perhaps he would wake up to find it was still the night before his ordeal and all was still to be gone through. Only half-conscious as he was lifted into the cart, he thought he heard Minos say:

'The gods go with you, Theseus, as they clearly have been with you. I believe Poseidon meant to forgive me my long-ago mistake and sent you for the purpose. May he give you calm seas and fair winds for Athens!'

He did not hear Minos take tender leave of his daughter, nor see him walk quietly away in the darkness towards the palace, where he was greeted by the violent grief of his wife who had been brought off the roof by Phaedra but was now convinced that her son was dead. But where was Phaedra to comfort her? Minos had the palace searched, but she was not to be found. He guessed then that she had gone with the Athenian girls and would already be on-board the ship and sailing out of the harbour. For a moment or two he considered ordering his own ships to overtake it and bring her back, but how could he do so without bringing back Ariadne, Theseus and the Athenians too? No, he must wait until morning before sending his fleet in pursuit or all his plans for Ariadne's future and the future of relations with Athens would go awry.

So Theseus had gone off with both his daughters. He smiled, was almost inclined to laugh. The gods were so tricky. They gave with one hand what they took away with another. A white bull which you failed to sacrifice led to a bull-headed stepson, whose long-awaited removal gave you a husband for your daughter, but lost you another daughter. And what on earth would the foolish Phaedra do now, an unmarried girl in a foreign city? And what could he do to placate the desolated Pasiphaë? It was no laughing matter.

6. THE ISLAND

The Athenian ship headed due north through the night and was well clear of Crete by dawn. Theseus himself was still feverish, watched over by Ariadne. She did not reveal to the master of the ship that her father had not only authorised but assisted their escape, so that the sailors as well as the former prisoners were constantly expecting pursuit and, since there was little wind to fill the black sails, rowed with special vigour. The seven Athenian girls even took turns with the youths, but could not quite understand in the darkness why there seemed to be eight of them. Only when it grew light did they see that their extra companion was Minos' daughter Phaedra and, fearing that she was a spy and would somehow bring about their recapture, wanted to throw her overboard. The sailors and youths, however, protected her and Phaedra explained that she had known of the plans for the escape and had helped her sister, so that she would herself have been punished once the escape became public.

Ariadne, always at Theseus' side, did not discover that Phaedra was on board until much later, when the ship put in for food and water at the island of Naxos. Theseus was now out of danger and wanted to accompany Ariadne ashore to make the sacrifice she had promised to Aphrodite, but when she found that Aphrodite's temple was on a promontory many miles from the port, she refused to let him in case his wound reopened or his fever returned. Exhausted, but determined nevertheless to keep her promise to the goddess, she went to the group of Athenian girls, who remained on-board while the sailors brought on the supplies, to ask them to care for Theseus while she was gone, and was astonished and dismayed to discover her sister among them. From the time when she was called to Minos' study to meet Theseus and make plans for his escape Ariadne had scarcely slept. She had watched his encounter with the Minotaur, waited half the day in a state of tense anxiety beside the door to the labyrinth, conducted the Athenian girls to the rendezvous, tended Theseus night and day on the ship and could perhaps be forgiven for the bitter fury of her reaction.

'You! What are you doing here? I know you fancy Theseus. But is it you or me that our father chose to marry Theseus? How dare you smuggle yourself on to our ship? How dare you leave our mother in her distress?'

'What hysteria!' said Phaedra. 'You sound just like Mother. Why should I be left to look after her when you are flying off with the hero? I'm not trying to take him away from you ...'

'Are you not?'

'Only trying to take myself away from that mad woman at home.'

'Lies! You love him.'

'What if I do? Can I help that? And what can you do about it?'

'I shall make him leave you here.'

'How will you make him? He's not so cruel.'

'It will be you or me. He will have no alternative. You'll see. Your nasty little adventure ends here on Naxos.'

Telling the girls that her sister was on no account to be allowed near Theseus, she left Phaedra in tears and went ashore. There she hired a donkey and a guide and rode out to Aphrodite's temple to make her sacrifice with the help of the priestesses who looked after it.

But she had not told the master of the ship what she was doing and when the supplies had all been brought on board he was anxious to leave, afraid that the Cretans might still be in pursuit. Theseus was asleep. As the ship began to leave the quay, both the girls and the young men told the master that Ariadne had not returned and that he must wait for her. Grumbling and uncertain, he told his men to tie up again, but scanning the horizon for Cretan warships and ever more nervous as time went by, he insisted on waking Theseus, who leapt up and said he would go and look for Ariadne himself. But as he was about to go ashore, pushing his way through the knot of girls who tried to dissuade him, he suddenly saw Phaedra standing alone at the ship's rail. Unlike Ariadne, he was pleased to see her and immediately accepted her tearful explanation.

'Of course you had to leave Knossos,' he said, 'and I will make sure that when we reach Athens you are treated with great honour as one of our saviours and, if it is your wish, I will find you a suitably noble husband.'

Phaedra told him of Ariadne's anger and that she had threatened to make him leave her behind on Naxos, and Theseus promised that he would do no such thing. Then, hiring a horse and getting directions to the temple of Aphrodite, he set off at once to bring back Ariadne. But the girls on the ship, afraid that he was still not well enough for such a journey, persuaded their male companions to follow him.

Ariadne, however, was not at the temple. Her guide had deceived her. Instead of leading her to the temple of Aphrodite, he had taken her in another direction to a temple of Dionysos, which was in the care of his own relations, intending that they, rather than the priestesses of Aphrodite, should benefit from the sacrifices to be paid for by this foreign princess. When Ariadne discovered that she had been guided to the wrong temple, she angrily demanded that the guide take her immediately to the right one and he, concealing his own anger, pretended to do so, but led her instead into a dense wood where they had to dismount from their mules. As they reached the far edge of the wood and the guide was holding her donkey for Ariadne to mount, he suddenly jerked the animal's bridle and, mounting his own, rode away with both donkeys, leaving Ariadne still struggling to her feet.

She wasted no time or effort in trying to pursue him, but only shouted after him that if this was the way he treated strangers who were only trying to pay tribute to the gods, the gods would surely punish him. Then, looking around her – she was on the slope of a hill above a fertile valley of vines and fruit trees – and glimpsing the sea in the distance, she began to walk towards it, sure that if she kept it always on her left she must eventually come back to the port.

Theseus, meanwhile, after reaching the temple of Aphrodite – his guide was a more honest man than Ariadne's – and learning from the priestesses that they had never seen Ariadne, began to fear that she had been kidnapped. He hurried back to the port so as to confront the king or whoever was in authority in the island and organise a search, but by the time he reached it his fever had returned and he was delirious. The Athenians carried him on to the ship, where Phaedra at once took charge of him, and it was she now who seemed to the master of the ship to be the only person he could ask for instructions. In fact he simply wanted permission to leave as soon as possible. The sun was sinking, there would be no hope of finding Ariadne until the next day and meanwhile they would give the Cretan warships another eight hours at least to catch up with them. Phaedra hardly hesitated. She remembered vividly her sister's last words to her and the venom she had put into them; and besides, the love she had felt for Theseus ever since she first saw him and had suppressed, partly in case he was killed by the Minotaur and partly because her elder sister had the prior claim, now flamed up and burnt away any affection she had left for Ariadne.

'We must go,' she said to the master. 'My sister could not want us all to be recaptured just because she has got herself lost. Theseus himself is seriously ill and must be seen by doctors as soon as possible. Athens can surely send another ship back to Naxos to fetch my sister in a few days' time.'

The master gave his orders, the ship left the quay and headed out of the harbour into the sunset. From a headland above the sea, Ariadne, who had at last come in sight of the port and stopped briefly to rest, saw it far out on the dark water, silhouetted against the red horizon, and recognised it by its black sails.

7. THE SAILS

The rest of Ariadne's story is obscure. Some say that she killed herself in despair, others that she was already pregnant and died in childbirth, but most people prefer the dramatic change of fortune depicted by Titian's painting *Bacchus and Ariadne* in London's National Gallery. Ariadne, still gazing desperately out to sea after the departing ship, is surprised by Dionysos (also called Bacchus) and his ravers – maenads, satyrs, old Silenos drunk on a donkey, Dionysos himself leaping out of a chariot drawn by cheetahs – and becomes the bride of the god instead of Theseus. This outcome must have been foreseen both by Dionysos himself and by Aphrodite, if it was not actually arranged between them, and if Aphrodite was offended by Ariadne's broken promise of a sacrifice in return for the safe delivery of Theseus, she clearly did not blame Ariadne. It was Phaedra, far in the future, whom she punished.

In Athens the return of the ship was awaited by the whole population with feelings between hope and despair. King Aegeus kept watchmen on duty along the south-east coast of Attica as far as the rocky headland of Sounion which, restless and apprehensive, he often visited himself in the hope of being the first to see the white sails signalling his son's success. He saw, of course, many vessels with white sails, since most of the traffic into Peiraias or Corinth from Euboia, the Black Sea, Asia Minor or the Cyclades and Sporades islands passed that point. But one day he happened to be at Sounion when the watchman, with sharper eyes than old Aegeus, tugged his sleeve and pointed. The ship just coming into sight had black sails. Aegeus stared with growing dismay as it came nearer. Must it be that Theseus and all his companions were dead, that the dreadful yearly sacrifice of seven youths and seven virgins to the Minotaur would continue? Now the ship, its fatal black sails filled with a stiff south-easterly breeze, was near enough for Aegeus to see that it was the very same ship – he recognised the serpent's head on the prow, the royal device of the House of Erechtheus – that had left Athens for Crete. He could see small figures on board, but they were too far away to be identified. Surely if Theseus and his companions were still among them, they would be waving in triumph to the people on the shore? But of course they would not, could not, since they had not changed the sails. The message was clear enough, he had devised it himself: all were dead, all was lost. Aegeus, his eyes blind with tears, stumbled to the edge of the headland, glanced once more at the ship – perhaps he had been mistaken, perhaps they were changing the sails even now – no, they were black still – and jumped to his death. His shattered body was recovered by his grieving servants from the rocky surf below and carried back to Athens.

The news spread quickly and there were few people on the quayside at Peiraias to greet the ship with black sails, which no one on board had remembered to change, which no one on shore wished to be reminded of. Theseus, limping on to the quayside, almost himself again, followed by the six youths and seven virgins, brought the place to life. Messengers ran to Athens, and by the time the hero and his companions, with Phaedra at his side, were half way between Peiraias and the walls of Athens, the population was pouring out to greet them. Theseus made thanksgiving sacrifices for their safe return, but forbade any great celebration in the shadow of the king his father's death, for which, bitterly blaming his own carelessness, he accepted full responsibility. As for Ariadne, having already exchanged one Cretan bride for another, Theseus had not yet worked out what he would do if the first were found and brought to Athens, but did not entirely blame himself for abandoning her, since it was not he but Phaedra who had ordered the ship to sail away. He held a magnificent funeral for his father, and after a suitable interval married Phaedra. Did he wait to do so until he had sent a ship from Athens to Naxos to search for Ariadne? Phaedra, never forgetting her sister's last words to her and considering that Ariadne had been justly done by as she would have done, might well have discouraged him, but whether he did send a ship or not, one way or another she was not to be found.

Ariadne was thus the second woman whom Theseus managed to leave behind, the first being Sinis' daughter Perigune. His treatment of women in general – there were many others more peripheral to his story whom he loved and left – gave him a bad reputation. But was his womanising any worse than Herakles'? The difference was really one of character, or at least of how their respective characters were perceived. Theseus appeared to be more calculating, more self-interested, emotionally colder. Herakles' warm, humorous, generous personality seemed to make his abandonment of women less deliberate and more forgivable.

But Theseus was now King of Athens and, whatever his personal failings, he soon began to achieve politically what Minos had foreseen. Athens at that time was only one of a dozen small towns and districts in Attica, linked by common interests but each wary of the rest and unable to present a single front to the outside world. Theseus, inspired by what Minos had done for Crete and riding on his fame as the conqueror of the Minotaur, built up the military strength of Athens on the basis of a form of conscription. Recalling his own period of training in Troezen before setting out on his journey to Athens and the brief experience of it he had given his companions on the voyage to Crete, he ordered that every male child reaching the age of sixteen should do a year's military service and every citizen under 40 years old should attend a military training camp for a month during the winter, when they were not required on the land. He then persuaded or forced the rest of Attica into a union ruled by himself and imposed the same rules for military service on all his new subjects. He made many local enemies, less among the common people than among landowners and noble families with private interests to protect, but, as his encounters with the brigands along his road to Athens had shown, he was ruthless towards anyone who stood in his way. Opponents either knuckled down or fled or died. As long as Minos lived there were no further Cretan attacks and even the beginnings of trade between the two kingdoms, and Athens soon had a navy strong enough to beat off any invaders from the sea.

Minos himself, meanwhile, had trouble not only with his wife but also his subjects, when it became known that Theseus had killed the Minotaur and escaped with all his fellow prisoners and both the princesses. Minos concealed his own part in the escape by executing the guards who, on his orders, had released the prisoners and taken them to the harbour, and he put the blame for the whole affair on his lovesick and wayward daughters. He was said to have punished Daidalos for suggesting or even providing the thread by shutting him and his son Ikaros in the labyrinth, from which they escaped with artificial wings. That seems unlikely. How did Daidalos in the labyrinth come by the materials with which to construct such wings and how, even from the open space at the centre, could they have achieved lift-off? Certainly Minos' relations with Daidalos were strained, but if he ordered Daidalos and his son Ikaros to enter the labyrinth it was no doubt because Queen Pasiphaë was insisting that her son's body be brought out for burial and Minos judged that to be a fitting punishment for Daidalos. He could find his way along the thread left behind by Theseus, and Ikaros would have gone with him to help him carry or drag the monstrous and by now fly-blown corpse.

To be compelled to do such dirty work as if he was a common slave was quite enough to convince Daidalos that it was time to leave Crete and, returning angrily to his workshop, he immediately put his mind to the logistics. They were not simple. He would have to leave the island in secret and go to some place beyond the reach of Minos' power. He could hardly commandeer a ship, nor could he build a large enough one by himself. Flying was the obvious answer, except that no human without the help of the gods had ever done it. Daidalos determined to be the first and he devised two pairs of wings, one pair for himself and one pair for his son.

It must have taken him a long time to collect enough feathers and then to assemble them into viable wings, using wax to hold the feathers together. But when they were finally completed the father and son took them by night to the top of the nearest mountain and as soon as it grew light, launched themselves into the air, finding, as with all Daidalos' inventions, that they really did work. But although Daidalos reminded Ikaros that the wings were made with wax and he must not fly too near the sun, the boy was too excited, too exhilarated, too young to heed the warning, and somewhere over the sea near the island of Samos he soared up high above his father and suddenly saw feathers floating away all round him. The next moment he was dropping and by the time he plunged past Daidalos in a cloud of loose feathers it was too late. Far below, Daidalos saw a little plume of water and Ikaros was gone.

They must have been heading towards Mysia or Thrace or even the Black Sea, but now for some reason, perhaps that he no longer cared where he went, Daidalos turned westwards. He landed at last in Sikania (modern Sicily) and was welcomed by Kokalos, king of the Sikani.

Minos was surely a little unhinged by now, for old as he was, hearing that Daidalos had taken refuge in Italy, he went after him in person and, having tracked him down to Sikania, demanded his extradition. Kokalos refused and Minos was murdered by another of Daidalos' inventions: a hot shower of boiling water.

8. THE MISTRESS

While he was still working to unite his people, Theseus heard that an invasion force of Lapiths from Thessaly, led by their king, Peirithoös, had appeared on the northern border of Attica. He was pleased. If anything could persuade the people of Attica that they needed to be united, it was just such an outside threat. Furthermore, he could test the quality of his new army of citizen soldiers in a serious battle. Up to now they had only been required to put down a few local insurrections. The two armies met near the plain of Marathon, where many centuries later the Athenians were to win their great victory over the invaders from Persia. Peirithoös, whose intelligence service must have been poor, had not expected to meet anything but sporadic resistance, and was disconcerted to see a well-armed and well-disciplined force lined up against him. His own troops were mostly cavalry, brave and dashing individuals who were accustomed to skirmishing but had no experience of a set-piece battle. They rode furiously at the Athenian ranks and, failing to break them, retired in disorder with many losses. Peirithoös, seeing the enemy preparing to advance and with nothing to stop them but his own royal guard, sent a herald to Theseus asking for a truce. Theseus accepted, the two kings met, immediately liked one another and became such friends that soon afterwards, when Peirithoös was getting married, he invited Theseus to the ceremony. Their friendship became even closer after that, since it was the infamous occasion when the centaurs, also guests at the wedding banquet, became drunk and tried to rape the bride and any other Lapith women they could get their hands on. Theseus was prominent among those who beat them off.

Peirithoös seems to have been a restless, rash and audacious person with a great influence over his new friend, and before long he was suggesting that they should mount a joint expedition against the Amazons, whose territory lay on the south coast of the Black Sea. These militant women, he pointed out, were taking revenge for Herakles' theft of the belt of Ares and the killing of their queen, Hippolyte, by interrupting the lucrative trade between Greece and other Black Sea kingdoms. Theseus, confident now that his own kingdom was in good working order and perhaps keen to make his mark on a wider world, agreed.

The combination of Theseus' steady infantry and Peirithoös' enthusiastic horsemen proved an instant success in their first battle, in which Antiope, Hippolyte's sister and successor as queen, leading a cavalry charge against the Athenian line, was captured. The invaders did not stay to conquer the territory or even risk a second encounter, but, content to have inflicted such a humiliating check to these women's military pretensions, boarded their ships and returned home with their captive. The Athenian troops sailed straight to Athens with the good news of their victory, but their king stopped off in Thessaly to stay a few months with his friend Peirithoös. Theseus had fallen in love with Antiope and she, as women tended to, with him. By the time they moved on to Athens, Antiope was pregnant.

Phaedra's response to this rival for her husband's love was inwardly volcanic, but outwardly dignified. She was no Medea, who when rejected by Jason murdered her own children and his new wife. Phaedra made no complaint to Theseus. She did not really blame him, whom she still loved, but rather the goddess Aphrodite, and in blaming her was also conscious of her own part in abandoning and displacing Ariadne. Above all, she did not want to be abandoned in her turn and hoped that her displacement would be only temporary. She simply ignored Antiope, as if she had been any ordinary slave girl brought back from a foreign war. Theseus perfectly understood both his wife's undeclared anger and the royal Cretan pride that made her hide it, and tactfully lodged Antiope in a separate building with her own attendants. Their son was born there, named Hippolytos after Antiope's elder sister, and brought up quite separately from Akamas and Demophoön, the two sons of Theseus and Phaedra.

The Amazons, however, led by Antiope's younger sister Oreithyia, were planning their revenge. First, they enlisted the Scythians as allies. These were wild nomads from the far side of the Black Sea who liked to scalp their enemies and drink out of their skulls and were always game for incursions into more civilised places where valuable plunder was to be had. Riding the long way round the Black Sea, past the land of the Golden Fleece, crossing the iced-over strait called the Cimmerian Bosporos at the entrance to the Maiotis Limne (or Sea of Azov), the Amazons joined forces with a band of Scythians and rode on southwards through Thrace and Macedonia to Thessaly, where they easily defeated the Lapiths and ransacked Peirithoös' territory. Then they rode on to Athens, where Theseus' citizen army was beaten and retreated to the Acropolis, while the Amazons occupied the rest of the city and sent a message that if the Athenians surrendered both Theseus and Antiope they would spare the rest of the population and return home.

Theseus consulted Antiope, who was already expecting their second child.

'Do you want to go home with your sister?'

'And with you?'

'Not with me. I undertook once to be fed to a man-eating monster. I don't mean to repeat the experience with a nation of man-eating women.'

'Would you let me go alone?'

'If that was your wish.'

'You've had enough of me?'

'Never. You are the love of my life, Antiope.'

'But you're still married to that Cretan woman.'

'Marriage is one thing, love is another.'

'Shouldn't they go together?'

'Who says so? The gods?'

'Then I will stay here with you, Theseus.'

'And may die with me at the hands of your own people and the wild Scythians.'

'So you do want me to go? '

'Not at all. But they are your own people, led by your own sister, and the choice to go with them or stay with me must be yours.'

'Then you and I will fight them together. And perhaps we shall win.'

So when the Athenians suddenly broke out of the Acropolis and attacked the adjoining hill where the Amazons were encamped, they were led by both Theseus and Antiope. Perhaps it was the sight of the queen they had come to rescue dealing death to their own ranks or the fiery strength of two such famous warriors in combination that took the heart out of the Amazons. At any rate, by the time one of the Amazon archers had shot down Antiope, they were already losing the battle. Oreithyia tried to rally them, but Theseus, seeing Antiope fall, became like a madman, and seemed to gain her strength as well as his own. Cutting down the woman who had shot her and every Amazon who stood in his way, he made straight for Oreithyia and was followed by close ranks of triumphant Athenians. Oreithyia's troops broke and scattered in front of Theseus' fury and Oreithyia herself fled with them.

The Scythians, encamped on the outskirts of the city, enjoying the plentiful wine and meat they had lifted from the Attic countryside, took no part in the battle, and, seeing that their allies were in flight, gathered up what plunder they could carry and galloped away northwards. Oreithyia took refuge in the small city of Megara along the coast to the west. Some of the Amazons fled north with the Scythians and settled amongst them, some returned to their own country with their lamentable news, many died on the battlefield or during the rout. Not until the Trojan War, many years later, were they once again a military force to be reckoned with, and then, siding with the Trojans, they suffered a further defeat when their new queen Penthesileia was slain by Achilles.

Achilles mourned the beautiful, brave woman he had killed, just as Theseus mourned her brave, beautiful predecessor, Antiope, who had fought against her own people for his sake, just as Herakles mourned her sister Hippolyte whom he killed without meaning to in the melée near his ship. These successive Amazon queens, dying by or for their hero-lovers, are a recurrent motif in the Greek stories and they pop up again in the Italian Renaissance stories of Ariosto and Tasso as pagans or Saracens fighting and loving Christians, and in the late twentieth century as bold and beautiful foreign vamps loved and destroyed by James Bond. Are they just male fantasies of dangerous temptation, of sweet, soft flesh concealed under armed and booted carapaces? Or the deeper truth of love between the sexes, who are in so many ways opposites and whose mutual attraction is also a battleground?

9. THE STEPSON

Theseus buried Antiope and the other dead Amazons with sorrow and ceremony. He even sent a message to Oreithyia inviting her to the funeral of her sister and promising to provide a ship to take her home. But Oreithyia could not forgive Antiope for fighting with the Athenians, nor did she think the Amazons would forgive her for their defeat. She rejected Theseus' offer, took poison and died. Phaedra behaved with her usual tact, showing neither pleasure nor sorrow in the removal of Antiope, congratulating Theseus on his victory without ever referring to the woman who had helped him win it, but when he suggested that Hippolytos might now be brought up with her own children she vehemently objected. Theseus did not insist; not wanting his son to be brought up in isolation in a household of servants, he sent him to his mother in Troezen, where his grandfather King Pittheus, at the suggestion of Theseus who would otherwise have succeeded him, made Hippolytos his heir. Phaedra, sure now that he would not be a rival to her own sons for the throne of Athens, was pleased.

She did not even mind when, many years later, Hippolytos returned to Athens as a boy of sixteen so that he could be trained, under his father's eye, in the military and gymnastic skills which Theseus had made compulsory for all his male subjects. His two step-brothers were a little older and had already been through this training, but without giving much satisfaction to Theseus. He considered them lazy and lacking in determination or courage, and often told them so brusquely and openly. Now in his middle age, Theseus was becoming something of a despot both to his family and his people. But he very much approved of Hippolytos, an extremely serious boy who was devoted to sport and physical exercise and already an accomplished archer, rider, charioteer and wrestler. Phaedra might easily have been jealous of the constant preference Theseus showed for this half-Amazon bastard over his own legitimate sons, but instead she found herself liking him. He had the striking good looks of his father, the man her mother had likened to Apollo and whom Phaedra had fallen in love with as soon as she saw him in the palace at Knossos. Hippolytos was particularly deferential to his stepmother, whom he expected to be his enemy, modest about his own abilities and even shy. He had been brought up, after all, mainly by his grandmother, loving but strict, and in common with most such boys was at ease with old women but nervous of younger ones.

Like all young athletes in those days, Hippolytos competed and exercised naked, and although the palace women were mostly out of sight in their own quarters, they were not confined to them as Muslim women were in much later times, nor, unlike Christian women, were they surprised or shocked by seeing men naked. It was entirely normal and gave them much cause for admiration, mockery and the humorous or wistful comparison of one man with another among themselves. The spectacle of Hippolytos, however, exercising as he often did in a courtyard of the palace, was special and he had a regular audience. They did not, of course, stand or sit around watching him – that would have been coarse and impolite – but they did peep round screens and through doorways or embrasures as well as pass that way much more frequently than when he was not exercising.

Hippolytos himself, intent on fine-tuning his body and improving his skills, seemed hardly to notice them. He was neither homosexual nor a narcissist, he had simply put sex aside for the present in his desire to match up to his father, much as his father at the same age had desired to match up to his cousin Herakles. He was also, of course, the child of an Amazon queen, high priestess of the virgin moon goddess Artemis, and though he could not remember his mother he knew of her heroism (from the Athenian point of view) and venerated her as much as his father. Amazons in general regarded sex only as the necessary prelude to creating more female warriors, and Hippolytos, if anyone had asked him, would probably have had a similar opinon about getting male warriors for Athens and Troezen.

Phaedra was amused by her attendants' interest in Hippolytos, which they did not express openly to her, but which she couldn't help noticing and overhearing. She herself sometimes caught sight of the naked athlete at his regular exercises, alone or with a fellow-athlete – it would have been abnormal to look away – but she did not deliberately spy on him as the other women did. Why should she? He was an unusually handsome youth, of course, but she was married to his still more handsome and very famous father and she did not need anyone else's love. Besides, Hippolytos was still a boy, younger than her own sons; she could admire his muscular physique and excellent proportions, his long legs and small buttocks, his golden hair, blue eyes and broad, open face, much as one might the painting or sculpture of an idealised god or hero.

And then one day Hippolytos returned to Troezen. His great-grandfather Pittheus was dying, and he would soon have to take his place as king. The women in the palace missed him badly. A mood between melancholy and irritability settled over the women's quarters and Phaedra, to her own surprise, found she shared it. It wasn't that Hippolytos had made any overtures to any of them or even exchanged words, except when directly addressed by his stepmother – he had offered them nothing more than a polite and fleeting smile – but that the courtyard was so abysmally empty. Life had left it, the epitome of life, the man who represented what man at his living best could be, young, strong, lithe, intelligent, idealistic.

When, not long afterwards, King Pittheus died, Theseus travelled by sea to Troezen for the funeral and much of his court, including Phaedra, went with him. Hippolytos, now king in his great-grandfather's place, organised the ceremonies and sacrifices and the burial with the same unostentatious efficiency he had brought to his own training. Theseus could only wish that it might be Hippolytus, rather than his eldest son Akamas, who would one day rule Athens. Soon after the funeral, when Theseus and his court were preparing to return to Athens, news came of the death of his friend Peirithoös' wife and Theseus sent the messenger back to say that he, who had attended their wedding and helped save the bride from the centaurs, would attend her funeral and offer what comfort he could to his grieving friend. Phaedra, however, surprising herself again, said that while he was away she would like to stay in Troezen rather than return to Athens immediately. Theseus too was surprised.

'It's quite a small town,' he said. 'What will you do here?'

'What do I do in Athens?'

'You preside over my court, you help the poor, you receive friends and take part in women's rites and mysteries – all the things that a queen is expected to do. But here in Troezen ...?'

'There is no queen in Troezen, is there? Your son is a man alone. I can perhaps bring a woman's touch to his palace and court until he finds a suitable wife.'

'My mother is here and will do that for him.'

'Your mother is old and – dare I say? – a little out of date. When you brought me from Crete you also brought much that was new and more civilised to Athens. Troezen strikes me as still quite primitive.

A lovely place, yes, and I like its old-fashioned air, but I'm sure your son will want to give it something of the style you and I gave to Athens.'

'Hippolytos is mainly interested in sport and hunting.'

But Theseus was pleased that Phaedra seemed to be so concerned for the welfare of Troezen and its new king, whom she clearly liked now in spite of his unfortunate origin. He said that she could stay in Troezen with two or three of her attendants – more would be too costly and invasive for such a small place – and when he returned from Thessaly he would come to Troezen to fetch her. Then he took affectionate leave of her and his mother and Hippolytos and boarded the ship for Athens with the rest of his court.

Hippolytos noticed, of course, that his stepmother stayed on after his father and most of the funeral guests had left, but having no notion of women's activities or what went on in their heads, simply accepted it as a given fact and left it to his grandmother, Aithra, to arrange for Phaedra and her two attendant women's comfort. He often went hunting, exercised every day in the gymnasium built by his great-grandfather and, apart from his royal duties of arbitrating disputes and judging crimes – of which there were few in Troezen – was busy supervising the building of a new temple to the virgin goddess Artemis, whom he worshipped with particular fervour.

Phaedra was now beginning to admit to herself, though not yet to her attendants, that she had not stayed in Troezen to help her stepson modernise it so much as simply to be near him. She did not like this realisation, she tried to suppress it and to laugh at herself, but every time she saw him and spoke to him, the dagger, as she thought of it, of her attraction to him sank deeper into her flesh. When she heard her attendants joking together that it was a pity Hippolytos exercised now in the gymnasium instead of his palace courtyard, she asked where the gymnasium was. They told her it was outside the town walls, next to a small house built by Pittheus as a retreat for himself when he wished to be philosopher rather than king. Finding that no one used the house since the old king's death, Phaedra asked Hippolytos if, now that it was high summer, she and her attendants might move in there, away from the heat inside the town. He agreed at once, only stipulating that, since the house was outside the walls, an armed guard should be posted there at night in case of pirates landing in the bay or robbers coming over the mountain.

'Pirates? Robbers?' said Phaedra. 'What have we to fear from them since Theseus was king of Athens and heir to Troezen?'

'Nothing that I know of,' said Hippolytos, scratching his fair curls, 'but I should not be able to sleep at night for anxiety if I left you unprotected.'

'Is that so?' said Phaedra. 'I had no idea you ever troubled your head about the weakness of women.'

'My father would never forgive me.'

'You are a most dutiful son,' said Phaedra, disappointed that it was not really her he was worried about, but how his father might react.

Phaedra and her attendants moved into the house and were rewarded almost at once by the sight of Hippolytos and several of his friends at their exercises. A small window of the house looked straight into the gymnasium's elegant pillared courtyard. Pittheus had no doubt planned it that way, so that he could keep an eye on the physical progress of his pupils, as he did on their musical studies in the Temple of the Muses, a mile away up the hill. Phaedra sat so often by this window when Hippolytos was in the gymnasium that her attendants could not help noticing and she herself, feeding her addiction to the sight of his naked body, began not to care that they did. Soon she no longer pretended to herself that she was not in love with him and was no longer ashamed to let her eyes fall from his face, red with his exertions, to his sweat-beaded chest and belly and powerful thighs, and allow them to dwell on that small bulging sac at the very centre of his body, and, drooping over it, the soft tube of flesh, like a snake's head protruding from its nest of fine golden hair.

Euripides, in his tragedy *Hippolytos*, makes this lust of Phaedra for her stepson the deliberate revenge of Aphrodite, in order to punish not Phaedra, who is merely her instrument, but Hippolytos for his one-goddess obsession with Artemis and neglect of herself, the goddess of love. Phaedra, however, remembering how her sister had gone ashore on Naxos to make a sacrifice to Aphrodite and how she herself had taken the opportunity of Ariadne's long absence and

Theseus' delirium to order the ship to sail away without her, believed that Aphrodite was punishing *her*. That didn't trouble her at all. The more her addiction to the sight of the naked Hippolytos took hold of her, the more grateful she was to Aphrodite. She had been an inexperienced girl when she fell in love with Theseus, now she was a mature woman who knew the pleasure of lovemaking with a lustful man. She longed to put her hands on this rejuvenated Theseus, to arouse that sleeping snake's head and give it exercises of its own.

The elder of her attendants, Evadne, seeing that her mistress was now sick with lust, refusing food, lacking sleep, unable to concentrate on anything but the view from that window, at last dared to speak:

'You love him, don't you?'

'And if I do?'

'You should do something about it.'

'What can I do? He's my stepson.'

'No blood relation.'

'Does that make it better, when I'm his father's wife?'

'Better or worse is not the question when love strikes so hard. You have to find a cure.'

'There's only one cure for this.'

'For him to make love to you.'

'Out of the question,' said Phaedra.

'Is it really? It's obvious that this boy has never slept with anyone. He doesn't have any idea of what pleasure it would give him. You could show him.'

'Yes, if he were willing. But he's not. Aphrodite means nothing to him.'

'You would be Aphrodite's ambassador, to bring him to her altar.'

'But how?'

'Let me speak to him!'

'Never! He'd be appalled.'

'Not if I found the right way of introducing him. Then it would be up to you.'

'No, no, no! We never had this conversation.'

'If you say so. But you can't go on like this and if you continue starving yourself and spending sleepless nights, you'll lose your looks and start to look like an old woman. And then what hope would you have of awakening him?'

Phaedra made no answer and turned away. But when she still refused food and became still more hollow-eyed and pale, Evadne decided that her answer had really been 'yes'. She intercepted Hippolytos on his way to the gymnasium and told him that her mistress was unwell and that he should call on her and discover what her trouble was. Hippolytos entered the little house, saw at once that his stepmother was not herself and sat down opposite her, with the window between them. The afternoon sun streamed through the window and cast a golden glow over Hippolytos as if he were indeed Apollo. Phaedra withdrew into shadow and stared at him in silence, as though she were in a trance.

'You are ill?' he asked.

'Not exactly.'

'Something is upsetting you?'

'Yes.'

'You're missing my father?'

'Yes and no.'

'Too hot?'

'I like heat.'

'Is there anything I can do to help?'

She shook her head so slowly and sadly that even Hippolytos, with no experience of women's moods and signals, was touched. He leaned across and took her hand.

'Let me help you!' he said. 'You know that since I lost my mother, you've been my mother.'

Phaedra cried out:

'No! No! I was never your mother. Antiope was your mother and then Aithra.'

'Yes, of course. But she was my grandmother. Since I grew up I've always seen you as ...'

'Not your mother!'

'No, I suppose not exactly.' Understanding that this word 'mother' distressed her, he tried to find an alternative. 'As – what can I say? As a beautiful, sophisticated woman. As the sort of wife I might one day hope for myself, if I was so lucky.'

He smiled and looked at her steadily, still holding her hand.

'That's how you see me?'

'Absolutely!' he said, pleased that she seemed pleased.

'I love you, Hippolytos,' she said, very quietly as if to herself.

'I know you do.'

'You know?'

'Because I love *you*. People, in my experience, don't love people who don't love them.'

Did she really mistake his meaning? The Greek verbs for friendly affection and sexual attraction are not, as in English, the same. More likely, in her desperation, driven mad by his close presence and the vengeful influence of Aphrodite, she chose to attempt the leap from one love to the other. Seizing with both hands the hand that still rested on hers, she kissed it passionately.

'I am in love,' she said, 'devoured by love, netted and speared by Aphrodite.'

Still he failed to understand her – how could he, from his complete innocence of the emotion?

'In love? What do you mean? With my father?'

'With you, Hippolytos, with you. The gods help me!'

Now he did understand. The shock stripped him of all the respect he had for her, of all his usual gentleness, of every idea he had ever had of how things should be. He pulled his hand away and stood up, knocking over the stool he had been sitting on.

'Revolting!' he said, 'horrible! filthy! You disgust me!'

He fled from the room, ran past the gymnasium, up the hill past the Temple of the Muses and beyond the town to his new temple of Artemis, nearly completed. There he flung himself down in front of the altar and prayed to Artemis for comfort and guidance.

Back in the little house beside the gymnasium, Evadne tried to console Phaedra. Phaedra would have none of it, none of Evadne herself, whom she blamed for precipitating this catastrophe. Raging, weeping, striking the walls with her fists and arms so that they bled, she drove her two attendants out of the house, telling them that she no longer needed them, they could go back to Athens or down to Hades.

'What do I need attendants for? I am no longer a queen, no longer the wife of a king, no longer even a woman. Something filthy, horrible, revolting! I disgust him! Yes, quite right, Hippolytos! I disgust myself.'

Evadne and her companion left the house and walked about disconsolately, not knowing what they ought to do. They needed help, perhaps even male help, to restrain Phaedra, but how could they get help without revealing the cause and spreading their mistress's shame all over Troezen? And even if they managed to conceal the cause, Phaedra herself in her unconstrained self-hatred would reveal it. An hour or two later, as the sun began to go over the mountain and parts of the valley fell into shadow, they returned to the gymnasium, where Hippolytos' friends, but not he, were exercising as usual, and came again to the house. There was no sound, not even of weeping. They went cautiously through the door. Phaedra was not in the room where she usually sat at the window. The door to her bedroom was shut. Evadne knocked but got no answer. She called Phaedra's name. Still no answer. She tried to open the door and found it locked, bolted on the inside. She called again, louder and louder, with no answer. They waited until the sun had disappeared behind the mountain and the whole valley was in shadow and tried again without result. The two women looked at each other and agreed without speaking that they should not wait any longer.

Evadne ran to the gymnasium and called out that the queen needed help. Several young men hastily put on their clothes and followed her into the house, then, at Evadne's urging, broke down the door of the bedroom. Phaedra had hanged herself from a beam by one of her own girdles.

10. THE LIES

Theseus returned from the funeral of his friend Peirithoös' wife to be greeted by the news of his own wife's death only a few days earlier. He would not at first believe that she had killed herself. Why should she do such a thing when she had been so happy in Troezen that she had asked to remain there? Hippolytos was absent. After leaving Artemis' temple he had gone into the mountains with a few servants, hunting deer, sleeping in the open, trying to cleanse himself in the realm of the virgin goddess from his encounter with what he saw as the terrible effect of Aphrodite's arts. He did not know yet that Phaedra was dead.

Her body had been placed in a cellar in the palace to try to preserve it from the summer heat, but it was already in a bad state. Theseus, however, insisted on viewing it and could no longer doubt, when he saw the mark round her neck, that it was suicide. But he was puzzled by her raw and bruised arms and hands. Evadne and Phaedra's other attendant were brought before him to give a full account of what they knew. They had already conferred endlessly about what they should tell Theseus and decided not to say anything about Phaedra's shameful love for Hippolytos, but to put her sleeplessness and failure to eat down to some unknown malady which she had refused to share with them. But when Theseus asked them sternly why her arms and hands were so damaged, they were taken by surprise. They had forgotten that and not prepared an explanation. They fell silent and looked at one another guiltily. Theseus, wrought up by what he had seen and by the inexplicable suddenness of his loss, became angry.

'You're hiding something,' he said. 'What was this malady? Tell me plainly and at once, or I shall have the truth out of you with torture!'

Evadne in her terror, still not wanting to shame her mistress, grasped at the first explanation she could think of.

'She was assaulted,' she said.

'What!'

'Someone attacked her.'

'Who attacked her?'

'A man.'

'What man?'

'You must ask your son.'

'I will ask him, but first I am asking you.'

'Her door was broken down – he seized her by the arms – she fought – he overpowered her – we two fled to get help – we returned and found her dead. Poor lady, she couldn't bear the shame.'

Driven by fear and the need to convince her more and more horrified and intimidating interrogator that she was telling the truth, she swam into a sea of lies that grew deeper and more treacherous the further she swam.

'Is this true?' demanded Theseus of her companion.

'Yes, yes,' she said, equally terrified and out of her depth.

'Then who was this man?'

'You must ask your son,' said Evadne.

Why did she repeat this when she must have known that Hippolytos would either say nothing or tell the truth? Probably, in the confusion of the moment, she hoped that he *would* tell the truth and that she herself would be spared doing so. Between Theseus and Hippolytos surely Phaedra's shameful secret could be buried with her?

'If my son knows the man who did this, why has he not arrested him? Why is Hippolytos not here? Why was he not here to tell me this dreadful news when I landed? I'm told he's gone hunting in the mountains. How could he do that in these circumstances?'

The women were silent, but at least Theseus was no longer glaring at them. His thoughts were on his son's strange behaviour, and he ordered men to go out in search of Hippolytos and bring him back immediately to Troezen. The women were sent to their quarters, while Theseus rode down to the house by the gymnasium to look at the scene of violation and suicide for himself. When he saw the broken door and the rumpled bed – its sheets bloodied by her abrasions – where Phaedra had tossed and turned in torment before deciding to end her life, he fully believed that the women had told him the truth.

Hippolytos was already on his way back to Troezen when he met one of the messengers sent to find him.

'Your father has returned,' said this man, 'and the queen –'

'Don't speak of her!' said Hippolytos, already regretting that he had not ridden much further afield, perhaps as far as the Arcadian mountains, so that by the time he returned she might have gone back to Athens with his father and he would not have to look at her again. Thus he did not learn of Phaedra's death until he entered the presence of his father.

'Why were you not here to tell me of Phaedra's death?'

'Her death?'

'You didn't know?'

'How did she die?'

'She hanged herself.'

Hippolytos knew immediately why she had done so. But still remembering only too clearly the way she had grasped his hand, the way she had thrust her face towards him, her exact words – 'with you, Hippolytos, with you. The gods help me!' – and his own feelings of shock and disgust, he could not find anything to say. Theseus was astonished.

'Doesn't that touch you at all?'

'I am very sorry to hear it.'

'She hanged herself in shame for what was done to her.'

'Done to her?'

'She was assaulted, forced, raped.'

'That cannot be.'

'What do you mean? Her door was broken down, her arms were wounded, her bed was rucked up and the sheets bloody. Do you suppose she did those things herself?'

'I put guards on the house at night to protect her.'

'This happened during the day.'

'Where were her women?'

'They ran away. But this is all beside the point. The women told me to ask you who did it. Who was the man who assaulted her?'

Hippolytos shook his head. He thought the women must be lying. He was sure that Phaedra's suicidal shame was not from being assaulted, but from declaring her love for him.

'Who was the man?'

'I have no idea.'

'Then why did the women say you knew?'

'I have no idea.'

Hippolytos was only half attending to Theseus' questions. His mind was wrestling with the problem of how he should deal with this news and with his father's ignorance of what lay behind it. He did not notice that his unsatisfactory answers and the neutral tone in which they were uttered were having an increasingly bad effect on his father.

'You sound as if you don't care, as if her death means nothing to you. What's the matter with you? Are you made of stone? Your stepmother, who loved you and asked to stay here in Troezen because she was so happy here, has hanged herself in shame. Who was the man who did this to her?'

'I know of no such man.'

'What do you mean? The evidence is plain. Are you saying it was a god?'

Hippolytos shook his head.

'Speak up!'

Theseus was shouting now with fury and Hippolytos thought that he must either tell his father the truth or remain silent. He shook his head again. Theseus seized his son by the shoulders and bellowed into his face:

'You don't want to tell me, do you? Why not? Because it was some friend of yours and rather than punish him, you rode off into the mountains and pretended you knew nothing about it. Are you fit to be a ruler? Are you fit for anything but killing deer? What sort of man are you? A miserable coward. At least your brave mother, Antiope, did not live to see this day!'

And now, too late, when his father was already so angry with him that he had lost all reason and judgment, Hippolytos decided that he had to tell the truth. Haltingly, clumsily, shamefacedly, he tried to do so, tried to express the horror he had felt when he understood what his stepmother's real sickness had been. Theseus stared at him with equal horror as Hippolytos stumbled to a conclusion:

'So I just pulled myself away and ran out and I suppose ...'

'Suppose what?'

'Suppose she just went into her room and ...'

'And broke the door down and tore at her own arms and left blood all over the sheets?'

'I saw none of that.'

'You saw none of that! Lies! Pitiful, shameful lies! Now I understand your cold demeanour, your reluctance to speak, your disappearance into the mountains. *You* did it! *You* assaulted her, *you* broke down her door, *you* forced her down on her bed and raped her! And now, barefaced, when I press you and you can see no other way out, you dare to put the blame on her.'

Theseus, bright red in the face, spitting and foaming at the mouth, lashed out at his son and when Hippolytos dodged and retreated, followed him across the room and again tried to hit him. But Hippolytos, stronger even than his strong father, caught his arms and held him off.

'You are wrong,' he said. 'I ran out of the house, as I said. I know nothing of the broken door or the blood. I could not bear to be near her after what she said to me.'

'And I can no longer bear to be near you,' said Theseus. 'Animal! Monster without shame! Liar! I would rather have had the Minotaur as my son, a man with a bull's head sooner than one with a bull's lust and a mouth full of such monstrous perversion. Go! Leave this city, leave this land, take yourself anywhere but where I can ever hear of you again! And may the gods punish you! Poseidon, I call on you. If ever you upheld the moral laws of the universe, if ever you favoured me and my ancestor Pelops, destroy this foul spawn of mine who destroyed my dearest Phaedra!'

Poseidon, god of earthquakes, answered with a rumbling shock that shook the ground and knocked them both to the floor. Hippolytos picked himself up and ran out of the room, then, going straight to the stables, he harnessed a pair of horses to his chariot, rode out of the city and galloped away northwards along the seashore.

Much of this violent interview, conducted in the main hall of Troezen's palace, which was only, after all, a large house, had been heard by others, and among those who rushed into the hall after the quake to help Theseus to his feet were two of the young men from the gymnasium who had broken down Phaedra's door and found her hanging. They had heard Theseus' shouts of rage and his false accusations – the whole house had heard them – and immediately asked Theseus, now seated and a little calmer, for permission to say what they knew. When they told him that it was they who had broken down the door at the request of Phaedra's two women attendants and that the women had never said anything at the time about her being assaulted, but only that she was not herself and they feared she might have done herself harm, Theseus began to suspect that he had made a mistake. The two women were summoned, questioned more closely and soon broke down and confessed that there had been no assault.

'And now tell me this,' said Theseus, 'and be careful how you answer, for if you utter any more lies or even equivocate you will be put to death: did my son Hippolytos visit his stepmother that day?'

'He did, yes,' said Evadne.

'Why? Be careful what you say! I want the exact truth or you die.'

'It was me,' said Evadne, 'that asked him to talk to her, because she was so ill, not eating, not sleeping ...'

'And then?'

'They talked together, sitting by the window, but we were not in the room.'

'Did you overhear what they said?'

'No.'

'Are you quite sure of that?'

'We heard his last words.'

'What were they?'

'Something like "you are disgusting". He was very upset and ran out of the house.'

'And she?'

'She was raving mad. She was beating the walls and crying and drove us out of the house.'

'And her arms were bleeding?'

'Yes.'

'What have you done to me with your lies?' said Theseus, rising abruptly from his seat. 'What have you done to my son who told nothing but the truth? Your lives will be spared, since I promised it, but you will be severely punished.'

He immediately ordered horsemen to ride out along every road and if possible overtake Hippolytos, tell him his father had been altogether mistaken, and bring him back to Troezen. Then he had an altar set up and made sacrifices to Poseidon, begging him to forget what had been demanded in ignorance and folly.

But gods can no more wipe out what has already happened than mortals can. The horsemen who took the northward road along the seashore found Hippolytos at the point where the road became little more than a track between the mountains and the sea. He was lying beside his wrecked chariot with his two horses standing by, still in their harness. He was alive, but his limbs were broken, his skull cracked, his spine twisted, his whole body blackening with bruises and leaking blood. A huge wave, he said, had suddenly risen out of the sea and surged towards him, the horses had panicked, the chariot struck a tree and then a rock and overturned, and the terrified horses had galloped on dragging the chariot and himself, tangled in the reins, for a mile or more over the rocky track. Some storytellers say that the wave contained a sea monster or a bull which vanished back into the sea as soon as Poseidon had accomplished what Theseus asked of him, but what need of more than a tsunami?

Hippolytos was brought back to Troezen, but only lived long enough to forgive his sorrowful father. Aphrodite's vengeance was complete, but why did Artemis do nothing to save her devoted follower? It may be that she in turn took revenge by bringing about the death of Aphrodite's mortal lover Adonis, gored by a boar and metamorphosed into the blood-red anemone that grows in the hills around our house, but his death is also attributed to a quarrel between Aphrodite and Persephone. Gods frequently fall out with one another, but seldom interfere with each other's schemes, perhaps because doing so would involve them in never-ending feuds and tear apart the whole fabric of their power. During the Trojan War, not long after this, the gods took different sides and many squabbles flared up and had to be stamped out by Zeus. Better the loss of one mortal, even the favourite of a particular god, than division in heaven. Mortals, after all, do not live very long and have to die one way or another. And there are always plenty more to come.

11. THE DAUGHTERS

Peirithoös sailed from Thessaly to Troezen to attend the funerals of his friend's wife and son and stayed some time to comfort Theseus. They spent the nights drinking together and the days sleeping off the effects. Theseus spoke very little, but sat staring into space in a trance of grief and alcoholic stupor. Peirithoös did most of the talking, and one night he proposed that now they were both widowers they should look about for new wives. Theseus at first rejected the idea outright, but Peirithoös was not discouraged and waited a week or two before mentioning it again.

'You and I,' he said, 'will soon be old. We only have one life. Are we going to waste our last opportunity, while we still have health and strength, to add to the stories they already tell about us, the battle with the centaurs, our expedition against the Amazons, the Minotaur?'

Theseus did not respond. He was thinking that his own name was much better known than Peirithoös' and that his friend was presuming a little too much in suggesting that their deeds were of equal weight. Apart from that, he was not proud of some of the stories in which he himself figured: the desertion of Ariadne, the death of his father because he forgot to change the sails, and now Phaedra's lust for Hippolytos, her suicide and his own disastrous treatment of Hippolytos. He smiled without humour and changed the subject. But Peirithoös returned to it a few days later.

'I have an idea,' he said, 'an absolutely brilliant idea. We will marry two daughters of Zeus.'

'How would we go about that?'

'The women I have in mind are Helen of Sparta and Persephone.'

'Isn't Helen the daughter of the King of Sparta, Tyndareus?'

'In theory. But it's well known that Zeus seduced her mother Leda and that Helen is really his child.'

'But still only a child. And as for Persephone, she's married to Hades and lives half the year with him in the underworld.'

'Precisely. Do you think she's happy down there with him? We'll fetch her up and give her a better life.'

'Persephone is an immortal. Why should she want to marry a mortal?'

'For the reason I gave. She cannot be happy to be queen of the shades, much better to be queen of the Lapiths or Athenians. But we'll try for Helen first.'

'How old is Helen?'

'Eleven? Twelve? She's said to be already a beauty and what better could she ask than to be the wife of either of us?'

'Her father – her theoretical father – Tyndareus, will hardly be looking for a husband for her yet.'

'No. We'll have to abduct her.'

Astonishingly, Theseus agreed to this hare-brained scheme. The years of political struggle in Athens had sapped his energy, and the deep wounds of Phaedra's shameful suicide and his own complicity in Hippolytos' death had damaged his self-confidence, as well as depriving him almost at one blow of the two people who meant most to him. He simply didn't care any more what he did or what became of him. Peirithoös' cheerful good fellowship made his life seem less empty. Peirithoös himself, on the other hand, unconsciously envying his friend's much greater fame and achievements, was glad of the chance to increase his influence over him and become inseparably associated with him. It was no doubt late at night and they were both quite drunk when they agreed that if they succeeded in seizing Helen they would draw lots for her, the loser taking Persephone. On their return to Athens, when they must have been more sober but hardly less misguided, they swore a solemn oath to help each other in abducting these two daughters of Zeus.

Entering the Peloponnese with a small force of horsemen, they rode down the central valley between the mountains (where the motorway runs now), through Arcadia into Lakonike. The city of Sparta had no walls, since the Spartans with their formidable military regime prided themselves on being strong enough to repel invaders from any of their surrounding territory. Riding swiftly ahead of their troops, Theseus and Peirithoös were lucky enough to surprise a group of women making sacrifices in the temple of Artemis on the outskirts of Sparta and to find that Helen was among them. They immediately seized her and galloped back to their troops, when the whole force returned northwards and were over the border into Arcadia before their pursuers could catch up with them. In the Arcadian city of Tegea they drew lots, as agreed, and Theseus won Helen.

But what was he to do with her now? She was more beautiful even than people had said or than her abductors had imagined, and, considering her sudden change of circumstances, extraordinarily calm, as if she already knew that all men everywhere would fall at her feet rather than harm her. Many years later, Homer tells us, after she had married Menelaos and been abducted by Paris, after the best warriors of Greece and Troy had fought and died over her for a decade, after she had been brought safely home from burning Troy, she was encountered by Odysseus' son Telemachos back in her husband's rich palace in Sparta. There she sat gossiping and telling stories, placidly reaching into her silver work basket for a golden spindle and a hank of blue wool. But now she was too young to marry and the Spartans would stop at nothing to get her back. Theseus decided that he could not keep her in his household in Athens or Troezen. He brought his mother from Troezen to look after her and hid them both in the small Attic village of Aphidna.

The success of this first phase of their piratical enterprise meant that Theseus had to keep his word and go down to Hades with Peirithoös in order to abduct Persephone. They went by a back route which avoided crossing the River Styx and reached the gates of Hades' palace, where they were received by the King of the Dead himself. Peirithoös had the nerve, citing instructions from an oracle of Zeus which were either an invention of his own or else deliberately intended by Zeus to bring him to grief as a punishment for his insolence, to ask Hades to his face if he would be so kind as to hand over his wife. Hades smiled under his black helmet and politely asked them both to be seated. They did so and found themselves stuck on the Chairs of Forgetfulness, from which Herakles rescued Theseus four years later, but where Peirithoös continued to sit for ever after.

12. THE ESTATE

The absence of Theseus on this ill-fated adventure caused him further disasters. First, the Spartans, led by Helen's grown-up brothers Castor and Polydeukes, known as the Dioskouroi (Zeus' boys), invaded Attica, discovered Helen's hiding place and took her back to Sparta. They also took Theseus' mother Aithra, to whom Helen had become attached, and made her Helen's permanent attendant. She even accompanied Helen to Troy, though she must by then have been extremely old. The loss of his mother and her reduction to the status of a servant was a greater blow to Theseus than the loss of Helen. His imprisonment in the underworld had brought him to his senses, and he could see now that Peirithoös had been a bad influence and that he should never have embarked on either of those foolhardy enterprises.

Secondly, by marching into his leaderless kingdom without meeting any serious opposition, the Spartans had demonstrated to the world and especially the Athenians that Theseus was a hero in decline. So that when he returned at last to Athens, he found that he was no longer its king. His cousin Menestheus had usurped the vacant throne. Theseus was now an exile.

Ageing and battered by ill fortune, for which he could only blame himself, Theseus, who had always counted on the gods' favour, now felt that the gods had deserted him and that his days of glory would never return. Making his way first to the island of Euboia, where his two sons had taken refuge from Menestheus, he and they boarded a ship sailing to Crete, where their uncle Deukalion, Minos' son and Phaedra's brother, had promised to give them asylum. A storm drove them off course – a sign, surely, of Poseidon's disfavour – and they landed on the island of Skyros. Here things seemed to look up. The king of the island, Lykomedes, was a close friend of Menestheus, but he welcomed Theseus with royal honours and when Theseus, his spirits reviving, suggested that he might after all settle here rather than in Crete, Lykomedes offered to show him an estate that might suit him. The island, he said, was well watered and fertile. In this northern part of it there was pasture for cattle and sheep, fruit trees and crops grew almost by themselves, bees flourished, while in the southern part there were forests of oak, pine and beech and also quarries of the variegated marble for which the island was famous. They walked up from the city of Skyros to its acropolis on a beetling precipice. Theseus, turning from the vertiginous view of the Aegean sea, named after his father, to look at the land, saw that his host had not deceived him about its beauty and fertility.

'What is this mountain called?' he asked, pointing to where the ground rose still higher to the west.

'Olympos,' said Lykomedes. 'But, of course, it's only a pimple compared to the mountain of the same name on the mainland.'

'Surely this is an Isle of the Blessed,' said Theseus, meaning the place, also called the Elysian Fields, where far out in the west, on the edge of encircling Ocean, some believed that the souls of fortunate heroes went instead of to Hades. 'I think even the gods may sometimes mistake your Mount Olympos for their own.'

'You are very kind.'

'I shall be more than happy to settle here and spend my old age growing fruit and keeping bees. Now point me out the estate you think might suit me!'

He was standing as he spoke near the edge of the precipice with his back to the sea. Lykomedes approached him as if to take his arm, but instead gave him a great shove in the chest, knocking him backwards.

'There is your estate,' he said, 'behind you!' and as Theseus staggered, trying to regain his balance, shoved him again.

Theseus fell, remembering how he had once treated a brigand called Skiron on his famous journey from Troezen to Athens much as this treacherous king of Skyros had now treated him, and thought that the curious similarity of these names bracketing the story of his life seemed to confirm that fate more than chance or their own intentions ruled the lives of men, before he was smashed on the rocks below.

A few years after his death, Helen, now grown into the wife of King Menelaos of Sparta, was abducted a second time and carried off to Troy by Paris, one of the many sons of King Priam. It was Theseus' usurping cousin Menestheus who led the Athenian contingent when Menelaos and his brother Agamemnon called all Greeks to unite in recapturing Helen and punishing Troy. Menestheus, unlike so many other Greek leaders, returned safely from the Trojan War, but he was not one of its famous heroes. Centuries later, when the Mycenaean age was almost forgotten and the power of Athens was rising, the bones of Theseus were discovered on the island of Skyros and transported to Athens for reburial. His mistakes and failings were forgotten or forgiven and the Athenians recognised that he was the dead hero they needed in order to compete with Argos and Tiryns, Mycenae and Corinth.

Were they the real bones of Theseus? Was there a real man called Theseus? Does it matter? Half the world probably believes that there was a real man called Sherlock Holmes who lived in Baker Street, London, and it is his statue, not his creator Conan Doyle's, that stands outside Baker Street tube station. Our lives disappear and can only be superficially reconstructed by archaeology and history. But stories, biographical or fictional or a mixture of both, tell us what we are and have been and probably always will be. Stories reflect our dreams and desires, our ephemeral relationships and secret selves as well as our actions and reactions. Stories are the inner substance of the cities and landscapes we inhabit, the pulse beneath the skin of our outward lives, the meaning behind all the things and routines that clutter our visible existence.

Sitting on this Arcadian terrace on the first evening of the New Year, with a view of the darkening sea and the mountains, with the scent of the last honeysuckle flower, with the laboured honking of the donkeys and the mewing of the goat's new kids, with the friendly New Year greetings of passing neighbours ('*chrónia pollá*'), Greece also gives me its substance, its pulse, its inner life in these stored, shared, continually retold stories, almost as changeable in shape as Nereus, the sea god encountered by Herakles, always in their essential character changeless.

Behind me on a higher terrace is an olive tree, the oldest in the village, four-and-a-half metres round its base, still bearing olives. Who planted it and when? Was it a seedling when Constantinople fell to the Turks in 1453 or is it older still, already growing when the feudal Franks ruled the Peloponnese in the thirteenth century? A dendrologist might know when it was planted, nobody can ever know by whom. But I can tell you its mythical ancestry. The first olive tree was the goddess Athene's gift to the new city of Athens.

GLOSSARY OF NAMES

These descriptions are only outlines, by no means definitive, since the myths were frequently altered, added to or varied according to period, locality and the imagination of poets and dramatists.

Abderos Friend of Herakles who accompanied him to Thrace to capture the four man-eating mares of Diomedes.

Acheloös River god in Aitolia, father of all Greek rivers. Competed with Herakles for the hand of Deïaneira.

Achilles Legendary warrior from Thessaly, chief hero of the Trojan War, in which, after killing the Trojan hero Hector, he was killed by Hector's brother Paris with help from the god Apollo, by an arrow in the heel, his only vulnerable point. His mother was the sea nymph Thetis; his father Peleus, king of the Myrmidons.

Admete Daughter of Herakles' cousin Eurystheus. She set Herakles his ninth labour: to fetch the girdle of Hippolyte, queen of the Amazons.

Admetos King of Pherai in Thessaly, whom Apollo served as a shepherd when he was being punished by his father Zeus for killing the Cyclops.

Adonis Son of the King of Paphos, loved by the goddess Aphrodite, but gored to death by a boar he was hunting. The red anemone was supposed to have grown from the place where his blood was spilled.

Aegeus Legendary king of Athens, father of Theseus. When Theseus returned from Crete but forgot to change the ship's black sails to white, Aegeus in grief threw himself off a cliff into the sea, giving his name to the Aegean.

Aeneas Legendary son of the goddess Aphrodite and her mortal lover Anchises. Fought for Troy in the Trojan War, escaped from the burning city and sailed to Italy, where he settled in Latium and founded the Roman race.

Aerope Granddaughter of King Minos of Crete, wife of King Atreus of Argos, mother of Agamemnon, Menelaos and Anaxibia.

Aeschylus (525-456 BC) Athenian dramatist and founder of Greek tragedy, in that he was the first dramatist to introduce a second actor. Author of the trilogy of tragedies, the *Oresteia,* telling the story of Agamemnon and his ill-fated family.

Aithra Daughter of King Pittheus of Troezen, mother of Theseus.

Agamemnon King of Argos, son of Atreus, grandson of Pelops. Commander-in-chief of the Greeks in the Trojan War. Husband to Clytemnestra and first cousin to Aigisthos who together murdered him on his return from Troy. Father of Iphigeneia, Elektra, Chrysothemis and Orestes. Brother of Menelaos, King of Sparta.

Agenor Intended bridegroom for Andromeda, turned to stone by Medusa's head.

Aigisthos Son of Thyestes, first cousin of Agamemnon and lover of Clytemnestra, he helped her murder Agamemnon on his return from the Trojan War.

Ajax

1. Mighty Greek warrior in the Trojan War. Son of Telamon, King of Salamis. Defeated by Odysseus in the contest for the arms of the dead Achilles, Ajax went mad and killed himself.
2. Greek warrior of the same name in the Trojan War, known as 'the lesser Ajax'. Son of Oileus, king of the Locrians. On the voyage home from Troy, his ship was wrecked and he was drowned.

Akamas Son of Theseus and Phaedra.

Akrisios King of Argos, son of Abas and great-grandson of Danaos. Akrisios' daughter was Danaë, who was visited by Zeus in the form of a shower of gold and bore Perseus.

Alcestis Queen of Pherai, wife of Admetos. When he was claimed by Death she took his place and was saved by Herakles.

Alkmene Mother of Herakles by Zeus and of Iphikles by her husband Amphitryon.

Alpheios River and river god in the Peloponnese. The river rises in Arcadia and flows westward into the Ionian Sea. The river god fell in love with the sea-nymph Arethousa and pursued her across the sea towards Sicily.

Amazons A legendary tribe of female warriors living on the south coast of the Black Sea.

Amphitryon Husband of Alkmene, father of Iphikles and stepfather of Herakles.

Anaxibia Agamemnon's sister, wife to Strophios, king of Phokis and mother of Pylades. Gave asylum to her young nephew Orestes after he had been smuggled out of Mycenae.

Anchises Mortal lover of the goddess Aphrodite, by whom he had a son, Aeneas, one of the Trojan warriors in the Trojan War. When Troy was sacked by the Greeks, Aeneas carried his father, by now an old man, out of the burning city and escaped.

Androgeos Son of King Minos of Crete, waylaid and murdered as he left Athens after his victories in the Panathenaic Games.

Andromeda Daughter of King Cepheus and Queen Cassiopeia, she was rescued from a sea monster by Perseus and married him.

Antaios A huge man, son of Poseidon and Gaia, living in Libya. He wrestled with every stranger who came his way and used their skulls to build a temple to his father. But he met his match in Herakles.

Antigone Incestuous daughter of Oedipus, king of Thebes, and his mother Iokaste. Her brothers were on opposite sides in a battle to capture Thebes. The attacking side was defeated and their uncle Creon, Oedipus' successor as king of Thebes, refused to allow the losing brother, Polyneikes, to be buried. Antigone defied her uncle and buried him. She was punished by being walled up in a cave, where she committed suicide with her lover, Haimon, Creon's son. Sophocles' tragedy *Antigone* tells this story.

Antiope Queen of the Amazons, succeeding her sister Hippolyte. Captured by Theseus and Peirithoös and became Theseus' lover, bearing him a son, Hippolytos.

Aphrodite Goddess of love, daughter of Zeus, known to the Romans as 'Venus'.

Apollo God of the sun, of the arts, of prophecy, medicine and disease.

Arcadia In ancient times the territory in the middle of the Peloponnese, without access to the sea. In modern Greece, a province extended to include Kynouria on the western coast of the Gulf of Argos.

Ares The god of war, son of Zeus and Hera. Like his half-brother Apollo, he was on the Trojan side in their war with the Greeks, though Homer has him ignominiously defeated when he joins the battle. He and Aphrodite, married to Hephaistos, were lovers. In some accounts he was the father of the Amazons. The Romans called him 'Mars'.

Argonauts The company of Greek heroes, under the leadership of Jason, who sailed in the ship Argo to steal the Golden Fleece from Colchis on the eastern shore of the Black Sea.

Ariadne Daughter of King Minos of Crete, who helped Theseus escape after he had killed the Minotaur. On their way back to Athens, she was left behind on the island of Naxos, but rescued by an even more powerful and prestigious lover – the god Dionysos.

Artemis Goddess of hunting, twin sister of Apollo, connected with the moon as he with the sun. Known to the Romans as 'Diana'.

Asclepios Son of Apollo by a mortal woman, taught medicine by the centaur Chiron, Asclepios was so good at healing that he could even bring patients back from the dead. Fearing that if this went on people would never die, Zeus killed him with a flash of lightning.

Athene Goddess of wisdom, of strategy and victory in war, industry and the arts, born from the head of Zeus. She was often sympathetic and helpful to mortal heroes, especially Perseus, Diomedes and Odysseus. Known to the Romans as 'Minerva'.

Athens Capital of modern Greece since 1834. In the fifth century BC a powerful city state and the heart of Greek culture.

Atlas A Titan, brother of Prometheus, who fought with the other Titans against the Olympian gods and was defeated. His punishment was to stand on a mountain in North Africa and hold up the sky.

Atreus King of Argos, son of Pelops and Hippodameia, father of Agamemnon and Menelaos. Constantly at odds with his brother Thyestes, the father of Aigisthos and Pelopeia, whom Atreus married as his third wife without knowing she was his niece.

Augeias King of the Epeans and owner of the filthy cowsheds which Herakles cleaned as his fifth labour.

Aulis Port on the coast of Boeotia, where the Greek fleets assembled before sailing across the Aegean to Troy.

Bellerophon Corinthian prince, engaged to Aithra, princess of Troezen and later mother of Theseus. Riding the winged horse Pegasos, Bellerophon overcame the monster Chimaera and performed many heroic deeds. But becoming too audacious he tried to ride Pegasos to the top of Mount Olympos. The horse, stung by a gadfly, threw him back to earth and he ended as a crippled and half-crazed vagrant.

Boreas The north wind.

Cadmos Legendary founder of the city of Thebes. All the gods came to his wedding with Harmonia, daughter of Ares and Aphrodite. Semele was their daughter.

Calchas Greek priest and soothsayer who accompanied Agamemnon to the Trojan War and told him that he would have to sacrifice his daughter Iphigeneia to Artemis if he wanted the wind that was against them to change.

Cancer The constellation of the crab, named after the giant crab which fastened on Herakles' foot during his battle with the Lernaian Hydra.

Cassandra Trojan princess, brought home to Mycenae by Agamemnon as one of his spoils of victory and murdered, like him, by Clytemnestra and Aegisthos.

Cassiopeia Wife of Cepheus and mother of Andromeda. Foolishly boasted that she and her daughter were more beautiful than the Nereids.

Castor Son of Leda, brother of Helen, twin of Polydeukes. Homer says his father was Tyndareus, some later storytellers make him the son of Zeus.

Centaurs A mythical people, half-horses, half-men, living in Thessaly, until driven out by the Lapiths after their disgraceful behaviour at the Lapiths' wedding feast for their king, Peirithoös.

Cepheus Father of Andromeda, husband of Cassiopeia.

Cerberos The enormous three-headed dog which guarded the gate of Hades.

Charon The boatman who ferried the souls of the dead across the River Styx into Hades. He was paid with the coins which were placed between the lips of the dead before burial.

Chimaera Fire-breathing female monster, part-lion, part-goat and part-dragon. Killed by Bellerophon.

Chiron A centaur and, unlike the other centaurs, immortal as well as wise and civilised. He was taught medicine, prophecy, music, archery and gymnastics by the twin-gods Apollo and Artemis. His own pupils included Achilles, Diomedes and Jason and he was a friend of Herakles.

Chrysothemis Daughter of Agamemnon and Clytemnestra, sister of Iphigeneia, Elektra and Orestes. She remained close to her mother in the years after her father's murder and did not join her brother and sister in the murder of their mother.

Clytemnestra Daughter of Tyndareus, King of Sparta, and his wife Leda, half-sister of Helen. Queen of Argos, wife of King Agamemnon. While he was away at the Trojan War she ruled Argos with her lover Aigisthos and when her husband returned murdered him in the palace at Mycenae. She was murdered in turn by her son Orestes.

Corinth A city-state on the north coast of the Peloponnese.

Creon Brother of Oedipus and succeeded him as King of Thebes.

Creousa Daughter of a king of Athens, raped by Apollo while gathering flowers on the Athenian Acropolis. She bore a son, Ion, in secret and Apollo had him transported to Delphi to serve in his temple there. When he had grown up, his origin was revealed and he became heir to the kingdom of Athens.

Cronos The youngest Titan, son of Gaia and Ouranos. Father of Zeus, who castrated and dethroned him.

Cyclops One-eyed giants, probably Titans, children of Ouranos and Gaia. Cronos threw them into Tartaros, but Zeus released them and they made thunderbolts for him, a helmet for Hades and a trident for Poseidon.

Cyparissos Grandson of Herakles, lover of the god Apollo. Cyparissos was a keen hunter, but killed his favourite stag by mistake and was so grief-stricken that Apollo compassionately turned him into a cypress tree.

Daidalos Legendary Athenian engineer, artist and architect working for King Minos of Crete. He created the labyrinth for the Minotaur. Later, when he fell out with Minos and was not allowed to leave the island, he made wings for himself and his son Ikaros so as to fly to another country.

Danaë Princess of Argos. Zeus visited her in the form of a shower of gold and begat Perseus.

Danaos Twin brother of Aegyptos. He quarrelled with his brother and fled to Argos. Aegyptos sent his 50 sons to marry Danaos' 50 daughters, but Danaos suspected treachery and told his daughters to kill their bridegrooms on the wedding night. All the Danaids did so, except for Hypermnestra who spared her husband Lynkeus. They had a son, Abas, whose son Akrisios was the father of Danaë.

Deïaneira Daughter of Oeneus, King of Kalydon. Wife of Herakles and unwittingly caused his death.

Delos Small island in the Aegean, legendary birthplace of the twin gods, Apollo and Artemis.

Delphi Site on the southern slope of Mount Parnassos of the god Apollo's principal temple, where his priestess and priests delivered oracles, usually ambiguous in meaning.

Demeter Sister of Zeus and goddess of agriculture, organic growth and family life. Mother of Persephone by her brother Zeus. Known to the Romans as 'Ceres'.

Demophoön Son of Theseus and Phaedra.

Deukalion

1. Son of Prometheus. When Zeus, angry with the human race, caused a flood to wipe them out, Deukalion and his wife Pyrrha were advised to build a ship by Prometheus and survived. When the flood subsided and the ship grounded on Mount Parnassos, Deukalion sacrificed to Zeus and pleaded for the human race to be restored. Zeus consented.
2. Son of King Minos of Crete.

Diktys Fisherman on the island of Seriphos who rescued Danaë and Perseus from their floating chest.

Diomedes

1. Greek warrior in the Trojan War, a favourite of the goddess Athene.
2. Son of the war god Ares and king of the Bistones in Thrace. His four man-eating mares were the target of Herakles' eighth labour.

Dionysos God of wine, fruitfulness and drunken frenzy. Son of Zeus and the Theban princess Semele. Known to the Romans and often to the Greeks too as 'Bacchus'.

Dryopes A Thessalian tribe, driven out of their territory by the Dorians. They migrated to various other parts of Greece, including the Peloponnese.

Elektra Daughter of Agamemnon and Clytemnestra, she helped her brother Orestes kill their mother in revenge for their father's murder.

Eleusis A town in Attica, famous for its temple of Demeter, the goddess of plenty.

Elis Kingdom, once known as Apia, in the north-west Peloponnese.

Epidauros Open-air amphitheatre near the north-east coast of the Peloponnese. Part of the sanctuary of the gods of medicine, Apollo and his son Asklepios. This was a huge health and fitness centre, the ancient equivalent perhaps, since it was also a place for worship, of the modern Lourdes in France. The stone theatre, built in the fourth century BC, seats 14,000 and is the best preserved of all Greek theatres. It has perfect acoustics and is still in use in the summer.

Erechtheus Another name for Erichthonios, but in later myths also his grandson.

Erichthonios First king of Athens, son of the blacksmith god Hephaistos. Brought up in the temple of Athene and credited with building a temple to Athene on the Acropolis (now the Parthenon).

Erinyes Also euphemistically known as Eumenides or 'Kindly Ones'. Ancient goddesses of the earth, older than the Olympian gods, who pursued criminals, especially those failing in duty to their parents. They pursued Orestes relentlessly after he had killed his mother. The Romans called them 'The Furies'.

Eunomos Boy serving the guests at a party in Kalydon. He spilled water over Herakles, who angrily cuffed him and unintentionally killed him.

Euripides Athenian tragic dramatist of the fifth century BC. Modernised tragedy by making it closer to everyday life and questioning the moral authority of the gods.

Europa Phoenician princess who travelled from Asia to Crete on the back of a white bull which turned out to be Zeus. Their child was King Minos.

Eurydice

1. Wife of the musician Orpheus.
2. Wife of King Akrisios, mother of Danaë, grandmother of Perseus.

Eurystheus King of Argos. His palace was at Tiryns, from where he sent his cousin Herakles out on his twelve labours.

Eurytos

1. A centaur who taught Herakles archery and tried to rape the bride of the King of the Lapiths.
2. King of the Thessalian city of Oechalia, father of Iole.

Evadne Attendant to Phaedra.

Gaia Mother Earth, the first being to emerge from Chaos, giving birth to Ouranos (Heaven) and by him to most of the other primal beings, including the Titans. The youngest Titan, Cronos, was the father of Zeus and the other major Olympian gods.

Ganymedes A beautiful youth from Asia Minor. Zeus fancied him and sent his eagle to carry Ganymedes up to Mount Olympos to be his cup-bearer.

Gorgons Three female monsters with wings, tusks, claws and serpents for hair, but otherwise more or less human faces. Two of them – Stheno and Euryale – were immortal, the third – Medusa – mortal. Whoever looked at their faces was turned to stone.

Graiai Three immortal old women, sisters of the Gorgons. Their names were Pephredo, Enyo and Deino and they had only one eye and one tooth between them.

Hades God of the underworld, also called 'Hades' by the Greeks. Brother of Zeus, he abducted his niece Persephone to be his queen in the underworld, causing his sister Demeter, Persephone's mother, such grief that she gave up on her responsibility for agriculture, crops and all growing things. The result was famine and desolation on earth and a failure of human sacrifice to the gods. Zeus therefore intervened and Hades agreed to let Persephone back to earth for half the year and so inaugurate the seasons. The Romans called Hades 'Pluto' and Persephone 'Proserpina'.

Hebe Goddess of youth, daughter of Zeus and Hera.

Hector Chief Trojan warrior, son of King Priam, brother of Paris, Cassandra and Polyxena. Killed by Achilles.

Helen Legendary beauty, daughter of Zeus and Leda, queen of Sparta. She married Menelaos, brother of Agamemnon, but fell in love with a visiting prince from Troy, Paris. They eloped to Troy, causing Menelaos and his brother Agamemnon to raise a Greek army and spend ten years besieging Troy. When Troy was finally taken and sacked, Helen returned to Sparta with her husband Menelaos and settled down to enjoy home life again.

Hephaistos Son of Zeus and Hera, the blacksmith god, lame and weak but married to Aphrodite, goddess of love, who cheated on him with Ares, the god of war. Hephaistos made a marvellously fine golden net which he threw over them when they were sleeping together and then brought the other gods to see them caught in each other's arms. The Romans called him 'Vulcan'.

Hera Queen of the gods, sister and wife of Zeus, goddess of marriage and childbirth. Because of her husband's constant liaisons with other women, both mortal and immortal, she was frequently in a state of fury and vengefulness, which she relieved by punishing the women and their god-given children. Herakles was a particular target. She was known to the Romans as 'Juno'.

Herakleidai Descendants of Herakles who claimed the kingdom of Argos. They invaded several times and were driven off, but eventually succeeded in defeating and killing Tisamenos, son of Orestes, and ruled over most of the Peloponnese. This story probably has some foundation in fact, representing the Dorian invasions which brought an end to the Mycenaean civilisation around 1200-1100 BC.

Herakles Legendary hero and demigod of superhuman strength from Argos in the Peloponnese. Son of Zeus and Alkmene. The Romans called him 'Hercules'.

Hermes Son of Zeus by Maia, daughter of the Titan Atlas. He was the gods' messenger and, because of his cunning and smooth speech, the god of politicians, public speakers, thieves, con-men and media. The Romans called him 'Mercury'.

Herodotus Greek historian and traveller, active in the fifth century BC, 'the father of history'.

Hesiod Early Greek poet, author of *Works and Days* and *Theogony*, probably active in the eighth century BC.

Hesperides Nymphs who guarded the golden apples given by Gaia to Hera when she married Zeus.

Hippodameia

1. Daughter of King Oinomaos of Elis, wife of Pelops, mother of Atreus and Thyestes.
2. Bride of Peirithoös, king of the Lapiths.

Hippolyte Queen of the Amazons, whose girdle, given her by the war god Ares, was acquired by Herakles as his ninth labour.

Hippolytos Son of Theseus and the Amazon queen Antiope. His stepmother, Phaedra, fell in love with him with disastrous consequences for them both.

Homer Epic poet, generally reckoned to be the author of both *The Iliad* and *The Odyssey*, but, since nothing is definitely known about him, almost as legendary as the characters and incidents of his great poems. Probably active in the eighth century BC on the east coast of the Aegean, then Greek, now Turkish.

Hyacinthos Son of a Spartan king and lover of the god Apollo. Killed while playing at discus throwing with Apollo, who turned him into the hyacinth.

Hylas Son of the king of the Dryopes, a beautiful boy with whom Herakles fell in love. Herakles took him on the voyage of the Argo but Hylas disappeared while fetching water for the ship on the coast of Mysia.

Hyllos Eldest son of Herakles and Deïaneira, leader of the Herakleidai.

Hyperboreans Worshippers of Apollo, who often visited them. They inhabited a land of perpetual sunshine ('beyond the north wind'), feeding only on plentiful fruits, never eating animals, peaceful, happy and long-lived, ignorant of violence, war and disease.

Hypsipyle Queen of Lemnos, the only woman on the island who did not murder all her menfolk, but hid her father. When the Argonauts visited the island on their way to Colchis, she slept with Jason and bore twin sons.

Ikaros Son of Daidalos, who made wings for them both so as to escape from the island of Crete. Ikaros, however, in his excitement at being in the air, flew too near the sun. The wax holding his wings together melted and he fell into the sea and was drowned.

Iolaos Son of Iphikles and nephew of Herakles, whom he helped to kill the Lernaian Hydra.

Iole Daughter of King Eurytos of Oechalia. Herakles competed at archery with her father and brothers for her hand in marriage and won. But Eurytos accused him of cheating and drove him out of the city. Herakles later killed Eurytos and his sons and took Iole to live with him, but he was by then married to Deïaneira and the consequences were fatal.

Ion Son of Apollo and the Athenian princess Creousa. Legendary founder of the Ionian race.

Iphigeneia Daughter of Agamemnon and Clytemnestra, sacrificed at Aulis to appease the goddess Artemis.

Iphikles Herakles' step-twin, born of the same mother, Alkmene, by her husband Amphitryon. Herakles' father was Zeus, who had taken Amphitryon's form and slept with Alkmene while her husband was away.

Iphitos Youngest son of King Eurytos of Oechalia. Killed by Herakles.

Iris Messenger of the gods and perhaps originally a goddess of rain, since the rainbow was supposed to be the path of her flight to earth with a message from Zeus or Hera to mortals, much as modern jet-planes leave a trail of vapour behind them in a clear sky.

Jason Legendary hero from Thessaly. Led the Argonauts to steal the Golden Fleece from Colchis, on the eastern side of the Black Sea (now Georgia) and was helped to do so by the local princess, Medea. But when they returned to Greece he married the daughter of the king of Corinth. Medea in revenge killed both her and her own two children by Jason.

Kerkyon King of Eleusis and keen wrestler, who generally killed his opponents. Theseus defeated and killed him on his journey to Athens.

Keyx King of Trachis, kinsman and friend of Herakles.

Kokalos King of the Sikani (Sicilians). Gave asylum to Daidalos after he left Crete.

Kynouria Mountainous district on the western side of the Gulf of Argos in the Peloponnese, part of Argolis in ancient times, now part of the modern province of Arcadia.

Kythera Small island off the south coast of the Peloponnese, where Aphrodite, goddess of love, according to one myth, was born from the sea foam. Homer, however, says that she was the daughter of Zeus and a sea-nymph called Dione.

Kyzikos King of the Doliones on an island of the same name as the king in the Sea of Marmara. Received the Argonauts hospitably, but after they had left and been blown back during the night, took them for enemies and was killed with many of his people in the ensuing fight.

Laonome Herakles' sister, married to the Lapith Polyphemos who accompanied Herakles on the first part of the voyage of the Argo.

Lapiths A people living in Thessaly, possibly the original prehistoric inhabitants. Best known for the wedding feast given by their king Peirithoös and his bride Hippodameia (not the same person as the bride of Pelops). They invited the centaurs, who became as usual very drunk and tried to carry off the bride and the other women present. A battle followed and the centaurs were driven out of Thessaly.

Leda Wife of Tyndareus, King of Sparta. Clytemnestra was their daughter.

Leda's other daughter, Helen, and her twin siblings Castor and Polydeukes were the children of Zeus, who ravished Leda in the form of a swan.

Leonidas Historical king of Sparta in the fifth century BC who held the enormous invading army of the Persians at bay with 300 Spartans in the pass of Thermopylae.

Lerna Town, now called Myli, at the head of the Gulf of Argos, next to the Lernaian Marsh, where Herakles performed his second labour, killing the Lernaian Hydra.

Leto Daughter of a Titan, mother by Zeus of the twin gods, Apollo and Artemis.

Lichas Young follower of Herakles, who took him Deïaneira's poisoned shift.

Lykomedes King of the island of Skyros, who received Theseus after his exile from Athens.

Maenads Ecstatic women, followers of the god Dionysos.

Makaria Daughter of Deïaneira and Herakles, his only known daughter.

Marathon The plain on the coast of Attika where the Athenians defeated the first great invading army of Persians in 490 BC. The modern long-distance race commemorates the messenger who ran from Marathon to Athens to bring news of their victory.

Marsyas A satyr (half-human, half-goat) or silenos (part-horse) who played the double flute with great skill and foolishly boasted that his music was better than Apollo's on the lyre. Their contest ended in his death by flaying.

Medea Legendary daughter of the king of Colchis in what is now Georgia on the eastern shore of the Black Sea. A sorceress. She helped Jason steal the Golden Fleece but when he deserted her for the daughter of the king of Corinth, she murdered both her and her own children by Jason. After that she fled to Athens and was given asylum by king Aegeos, until she conspired to poison his son Theseus and fled again to find refuge in Asia.

Medusa One of three monstrous Gorgons, the only one that was mortal. She had been a beautiful woman until she slept with the god Poseidon in one of Athene's temples. Athene punished her by making her so hideous that anyone looking at her was turned to stone and later sent Perseus to cut off her head. Athene then wore the head at the centre of her aigis or cape.

Megara Herakles' first wife, daughter of King Creon of Thebes. In a fit of madness caused by his perennial enemy, the goddess Hera, Herakles murdered Megara and their six children. He performed his Twelve Labours in expiation for this crime.

Menestheus Theseus' cousin and usurper as king of Athens.

Midas Greedy and foolish King of Phrygia whose choice of a gift from the god Dionysos was that everything he touched should turn to gold. He soon asked for the gift to be taken back, but was no wiser when asked to judge the musical contest between Apollo and Marsyas. He voted for Marsyas and Apollo gave him ass's ears.

Minos Son of Zeus and Europa. The great Bronze Age Minoan civilisation of Crete, which preceded and influenced the Mycenaean civilisation in the Peloponnese, was called after this king of Crete. He may have been a real person as well as a mythical one. His palace at Knossos was excavated and partly restored by Sir Arthur Evans. The legendary Minos married Pasiphaë, a daughter of Helios, the sun, and they had at least eight children, not including the Minotaur, which was the child of Pasiphaë and a prize bull given to Minos by the sea god Poseidon.

Minotaur Half-man, half-bull, the savage, man-eating son of Pasiphaë, queen of Crete.

Muses Nine divinities, originally nymphs of wells and springs, who presided over the arts, under the leadership of Apollo. Clio was the muse of history; Euterpe of lyric poetry; Thalia of comedy and bucolic poetry; Melpomene of tragedy; Terpsichore of choral dance and song; Erato of love songs; Polymnia of sacred songs; Ourania of astronomy; Calliope of epic poetry. They had a temple at Delphi near the Castalian spring on Mount Parnassos.

Mycenae A fortress city built on a small hill among the mountains north of the plain of Argolis. Centre of the Mycenaean civilisation in the late Bronze Age. Perseus was its legendary founder.

Myrtilos Son of Hermes, charioteer to King Oinomaos of Elis. After he had tried to rape Hippodameia, he was thrown off a cliff in Kynouria by Pelops. The Myrtoan Sea was called after him.

Narcissus A beautiful youth who fell in love with his own reflection in a pool, pined away and was changed into the flower of his name.

Nauplia The port of Argolis. Briefly capital of Greece from 1828-1834 after it gained its independence from the Turks. The Venetians occupied it before the Turks and made it perhaps the most elegant city in Greece.

Nemea In ancient times a valley in the state of Argolis, where Herakles killed the monstrous Nemean lion, whose skin he wore ever afterwards. Now famous for its vineyards.

Nereus Sea god with 50 daughters, the Nereids. Herakles went to him for advice on how to find the Hesperides, but had to wrestle with him first.

Like the other sea gods, Proteus and Glaucos, encountered by Odysseus and the Argonauts respectively, Nereus could change his shape at will.

Nessos Centaur acting as ferryman across the river Evenos. He tried to rape Herakles' wife Deïaneira and was killed by Herakles with a poisoned arrow.

Nestor King of Pylos on the western coast of the Peloponnese. The oldest Greek warrior in the Trojan War, he did not do much fighting but a lot of talking in councils of war, mostly about his own great deeds when he was younger.

Odysseus Legendary king of the small island of Ithaka, chief Greek strategist in the war against Troy. Due to the enmity of the sea god Poseidon he spent ten years returning home to his faithful wife Penelope.

Oedipus Legendary King of Thebes, who unwittingly killed his father and married his mother. His story is told by Sophocles in his great trilogy, *King Oedipus, Oedipus at Colonus* and *Antigone.*

Oeneus King of Kalydon in Aitolia, father of Herakles' wife Deïaneira.

Oinomaos King of Elis, father of Hippodameia, whose hand in marriage he promised to anyone who could defeat him in a chariot race from Elis to Olympia.

Olympia Site of the Olympic Games in north-west Peloponnese.

Olympos Mountain in northern Greece, home to the gods.

Omphale Lydian queen, whom Herakles served as a slave.

Oreithyia Succeeded her sisters Hippolyte and Antiope as Queen of the Amazons.

Orestes Son of Agamemnon and Clytemnestra, he murdered his mother in revenge for her murder of his father.

Orpheus Legendary musician, whose music charmed animals and birds and even the gods of the underworld. They allowed his dead wife Eurydice to follow him back to earth on condition he didn't turn back to look at her on the way up. He did and lost her a second time.

Ouranos Child and husband of Gaia. Father of Cronos, who mutilated and dethroned him, the same treatment afterwards meted out to Cronos in turn by his son Zeus.

Pan The Arcadian god of flocks and shepherds, forests and hunters, usually represented with horns and goat's legs and often playing the pan-pipes or syrinx.

Paris Son of King Priam of Troy. Three goddesses – Athene, Aphrodite and Hera – made him judge which of them was the most beautiful, offering various bribes in return. He chose Aphrodite, who promised him the most beautiful woman in the world as his wife. Visiting Sparta in the Peloponnese he collected his reward by eloping with King Menelaos' wife Helen. The outcome was the Trojan War and the eventual destruction of Troy.

Parnassos Mountain in Phokis on which Deukalion's ship grounded after the great flood. On its southern slope were Apollo's principal sanctuary and oracle at Delphi and nearby the temple of the Muses, beside the Castalian Spring. Hence Parnassos is always associated with the arts.

Peirithoös King of the Lapiths, friend of Theseus, who accompanied him into the underworld to kidnap Persephone.

Pelasgians Original inhabitants of Greece, before the invasions of the Achaians and later the Dorians.

Pelopeia Priestess and daughter of Thyestes, who raped her without knowing who she was. Their incestuous child was Aigisthos. Pelopeia later married, again in ignorance of their relationship, her uncle Atreus.

Peloponnese Literally 'the island of Pelops', named after the legendary ancestor of the House of Atreus. The southern area of mainland Greece, in ancient times joined to it only by the narrow isthmus of Corinth, now, since the cutting of the Corinth Canal in 1882-93, actually an island. The ancient states of Corinth, Achaia, Argos, Arcadia, Troezen and Lakonike (Sparta) were all in the Peloponnese.

Pelops Son of Tantalos and grandson of Zeus. As a boy he was loved by the sea god Poseidon. Married Hippodameia, princess of Elis. Ruled over the whole Peloponnese, to which he gave his name. Ancestor of Atreus, Thyestes, Agamemnon, Menelaos and Theseus.

Penelope Sister of Tyndareus, king of Sparta, and wife of Odysseus, king of Ithaka. He reluctantly joined the Greeks in attacking Troy and was away for twenty years: ten besieging Troy; ten contending with innumerable setbacks and adventures on the way home by sea. Penelope, the legendary faithful wife, kept her many greedy and lustful suitors at bay through all these years by telling them she must first finish weaving a robe for her father-in-law. Each night she unpicked the work she had done during the day. Her only son Telemachos was too young to drive the suitors out of the palace, but Odysseus returned at last in disguise and killed them with the great bow which none of them could draw.

Penthesileia Queen of the Amazons who fought for the Trojans during the Trojan War. Killed by Achilles.

Perigune Daughter of the robber Sinis. Travelled briefly with Theseus and bore his child.

Periphetes Hunchback robber encountered by Theseus near Epidauros.

Perseus Legendary hero and demigod from Argos in the Peloponnese, who decapitated Medusa, rescued the princess Andromeda from a sea monster and turned his enemies to stone with Medusa's head. Son of Zeus and Danaë.

Phaedra Daughter of King Minos of Crete and younger sister of Ariadne. She married Theseus, but fell fatally in love with Hippolytos, Theseus' son by Antiope.

Pholos A centaur, friend of Herakles.

Phyleus Son of King Augeias of the Epians, the man with the filthy cowsheds cleaned by Herakles.

Pindar Lyric poet from Thebes, active in the sixth century BC, author of *Triumphal Odes*, celebrating the winning athletes in sporting contests such as the Olympic Games.

Pittheus King of Troezen, son of Pelops, grandfather of Theseus. Famous for his wisdom.

Plato (428-347 BC) Athenian philosopher, teacher and pupil of Socrates. Among his many extant works are the Socratic dialogues. The philosopher Aristotle was one of his pupils.

Polydektes King of the island of Seriphos who gave a home to Danaë and the baby Perseus in the hope of making Danaë his wife.

Polydeukes Son of Leda, twin of Castor, brother of Helen. More often known as Pollux.

Polyphemos

1. The Cyclops who captured Odysseus and his ship's crew on their way home from the Trojan War.
2. A Lapith of the same name, brother-in-law of Herakles, who joined him on the voyage of the Argo.

Polyxena Trojan princess, sacrificed after the capture and sack of Troy as an offering to the dead Achilles.

Poseidon God of the sea, earthquakes and tsunamis, brother of Zeus. Known to the Romans as 'Neptune'.

Priam King of Troy, married to Hecuba. Their many children included Hector, Paris, Cassandra and Polyxena.

Prokrustes Hotelier at Korydallos. He gave his guests beds which were either too short or too long and adjusted the guests to fit the beds. Theseus stayed with him on his way to Athens.

Prometheus A Titan, brother of Atlas, who gave fire and other amenities, such as astronomy, mathematics, medicine, writing and metalworking, to mortals and was punished by Zeus. Chained to a peak in the Caucasus mountains, Prometheus' liver was pecked away each day by an eagle and restored during the night. This torture was to last until some other immortal should willingly take his place in Tartaros. Herakles killed the eagle and the immortal centaur Chiron, suffering from an incurable wound in his leg, agreed to take Prometheus' place in Tartaros.

Ptolemy Claudius Ptolemaeus, Alexandrian mathematician, astronomer and geographer of the second century AD. He catalogued and named the stars and constellations and wrote a textbook on geography.

Pylades Son of the king and queen of Phokis, first cousin to Agamemnon's son Orestes and his close friend, helping him to avenge his father's murder.

Python The monstrous snake which inhabited Delphi until Apollo killed it and made Delphi his own chief sanctuary.

Satyrs Nature deities of mountain forests and streams, followers of Dionysos. They had small horns, pointed ears, goat tails and permanently erect penises.

Scythians Wild horsemen from the shores of the Black Sea.

Semele Daughter of Cadmus and Harmonia, grandaughter of Ares and Aphrodite. Zeus loved her and she bore him the god Dionysos, but demanding to see Zeus in all his glory she was consumed by flames.

Silenos In the singular, the old obese man accompanying the god Dionysos. In the plural, nature deities connected with springs and running water, with the tail, ears and hooves of horses.

Sinis Robber on the Isthmus of Corinth who bent trees down, made travellers sit on them and catapulted them to death. Killed by Theseus on his journey to Athens.

Sisyphos King of Corinth, said to have built the city and improved its commerce, but accused of avarice, fraud and deceit. He was also said to have chained Death when it came for him, so that no one would die any more and would lose their fear of the gods. Death was set free by Ares, the war god, and Sisyphos condemned to eternal punishment in the underworld. He had to push a huge stone up a hill, but the stone always rolled down again just before it reached the top.

Skiron Robber on Mount Geraneia who made travellers wash his feet and as they did so kicked them over the cliff. Killed by Theseus.

Sophocles Athenian tragic dramatist of the fifth century BC, a generation younger than Aeschylus, half a generation older than Euripides. He increased Aeschylus' two actors to three and the Chorus from twelve to fifteen. The Athenians preferred him to either of his great rivals. Author of the *Oedipus* trilogy.

Strophios King of Phokis, married to Agamemnon's sister Anaxibia. Father of Orestes' friend and cousin Pylades.

Stygian Nymphs Guardians of the adamantine sickle, bat skin satchel and dragon-skin helmet of Hades. They lived beside the waterfall where the river Styx enters the underworld.

Styx The river in the underworld which the dead had to cross in Charon's boat. When the gods swore an oath, it was on the water of the Styx, fetched for the purpose by Iris.

Tantalos Son of Zeus and a mortal woman, much favoured by the gods until he became so overconfident that he invited them to dinner and offered them a dish consisting of the cut-up pieces of his baby son Pelops. The gods restored Pelops to life and punished Tantalos with everlasting hunger and thirst in Tartaros.

Tartaros The deepest level of the underworld, reserved for the harshest punishments and divided from the rest of Hades by a river of fire, Pyriphlegethon.

Tauros Cretan general. He defeated the Athenians and imposed their annual tribute to Crete, but was overcome by Theseus in a wrestling match.

Teutamidas King of Larissa. Held funeral games for his father during which Perseus, competing at throwing the discus, accidentally killed his step-grandfather, Akrisios, as foretold by the Delphic oracle.

Thebes City state adjacent to Attica. Oedipus was its legendary king.

Thermopylae Pass in northern Greece where Leonidas and his small force of 300 Spartans held the mighty army of the invading Persians at bay in the early fifth century BC.

Thespios King of Thespiae in Boeotia. The young Herakles happened to be in the area looking after his stepfather's cows and had killed a large lion which was harassing both Amphitryon's cows and Thespios' sheep. This was not the Nemean monster lion with its invulnerable skin, but a more ordinary one which lived on Mount Kithairon. Thespios had 50 daughters and, experienced shepherd that he was with an eye for a prize ram, liked the look of Herakles. So night by night for 50 nights he sent a different daughter in to Herakles and every one but the eldest bore a child. She bore twins.

Thesprotos King of Sikyon on the north coast of the Peloponnese. He and his wife adopted Thyestes' daughter Pelopeia after she had been raped by an unknown man, who was actually her father.

Theseus Legendary hero, son of Aegeus, king of Athens, and Aithra, princess of Troezen in the Peloponnese. He killed the Cretan Minotaur, became king of Athens and married Phaedra.

Tiryns A great palace fortress in Argolis, near the port of Nauplia, seat of King Eurystheus, taskmaster of Herakles' Twelve Labours.

Tisamenos Son of Orestes and his successor as king of Argos. Killed by the rival dynasty of Herakleidai, descendants of Herakles.

Troezen City on the easternmost peninsula of the Peloponnese, the so-called 'Claw'. Theseus' native city.

Trojan War The subject of Homer's great epic poem, *The Iliad*. The story of how Agamemnon led the Greeks to Troy and fought the Trojans for ten years in order to take back Helen – 'the face that launched a thousand ships' – belongs to myth. But the city of Troy, sited near the mouth of the Dardanelles on the north-west coast of Asia Minor, dominated the trade route to the Black Sea and was indeed destroyed in about 1230 BC. So the war may have been about trade and profit rather than adultery and abduction.

Tyndareus King of Sparta, married to Leda. Leda was ravished by Zeus in the form of a swan. Tyndareus was the father of the formidable Clytemnestra, but his other daughter, the beautiful Helen, was the child of Zeus.

Xerxes Persian king who invaded Greece in the fifth century BC with an enormous fleet and army. The fleet was defeated by the Athenians in the battle of Salamis (480 BC) and the army by a mixed Greek force in the battle of Plataia (479 BC) in Boeotia.

Xouthos King of Athens, husband of Creousa. Lacking any children, the couple went to Delphi to get advice from Apollo's oracle and found Ion, a temple servant, who was Creousa's long-lost child by Apollo.

Zephyr The west wind.

Zeus King of the gods, son of Cronos, whom he displaced, husband of his sister Hera. Zeus was the god of the sky. His brothers Poseidon and Hades were the gods of the sea and underworld respectively, and his sister Demeter goddess of agriculture and plenty. It was altogether a family affair. Zeus was the father of Demeter's daughter Persephone, who married her uncle Hades. Most of the other gods and goddesses – Ares, Athene, Aphrodite, Artemis, Apollo, Dionysos, Hephaistos and Hermes – were also the children of Zeus. So were many mortals, including Herakles and Perseus, by Zeus' brief liaisons in various disguises with innumerable women on earth. The Romans called him 'Jupiter'.

AITOLIA
PHOK
AKARNANIA
Ithaka
Mesolongi
Kalydon
Patras
Kephalonia
R. Piros
ACHAI
Mount Erimanthos
R. Selimus
Source of the River Styx
ELIS
R. Peneos
Zakinthos
R. Ladon
ARCAD
Olympia
Epea
R. Alpheios
MESSENIA
Kalama
Pylos
GULF OF MESSENIA
GREECE
BULGARIA
MACEDONIA
ALBANIA
THRACE
TURKEY
MACEDONIA
Thasos
Mount Olympos
Mount Athos
Pindos Mountains
THESSALY
Lemnos
Troy
Larissa
AEGEAN SEA
Corfu
GREECE
Pherai
Lesbos
Lefkada
Mount Parnassos
Thermopylae Pass
Skyros
Chios
LYDIA
ATHENS
Peloponnese
Andros
Samos
IONIAN SEA
Delos
LYCIA
Seriphos
Naxos
Kos
SEA OF CRETE
Rhodes
MEDITERRANEAN SEA
Knossos
Crete
Karpathos